Praise for *The D[...]*

'Neil Lancaster is one of th[...] crime writers in the UK right [...] procedurals I've read in a lo[...]
M. W. [...]

'A tense and twisty thriller that had me gnawing my fingernails one minute and laughing out loud the next'
Marion Todd

'Action-packed & lightning-paced with some of the best dialogue I've read. I'm a huge fan of Lancaster and he's a true rising star in crime fiction. Explosive & compelling'
Helen Fields

'As hard as it is to believe, these books just get better and better'
Tony Kent

'A wickedly clever and riveting thriller'
Graham Bartlett

'A gripping read that feels entirely authentic, seasoned with lovely flashes of humour'
Cass Green

'Smashed through it, top work!'
Callum McSorley

'Neil Lancaster has an unerring ability to keep the pages turning. And he's produced another belter of a book'
John Sutherland

'Breakneck pacing combined with devious plotting and compulsive narrative hooks you from the first page'
Neil Broadfoot

'Yet again, Lancaster has knocked it out of the park, over the main road, and into somebody's back garden!'
Paul Gitsham

NEIL LANCASTER is the No. 1 digital bestselling author of both the Tom Novak and Max Craigie series. His first Craigie novel, *Dead Man's Grave*, was longlisted for the 2021 McIlvanney Prize for Best Scottish Crime Book of the Year. The second Craigie novel is *The Blood Tide*, which has topped several ebook and audio charts, and was also longlisted for the McIlvanney Prize, and shortlisted for the Dead Good Readers Award. He served as a military policeman and worked for the Metropolitan Police as a detective, investigating serious crimes in the capital and beyond. As a covert policing and surveillance specialist he utilised all manner of techniques to investigate and disrupt major crime and criminals.

He now lives in the Scottish Highlands, writes crime and thriller novels, and works as a broadcaster and commentator on true crime documentaries. He is a key expert on two Sky Crime TV series, *Meet, Marry, Murder* and *Made for Murder*, and will shortly be appearing on a BBC true crime show, *Big Little Crimes*.

𝕏 @neillancaster66
[f] @NeilLancasterCrime

Also by Neil Lancaster

The Max Craigie Novels
Dead Man's Grave
The Blood Tide
The Night Watch
Blood Runs Cold

The Tom Novak Novels
Going Dark
Going Rogue
Going Back

NEIL LANCASTER

THE DEVIL YOU KNOW

ONE PLACE. MANY STORIES

HQ
An imprint of HarperCollins*Publishers* Ltd
1 London Bridge Street
London SE1 9GF

www.harpercollins.co.uk

HarperCollins*Publishers*
Macken House, 39/40 Mayor Street Upper,
Dublin 1, D01 C9W8, Ireland

This edition 2024

1
First published in Great Britain by
HQ, an imprint of HarperCollins*Publishers* Ltd 2024

Emojis © Shutterstock

Copyright © Neil Lancaster 2024

Neil Lancaster asserts the moral right to be
identified as the author of this work.
A catalogue record for this book is
available from the British Library.

ISBN: 9780008551346

MIX
Paper | Supporting
responsible forestry
FSC™ C007454

This book contains FSC™ certified paper and other controlled
sources to ensure responsible forest management.

For more information visit: www.harpercollins.co.uk/green

This book is set in 11/16 pt. Sabon by Type-it AS, Norway

Printed and Bound in the UK using 100% Renewable Electricity at
CPI Group (UK) Ltd, Croydon, CR0 4YY

To my dear mum, Brenda Lancaster. I miss you every day

Prologue

BEATA DABROWSKI SWIPED at the tears that were streaming down her face, feeling the flush of heat on her cheeks as she hurried out of the grimy town centre. It was a balmy summer evening, but she didn't really notice as she swallowed a sob – the door was held open for her by a smiling young woman.

She halted suddenly on the pavement, looking at, but not really seeing, the pulsating traffic in central Glasgow. She ignored the drunken shouts of the revellers pouring out of the pubs, all heading for the late bars and clubs. She just stood, stock still as young men and women, dressed in their Friday-night finery, swept all around her, like an inrushing tide washing around a half-buried rock.

She was alone, completely isolated in this sea of humanity, whereas ten minutes ago, she genuinely thought that her new life was about to begin.

She felt a flush rise from her stomach. Nausea gripped as his words, spoken just a few minutes ago, returned to her.

'I'm sorry, darling. I just can't. I just can't leave her and the kids. It'd break them, and it'd finish my career forever. I'm so sorry, much as I love you, it's over.' His voice was simpering, and sympathetic, but she could see it. She could see it in his eyes, the same deep, dark blue that had first captivated her. He didn't care. He didn't give a shit. He'd had his fun, but now he was going to discard her like he'd discarded many over the years.

She felt the sorrow begin to mutate as she stood there, tense and quivering like the string of an archer's bow before an arrow is released. She'd screamed abuse at him, as he sat on the rumpled bed, the musk of sex still redolent in the seedy hotel room. His face registered surprise at first, which soon relaxed into mild amusement, only to be replaced by scorn and disdain, demonstrated by the sneer she'd seen many times in the past. Although it had normally been reserved for his opponents, or those who displeased him, rather than her.

'Go on, fuck off out of here then, you Polish slag. You were only an easy shag, and not a great one at that.' His face wore a contemptuous, shit-eating grin as he stood, the sheets falling away from him revealing his pudgy middle-aged form.

'You'll be sorry. You'll be very fucking sorry, you think I don't know what you do, eh? You think I don't know that you wash money for big criminals? You think I'm always asleep, but I hear your phone calls. I know who you work for,' she'd hissed, her face contorted with rage, trying desperately to hold back the tears that were threatening to overwhelm her.

'Oh, I doubt it very much, old girl, you're not the first I've dealt with. Remember who's been paying the rent on your scummy little apartment and keeping you in stupid handbags. Maybe start looking for somewhere new to live, eh?'

Beata felt her cheeks begin to burn; how could she be so stupid? Her apartment, her whole life was paid for by the bastard. She had few friends, and all her family were back in Poland. She was suddenly disgusted with herself that she'd been so foolish as to put all of herself into this man.

'Bastard,' she spat, tears running down her face.

'Don't be silly, Beata. It had to end one day, we've had our fun, and now it's time for you to run along, there's a good girl.' He paused, a vulpine smile spreading across his thin lips.

'Fuck you,' she'd said, her voice cracking, before she turned and stormed out of the hotel room, slamming the door behind her.

'I'll fucking show you,' she growled to herself, her voice loud enough to cause a young reveller wearing an inflatable sumo wrestler suit to stop and stare.

'Talking to me, hen?' he slurred, his eyebrows raised in surprise and an amused lop-sided grin on his bright red face.

'Sorry, no,' she stuttered as she began to walk away from the hotel, head down, her pace increasing as she joined the throng of pedestrians in the warm Glasgow evening. Her steps became quicker as she rounded the corner towards the dimly lit side street where she'd parked her car. It was always this way. The same low-key hotel, where he seemed to know the manager, it had no on-site car park, and no CCTV. He was careful, as a man in his position would be expected to be, and there never seemed to be a bill to pay. 'Never you mind that, my dear, all taken care of with no paper trail,' was as close as she ever got to an explanation. As a final insult, he always insisted that they arrive and leave the hotel separately. It made her feel dirty and cheap.

As she approached her car, a little Renault, she was rummaging in her bag for the keys when she heard a vehicle pull up. She turned to see an old, battered white Transit van alongside her, the window down and a man looking at her, his smile revealing white, even teeth.

'Are ye moving, hen? Nae parking spaces around here,' he said in a heavy Glaswegian accent.

'Yes, I'm going now,' she said, blipping the car open.

'Stoatin, I'll just back up,' he said, grinning widely.

She turned back to her car and in the gloom, felt for the handle, opening the door wide and throwing her bag inside.

Suddenly, and with terrible force, she felt an impossibly big and strong arm encircle her neck and she was jerked back from her car so hard that her feet left the damp cobbles. She heard the van door slide open and she was dragged inside with horrifying speed, the backs of her stocking-clad legs bashing painfully against the edge of the door frame. She was dumped onto the flat sheet-metal floor of the van in an undignified heap. She opened her mouth to scream, but the arm just tightened, and no sound came out. Her head swam as the blood supply was interrupted – the arteries in her neck constricted. Her vision failed, and then everything went black.

She could have been unconscious for just a few seconds, or possibly an hour, but when she blinked, a harsh overhead light in the windowless van was blindingly bright. She was sitting on the cold floor of the vehicle, her wrists secured with plastic ties, and a man was looking at her with deep, sad eyes. His face was huge, jowly and covered in hard stubble. His eyes were hooded with heavy lids that gave him a sorrowful expression, but the dark pools glittered with something sinister.

He let out a long, sad sigh before he spoke, his Glasgow accent strong. 'Ye, cannae do this, ye ken, missie. Ye cannae threaten the boss,' he said in a dark, nasty growl. He had a phone in his hand which he was fiddling with.

'I'm sorry, I'm sorry . . .' she began to blurt out, but the sad-looking man just raised his hand laconically.

'Dinnae want to hear it, lassie. He's no' happy, so what do we do, eh?' he said without looking up.

'I'll say nothing, I promise, I promise I'll say nothing,' she said, the terror descending on her like an icy blanket.

Sad-face just sighed deeply and raised a massive fist which he used to rap on the screen that separated the load bay of the Transit from the driver's compartment. The engine barked into life and the van moved off.

'Where . . . where are you taking me?' she said, her voice trailing off to barely more than a whisper.

He said nothing, just stared at her for a full ten seconds before raising the phone and pointing it towards her. He nodded, almost imperceptibly over her left shoulder. She became aware of another looming presence behind her and she turned to look, a sick feeling rising in her churning stomach.

There was a sudden crackle and a rustle and then she felt a plastic bag being pulled over her face and cinched tight. She tried to scream, but as she inhaled, the plastic was sucked into her mouth and she retched, vomit exploding from her. With nowhere to go the thick mucus went up her nose as she breathed in, the panic rising. She tried to cough, but the thick plastic allowed nothing to escape, and she felt the vomit in her lungs, just as her vision began to cloud again.

The final thing she saw, through the clear plastic bag, were those sad eyes, a phone to his ear as he surveyed her with little interest. She stopped struggling, defeated.

'It's done, she'll no' be found,' were the last words she heard as the blackness swept over her like a warm, enveloping blanket.

1

Now

LEO HAMILTON STARED across the table at his client, Davie Hardie, in the legal visits room at Shotts prison. The high-ceilinged room was echoey and depressing, with scuffed walls and peeling cream paint, flecks of which were scattered on the dusty linoleum floor. Davie picked at a fissure in the scratched Formica table top as Leo felt some degree of shock at what he'd just heard from his client. He'd acted for the Hardie family for many years, thought he knew all the dark secrets, but he didn't know this one.

'Are you sure about this, Davie?' Leo asked, feeling a flutter of nerves in his belly. What Davie had imparted was something that he'd never expected to hear in his twenty-year association with the Hardie family. In the past, instructions had always come from Tam Hardie Senior, then after his death, Tam Junior. He'd had very little to do with either Davie or his older brother, Frankie, but as Tam Junior had disappeared without trace after being sprung from Saughton a couple of years ago, he guessed that he now took his instructions from whoever delivered them. His firm still had a sizeable amount of money on account from the Hardie legal trust, so he was duty bound to act on his client's behalf.

'Aye, of course I'm fucking sure. I'm only a couple of years into a twelve stretch.' Davie's face was hard and grim, and Leo could sense the bitterness.

'Not gonna lie, Davie, you were lucky to only get twelve. I'm not a bragging man, but keeping you out of the murders your big brother was convicted of was a work of legal genius.'

This was at least very true. Tam Junior had been convicted of murder, attempted murder and conspiracy to murder in revenge attacks after his father had been murdered in that remote Caithness graveyard. Keeping the two brothers out of that had been his finest hour, professionally speaking.

'Aye, you did good work, and were paid for it well, so I need you to excel yourself this time, Leo. The chances of me getting out of this shite-hole in the next ten years are remote to say the least. No way will any Hardie get out of jail early, will they?' Davie sat back in his chair and rubbed his face, before fixing Leo with a firm stare. 'Look, I know stuff that the cops will want to hear, Leo. I can clear up a big murder from years ago that the cops don't even know happened. They just think it's a missing person, but it's not and I know all the details.' An amused look overtook his lean, sharp features.

Leo narrowed his eyes. 'Go on.'

'Pa made it happen, and I know where the body was got rid of. Trust me, this is fucking dynamite stuff.'

'What do you want in return? I can't see the cops wanting to do you any favours, Davie. As you rightly pointed out, you're a Hardie.' He produced a gold pen from his pocket and poised it over the legal pad that was on the table.

'This is big, Leo. Bigger than anything they could fucking imagine. Someone went missing years ago, and said individual was put in the ground by someone working for my late Pa. He sorted it as a favour for one of his acorns that has since grown into a massive, huge great oak-fucking-tree.'

Leo felt his stomach tense a little. Davie wasn't given to hyperbole. 'Like how big?'

'Put it this way, it makes the bent cops Max Craigie brought down look like fucking traffic wardens. Make the call and tell them Davie Hardie wants to do a deal. But I want out of this bogging shite-hole.'

'I'll need to know more if I'm to approach the cops.'

'Not yet, Leo. I need an agreement before I blether about that, but it'll shake Scotland to its foundations.'

'What does Frankie think of this?'

There was a long, frigid pause in the grim room. 'He doesn't know about it, yet.'

'Are you going to tell him?'

'Aye, I will. But not yet, if he wants to come on board, we can both get the same deal.'

'And if he doesn't come on board?'

'Cross that bridge when we get to it, but I'm getting out of this bloody place, Frankie or no Frankie.'

'Davie, you could give them Lord Lucan and you'd not get out of here, you must know that. We managed to keep you and your brother out of all the murders, and your brother's stupid obsession with Max Craigie, but you still got twelve years for serious drug offences. You won't get parole for some time yet. The earliest I can imagine you even being considered is another four to five, and even then, it's debatable.'

Davie looked up from the table, and a slow smile spread across his face. 'Aye, but if I give them something big, showing cooperation like, and regretting my former life, I could get a transfer, eh?'

'Well, possibly, but they'd need a lot of convincing. Where?'

'Castle Huntly. I've heard good things about it, and it's close to the missus. A key to your cell, cooking facilities and shit like that. I can't stick another four years in this shite-hole. Twenty-three hours banged up a day, one shower a week, no gym, shite food and it's getting too fucking dangerous with the Albanians in here.'

'That bad?' Leo pulled a face and couldn't shake the thought that the younger Hardie wasn't a patch on his missing big brother. No way would Tam Hardie have backed away from a confrontation with the Albanians. He'd have relished the battle, whatever the cost. The boys still had access to money, and he was still their lawyer.

'Worse, and with Tam still missing, mine and Frankie's influence has gone. It's a nightmare, and the missus has made it clear that she'll only wait for so long. Four or five more years of her visiting me here is too fucking long.' Davie's eyes dropped to the table again, and Leo could sense worry in the man.

'You'll still be in jail, Davie. Is it worth the risk of dealing with the cops? Max Craigie wouldn't believe it for a minute, and he'd never leave you alone.'

'At Castle Huntly you get weekends at home, Christmases outside, day release for work, all sorts of stuff. I could do enough to keep Elizabeth happy whilst I see out the next four years, Leo. I can't be here much longer before some bastard napalms me. I'm not Tam.'

'And what about Craigie?'

'No Craigie. I won't deal with that bastard. I'm still not convinced that he didn't fucking kill my brother, it's too much of a coincidence. You must have a contact in the force you can go to. Someone with clout?'

'I have people I can call, of course, but are you sure?'

'Aye. I'm positive. Make the call, but no Craigie. He can't even know about this, or it's all off. I can take the police to the spot where this person was buried, they'll never find them otherwise.'

'The cops are going to want to know how you know all this, and if they think you're involved then you could be in a worse situation than you are now, you sure you want to take the risk?'

'Dead fucking sure. I want an immunity deal. I know about the job, I've seen the proof and I can serve it up to the cops on a plate.'

'You'll get nothing if they prove you were involved. Are you sure you want to pull off that plaster?'

Davie nodded, confidently. 'I didn't kill her, but I know all the details. If you can get me immunity, I'll tell them fucking everything, but otherwise I'll say nothing, and she can stay in the ground forever.'

'Her?'

'Aye, her. Look for the missing person case of Beata Dabrowski.

I know where she is, and I know who killed her, and more importantly, who wanted her dead.'

'I remember. Polish girl who went missing after a night out. It didn't make much of a splash, as far as I recall.'

'No, it didn't. She was a working girl, with no family or anything to make a fuss, but one of her punters was a big fish, who is much bigger now.'

'You know they'll suspect you of involvement, right?'

'Obviously, but I have a cast-iron alibi, Leo.'

'Which is?'

'I was in Spain when she went missing.'

'Fortunate. Can you prove it? They'll check flight records.' Leo began to scribble on his legal pad.

'I didn't fly. We took the ferry and drove, so it won't be on flight records, but I'll have proof, don't fret.'

'You'll need it. Give me the abridged version, then.' Leo's pen was poised over the pad.

'Pa subcontracted the hit out to a bad motherfucker from Glasgow via Jack Slattery. You remember that daft bastard? Bent ex-cop that used to work for Pa, now doing twenty-five years in Saughton.'

'How could I forget.' Leo scratched away on the paper, head down, the gold pen flashing in the harsh overhead lights.

'Aye, well, he's out of the picture, but the subcontractor is a right evil bastard who's still out there, ex-army or something, but seriously connected all over and yet, somehow still well off the cop's radar. He's like a bloody ghost: arrives, does his thing and then leaves no trace. He'll kill anyone for a bit of coin.' Suddenly, Davie looked a little pensive, as he paused, the cogs almost visibly turning.

'Davie?' Leo looked up, noting the slight furrow on Davie's brow. *Definitely not his brother*, he thought.

'He used a couple of heavies, one to drive the van, the other suffocated her with a plastic bag whilst he watched.'

'And you have proof of who killed her?'

'I do. There were three people who were there when the lassie was killed, and I know who they all are. The mannie who drove the van is called Mitch, but he's gone straight, and is a builder in Newcastle. Billy Watson was the one who put the plastic bag over her head, but he got on the skag and died of an overdose a few years ago. Droopy is on the out, still in the same line of work.'

'Droopy?'

'Aye, Droopy, because he looks like that cartoon dog with a sad face. Once I'm out of here, and my parole date is sorted I'll give them the lot. My pa always kept proof when he did favours for his acorns, and I know exactly where it is.'

'What type of proof?'

Leo scratched at his forearm, before continuing. 'The best kind. It's on film. Pa always wanted proof when he subbed a job out, so it was filmed by Droopy and sent to Jack. Jack then gave it to Pa, who downloaded it onto an SD card.'

'How's that tie it to the main man?'

A long, slow smile stretched across Davie's face. 'Pa was a careful man, and he knew everyone in Glasgow who mattered. He knew exactly which hotel, and even which bloody room that the man took Beata to for their "liaisons".' Davie mimed quotation marks with his fingers, and took a sip of water from the plastic cup on the table.

'Tam Hardie was a smart man, Davie.' Leo nodded approvingly, but a huge part of him wasn't sorry that Tam Hardie Senior was no longer with them. Leo had his own skeletons, and it was likely that Tam knew all about them.

'Aye, Pa loved having leverage over people, whether they were with him or against him. He was very careful, and very organised, and always thought long term.'

Leo shook his head in grim admiration. They didn't make them like Tam Hardie any more. 'Aye, he was a canny bugger, your dad. So, who's the main man?'

'Not yet, Leo. Not even for you, it's too big. This man will pay massive money to make this go away, and I'm keeping my powder dry, as Pa used to say.'

'Okay, but I need to give the cops enough to motivate them.'

'Give them the bare minimum for now, no names apart from the dead girl. That'll be enough to whet appetites and to get things moving.'

'Okay, I'll make a call, but it'll need to be of the highest public interest for the cops to bite.'

'They'll bite. Put it this way, Leo, when word gets out who it was, it'll be on the front page of every newspaper in the fucking country.'

2

LEO HAMILTON WAS still feeling uneasy as he left Shotts prison and walked to his waiting BMW in the car park. The sky was as dark as flint, and it looked like snow could be coming. He shivered as he removed his heavy wool coat, threw it onto the back seat of the car and eased his considerable bulk behind the wheel, settling into the plush leather.

Davie Hardie's dealing with cops was an anathema, even when in jail with years left to serve. He wondered for just a moment what Tam Senior, God rest his wicked soul, would think of it. He also couldn't help but wonder what Frankie would think. Should he tell him? He clicked his tongue as he considered the ramifications. On the one hand, there was the Hardie family honour that had been so important over the many years he had worked for them, but then there was the two hundred grand stuck in his client account, placed there a few years ago by Tam Senior. It had crossed his mind to do something with it a few times, but as Tam Junior was still missing, the prospect of incurring his wrath by stealing from him made Leo shudder. The description of what he'd done to Turkish Joe had removed any doubts as to whether he was a chip off the old block. A smile stretched across his face. That was two hundred thousand that could easily be burnt through with complex immunity negotiations, briefing counsel, maybe some private investigator fees. It was an easy choice. He'd let Davie tell his brother and deal with the consequences. Business had slowed down since his best client had died, and then his heir had disappeared in very strange circumstances.

He scrolled through his phone, looking for a name from the past, his thoughts racing. The meeting with Davie had been unexpected and frankly quite odd. He wasn't the hard-faced enforcer that he'd been when Tam Senior was running the show. The rumours of what Davie Hardie was capable of had been frankly terrifying, but he looked like a spent force now. He was different. His eyes had none of the old fire in them, and he was half the man he'd been before DS Max Craigie had brought the whole house of cards crashing down.

Leo looked at his phone and opened an internet search engine. He typed in 'Beata Dabrowski' and took in the six-year-old news reports detailing her disappearance. 'Sex worker goes missing in Glasgow. Friends worried for thirty-year-old Polish woman not seen for a week', read the BBC News headline, which was accompanied by a professional photograph of a strikingly attractive dark-haired woman, with a beaming smile. What was notable was the absence of coverage beyond the initial reports. A young woman goes missing in the centre of Glasgow and it caused barely a ripple.

Leo sighed as he found the contact he was looking for. He'd dealt with him on a few occasions, and he'd been useful in making one or two situations with the Hardies become a little more manageable. He wasn't corrupt, but he was 'approachable', if he felt that it would advance his cause. He pressed the dial button on his phone and listened to the ring tone in his ear.

'DCS Wakefield speaking,' came the resonant voice.

'Miles, it's Leo Hamilton.'

'Leo? Why are you calling?' The voice tightened.

'Davie Hardie, he wants to do a deal, and it's a big one.'

'A Hardie wants to do a deal?' Wakefield sounded shocked. 'I'm not sure that there's much we can do for Hardie. Let's not forget, they were convicted of conspiracy to import huge quantities of drugs. They did well not to get twenty years.'

'I know. Unexpected, but he's ready to name names. A missing person from six years ago isn't missing, she's very dead. Mr Hardie knows where she is, and who put her in the ground, and he wants to do a deal. He wants immunity for any part he may have played, which I understand is that he knows it happened and hasn't grassed. He wants a guarantee on his parole date, and he also wants to move to Castle Huntly for the rest of his sentence.'

'You know I can't make these deals, right?'

'I know. Make some calls, okay.'

'I'll need to know more.'

'Not yet, Miles. My client is very wary, but I can tell you that the person who ordered and paid for the hit on the deceased, and I use the word "deceased" advisedly, is someone of significant note, you understand me?'

'I think so. Is he up for being visited?'

'He'll need an initial visit, and he'll also need to be taken out of jail, to identify a disposal site. Two caveats, though.'

'I'm listening.'

'One, I have to be present at all times, whatever it is that's happening. I need to be there, okay?'

'Understood, and two?'

'No DS Max Craigie anywhere near it. Craigie cannot learn what is happening. He's not independent, Miles. We believe that he has a large axe to grind against my clients caused by his confrontations with the now missing Tam Hardie. My client doesn't trust him, and worse, he feels that Craigie could be responsible for his brother's disappearance. This is non-negotiable. Is that clear?'

Wakefield paused at the end of the line and exhaled deeply. 'I'll make some calls, but this is going to have to go to the top, Leo. Craigie and his team have the ear of the Chief Constable. They've been highly effective, and those above me may think that Hardie shouldn't be making demands when he's currently serving a long sentence.'

'Well, make it clear to the bosses that this is a pre-requirement for the significant new evidence that Mr Hardie can provide. Let's be fair, Miles, imagine that it was leaked to the press that Police Scotland weren't taking seriously the claims of a prisoner, who has since rediscovered his Christian faith and wants to cleanse his soul for redemptive purposes. They'd go fucking nuts, Miles.' Leo sniggered.

'What, Davie's found God?' Wakefield said incredulously.

'I've no idea. I doubt it, but imagine how the press will leap on it. "Convicted gangster who finds God is spurned by Police Scotland when trying to clear up six-year-old missing persons case of woman believed dead. Dodgy dealing with powerful individuals suspected, leading to claims of corrupt practice within Police Scotland." Think about the headlines, a photograph of you alongside the photograph of the deceased victim. She's very beautiful, Miles. It'd be a hell of a scoop.' Leo chuckled again, a nasty throaty sound.

There was another long, deep sigh on the end of the line. 'Leo, are you blackmailing me? Because I can get down and dirty in the trenches, if I need to.'

'As if, old man. Just no Craigie, or anyone from his team. We'll deal with anyone else, but not him, or anyone he works with. You must have other trusted cops.'

'Aye, of course I do, but I'll need to escalate this. When can you get us a name?'

'Right now. Beata Dabrowski.'

'I remember her. Polish girl who went missing in Glasgow a few years ago, yeah?' said Wakefield.

'That's the one, she was a sex worker, and disappeared into thin air. Never seen again in Glasgow, or home in Krakow. Well, my client knows all the details and he's willing to talk, but only if the deal can be done. He knows where she is, who killed her and who ordered her death, and one last thing?'

'Go on.'

'He can prove it.'

3

DCS MILES WAKEFIELD was sitting in his office on the sprawling crime campus in Gartcosh, east of Glasgow. He looked at his phone as the call ended, frowning at the familiarity of the slimy lawyer, who seemed to think he owed him a favour. True, he had greased the wheels in the past once or twice, but nothing illegal, but he realised this new information could be dynamite. There was no choice, he'd have to speak to the Chief.

He dialled the Chief's office, and as usual the call was taken by his PA, Margaret.

'Margaret, Miles Wakefield, is the boss about?'

'Hi, Miles. No, he's on leave, sunning himself in Tenerife right now.'

'Ach, of course, I remember now. Is Louise Campbell at the helm?'

'She is, but she's in her own office down the hall, still settling in after her transfer.'

'How's she getting on?'

'Bit of a change from the Met, but she's smart as a whip, if a little spiky.'

'Well, she left Scotland a long time ago. She was sergeant in Strathclyde when she transferred south, right?'

'That's right. She's on her fourth force now,' said Margaret.

'I did hear. Is she in?'

'She is, but her diary is a bit chock-a-block, something urgent?'

'Aye, urgent and sensitive.'

'Okay, I'll have a word in her ear and see if I can squeeze you in. When are you coming?'

'As soon as I can get there from Gartcosh, if that's okay?'

'I'll let her know.'

*

Deputy Chief Constable Louise Campbell sat across the wide teak desk and appraised Miles Wakefield, who had a cup of coffee in his hand and a notebook open on his lap. She was small and compact, immaculately smart with neat bobbed hair and she wore a blue business suit with a tastefully sombre blouse. She smiled widely when they were introduced, showing even white teeth. Despite twenty-five years in southern England, her accent was still softly Scottish, but it carried an edge of steel. She was a true careerist, service in London and several provincial forces as she climbed the ladder with her eyes on the top job, wherever that may be.

'Okay, Miles, forgive me, but this is a little irregular, no? A somewhat shady lawyer for two convicted gangsters who had corrupted senior officers in this very force contacts you direct about this extremely sensitive situation rather than use a more formal avenue of approach?'

'I get it seems a bit iffy, boss. I've known Hamilton for some time when I was a DI investigating the Hardie family and he was representing them on a money laundering situation, and of course I oversaw the case that landed them in jail. Seems he still has a number for me, so as the situation with Davie Hardie is a little sensitive, he came direct. Our association has only ever been professional.'

'I'm not suggesting anything other than that, Miles. I've read about the Tam Hardie Junior investigation. He's still missing after his escape from Saughton, I understand?'

'Aye.'

'Is the lawyer straight?'

Wakefield grimaced. 'Put it this way, we have no evidence of malpractice, but a bent cop in custody at Wick who he was represent-ing managed to get hold of a razor and cut his throat in prisoner transport, and the last person he was alone with was Hamilton. Nothing could be proved, but you don't represent a family like the Hardies for as many years as he has without learning a few strokes.'

'But this is a genuine misper case?'

'Aye, six years ago. Polish sex worker, no trace ever found of her, but there was some evidence that she was planning on returning to Poland.'

'What evidence?'

'Hasty packing, no passport found, and the computer at her tene-ment had searches for flights, and she had registered on some job sites in Krakow. A friend at the time said that she was pretty depressed and was in a fair bit of debt, which is borne out by her financials. Several maxed out credit cards and a heavy overdraft. Her pal said that there was a man, but no details were known. I guess she didn't fit the profile that would attract attention and go viral. It seems that from what I can see, she just disappeared, and no one cared enough to keep it in the public arena. Shame, but the way it is, boss.'

DCC Campbell nodded sadly and paused. The harsh realities of missing persons hung unspoken in the office. Some attract massive public attention, whereas others attract none. A Polish sex worker was unlikely to garner significant public sympathy, and could easily join the many missing persons who are never found, and simply disappear without trace. 'Yet Hardie's claim is that someone notable has had her murdered, yes?'

'Well, he says that he can lead us to the body, and that he knows of evidence which will expose who's guilty, so I think we have to go with it. Hamilton is threatening to go to the press if we don't, and those are headlines I suspect we don't want with the corruption scandals that have been unearthed by DI Ross Fraser's team recently.'

'Yes. I've read about those, and it's part of the reason I've been brought in. I can't say I'm totally comfortable with a small team sitting outside of professional standards oversight and seemingly with minimal supervision. Doesn't assist a corporate approach, but I can see why Mr Macdonald felt the need at that particular moment in time. Hopefully with the processes I'm implementing it won't be necessary for much longer. Okay, Miles, I'm happy for you to take point on this. Do you have anyone in mind to make first contact with Hardie?'

'Yes, ma'am. I'll have DS Lenny Maxwell and DC Ann Laithwaite from Covert Source Management make the approach at Shotts and we can take it from there. Both are first-rate tier three and four interviewers, and are used to the most sensitive of tasks so can handle anything.'

'That's good. I want you to oversee it until we know what we have. Once we have clarity, we can appoint an SIO and have a team take primacy for the homicide investigation if that's what we have. I don't want a massive operation, only to find that Hardie is leading us down the garden path, just the bare minimum to make sure it's safe.'

'How about Craigie?'

'Well, I think it's wise he and the whole "Policing Standards Reassurance Team",' she said, using her fingers to indicate speech marks, 'are kept well away from this. When we consider the confrontations between DS Craigie, and for that matter DC Calder, and the Hardie family it would be very easy for allegations to be made of prejudice. I want this to be kept covert and low key, and I want you to report direct to me, Miles.'

'Understood.'

'Last thing we need is a big tabloid splash about investigations that aren't dispassionate or are influenced by prejudice. Get Hardie interviewed, and then get him out to identify the disposal site. If that bears out, then we're on. Have you spoken to the Crown Office?' She looked directly at Miles, her dark brown eyes boring into his.

'Not yet.'

'Okay. Leave that to me, the new Crown Agent, Finn Townsend, has only recently been appointed, and he's made it clear that he wants early briefings on matters such as this. I don't think we need to do it until we've looked into the veracity of this claim. We all know that it can be a little leaky in that building, and it isn't the time until we have a body. Without a body, there isn't a case, is there? I mean, it's not as if Hardie is exactly an ideal witness.' It was a statement rather than a question.

'I'd call that an understatement, boss.'

'Legally, I don't think this will be much of a challenge as long as there is no involvement by Hardie. He's not going to be getting released early, just moved to a more favourable environment and his parole date fixed. The Crown Office can make the call on immunity once we know more, but any evidence that he was involved at any significant level, then the deal's off, as far as I'm concerned. Any suggestion of that, and he'll become a suspect as much as anyone else. We have to be totally above board, and investigate this matter without fear or favour, is that clear?'

'Crystal, ma'am.'

'Good, I'll need something in writing with as much detail as you can muster by end of play today, okay?' She lowered her eyes to her computer that sat on her desk, indicating that the meeting was over.

Wakefield stood, nodded and left the office, feeling the Deputy Chief's eyes burning into his back as he exited. He pulled his phone out of his pocket and dialled.

'That was quick, Miles,' said Leo Hamilton.

'We're on. Craigie and his team are out of the picture, when's your man ready to talk?'

'As soon as you can get someone into Shotts. It'll need to be totally under the radar, and I have to be there.'

'When can he give us some more details?'

'Once we have a deal signed and delivered.'

'Leo, you're being unreasonable here. No way will the Crown Office sign off on an immunity deal without knowing what the evidence is likely to be.'

Leo guffawed. 'Worth a try, old man. Look, he'll be ready as soon as it can be arranged. But remember, no Craigie, and no one associated with him. My client doesn't trust him. He'll be able to take you to the deposit site, and once the body's found you'll know that he's playing with a straight bat. From there, we can start to talk about the deal, and how my client protects his interests before he gives the evidence. Incontrovertible proof of who ordered the killing, and who enacted that order.'

'Do you know who, Leo?' said Wakefield, his voice even.

'Being honest, no, I don't. Davie trusts nobody, and that pretty much includes me. Once his agreement is signed and sealed, he'll tell all. When can you get the first visit done?'

'Two days.'

'Who are you going to send?'

'DS Lenny Maxwell and DC Ann Laithwaite, both very good cops. They're used to doing complex debriefs, supergrasses and things like that.'

'I've encountered DS Maxwell, he's a sharp operator. Two days it is, which by my watch makes it Wednesday. I'll clear my diary.'

Wakefield smirked. 'Way I hear it, Leo, your diary is pretty empty at the moment.'

'Well, when your biggest clients either get locked up, or mysteriously disappear from a boat in the North Sea having been sprung from jail, it does tend to affect one's workload a tad.' The lawyer's voice was tight and without humour.

'So, this is manna from heaven for you then, Leo, eh?' Wakefield felt a smile stretch across his face, as Leo's work had dried up since the Hardies were taken out of the picture. It was always likely that he'd be seen as toxic.

'Not complaining. Makes a change from chasing ambulances and sorting out wills. Tell me as soon as you have a plan, but you'll have to find a way of doing this on the downlow. Davie isn't as influential as he once was, and you know how prisoners feel about snitches?' Leo chuckled. 'Snitches get stitches, or more likely in Shotts, they get a jug of boiling water laced with sugar in the puss.'

4

IT WAS A cold, crisp winter morning when Janie pulled up in the car park on the parade square at Tulliallan Police College. Max stifled a yawn as Janie silenced the strange pounding beat and weird repetitive bassline of some music that was blasting out of the big car's speakers.

'Thank God for that. What a bloody racket, what was it?' said Max, looking at the pale and tired face of his work partner of the last few years.

'Philistine. The Fall, "Eat Y'Self Fitter". Classic stuff, didn't you find the bassline almost hypnotic?'

'I found it utterly shite.'

'Yeah, but you like Radiohead, so your opinion is questionable.'

'What's wrong with Radiohead? You look knackered, by the way. Eyes like pish-holes in the snow.'

'Have you looked in the mirror, sergeant? Of course I'm knackered, we've just spent a week with basically no sleep as our bumptious and permanently angry leader wanted us doing surveillance on a suspected bent cop, who turned out to just be bone-idle as opposed to corrupt. Anyway, to finish the music critique, Radiohead are pretentious and predictable, and did you know that both David Cameron and Nick Clegg chose Radiohead tracks for their Desert Island Discs?' She turned to look at Max, her lassitude dissipating at the prospect of a discussion on the merits of various music genres, of which she was a self-proclaimed expert.

'Funnily enough, no.'

'So, your musical taste mimics dodgy Tory MPs, which practically proves you're a Tory.' She nodded almost in satisfaction.

'Wasn't Clegg Lib Dem?' said Max, opening the car door, but turning to look at Janie, one eyebrow raised.

'Well, possibly but he chased the power with the coalition of 2010. Total sell-out,' she said, getting out of the car.

They both began the short walk across the parade ground car park towards the hulking castle that housed the small, poky and depressing office of the Policing Standards Reassurance Team, which had been formed by Chief Constable Chris Macdonald to tackle the corruption that others couldn't. The name itself was covert, being so tedious that no one would want to know anything else about it.

'Weren't you about fourteen in 2010?' said Max, falling into step alongside Janie as they crossed a grassy patch towards the main entrance of the castle.

'Thirteen, actually.'

'And you were interested in politics?'

'Always. Weren't you?'

'At thirteen? No chance, I was too busy drinking cider in the forest, or boxing. Isn't that Barney's van parked in the disabled bay?' said Max, pointing at a blue VW camper van that was sitting inert in front of the sprawling building, a long orange cable snaking towards a window where it disappeared inside.

'Looks like our elderly ex-spy is abstracting electricity from the Chief Constable,' said Janie.

'Doesn't he ever go home to Leeds?'

'Not recently, as far as I'm aware. He's an odd bugger.'

'I know, but he's been in that van for months now. I don't think he's been home for ages, I mean, where does he shower or wash his clothes?'

'He's the product of fifty years being secret all the time, living in the shadows and smoking consistently.'

Max knocked on the side of the van, the sheet metal rattling as he did.

'Morning, troops. Brew?' came a cheery Yorkshire-accented voice from within the van. There was a clunk as the door slid open and Barney appeared, a broad smile stretched across his lean, weathered face as he sat on the reversed driver's seat that butted up to a folding table, a chipped tin mug in his hand. Typically, there was an unlit roll-up pursed between his lips, which he applied a flame to from an old, battered Zippo. He inhaled with deep satisfaction, the smoke wisping out of his nose. Barney was an ex-MI5 technical specialist who after retirement had found himself bored and frustrated, so had set up as a freelance technical consultant. He had been amongst electronic surveillance his whole life, and there wasn't a premises, car, hotel, home or computer that he couldn't bug, hack or put a camera in.

'Is that a brew made using the Chief Constable's electricity?' asked Max.

'And it's all the more refreshing for it,' Barney said. He was still dressed in striped pyjamas, one of the legs of which was tied up below where his lower leg should have been. Despite working together for some time, they'd only just learned that Barney had lost his leg below the knee during the Iraq conflict in the 1990s and wore a prosthesis. He'd never bothered to tell them as he didn't want to make a fuss. This was typical for Barney, he never showed a great deal of emotion, beyond a wry chuckle, and certainly had never been seen to panic, or get flustered under even the most intense operational stress.

'Typical Yorkshireman, short arms, deep pockets,' said Max.

'Coming from a Scot, I'll take that as a compliment, lad. Now do you two want a brew, or not?'

'Not with you smoking in there, my clothes will stink for the day,' said Janie, wrinkling her nose.

'Stop moaning, not like you've paid for it, is it?'

'Well in that case, I'll say no,' Max replied. 'In any case, I want a decent coffee, and there's a machine in the office, and you only have instant pish. See you inside. Our bumptious and irascible leader wanted an early meet about something and he's waiting impatiently. The Chief's away, and I think he's hoping that we could have a short day, followed by a few days "working from home".' Max waggled his fingers.

'Where's the Chief?' said Barney.

'Holiday. New DCC who's recently transferred from the Met has the reins, and I don't think she's overly keen on our existence, as she's lead for professional standards. I think there's some chest-beating going on as she tries to assert herself.'

'Do you know her?' said Janie.

'Only by reputation.'

'Meaning?'

'Efficient, ruthlessly ambitious and doesn't suffer fools gladly. In fact, don't look now, she's coming this way. A skipper in Strathclyde before she headed south on the promotion trail, wants to be commissioner, I hear.' Max nodded towards the car park, and at the neat form of DCC Campbell walking across the car park towards the entrance of the Castle. Barney, half pulled himself out of the open van door and stared at the approaching figure.

'Barney, I said *don't* look now, not obviously stare at her. You're supposed to be an expert in being covert,' said Max, shaking his head.

As they stood there a post office van drove up and parked next to Barney's van. A short, uniformed man with a shock of red hair jumped out, went to the back of the van and opened it, whistling tunelessly.

Barney continued to puff away as the DCC approached, a look of distaste on her face as she took in the unusual scene of a pyjama-clad amputee puffing on a hand-rolled cigarette, whilst hanging out of a camper van door.

Her eyes fell on Max. 'DS Craigie, isn't it?' she said, her accent soft, yet it had a steeliness to it.

'Yes, ma'am. This is DC Calder, and this is Barney, our technical expert.'

'Now then, love,' said Barney, pulling the roll-up from his mouth, a big beaming smile across his leathery features and tendrils of smoke wisping from his lips.

The DCC's lips curled in displeasure, her eyes narrowing with deep suspicion.

'Why is this van parked here?' she said, looking at Barney's VW, and then at the orange cable that snaked across the pavement and into a window of the building.

'Close t' leccy. It were brass monkeys last night and I'd have frozen me knackers off without some heat,' said Barney, his accent growing.

'Sorry, you mean you slept here? In a disabled bay? Powered using electricity from the building?' she said incredulously.

'Aye. Late finish and I were cream-crackered. Pleased to meet you, by the way.' Barney's smile widened.

DCC Campbell opened her mouth to remonstrate, but she then snapped it shut, her eyes flinty. 'Is DI Fraser in?'

'Yes, ma'am. I spoke to him fifteen minutes ago,' said Max.

'Is one of you called Barney Illingworth?' They all looked towards the postman, who was scratching his red thatch, a briefcase-sized parcel in his hand.

'Aye, that's me, lad,' said Barney.

'Parcel for you. Never had an address like this before, "Blue VW Camper Van in front of Tulliallan Castle", even has your registration number on it. Sign here,' he said with a chuckle as he handed a small smartphone to Barney, who squiggled on the screen.

'Nice one. A new toy to play with,' said Barney as he handed back the smartphone and accepted the parcel.

'I'm not awake enough for weird deliveries like this,' said the postie, shaking his head and returning to his van.

'Are you actually living here?' said the DCC, turning to look at Barney, her brow furrowed with confusion.

'Nay, love. Just a temporary fix whilst I'm helping out,' said Barney, looking at the package with relish.

DCC Campbell opened her mouth, her eyes flashing displeasure, before she seemed to change her mind. She shook her head. 'I'll take this up with DI Fraser, but this is a place of work, DS Craigie, not a campsite. Get the van disconnected, and get it appropriately parked.' She turned on her heel and strode off, her steps purposeful and quick.

'I don't want your coffee, but maybe we'll have a tea, Barney. I think staying away from the office for a while may be a good idea.' Max winced.

'Aye, a carpeting from the DCC is no way to start the day, is it?' said Barney, chuckling.

'I cannot believe that you've had the bloody postie delivering to you in your van, outside Police Scotland HQ,' said Max, laughing.

'Good bit of kit, this. It'll be really useful, and I wanted to mess with it. Particularly if we have some downtime.'

'This is guaranteed to put Ross in a bad mood before we've even got in, and he'd been edgy, anyway. I think Mrs F had been moaning about the hours,' said Janie.

'Unsurprising, Katie hasn't been that impressed, either. We could do with some time off,' said Max, accepting a steaming mug from Barney.

'I can't say that Melissa has been that happy either, so another vote from me for downtime.'

'All these ties you folk have. Should be like your Uncle Barney.'

'What, living in a tiny van and pishing in a bucket?' said Max.

'I resent that. It's compact and bijou, not tiny.'

'Barney, when did you last go home?' said Janie.

'Not recently.'

'Why?'

'No point, I'm always working here. I also like the van, I have me fags, a beer now and again, and maybe a little punt on a horse. Don't need owt else.' He shrugged.

'But surely you have a home to go to?'

'Well, there's a house, but I've always lived out of a suitcase, and I like to keep on the move, so it suits me, I guess.'

'No one at home waiting?' asked Janie.

'Not for a long time, love.'

Max was preparing a follow-up question to this odd exchange when his phone buzzed in his pocket. He looked at the email icon on the screen, opened the app and saw a new message, but there was no return email address, just a long series of numbers and characters. His memory flared at the seeming gibberish. He tapped it and his unease grew. There were just four words in it.

We need to speak

Max stared at the screen for a full five seconds, before the message simply vanished before his eyes.

'You okay, Max?' said Janie, a flicker of concern on her face.

'All good, see you back in the office. I need to make a call.' Max drained his scalding tea and handed the mug back to Barney. He walked off towards the side of the building and dialled a number from his contact list that was titled simply 'BF'.

There was a single tone before the call was answered.

'Max?' the soft, Caithness accent of Bruce Ferguson was instantly familiar.

'Bruce. Unusual for you to contact me,' said Max, feeling a brief flip in his stomach. Bruce Ferguson was the brother of a victim of the Hardie family. He was also an ex–special forces operator and currently the head of security for a Russian oligarch and telecommunications magnate. He had access to data and intelligence that most law enforcement and intelligence agencies would long for, but he wasn't prone to impromptu catch-ups. When Bruce called, he called for a reason.

'Aye, I know, but this is important, are you clear and free to speak?'

'Yes, I'm good,' Max's heart thumped in his chest. Bruce Ferguson never just called for a blether. He called when something bad was happening.

'We have a serious problem. More pointedly, you have a serious problem. We need to meet.'

5

DAVIE HARDIE SAT across the same chipped and scuffed table as a couple of days ago when he'd dropped the bombshell that he wanted to cooperate with the cops. The difference this time was that Leo was sittting next to him, and they were facing two officers, who were surveying him with interest. An air of tension was almost palpable in the stuffy, gloomy room. A small tape machine was on the table, a light blinking on the top.

The cops who had identified themselves as DC Ann Laithwaite and DS Lenny Maxwell had shown no emotion as Leo had made the pitch to them. Davie would take them to the deposit site of Beata Dabrowski, and once it was confirmed that he was telling the truth, and the deal was ratified, he would offer full evidence of how she got there, and more importantly who ordered it.

'But my client won't say another word beyond that until we have a signed deal from the Crown Office that he will not face prosecution, and that parole requirements are met.' Leo sat back and cupped his chin with his hand, waiting for a response.

DS Maxwell paused and observed Davie and Leo in turn before speaking. He was a well-fleshed middle-aged man, smartly dressed in a blue suit and open-necked shirt. He looked tough and seasoned, and his eyes had the weary gaze of someone who had seen and heard it all. DC Laithwaite was much younger, immaculately dressed in a grey business suit, with neatly styled hair, and she wore dark-framed spectacles. She glanced at her partner and shrugged.

'Thing is, Davie. The Crown Office will want a little more before committing to anything. At the moment, we just have words, but almost no detail. Just a name, and before we can present this up the food chain, we'll need convincing that you played no active part in the murder.'

Davie didn't speak. He just looked at Leo and raised his eyebrows.

'My client can take you to the body deposit site. His late father always kept an accurate and secure record of details and circumstances when he organised services such as these for individuals. My client has had sight of these details, knows exactly where the victim is hidden, and he has digitally recorded evidence of what happened to Miss Dabrowski six years ago.'

'Why did he keep such details? Surely that would be a huge risk?' said DC Laithwaite in a strong Glaswegian accent.

Leo opened his mouth to reply, but Davie put a hand on his solicitor's arm and nodded. 'I've got this, Leo. Officer, my father was a meticulous man, and he always kept receipts when he undertook his many activities. Despite his tough upbringing and age, he was technically smart and astute. Any favours he carried out, he would expect his pound of flesh in the future, so his record-keeping was to ensure that any debts, whether financial or not, were paid. The person who benefited from the death of Miss Dabrowski is now a very powerful individual, and my father wanted to ensure that should he need payback, he would have something to motivate cooperation, if you understand.'

'And you are offering to reveal this to us?' said Maxwell.

'As long as I get what I want.'

'And what is that, exactly?'

Davie nodded at Leo.

'Firstly, a guarantee of immunity from prosecution from any complicity in the death of Beata Dabrowski,' said the lawyer.

'It's not as simple as that. If there's evidence to link your client to the murder conspiracy, then there's no immunity deal in Scotland that will cover that,' said Maxwell.

'There's no evidence that my client had any involvement, because he *had* no involvement. He was demonstrably, and provably, in Spain at the time she went missing. He did not know that the murder was going to happen, and he played no part in the planning or commission of the abduction and subsequent murder, and only learned of the details afterwards when he was made aware of the compromising material. His late father passed the material on when he became aware of the terminal nature of his cancer diagnosis. He wanted his offspring to be able to leverage the evidence in the furtherance of their organisation's objectives, should it become necessary in the future.'

'That's a fancy way of saying that Tam Hardie handed over a loaded gun to his boys before he died.'

'Fair point, well made, DS Maxwell. The fact remains that my client has incontrovertible proof that a hugely influential individual solicited a murder that was subsequently carried out. He can take you to the body to prove he is genuine, and when the deal is signed, sealed and delivered to my satisfaction, he will supply this evidence.'

'Okay. We need to report back on this and seek advice, but in principle this should be acceptable. When will you be ready for phase one?' said Maxwell.

'As soon as you are. This shite-hole has lost its appeal.' Davie shrugged.

'Yes, we're ready, but remember our other caveat. No DS Max Craigie, and no one associated with him. He is toxic for my client, and we have grave concerns as to his independence.' Leo Hamilton looked pointedly at the two officers.

'I can assure you that we're taking point on this, and we're reporting directly to Detective Chief Superintendent Wakefield who in turn is reporting to the Deputy Chief Constable. We can do this in two days, if that suits your schedules?' said Maxwell.

'That's acceptable.'

'Any hints as to what we will need to bring?'

'Aye, you'll need a wee boat, and you'll need a diver,' said Davie.

'A diver? She's in water?'

'Why else would I say you'd need a boat?'

'Can't you narrow it down a bit more? It's Scotland after all. Known for its coastline and a myriad of lochs. How many divers? How many boats? It sounds like it could be a big logistical exercise,' DC Laithwaite pressed.

Davie looked at Leo and raised his eyebrows, questioningly. The lawyer nodded.

'Well, the specifics of getting her out of there are up to you lot, but she's in the White Loch close to Newton Mearns, but it's a decent-sized loch, and you'll never find her without an exact location. I know that location, and I'll point it out when I'm there.'

'You could just describe it to us,' said Maxwell.

'I could, but I can't describe it properly. I need to see it with my own eyes, plus I don't trust anyone. I want to be there when it happens, so no bugger can plant incriminating evidence, or any shit like that.'

'Davie, Davie. I'm hurt you'd think such a thing,' said Maxwell, a mock hurt tone in his voice.

''Course you are. This must be done my way, or I'll say nothing more, and Leo here can leak to the press how you're ignoring my desire to assist the good people of the polis and bring closure to poor Beata's family in Poland. How would that sound, eh?'

'Fine, we're ready to go, make sure you are.'

'There's one more thing,' said Leo. 'No big circus, no helicopters, no coachloads of armed cops, not until Mr Hardie has left, in any case. We don't need his photo in the national press, do we?'

'Don't worry, it'll be low key. Last thing we need is a big splash until we know what we're dealing with. We have a cover story ready to go, and you'll be taken out of the jail on the pretext of a hospital appointment, so you'll need to come up with something believable to your co-inmates. Maybe start pulling a pained expression and say that your piles are playing you up,' smirked Maxwell.

'Aye, right,' said Davie without a flicker of emotion.

'When will you give us the full picture?' said Maxwell.

'Only when the Crown Office sign the deal off. We'll agree to an initial exploratory interview after the site has been identified, you'll need a secure and discreet location for this. My client will give details of how the body was deposited, and who was present. He will not disclose who ordered the killing until we have the agreement in hand.' Leo scratched at his legal pad, before looking up at each officer in turn.

'Anything more specific?'

'I'll tell you when appropriate. I don't want you buggers to screw me over,' Davie's bottom lip protruded, a touch.

'Are there interview facilities nearby?' said Leo.

'Kilmarnock police station. Pretty quiet there, and we could probably clear the place,' said Maxwell.

'That's acceptable.' Leo nodded.

'One thing, Davie. We're not daft, and if you're trying to pull a fast one, you're making a big mistake.'

Davie chuckled. 'As if, officer. As if. Get this right, and your next promotion is in the bag, once it comes out who you can bring down. This will go down as the biggest collar in the history of Police Scotland.'

6

DAVIE HARDIE WAS struggling to keep the smile from his face when he was escorted back onto the wing, which was a hive of activity as association was in full swing. There were card games, pool matches and even some chess underway. Small knots of prisoners hung around in corners, chatting conspiratorially, and a faint acidic tang of spice filled the grimy space.

'Davie, where ya been, man?' slurred a small, elderly prisoner, his eyes glazed as he stared blearily at Davie, who had paused to look at the prisoner with a touch of amusement.

'Healthcare, Patsy. You pished again?' he said, a smile stretching across his face. Patsy was always drunk, generally on hooch that one of the other cons somehow managed to brew up in his cell during the long hours of bang-up.

'Pished? Ye cheeky basa' I'll have ye ken that I've nae touched a fucking drop, man. Shh,' he said as he swayed, before adding in a whisper that could be heard even over the prison chatter, 'Ya want a bit? I've a bottle of pruno I could let you have, man. Cheap as chips,' he said, using the slang word 'pruno', for the homemade hooch brewed using apple juice and yeast. As the much smaller man spoke, a fetid waft of alcohol-laden breath almost smashed Davie in the face.

'I'm good, Patsy. Now, fuck off, your breath stinks, man. I need to make a call.'

'Ach, ye young 'uns have nae style,' he said as he staggered off, looking for someone else to buy his hooch.

Davie walked up along the wing to where there was a short line of prisoners waiting for the three phones that were bolted to the wall, each covered with a canopy that was designed to offer a little privacy. Ignoring the queue, Davie strode to the front and approached the closest booth, where a small young man was tucked into the hood, whispering into the receiver. Davie tapped him on the shoulder. The prisoner flinched, as if the phone had suddenly become electrified.

'Jesus, Davie. You scared the shit out of me,' he said. He had a smooth face, only marked by a thin scar on his forehead.

'I need to make a call, Mikey. Hang up.'

The smaller man placed the receiver back on the cradle, his face turning white rapidly.

'You have any credit on your account?'

'Aye, a wee bit.'

'I don't even need a minute. Is my man still on your contacts list?'

'Aye, of course.'

'Good, now fuck off,' he said, handing the smaller man a pouch of tobacco, which he tucked into his pocket before moving away. Davie lifted the receiver and tapped in the code that had been issued to Mikey, but had been shared with Davie for a little tobacco every now and again. Davie always assumed that any calls he made would be intercepted by the prison security division, so it was prudent to use someone else's PIN, and have the other inmate add your contact to their list of approved numbers. It was a simple way of avoiding being eavesdropped on, and as Mikey was only inside for death by dangerous driving, there was no way he'd be intercepted.

There were clicks in Davie's ear as he dialled, and a short pause as the call was connected and began to ring. As it was answered there was a further pause, as the automated system informed the call recipient that there was a call from HMP Shotts waiting should they wish to accept it.

'Yes?' A male voice at the other end of the line responded. Flat, unaccented and unfathomable.

'Two days. The White Loch.'

'Time?'

'Unknown.'

'No problem, we can monitor.'

Davie hung up, turned on his heel and strode off, a grin spreading across his face.

7

IT WAS THREE hours later when Max sat down at the meeting point arranged with Bruce Ferguson at the café just inside the entrance of Glasgow Airport. The large chain coffee outlet was bustling with eager travellers and weary returning holidaymakers, with their polar opposite expressions of either excitement at going on holiday, or dismay at coming back to the cold, frigid Scottish morning.

Max sipped his scalding hot Americano and looked at the arrivals gate with interest. Bruce hadn't specified a flight number, and Max doubted whether it would be a scheduled flight in any case.

He only had to wait a few more minutes before the gates slid open and the wiry form of Bruce Ferguson appeared, casually dressed in jeans and a blue polo shirt, and hauling no luggage beyond a small laptop case, which he wore across his shoulders. He immediately spotted Max and nodded as he approached, extending his hand.

'Max, good to see you,' he said, a smile flashing across his deeply tanned and lined face. His eyes were pale blue and creased with crow's feet and they twinkled with a mixture of intelligence and humour.

Max gripped his hand, which was firm and dry but with none of the macho test of strength. As always, he exuded utter self-confidence that was just softened by his disarming smile.

'You too. Coffee?'

'No, I'm good, full of the bloody stuff from the flight. It's bloody Baltic here, man.' He shivered as he reached into his bag and pulled out a Rab microfleece, which he put on.

'Been somewhere warm?'

'Much warmer than here. This is just a flying visit, as soon as we're done here, I'm going back through and I'm heading down to London.'

'So, what's so important you couldn't tell me over the phone?'

'I need to talk to you about Hardie.'

Max opened his mouth, his stomach gripping at the mention of the name. The Hardie family that tried to kill him, twice. A Hardie almost killed his closest friend and terrorised his elderly aunt. Max tried to formulate the correct words, but all he could do was stare at the ex–special forces operator.

'You okay, Max? You've gone a bit pale.'

'But we all know what happened to Tam Hardie,' stuttered Max.

'Aye, we do, but I'm not talking about Tam Hardie.'

'Who then?'

'His brother, Davie. You know, I will grab a coffee, you want another?'

Max shook his head, as Bruce made his way up to the counter and stood in the small queue looking at his phone.

Davie Hardie? Max's mind flared back to his few encounters with the younger Hardie boy. Max almost struggled to picture the man, who was bigger than his late brother, but without the brooding menace. Despite suspicions that Davie had taken part in many acts of unimaginable brutality, he looked softer than Tam Hardie. Max hadn't attended the trial, preferring to stay in the shadows, but Davie's lawyer had managed to plea-bargain his way to twelve-year sentences for Davie and Frankie, and everything he'd learned was that the remaining Hardie boys were a spent force.

'Sure you're okay, Max? Look like you've seen a ghost, or it could be that I've been hanging about with tanned people in the Canary Islands for a few weeks.'

'I just hadn't expected you to be wanting to talk to me about a Hardie, especially after our last communications about them,' said Max, referring to the video of Tam Hardie Junior disappearing beneath the grey waves of the North Sea, having been tossed overboard from a fishing vessel that he'd thought was his rescue vessel. Bruce was certainly not the forgiving sort.

'Aye, well, that's as may be. But there are two Hardies left, both in Shotts jail right now, and I tend to keep a watching brief on what's going on. You know, a few key words here, a little algorithm there and a bit of background metadata surveillance that my boss is happy to help with via his backchannels. I'm convinced something is occurring with Davie Hardie.'

'How?' said Max, trying to keep the emotion that was beginning to nip at him from his face.

'I think he's doing some kind of a deal. Leastways, he's trying to convince your firm that he wants a deal.'

'How are you doing this, Bruce? I wouldn't be able to get this kind of intel.'

'Well, the snidey lawyer still has both Hardies as clients, and I know he's as corrupt as they come, so I focused my attention on him as I can't get into the prison phones system. Leo Hamilton was receiving plenty of calls from both in jail from their prison accounts, which I can hear if they call in to Hamilton. He gets an automated message first, and then he has to agree to take the call from the jail. I managed to get an alert on his phone which triggers when called by the jail. Well, in reality, it was a while ago, when they were appealing conviction and then sentence, but the calls had mostly dried up. He still has plenty of their cash on account, so he visits every now and again, probably to justify a retainer fee.' He paused to sip his coffee.

'Remind me to never piss you off.'

Bruce smiled. 'Well, as I say, I've been listening on the downlow, and something is definitely happening. His slimy lawyer visited the other day, and then made a call to a cop. A senior cop called Wakefield; do you know him?'

'Possibly,' said Max, trying to keep his voice even at the name of Chief Superintendent Miles Wakefield.

'Well, apparently, Hardie is offering to give up a murder facilitated by his late father that was done on behalf of someone who is now a public figure, and things are in motion. It seems a woman called Beata Dabrowski went missing six years ago but was actually murdered. Have you heard about it?'

'I've a vague memory about a Polish misper.'

'I meant about Hardie doing deals with you lot.'

'Not a dicky bird,' said Max, feeling his face redden.

'Would that be normal?'

'Maybe, maybe not.' Max's mind began to whirl. As the person at the forefront of bringing the Hardie family down, he hadn't been consulted and that seemed strange.

'Obviously, I'm trying to knit a complete picture together from incomplete intelligence, but his lawyer went to the prison early today, together with two cops whom he'd arranged to meet and get in the jail covertly. DS Lenny Maxwell and DC Ann Laithwaite, you know them?'

'Covert Source Management team. I know of them; they have a good reputation.'

'Wakefield and Hamilton organised it a couple of days ago.'

Max just shrugged.

'Well, as it was a face-to-face meeting, and they wouldn't have phones in the jail, I've no idea what's said, but I may have heard a call between the lawyer and the senior cop.'

Max raised his eyebrows but still said nothing, the name Miles Wakefield swirling in his mind.

'Well, it seems to me that Davie is offering chapter and verse on this old murder for an easier ride in jail, and early parole.' Bruce sipped at his coffee, but kept his eyes locked on Max's as he drank.

'Shit.'

'My sentiments exactly. I don't buy it for a second, do you?'

'No. No way would a Hardie grass. It's in their DNA that you never help the police. Ever.'

'I'd say he's planning something.'

'Any suggestions on the phone calls that Hamilton is in on it?'

'Nothing.'

'So, all we have is our inbuilt mistrust of Hardie,' said Max.

'Basically, yes. Can you do anything about it?'

'I can ask, but if we've not heard anything, I'd say that we're being excluded for a reason.'

'You'll try, though?'

'Damn right, I will.'

'I know I don't need to say this, Max, but you can't mention my name at all. We're both breaking a shitload of laws, me by these illegal intercepts, and you taking the intelligence and not arresting me, right?'

'I know. I know, thanks for the heads-up, Bruce. Are you heading straight off?'

'Aye, in fact I need to go and check in again. Plane leaves imminently, well, as soon as I get back on board, anyway.'

'So, you came here just to see me?'

'Just a minor diversion, pal. Now, do something about this, Max. If Hardie gets out, I'm not just gonna let it lie, you know that, right? He's part of the reason my brother ended up dead, and if they got a chance, they'd kill me.'

'What about the cops?'

'What, you're hardly in a position to grass me up, are you?'

'I guess not, but I can't stop others from acting against you. If you start doing questionable stuff with your irregularly sourced intelligence. I'm grateful for everything you've done for me, but there are others in Police Scotland who won't have the same attitude as me.'

'You think that bothers me? With the way I live, they'd never trace me, Max, and I think you know that. Put it this way, I'm not letting those bastard Hardie boys get out of prison a minute before they're due out. They managed to escape the most serious of the charges, but they have to do every bloody minute of the time for what their family did to my brother.'

Max looked at the tough and grizzled ex-commando. He took in the rope-like muscled arms, lined face and steady eyes that managed to combine humour with cold-hearted ruthlessness. Even though Max was breaking laws just by speaking to Bruce Ferguson he felt no conflict and he knew that he trusted him as much as he trusted anyone in the police. He was ruthless, he was a killer, but he was a force for good.

'Yeah, I know that, Bruce.'

8

DAVIE HARDIE WAS snoozing on his bed in his single cell when there was a thump on the steel door, which then sprang open, banging hard as it smashed into the metal bed-frame.

'Jesus suffering fuck,' he blurted out, leaping to his feet with his fists balled, ready to fight.

'Sit down, ya fuckin nugget,' came the voice from the doorway.

Davie rubbed his bleary eyes to see the large form of his brother looming over him, a scowl on his face. Initially after their sentence they'd been at separate prisons, but once the police realised that having them together presented no specific threat, Davie had joined Frankie at Shotts. They hung about a fair bit, often eating together, or playing pool, but mostly they kept their heads down.

'What's with the noisy entrance, bro? You could have just fucking knocked.'

'You fucking know what.' His face was flushed red, as it always was when he was angry.

'Who's pissed on your bonfire, man?' said Davie.

'Don't give me that shite. Anything you want to tell me, brother?'

'No idea what you're fucking on about.'

'Don't bullshit me. You think I don't have sources in this fucking jail, you've been seeing Leo, haven't you?'

'No.'

'Fucking liar,' Frankie growled, shoving at Davie's chest with his open palms.

Davie staggered backwards, falling onto his bed. His brother had always been the biggest of all three of the Hardie boys, and he knew that he'd be bested in a physical confrontation.

'Frankie, I . . .'

'Shut the fuck up, nae more fucking lying, or so help me we're gonna have a square go right here, right now.' Frankie towered over Davie, still sprawled on the bed, his face contorted with rage.

'I just wanted to check something out with him . . .'

Frankie didn't let him finish his sentence. 'Bullshit, you've also just been seen by two cops, and don't fucking deny it. One of the screws told me. What the fuck are you doing? Please don't tell me you're helping the polis, man. Anything but that.' Frankie's eyes were hard and flashing, the fury evident in them.

Davie sighed and sat up on the bed. 'Sit down, bro, and I'll explain. I was going to tell you, I promise.'

Frankie uncurled his fists, the white knuckles softening as the blood returned to them. He pulled the upright chair away from the desk and sat on it, his body still tense. 'This better be fucking good, Davie.'

'Look, I can't handle it in here much more, man. Elizabeth is getting pure crabbit with me, and I need to go somewhere new. I've a plan, and it can include you. We can both get out, and get transferred to Castle Huntly, and get parole dates fixed. Leo has confirmed it and there's a cop who's willing to go for it.'

'Go for what, for Christ's sake? In exchange for what, Davie? What the fuck have you agreed to?' His eyes were bulging out, and his breathing was short and staccato.

'Remember that Pa sorted out a major problem for someone six years ago? Polish girl was taken care of because one of his people wanted her out of the way?'

'Aye, vaguely. I remember Pa talking about kompromat on some bigwig.'

'That's the one. Pa always called him The Ace.'

'I remember, but you know how it was. Pa and Tam kept lots between themselves, so I don't know much.'

'Well, I've a plan to use it, and it involves the cops, but we need to keep our fucking voices down. You know what it's like in here, Frankie. In exchange we'll get immunity, and we just have to do two to four years at Castle Huntly. It's a bloody breeze in there, man. Your own key, cooking facilities, unlimited gym and even better, regular home leave, and Christmas at home. Elizabeth will leave me if I have to do another eight to ten in this shite-hole.' Davie's eyes were pleading.

Frankie said nothing. He just sat staring at the wall above Davie's head, breathing evenly, a palpable strain in his face. All of the jail noises of shouting, music, clattering and doors banging were zoned out and there were just the two brothers, in that grim cell with the tension almost crackling with its intensity.

Suddenly, and with almost impossible speed, Frankie rocketed to his feet and his open hand whipped out and connected with Davie's cheek with a sound like a pistol shot. Davie's head rocked to the side, but he did nothing. He didn't retaliate, he didn't cry out, he just sat there, his eyes fixed on his brother, tears brimming in his eyes.

'Listen to me, Davie, and you listen well. You are sullying our fucking family name, if you help the bastard polis. Our pa would be spinning in his grave if he knew that one of his sons was grassing. Hardies don't grass, Davie. Hardies. Don't. Grass. Of all the rules in the book, that one is written in big fucking bold letters, and you're considering going against everything our family has ever stood for. You've broken the code,' Frankie said, drawing himself to his full height, his chest puffed out and his face brick-red.

'Frankie, I . . .' but Davie couldn't get the words out.

'I dinnae want to hear it, man. The only thing I want to hear is, "I'm no helping the fucking polis." That's it,' Frankie said, his voice tight and hoarse, the veins protruding on his neck, and his teeth gritted. The loathing came from him in palpable waves.

'It's not so easy for me, man. I've a wife, you don't. She'll fucking leave me, and I cannae have that. She's all I have left. Our name means nothing any more, and it certainly won't after another eight in here. The Albanians will already have taken over.' He shifted his gaze down onto the coarse bedspread, but he said nothing, his face pale and a slight tremble detectable in his shoulders.

Frankie almost growled, the loathing evident in his face, 'Say that again, and I'll fucking kill you, right now.'

Davie said nothing, just continued to stare at the bedspread, a solitary tear falling onto his grey joggers.

Frankie looked down on him, scorn in his eyes. 'You're no longer my brother. You're dead to me.' He turned on his heel and walked slowly, and calmly, out of the cell.

9

'OH WELL, LOOK what the fucking cat dragged in. Detective Sergeant Craigie has at last deigned it timely and appropriate to grace us with his presence. Only half a day late, Craigie, anyone'd think you've been bloody working hard. I want to say thank you, DS Craigie, we are honoured that you've lowered yourself sufficiently to come to our humble office. Get the bastard kettle on,' said Detective Inspector Ross Fraser, looking up through his bushy, untamed eyebrows, a phone receiver clamped to his ear as Max walked into their office in the bowels of Tulliallan Castle.

'Hey, Max-dude. Where's the tardy doughnuts?' Norma piped up from behind three large monitors, her impish face peering around the edge of the largest one. Norma was the team intelligence analyst and researcher who Ross had recruited from the National Crime Agency. She was hugely capable and could decipher and interpret the most complex intelligence from multiple sources and come up with a concise and cogent briefing document within a startlingly short timeframe, but only if she was regularly supplied with cakes, sweets and biscuits.

By way of an answer, Max produced a pack of Tunnock's teacakes from his rucksack and tossed them onto her desk.

'Ah, man. All is forgiven, be late any bloody time if you're bringing teacakes,' she almost squealed.

Max just smiled weakly and walked over to the small, dented and ancient-looking fridge, on top of which was a tray cluttered with dirty mugs and an old stainless-steel kettle.

'Mugs are bloody bogging,' said Max, looking at the scummy selection of chipped china.

'Well, you know where the sink is, or is that too lowly for someone with a high-maintenance supermodel's regard for timekeeping, eh?' said Ross, scowling at the phone, before slamming it down hard into its cradle. 'Why does nobody ever answer the bloody phone? It stresses me out. Pass me a teacake, my blood sugar's dropping, and I need tea and sustenance. Come on, tea. Chop-chop.'

Ross looked tired, his face was craggy and pale, and he looked even more dishevelled than normal. His shirt was creased, and there was a button missing where it bulged against the pressure of his belly, exposing white, hairy flesh.

'Don't you want to hear why I'm late?' said Max.

'Of course, DC Calder was being deliberately evasive when I asked her, so I was going to do it over a nice cuppa, but as you seem to be eager to get to the bollocking, let's go for it. Where the fuck have you been?' Ross said, a touch of humour creasing his face as he caught the foil-wrapped teacake that Norma had tossed to him.

'I've received some concerning intelligence from a source.'

'What type of source, human or electronic?'

'Can I answer that a bit later?' said Max.

'Why?'

'Because it's a little irregular, and I need time to think about how I describe it.'

'Is it reliable?'

'Very.'

'How can you be so sure?' said Ross, taking a big bite of the chocolatey dome, the white fluffy interior spilling out and smearing on his lips.

'Because it's been very reliable in the past, but is a little . . .' Max paused to consider, 'can I say, shy?'

Ross's brow furrowed in confusion. 'Craigie, I know you're a weird bugger, but I also am aware that you have a knack for getting intelligence right. If I'm to do anything with whatever it is you're going to tell me, I probably need to be able to categorise the source, and then evaluate it. You know, National Intelligence Model and all that shit, the College of Policing are particular about it.' Ross licked the white fluffy centre from his lips.

'Okay, can I say a community contact?'

'Call it what you bloody like, man. Just tell me what the intelligence is, and we'll worry about the attribution and evaluation later.'

'Okay, but you're going to have to trust me on this one, it's a big deal, and I trust the origin of the info.'

'Pal, you're being deliberately obtuse here. Just spit it out.'

'I think that Davie Hardie is going to try to escape from prison.'

A sudden silence descended on the room, as everyone stopped typing.

'What, that brother of Tam Hardie?' said Barney, from his customary spot on a worn armchair in the corner of the room.

'That's the one.'

'Shit,' said Ross.

'I'll make the tea,' said Max.

10

STEVEN 'MITCH' MITCHELL threw the last of his tools in the back of his battered white van and slammed the door shut. He zipped up his jacket against the cold and turned to face the grey-haired and elderly householder who was standing on the doorstep, nodding and smiling.

'Thanks for such a grand job, Mitch. The new kitchen is marvellous, and I'll recommend you to everyone at my book club.'

'Grateful, Mrs Lyons. I'm glad you like it.' He smiled, brushing sawdust from his trousers.

'When can you fit the new flooring?'

'It's on order, so probably the week after next. I'll get it fitted as soon as it's in, I promise,' Mitch said, and scratched an itch in his ear.

'You're an absolute darling. Let me know, yes?'

'Will do Mrs L.' He climbed into the driver's seat, started the ropey-sounding engine and headed off, returning Mrs Lyons's wave. He sang along with the radio, as Adele burst out of the speakers, feeling once again relief that he was no longer in the game. He was finally enjoying being on the straight, and away from all the problems that his former life had brought with it. He was excited about getting home early and he was going to grab a lightning shower, and then set about making dinner, so that Abi would have a meal waiting for her when she got home. His smile widened at the thought of his lovely wife. She'd saved him from his former life and shown him that there was a better way to live. He actually enjoyed his job now, fitting kitchens, floors, shelves and the like. It was honest, and it gave him satisfaction.

The journey home took only ten minutes, as the traffic was light, and he yawned as he pulled onto the drive of his newish home on one of the recent developments to the east of city. He switched off the engine and fumbled for the front door key.

Although Mitch had left the life of crime a couple of years ago, he still had a sixth sense for when things were wrong, and he knew something wasn't right, now. He looked at the house, reaching down into the footwell, where a socket wrench had fallen earlier, and he was reassured by its cold heft in his calloused hand.

He wracked his brain, trying to identify what was different that was making his hackles rise.

Then he saw it.

The side gate to the left of the house. The wrought-iron latch handle was askew. He'd fitted the gate himself after they bought the house, but it was rarely used, and the latch was normally parallel to the ground, but it was at a slight angle. Someone had opened the gate, or at least attempted to do so, which was unusual, as it was bolted shut on the other side.

Mitch got out of the van, the wrench still in his hand and walked from the van to the gate. He reached out and lifted the latch, noiselessly. The gate swung open, and his heart lurched. No one ever opened that gate apart from him, when mowing the lawn. Being the depths of winter, it hadn't been opened for months. Someone had opened it, either from the other side, or by climbing, or by reaching over to pull the bolt back. But why? Burglary was uncommon in this area, but they weren't unheard of. If there was a bastard burglar in his house, he was about to get a nasty fucking shock, thought Mitch as his grip on the wrench tightened, his knuckles whitening. He lived a law-abiding life now, but he would protect his wife and home with his life, he thought as he felt sweat begin to prickle on his spine, and a flush of blood rise in his face. He'd been a good fighter in his time, and this fucker was going to regret ever breaking into his house. He pushed at the gate and stormed the path that led up the side of the house. When he reached the back, he saw with horror, which soon morphed into fury, that the back door was open and shards of glass were under his feet, crunching like hard ice. He growled, trying to keep the fury from exploding out. Stealth was needed, just in case the bastard was still inside. He pushed the UPVC back door open, and it swung smoothly on well-maintained hinges. He eased into the kitchen, trying to stop his footsteps cracking the toughened glass that was strewn all over the hard-tiled floor.

He steadied his breathing, trying to control it, ready to deal with whatever came next, when there was a chink of glass behind him. His heart jumped into his mouth as he turned, raising the wrench, a snarl on his face.

'Hello, Mitch,' came a deep, sonorous voice, tinged with the dark streets of Glasgow. Mitch looked at the newcomer who was standing six feet away on the garden path. He took in the heavy, hooded eyes, drooping jowls and deeply lined forehead of the expressionless face.

'Droopy . . .' he began, his heart lurching as dread instantly gripped him like an icy fist.

'Bye, Mitch,' said Droopy, who quickly raised his hand. Mitch just had time to recognise a long-barrelled pistol with a bulbous silencer on the front. It coughed once, bucked in Droopy's hand, and a bullet smashed into Mitch's forehead. He fell like a dropped sandbag, dead before he hit the floor.

11

MAX STARED AT Ross, who was chewing thoughtfully on another Tunnock's teacake, his mug in his hand, eyes half closed, contemplatively, as Max spelled out the intelligence given just an hour ago by Bruce Ferguson. The only bit he left out was Bruce's name, and the fact that illegal phone intercepts were the source of the information. Intercepts are tightly controlled, can never be openly referred to, and are only authorised at the highest level. Max trusted Ross more than anyone else he could think of but telling him about 'unconventional' telecommunications intercepts would put him in a difficult position.

Ross brushed away the inevitable chocolate crumbs that had landed on his shirt, wiped his mouth and spoke, his voice calm. 'Right, let me get this straight. Your source, whoever the fuck it is, has mysteriously sourced intel that Hardie's slimy lawyer is negotiating with the cops, and more specifically Chief Superintendent Miles Wakefield, and the CSMU to identify a misper, who is in fact a Polish murder victim topped on the orders of some bigwig?'

'Aye, that's about the size of it.'

'It's not that much, is it?'

'Can you see a Hardie cooperating with cops?'

'No, it's absolute mince, pal. I've been in this job a long time, and no Hardie has ever helped the cops. He's planning something.' Ross rubbed his hair with his hand.

'Any suggestions on how to handle it?' asked Max.

'This calls for my legendary tact in finding out shite like this. Trust me, I know everyone, and the reason I've survived as long as I have in the job is my tactful, sensitive diplomacy. I'll make a call.'

'Who to?' said Janie.

'Miles Wakefield. I've known the dickhead for decades, and he'll level with me. I want to know why we're not taking point on this, or at the very least being heavily consulted. We, after all, banged the bastards up.' He picked up his phone from the desk and dialled, pulling himself to his feet with a half-strangled groan and moving towards the door with a slight limp, wincing a little as he did. 'Miles, you old bugger, I'm hearing rumblings about Davie Hardie,' he almost bellowed as he left the office.

'The legendary tact,' said Max, shaking his head.

'How does he get away with being so rude to senior officers?' said Janie.

'I reckon he knows where all't bodies are buried,' said Barney, who produced his scratched and worn tobacco pouch and began to roll a cigarette, almost meditatively.

'Anything on the supposed victim?' said Janie, looking at Norma.

'What makes you think I've been looking already?' said Norma, peering from behind her screens, her glasses a little askew on her nose.

'Because you always do. I bet you've half a profile compiled on the case already, just by listening in.'

'Well okay, I've had a wee peek. Not much to it, really. She was living in a rented place in Glasgow. She went out one afternoon, her pal spoke to her on the way, and she thought it was to meet a man. There had been talk of an affair or something, but her pal didn't know. She'd been a working girl, self-employed type using websites for a time, but had stopped a while before she disappeared. When her pal tried to call her, her phone went to answer machine and never came back on. Some evidence of hasty packing, and of an intention to travel, but she never showed up anywhere again. No sign of travel on border targeting, no banking activity, and no phone traffic after the day she disappeared. A big fat mystery. She was a bonnie wee thing,' said Norma, shaking her head.

'Any boyfriend?'

'Not that I can tell, but the friend thought there was someone. One interesting thing.'

'Go on?' said Max, sipping his tea.

'She was receiving money each month from a UK bank account that stopped as soon as she disappeared, the same with the rent payments that came from the same account. All stopped,' said Norma, tapping at the keys, the familiar look of total concentration on her face.

'Was anything done with that? It doesn't seem right to me,' said Max.

'It looks fairly half-arsed as far as misper investigations go. It was quickly downgraded to medium risk, and then they took DNA samples from the flat, you know, hairbrush and toothbrush, and a profile was developed in case any body was found, but after that, nada. I think that they just thought she'd fled.'

'That's not a great example of a misper inquiry, is it? The money should have been followed up, at least. Can you have a look at the bank account, Norma?'

'I can send the enquiry out. It could just be that she stopped the payments herself, once she knew she was going.'

'It looks like she fled in a hurry, without her computer, and without mentioning it to friends, so how could she shut those accounts? It doesn't seem right.'

The door to the office burst open, and Ross limped in, his scowling face red as a tomato. 'That's bullshit, Miles. Since when does a fucking villain like Hardie dictate who investigates, eh?'

He looked at Max and shook his head, angrily, the tinny voice on the other end of the line was almost audible, and it didn't sound happy.

'No, it's shite, Miles. We put Hardie away, we should at least be able to be briefed on it.'

There was another pause, as Miles spoke.

'DS Craigie had a tip-off, that's all. We just want to have a poke around. What do you mean, not trusted? I'm not having that, Miles . . .' Ross's face flushed an even deeper shade of red, before he yelled down the phone, 'Well, fuck you, too then.' He threw the phone down on his desk.

'Well, your legendary tact went down well there, Ross,' said Barney, chuckling in his armchair.

'Piss off, Grandpa. We're off the case, not that we were ever on it.'

'What, why?' said Janie.

'Hardie seems to be calling the shots. He's demanding no involvement by Max, and no one who works with him. We're ordered to stay totally off the case, direct from the DCC.'

'What?' said Janie, incredulously.

'Exactly that. Miles and the DCC are letting him run the bloody show.'

'He's planning something, Ross. He's planning something big, and that's why he doesn't want us anywhere near it. He knows we won't believe his bullshit. Can you appeal this?' said Max.

'I'm going to do that, right now, but as I've already had one carpeting from the DCC about our one-legged spy abstracting electricity, I suspect it won't do much good.' Ross reached for his phone again and dialled.

'Margaret, it's Ross Fraser. Is the DCC in?' He paused, his face frozen in mild surprise as the tinny voice spoke.

'On our way.' He hung up and looked at Max. 'Margaret was just about to call us. She wants to see you and me now. Looks like Miles cliped on us, the bastard.'

12

MAX AND ROSS were quickly ushered into DCC Campbell's office by the nervously smiling Margaret, who notably didn't offer coffee. A meeting without coffee was always ominous.

'Sit down, both of you,' said the unsmiling DCC Campbell, who didn't look up from a document that she was studying.

Max glanced at Ross, who just shrugged as they sat down on the two hard chairs that had been positioned six feet directly in front of the huge walnut desk. She continued to read the document in front of her, flipping the pages with apparent bored interest. The room was overpoweringly quiet as she continued to go through the sheaf of papers. This was a classic senior-officer tactic to assert her power. By ignoring them, as she was clearly doing, she was making it clear who was in control. Ross looked again at Max and smiled, shaking his head at this pretentious display.

The silence was thick and unpleasant, but Ross didn't seem in the slightest bit fazed, and his eyes twinkled with amusement. DCC Campbell was clearly making a point.

When she spoke, she didn't look up from her document. 'Ross, just what the hell is happening on your team?'

'Beg your pardon, ma'am?' said Ross, his face impassive and his voice even.

When she eventually raised her eyes, they were flinty and hard. 'You know what I mean. I had to take you to task this morning because one of your staff is camping out in the car park as if this is a caravan site and stealing electricity for goodness' sake, and now I hear from DCS Wakefield that you're interfering in a covert investigation. To make things worse, DS Craigie, you seem to be accessing highly sensitive intelligence from questionable sources. So, Ross, I ask again, what the hell is going on with the Policing Standards Reassurance Team? Because nothing I have seen so far is in any way reassuring me.'

Surprisingly, Ross kept his cool. 'Ma'am. DS Craigie received the intelligence anonymously, so quite reasonably raised it with me. We have detailed knowledge of the Hardie family, being responsible as we were of bringing them down. It doesn't feel right that Hardie is setting the parameters of the investigation. We should be involved. We have knowledge and experience of that family that DS Maxwell doesn't. Hardie has an ulterior motive, I guarantee it.'

'Well fortunately, Ross, this is my decision to make, and the possibility of Hardie leading us to an unsolved murder of a foreign national is too important. Hardie has made it clear that your team, and in particular DS Craigie, is not to be involved in any way or the deal is off. Can you imagine the media attention? With all the corruption scandals Police Scotland have had recently, it'd be a blood bath.'

'Aye, scandals, that my team uncovered. We've done more to clear up corruption than any other bugger in recent years. Your predecessor for one,' said Ross, his voice tightening as he referred to the previous DCC who had been uncovered by the team.

'Don't take that tone with me, DI Fraser. Yes, I've been made aware of your successes, but there are also many questions I'd like answering about those, as many of the details don't add up. I am now lead for professional standards, and I'll be making representations to the Chief Constable about your team. My submission will be that you should be part of my portfolio for reasons of scrutiny and accountability.' Her face had begun to redden, just a touch, and her jaw was set tight.

'Well, I'm happy for any and all types of scrutiny, ma'am. I answer direct to the Chief Constable, and it was his decision to form the team. I believe we still have his confidence.' Ross's eyes blazed as they met hers.

Campbell broke first and turned to Max. 'DS Craigie, what did you say the source of the intelligence was?'

'Anonymous, ma'am.'

'Anonymous how?'

'Phone call from a withheld number, I believe through a web-based call.'

'Do you have a way of returning the call?'

'No, ma'am.'

'Well, if you do, you are to hand it over to DS Maxwell, is that clear?'

'Perfectly, ma'am,' said Max, flatly.

'Now, I will only say this once. Ross, your team is to have no part in this case. Any intelligence you receive must be shared, along with source details to DCS Wakefield. When I say no involvement, I mean exactly that. No poking about, no rattling cages, or shaking trees. Nothing. This is too important, too high profile, and is the sort of thing that costs careers. Am I clear?'

'Crystal clear,' said Ross.

'Now, I've been made aware of the excessive hours you've all been working, so I want you all to take the rest of the week off. Go and spend time with your families. We'll meet next week, and I'll want to review your team's performance, and how I think we can improve, moving forward.' Her eyes lowered to her report again, indicating clearly that the meeting was over.

Ross looked at Max, raised his eyebrows and shook his head as they stood up.

'Oh, one more thing,' said Campbell.

'Ma'am?' said Ross.

'Your camper van—dwelling technical man, Bobby?' Her eyes narrowed.

'Barney, ma'am.'

'I'm having vetting look at him, as I'm not comfortable with the idea of a man with access to such sensitive material and equipment living in a camper van.'

'Is that necessary, ma'am?' said Ross, his brow furrowing with confusion.

'Yes, I believe so. I'm going to be looking at all staff working in professional standards as well as other sensitive roles, including your staff. I want a clean bill of health on all the workforce in such sensitive roles.'

'That seems a little like overkill, ma'am?'

'I disagree. Vetting have already informed me that Barry—'

'Barney, ma'am,' interrupted Ross.

'Okay, fine. Barney has some significant debt issues. His house in Leeds was repossessed not so long ago. Were you aware of this?'

Ross just stood there, open-mouthed.

'I can see not. You need to be aware of what your staff are doing, Ross. Debt is a serious driver for corruption, you know.'

Ross's face flushed. 'Barney is a freelance contractor. He's the best in the business and he's been vetted to the highest level with the security services for decades.'

'Well, his vetting is being renewed now, so I advise you speak to him to see if there are any other surprises. Now, if you'll excuse me, I have things to do.' Her head bowed again, the tension almost crackling in the room.

Ross opened his mouth, his teeth bared in a snarl, but Max took his elbow and led him away before the anger he could see welling up overflowed. Ross didn't resist.

'What now?' said Max as they left the office, nodding at Margaret as they passed through.

'You heard her ladyship. We're taking the rest of the week off, but not before I tear that senile, one-legged old spy a new arsehole.'

'Maybe make sure he's okay first, Ross?' said Max, softly.

'Aye, right, I'm feeling really bastarding sensitive after that bollocking. Fucking second in a day, because of that old duffer.'

'So, are we just going to let Hardie do whatever he's planning?'

'I don't see what else we can do, Max. If we go off-books, we're liable to all get bloody sacked. Can you imagine how Mrs Fraser would take that? "Sorry, hen. I cannae pay the mortgage this month as I got canned." Same goes for you. We leave it to them and pick up the pieces when they inevitably fuck it up. Or, alternatively, maybe Hardie actually is just trying to horse trade for early parole, and a cushy regime.'

'You believe that?'

'Does the Pope shit in the woods?' said Ross, wincing as he limped down the corridor.

'Erm, no?'

'Well maybe, but I'm fairly confident he has a gold cludgie in the Vatican.'

'So, what do we do?'

'Max, seriously, pal. We go home, and we stay out of it. If your "anonymous source" contacts you again, you'll just have to give him Lenny Maxwell's number. It's not worth your job, and there's no doubt that DCC Campbell would take the greatest of pleasure in getting us the tin-tack, as your cockney former colleagues would say. It's a slam dunk gross misconduct, sacked, ruined pension and divorce certainty. So, I'm going home. I'm gonna look after my kids, mow the lawn and prune the fucking roses.'

'Firstly, it's winter, so there's nothing to mow. Secondly your kids are in their thirties, and will be at work. And you have no roses that I can recall,' said Max with a chuckle.

'Aye well, piss off home, and stay out of this job, Max.'

'I will,' said Max, avoiding Ross's eye.

'I mean it, man. Stay away from anything to do with Davie and Frankie Hardie, slimy bent solicitors and the like, okay?'

'Fine,' said Max, wondering if it was true.

'I'll have another word with Miles and tell him to watch his back, but I think after my slightly disrespectful encounter earlier, he may not be that receptive.'

'Aye, your tact and diplomacy really worked a treat,' said Max, smiling.

'Maybe I should think before I swear at senior officers. I'll call him and eat a bit of humble pie. Maybe tell him to take some backup, but he wasn't in a listening mood earlier.' Ross shook his head ruefully.

'What's done's done. Come on, let's get back to the office, and get everyone home.'

13

MAIRI MALONE WENT to the combination-lock key box by the back door of the small, pebble-dashed bungalow in a quiet side street in one of the better suburbs of Glasgow. She positioned the numbers into place until the box sprung open revealing the solitary key inside. She took the key and slid it into the lock, the door creaking arthritically as it swung open. She stepped in, her nose wrinkling at the smell, which was the familiar pungent mix of piss and biscuits underpinned by the tang of cleaning products deployed to combat the ever-present unpleasant odour.

'Hector? It's just me, Mairi,' she said, closing the door and tucking the key into the pocket of her purple tabard that had 'Alba-Care' emblazoned on the breast pocket. An ID badge on a bright purple lanyard was around her neck, declaring that she was Mairi Malone, together with a photo of her smiling, broadly.

'Hector, will you look at the state of you, man?' she said, striding into the cluttered room, clucking at the tiny and almost skeletally thin man who was sitting in the high-backed Shackleton chair in front of the two-bar electric fire. The carpet was worn and wildly floral, and the curtains were a deeply clashing geometric-shaped mess. The TV, which looked almost as old as Hector, was switched on, but the sound was turned down, with subtitles slashing across the flickering screen. Hector was pretty much deaf, despite the hearing aids that protruded from his ears that seemed far too large for his tiny head, which was covered in a silver-grey halo of fine, almost baby-like hair.

'Mairi, my darling, I didnae hear you come in. I'll get Morag to put the kettle on.' He turned to face her, his face lighting up at the sight of his home carer.

'Oh, Hector, hen. You remember that Morag's no longer with us, she passed ten years ago,' she said, sitting next to him on an upright chair, and stroking his hair, affectionately.

'Ach, yes. Of course, she is. I just forgot for a moment. Is it bath day?' His rheumy eyes appraised her from behind thick semi-tinted spectacles.

'It is, you look bogging, man. And you need a shave, look at them whiskers. If you're to go to the day-centre later, you'll need to scrub up, eh?'

'Aye, you'll be right, hen. Now will you run a bath for me?'

'That's why I'm here, Hector. Have you eaten?'

'Aye, young lady came in this morning and made me breakfast, and I think I have soup and sandwiches for lunch.'

'You do, and I'll heat it up after your bath, man. Come on, now you're a bit whiffy, man. I'll go and run it now and you can have a soak whilst I fix lunch.' Mairi ruffled his hair, and headed to the tiny bath-room. He was a nice man, Hector. Never inappropriate and, despite occasionally forgetting that his wife had passed away some time ago, was almost always cheerful. She quickly ran the water, adding some bubble bath, which Hector always loved, and she carefully checked the temperature with her elbow. She smiled at this, as it reminded her of what she did for her kids, and it struck her as prophetic how more child-like her clients became as they got closer to death.

Quickly striding back to the living room, she saw that Hector had managed to stand, and was moving towards the door, his walking stick clasped in his bony hand.

'All ready for you, hen. I'll help you get in and then get your lunch sorted.'

'Aye, but no peeking, ya ken. I know what you're like, Mairi Malone.' His eyes twinkled mischievously.

'Och, Hector. You're far too young for me.' Mairi giggled as she took his arm and steered him to the bathroom. She then followed the familiar routine of helping the skinny, arthritic old man into the chipped and worn aubergine-coloured tub, with her eyes closed, as he lowered his undernourished frame into the bath. Once in, he said, 'Okay, open now' as he sat there, tiny and frail and almost up to his neck in bubbles.

Mairi opened her eyes and grinned. 'Now make sure you get into all the creases and wrinkles. Need you smelling all fresh for the ladies. I see you have your aftershave all set and ready to go,' she said, pointing at a bottle of Old Spice.

'They can't resist it, hen. Now scoot whilst I perform my ablutions,' he said, nodding at the door.

Mairi chuckled as she left the bathroom and returned to the living room. She cleared up a dirty cup and saucer, and a plate with a half-eaten piece of toast on it and took it to the tiny galley kitchen, which looked like it hadn't been updated since the bungalow had been built. She went into the fridge and pulled out a clingfilm-wrapped sandwich on a plate, and then found a can of tomato soup on the kitchen table. She opened it with a can opener that was laid out on the side. Poor old Hector's arthritis meant that he could not open a can without help, so she quickly removed the top and tipped the bright red liquid into a saucepan, and put it on the stained hob on low.

Her phone buzzed in her pocket. Looking at the screen she frowned at the message. **I need it now**, was all that the message said. Feeling a sick sensation in her gut, she tucked the phone back in her tabard pocket.

She went to the drawer in the kitchen dresser and pulled it open. She knew what she'd find in there. She pulled out a large leather wallet, which she opened. Inside was a passport and driving licence in the name Hector MacFarlane. She pulled out her phone and engaged a scanner app. She quickly scanned the driving licence and the details page of the passport, which bore a faded photo of a much younger looking Hector. As she leafed through the passport, she couldn't help but be saddened by the stamps on almost every page showing how much Hector had travelled until his arthritis had put a stop to it all, and it only increased her shame at what she was doing. She looked at the big stack of unopened mail on the dresser top and flicked through it until she found what she was looking for. She ripped open the envelope, and pulled out Hector's council tax bill. She scanned this as well and saved the image to her phone, before sliding the bill back into the envelope and tucking it into the stack of mail. Hector did have family, but not nearby and his son took care of all his bills remotely. No one would notice that the bill had been opened, and if they did, so what? There was no fraud, nothing was being stolen.

She quickly opened WhatsApp and composed a reply to the message she'd just received from a number that was just saved in her phone as 'D'.

Passport, driving licence and utility. Enough? and pressed send. Her face flushed as she tucked her phone away again. This wasn't the first time she'd done this for him. He could be very persuasive, and it was hard to say no. Nothing was being stolen, no one was being defrauded. 'Borrowing an identity for a wee while', was how he had sold it to her, and she'd make a little bit of coin out of it. Her pay was so low that a thousand quid just for a single message wasn't money she could turn down, was it?

She tucked the passport and driving licence away in the wallet and returned them to the drawer, closing it silently. Not that she needed to, Hector wouldn't hear a thing. She stirred his soup, a feeling of shame washing over her like a harsh, sticky blanket.

'Mairi, I'm ready, hen,' came the croaky voice.

She shook her head to clear the fog. No one was getting harmed; it was just borrowing an ID for a while. No harm, no foul, she thought before squaring her shoulders to go and see to lovely Hector.

14

LC-Campbell, Louise <Louise.Campbell@scotland.police.uk>
To: <Finn.Townsend@copfs.gov.uk>
Cc: <Mark.Jacobs@copfs.gov.uk>
Subject: David Hardie – Debrief and immunity exploratory exercise

Dear Finn,

It was lovely to meet you and Mark earlier today, and thank you so much for the warm welcome that the Crown Office has extended to me. In my role as lead for criminal justice support, I am keen to develop a close relationship with yourselves as Crown Agent and COPFS generally to ensure a joined-up approach which will help strategise a formal, corporate procedure.

Just to summarise, the case of Hardie to ensure we are all aware of the terms of reference.

A scoping interview will be undertaken with David Hardie, currently serving a twelve-year sentence for drug trafficking offences. He will be covertly interviewed within the prison estate by DS Lenny Maxwell, and DC Ann Laithwaite, both of Covert Source Management Unit, overseen by DCS Miles Wakefield. Hardie will be legally represented at all times by Leo Hamilton, of Hamilton and Partners solicitors.

Post interview evaluation will be sent to yourself and Mark Jacobs, Advocate Depute, for consideration.

In the event of a reliable indication that prima facie evidence

*exists to indicate that remains of Beata Dabrowski (BD) are locat-
able, an operational plan will be devised to produce Hardie from
HMP Shotts in order to identify the deposit site for BD. The operation will be fully risk assessed, but as it stands, it appears to be
a wholly proportionate exercise.*

*Upon successful identification of the remains of BD, the proposal
by Leo Hamilton will be considered as a matter of urgency by
yourself in conjunction with Mark Jacobs.*

*Once the agreement is signed, a full debrief of David Hardie
will be undertaken at a secure facility, which will include digitally
recorded evidence, along with an ABE standard debrief, which will
be evidentially sound.*

*This will enable a further strategy to be devised to locate as yet
unidentified suspects in the case of the disappearance of BD, and
bring them to justice.*

*You will both agree that this exercise is of the highest importance,
and is of high levels of public interest, if the allegations being made
by Hardie have any credence. Police Scotland has suffered some
PR disasters over the last few years, and I want us to be squeaky
clean in our handling of it.*

We'll speak again, once we know the results of the initial debrief.

Warm regards,
Louise Campbell

Louise smiled as the 'whoosh' from her laptop indicated that the email
had been sent. She had only arrived in Scotland a few weeks ago and
already she had one of the biggest scandals land right on her desk,
at a time when the Chief was sunning himself in Tenerife. If things
went well, this case could almost be done and dusted before he got
back, and all the credit would be hers. Just perfect timing, to be seen
as a new professional standards broom, when Police Scotland had
been riven with corruption scandals, and if Hardie was to be believed,

a significant public figure was at the centre of this inquiry. She smiled, as she stood up and walked to her Nespresso machine, slotted a pod in the slot, placed a cup under the nozzle and pressed. A small, thick stream of coffee drizzled into the cup, almost like treacle, filling the room with the heady aroma.

She inhaled deeply and took a sip, a tingle of excitement in her stomach at the prospect of landing in her new force with such a bang.

There was a ping, as an email arrived, she returned to her leather chair and sat down.

FT-Townsend, Finn <Finn.Townsend@copfs.gov.uk>
To: <Louise.Campbell@scotland.police.uk>
Cc: <Mark.Jacobs@copfs.gov.uk>
Subject: Re: David Hardie – Debrief and immunity exploratory exercise

Hi Louise,
Thanks so much for your prompt action on this.
   Agree with all your points, of course with the caveat of the principle of habeas corpus. No body, no case.
   I look forward to hearing the results of the scoping exercise, but I see no problems. Hardie would possibly be eligible for parole in another few years anyway, and moving him to Castle Huntly will be a simple process. I'm actually surprised that he isn't asking for more!
   Any immunity deal will inevitably have to be signed off by the Lord Advocate, but I foresee no problems if Hardie is true to his word.
   Maybe lunch soon?

Warm regards,
Finn

Campbell smiled at the overly familiar reply from Finn Townsend, which almost had a suggestion of flirting in it and actually made her chuckle. Typical man, thinking with his dick after just a short meeting. She knew how to manipulate men, and she knew that she possessed more ability in her well-manicured little finger than half of the boys-club senior officers. She was destined for the top, she had always known it, and this could be the next step on the ladder to her ultimate aim.

She sat back in her chair, and smiled. By the time Macdonald was back, they might even have people arrested, and a big media splash ready to go.

Police Scotland being the second biggest force in the UK wasn't the only reason she'd taken this role as DCC. She knew that Chris Macdonald's initial contract date was looming. A few big splashes like this, and she'd be in prime position to sweep in.

Chief Constable Louise Campbell had a nice ring to it.

15

DAVIE HARDIE WAS sitting on his bed, looking at, but not seeing, the television which was showing some kind of antiques challenge, when there was a tap at the slightly ajar door.

'Yeah?' he said not looking from the TV.

A prison officer pushed the door open; he was a small and wiry man whom Davie hadn't seen before.

'Hardie?'

'Aye.'

'My name's Mr Dixon from prison security. Your hospital appointment has been confirmed for tomorrow morning at Queen Elizabeth. You'll be collected at ten so be ready to move, okay?'

'I'll be ready, guv.'

Dixon nodded, turned on his heel and left the cell without another word. This was often the case with the security screws at the nick. They kept out of the way a lot of the time, but when they came, it signalled something was going to happen.

Davie smiled to himself, before standing up to follow in Dixon's footsteps. He went out onto the metalled landing and descended the staircase before heading for the line of phones. One of the younger inmates was deep in conversation on the middle of the three phones as Davie walked up and pressed his hand down on the cradle.

'Hey, for fuck's—' He stopped, his face twisted with anger, but his eyes widened, and the angry look turned to one of contrition when he saw who it was who had cut off his call.

'I'll be one minute, piss off,' Davie said, entering Mikey's code, and then dialling. He listened to the dial tone, followed by the pause as the recorded message was played.

'Yes?' The same flat voice as before.

'Tomorrow, leaving at ten. To the White Loch, and then on to Kilmarnock cop shop for interview,' he said, trying to hide the smile he felt spreading across his face.

'Understood.' There was a click as the call was disconnected.

Davie turned and began to retrace his steps back to his cell, a spring in his step as he broke out into a tuneless whistle.

He didn't notice his brother watching intently as he stood by the pool table with the younger prisoner whose call had been interrupted.

16

MAX HAD JUST finished working out in his makeshift gym in the garage at his farm cottage in Culross when his phone rang. He picked up the handset from the weights bench and looked at the display. There was no number.

'Yeah?' he said as he answered it.

'Is there something you need to tell me?' said Bruce Ferguson.

'Is this line secure?' said Max, still slightly out of breath, sweat cold against his cheek where the phone was against the skin.

'Max, it's me you're talking to here, man. VPN enabled and web-based; GCHQ wouldn't even be able to hack it.'

'Good, and what do you mean?' said Max, guardedly.

'I think you know what I'm talking about. Hardie's getting out of jail tomorrow, to go to identify the burial site. Are you involved?'

Max sighed and rubbed at the dull ache that was beginning to appear at the back of his head. 'I didn't even know about it. We've been ordered off the case, totally. Literally forbidden on pain of getting sacked from having any involvement at all.'

There was a long pause at the other end of the line.

'Bruce?'

'I'm still here. This is madness, Max.'

'Tell me about it. We made a fuss, but the new DCC is looking to make a name for herself, and she wants us nowhere near it. It also sounds like she wants us disbanded.'

'Can't you go over her head?'

'No. Chief's on holiday.'

'He can't be allowed to escape, Max.' Bruce's voice was edged with steel.

'Well, we're out of the picture, completely. We've been ordered on leave.'

'Isn't that a bit concerning?'

'What being on leave?'

'No, the timing of it. A Hardie being taken from prison on a bullshit story, you get removed from the case and now they put your whole team on leave. That stinks.'

'Nothing I can do about it.'

The ex-commando exhaled with frustration. 'You know my feelings on this, Max. I won't have a Hardie running around the place, free. No fucking chance.'

'My advice is to stay out of this, Bruce. It's really big, and is being scrutinised at the highest of levels. I can't protect you, if you do anything daft.'

'I'm not asking for anything. You take care, Max. An angry Hardie on the loose is a threat to you, as well as to me. Those bastards couldn't forgive a two-hundred-year-old feud, and they won't forgive you.' The line went dead.

17

JACK SLATTERY SIGHED as he ascended the stairs towards his cell at Saughton jail, his plastic tray in hand. The hollowed-out compartments in the tray were filled with his evening meal, and it didn't look appetising to say the least. Some grey meat stew that was on the menu as 'stovies', a couple of soft oatcakes and a jam roly-poly, with congealing custard. He also clutched a plastic bag that contained his breakfast for the morning. A bag of cereal, some milk and an apple. It wasn't much, and he was thankful that his cell contained a supply of Super Noodles, some tinned tuna and a variety of biscuits, all bought with his canteen allowance, or bartered with other cons. He was adept at trading for food, as he wasn't a junkie, but managed to get spice smuggled into him via an approachable officer. He then would sell it on to the jail's junkies to keep him in tobacco and extra food. Despite being an ex-cop, his years of associations with the Hardies and a couple of other criminal gangs meant that he was off-limits to the hot-heads. He mainly kept his head down, and rarely got into confrontations.

But it was still hateful in here, and he had at least eighteen years left to go. Eighteen years of at least twenty hours a day in bang-up, often twenty-three. He cursed his luck in getting involved in the Hardie business, and even more, the fact that it brought him up against that bastard Max Craigie.

He pushed his door open and was thankful that his pad-mate, the overweight and malodourous scumbag 'Shorty' Maguire was nowhere to be seen, which was in itself unusual. What wasn't unusual, however, was Galbraith, a big unit of a con from the ground floor, who was currently sitting on the chair in his room, an open can of tuna in one hand, and one of his forks in the other, as he chewed away.

'What the fuck are you doing in here, Galbraith? And that's my bloody tuna,' said Slattery, placing his tray on the table and tossing his breakfast bag on his bed.

'Bit hungry, Jacky boy. You've plenty, and Shorty didn't think you'd mind.' He smiled as he shovelled in another forkful, moving the jagged edge of the lid to one side to allow access to the last of the meat.

'You cheeky bastard, who the hell do you think you are, man?' Slattery said, bristling with anger, his face flushing, but a knot of fear forming in his gut. He knew nothing of Galbraith other than him being a lifer from Aberdeen. He was a big lad, full of muscles, and with that hard, grizzled look of someone who'd seen his share of life.

'Jack, old son. You worry too much, I've a message to deliver, the tuna was just a bonus whilst I was waiting. I got peckish.'

'A message?'

'Aye, an important one, from an old pal of yours.'

'Well, tell me the message and fuck off. And you owe me a can of tuna.'

'Fair enough.' Galbraith stood and smiled. He was utterly relaxed, with an amused look on his meaty face. Slattery didn't notice what he was holding in his hand until the sock, containing two further cans of tuna, flew through the air, propelled with massive force, until it connected with his temple, dropping him to the floor like a collapsing shop dummy. Sparks flew in his head, like fireworks, and his vision began to darken.

A voice emerged into the darkness. 'Droopy sends his regards, Jack,' said Galbraith as the wickedly sharp and jagged tuna can lid was sliced across his windpipe, and warm blood exploded from his carotid artery.

18

MAX STEPPED OUT of the shower and began to towel himself dry, his thoughts whirring after the conversation with Bruce. Could it really be that Hardie would help the cops? Stranger things had happened, but it didn't feel right at all. Not snitching was in the Hardie DNA, but he was forced to accept that he had nothing to base that on other than his prejudice against the family.

He was pulling on his jeans when Nutmeg flew into the bedroom, tail thrashing wildly and jumping on the bed, trying to leap into Max's arms.

'Hey, Nutty, settle down, eh?' he said, tickling her ears.

'Hey, mister, you're home early. Is this some kind of miracle?' said Katie, coming into the bedroom dressed in her business suit.

'Rest of the week off,' he said, kissing her on the mouth.

'What? As in leave?' she asked incredulously.

'Sort of.' Max's voice was slightly hesitant.

'You've not been suspended or something again, have you?' she said, puzzlement in her eyes.

Max laughed. 'Why would I be suspended?'

'Well, sudden, unexpected leave is hardly the norm, is it?' she said, stripping off her jacket and slotting it on a hanger.

'Well, not exactly. We've been caning the hours.'

'Don't I know it; I was thinking of calling missing persons.'

'Aye, well. DCC sent us all home, plus there's some rumours about one of the Hardie boys in prison.'

'What kind of rumour?' Katie's eyes widened in alarm. The Hardie name always had that effect.

'Ach, it's nothing,' said Max, pulling his T-shirt over his head.

'Max?' said Katie.

'He's getting out of jail about an unsolved murder.'

'What, voluntarily?'

'Supposedly.'

'Is that credible?'

Max just shrugged, and yawned deeply, fatigue descending on him all of a sudden.

'Max, are you okay?'

'I'm just tired, but I don't buy it for a second. Hardies don't help cops. They don't grass. Not ever,' he said, looking up at his wife, who had unbuttoned her blouse and was turned to him with concern in her beautiful eyes, her choppy hair, all tousled. A sudden wave of desire washed over Max, and he took Katie's hand in his, kissed it and gripped it tightly, moving closer until they were inches apart.

'Again, Craigie? Even with your daft hours, we've been at it regularly, no wonder you're always tired,' she said, a mischievous glint in her eyes.

Max returned her smile and kissed her again. She encircled his waist with her toned arms, and they fell onto the bed in a tangle of limbs, their lips locked onto each other's.

*

'Dippy man, look at me. Look at me, pal, stay awake. You're gonna go home, back to the shite-hole you live in, bud. You're gonna be good, man.'

Dippy opened his eyes, and his pinprick pupils were full of confusion as the medic tried to get a line into his arm to replace the fluids that were still flowing out of him onto the sand. 'Max . . .'

'Dippy?'

'Max . . .' His voice dropped an octave and was only just above a hoarse whisper.

'Come on, look at me, pal.'

Dippy's eyes glazed and the faraway look became an empty one. Something changed. A light went out.

Max yelped as he was jerked into consciousness. The dream ripped him from sleep, like being violently pulled from a deep, black hole. The smell of the Afghan desert was redolent in his nostrils, the stench of Dippy's blood that was congealing in the hard, desiccated dirt. The colours were vivid, almost technicolour in intensity and his heart was beating rapidly, a cold, mucky sweat lathering his body.

'Max, you're okay, babe. It's just the dream.' Katie threw her arm across his chest, and stroked his forehead, the sweat beading on his skin.

Max inhaled, deeply, the only light in the room coming from the digital clock, which try as he might he couldn't focus on, feeling the panic beginning to subside as his wife stroked his brow, her soothing voice easing the fear away.

'You're okay, babe. I'm here.' Her voice was soft and warm, like a balm.

'What time is it?' said Max, his throat dry and cracked.

'Half nine. We both drifted off,' said Katie.

'Afterwards, not during, I hope,' said Max, a smile returning to his voice.

'Most definitely afterwards. You hungry?'

'Starving.'

'What do you fancy?'

'Apart from you?'

'Goes without saying.'

'Pizza?'

Katie wrinkled her nose. 'Nah, I'm off cheese.'

'What, you, off cheese? Never thought I'd hear that.'

'You go shower, sweaty-man. I'll go rustle up something to eat,' she said, switching on the bedside light and reaching for her towelling robe that was on the floor. She threw it around her shoulders, pulled it tight against the chill of the room and winked as she headed out of the bedroom.

Max lay back and stared at the ceiling, his mind whirring with thoughts of Hardie, which had come crashing back into his life since Bruce's call. He was just throwing back the duvet to go shower when his phone began to buzz and dance across the bedside table. He peered at the display.

'Janie, what gives? You do realise what time it is, right?'

'Of course, but as we're on leave, I thought I should mention what I've just heard. You remember Pete Barr?'

'No, should I?'

'Maybe not. Prison liaison officer for Saughton?'

'Of course. Grey-haired old fella.'

'I think he's a similar age to you.'

'Shite, hard paper-round?'

'Whatever. He called not long ago with some disturbing news.'

'What?'

'Ex–Detective Sergeant Jack Slattery was murdered in his cell just a few hours ago.'

'What?' Max's gut lurched.

'That was my reaction.'

'Shit.'

'Shit, indeed. Apparently, he was found in his cell during lockdown with blunt force trauma to the nappa and someone had cut his throat with a tuna can lid. He was barely alive, so they did the whole first-aid thing, and rushed him off to healthcare, got an IV into him, but died in the ambulance on his way to hospital.'

'Any suspects?'

'Aye. Clear as day. Looks like a big nasty lifer called Galbraith did it. No attempts to be sneaky for CCTV on the landing, and he was found a few minutes after covered in blood. Turbo team took him out, but he didn't resist. He just smiled his way through it all and has just said that he killed him because he was a pig.'

Max sat there on the bed, his heart pounding like a drum. This had to be connected to Hardie. It just had to. 'Any links to what we've been conveniently sidelined from by the powers that be?'

'If you mean Hardie, then no. Well, they know basically bugger all at the moment. It's only that Pete is a mate that we've heard about it at all.'

'Does Ross know?'

'I bet he doesn't. He was off intending to keep Mrs F happy for the rest of the week.'

Max began to scratch at his scalp, which was still sticky and damp as he attempted to get his brain to operate. Jack Slattery, ex-cop and fixer for both Tam Hardies. A man with fingers in every pie possible before his incarceration, and a man with a major grudge against Max, in the same way that the Hardie family did. The memory of the confrontation with Slattery behind his house, the revolver pushed into his face, swam into Max's mind. Could there be a link?

'Max?' said Janie.

'Yeah, still here, just trying to organise my thoughts. It has to be connected, don't you think?'

'Well, as an ex-cop, Slattery would have always been something of a target. You could make the observation that this was almost inevitable, right?'

'Yeah, but he was Hardie's man. He was Hardie's tame ex-cop, so I can't see that. It just seems far too convenient, timing-wise.'

'But why, Max? Let's say that Hardie is planning to bust out of jail, why would he want Slattery dead?' said Janie, her voice hesitant, and Max could almost hear the cogs turning.

'I don't know, but maybe there's something else at work here.

89

Maybe someone wanted Slattery dead because of what he knows, not because of who he was, and maybe it isn't Hardie.'

'Then who?'

'Janie, I have no bloody idea. I'm gonna call Ross.'

'Is that wise?'

'Well, if it's connected, he needs to know. At the very least it should be flagged to the team who are taking Hardie out tomorrow.'

'Okay, I've asked Pete to keep me in the loop.'

'Thanks, speak later.'

Max dialled Ross, who quickly answered. 'You may have no fucking life, Craigie, but I am happily watching a movie with my dear wife, and a very choice glass of red wine, so why are you bleeding bothering me?' Ross's voice had a melancholic edge to it, and Max suspected that his boss had consumed more than one glass.

'Janie's heard from her prison contact that Jack Slattery has just been murdered in Saughton,' said Max, without preamble.

'What?' said Ross, the incredulity masking the mild slur in his usually hoarse and caustic timbre.

'Aye.'

There was a long pause on the line punctuated only by Ross's heavy breathing.

'Fucking hell, how?' he said, eventually.

'Janie only has sketchy details, but blunt force trauma followed by cutting his neck with a tuna tin lid.'

'I remember Galbraith. A gun for hire, and he's an evil bastard who was unlikely to see the outside world ever again. Killed two in a gang dispute a decade ago, but I didn't think he was connected to the Hardies at all. Jack was a dirty, corrupt and amoral bastard, but he didn't deserve that.'

'Aye.' Max felt the phone buzz against his cheek, looking at the screen he saw that there was a WhatsApp from Janie with a photo attached. 'Hold up, Ross. Janie's sent a message. It may be an update.' Max opened the message which had a single line of text under the photo. **Pic from Phil of cell after body removed**. The photo was pin-sharp and lurid and showed an empty single cell. The bed was covered by a plain duvet cover that was saturated in blood, matched only by the dark, congealing puddle on the hard floor. There were footprints everywhere in the gory mess and discarded first-aid detritus. There was no body visible, it clearly having been removed. However, it wasn't the gore on the floor, or the bed, or the discarded first-aid equipment that made Max's stomach lurch. It was what was on the wall, smeared in blackening blood. Max felt an icy hand grip him, and sweat began to form on his spine.

PIGS WILL BE BLED

Max paused, his heart thumping as he looked at the macabre daubing on the chipped paint of the cell. The post-dream feelings flared in his mind, which he forced down. The sight of blood often did this, and he swallowed against the rising taste of bile in his throat. He squeezed his eyes shut, and breathed deeply, in for four, hold for four, exhale for four.

'Max? What are you playing at, you fucking nugget?' came Ross's tinny voice from the speaker. Max shook his head and forwarded the message to Ross, and then put the phone back to his ear. 'I've sent you a message. Photo from Slattery's cell after the event.'

'Fucking hell,' said Ross. Immediately there were repeated beeps and clicks as Ross tried to bring the message up, followed by a muffled 'piece of shite phone, why can't it have buttons that fit my bastarding fingers?' before there was silence again, punctuated only by Ross's rasping breath.

When he spoke, his voice was low, tense and almost sad. 'I'll make a call and get back to you.'

Max sat on the edge of the bed, staring at the plain white wall in front of him, when Katie came in the room followed by Nutmeg, her soft feet padding on the carpet before she leapt up on the bed alongside him, tail twitching and her cold nose nuzzling his hand. Max instinctively tickled her silky, soft blonde curly ears.

'Max?' said Katie, concern in her voice.

'It's nothing,' said Max, but even as he said the words, he knew that they were not true.

'Max?' repeated Katie, her tone longer and lower, demanding a response.

'You remember Jack Slattery?'

'Yes, of course. The ex-cop who broke in here and planted drugs?' Her face screwed up with distaste.

'Amongst other things, yes. Well, he's just been murdered in prison.'

'Oh my God, how?'

'Still working it all out, but he was hit over the head and stabbed,' said Max, leaving most of the details out. His wife had seen things that she shouldn't have since she'd become involved in the last big case. Despite his utter respect for her humanity, strength and kindness, he wanted to protect her from the darkness. He wanted to shield her from the prospect of harm coming to them. He wanted to stop his stupid job causing his beautiful, strong and kind wife being exposed to the dark world that he was forced to operate in at work. He looked at her, and felt a surge of overwhelming love. He took her hand and kissed it gently.

'Oh Max, your job is just so awful. Why was he killed and are you going to be involved in it?'

'I don't know. We're being kept out of it all so far, but maybe this will catapult us back into it.' He continued to stroke Nutmeg's ears as he stared at the wall, his mind turning, his thoughts dark. He breathed in slowly and softly for four, paused for four, and let it out again.

His phone buzzed again. 'Ross?'

'I've just spoken to Miles Wakefield, and he wants to know how you found out about it,' he said, getting straight to the point.

'Why the hell does that matter?' said Max, confusion flaring in his mind.

'He got crabbit about us interfering in shit that doesn't concern us, as bloody usual. To be fair, it sounded like he was in the pub, and he sounded pished to me.'

'What did you tell him?'

'To go forth and multiply.'

'I'm sure that'll have helped.'

'Possibly not, I suspect that I'm going to get cliped on again. He's turned into a right grass, that bugger has.'

'So?'

'So, what?' said Ross, his voice full of irritation.

'So, what are we doing about it?' said Max.

'Nothing.'

'What, just nothing?'

'What do you expect us to do? A murderous bastard kills a corrupt ex-cop in jail. A MIT team is being formed and they'll deal with it. Probably very quickly if what I'm hearing is correct. We're just another unit within Police Scotland, we're not a posse in the wild west. We do as we're bastard told, or we end up at the end of the dole queue, pal. Now go to bed, and stay out of this case, and tell that busybody Calder the same. Am I clear?'

'Crystal.'

'Good, now piss off. See you next week.' There was a click and he was gone.

'That sounded typically Ross,' said Katie.

Max said nothing, just closed his eyes and rubbed hard with his hands. The whole situation was surging in his mind, and he knew he was missing something. Something was staring them in the face, and he couldn't fathom what it was. A mix of frustration and anxiety began to rise inside him, and he knew there was only one thing he could do to make it stop.

'Max, is everything okay?' said Katie, reaching her hand out to his bare thigh.

Max shook his head, vigorously, trying to shake the fog that was descending. 'I'm going for a run.'

19

DAVIE HARDIE SAT in the back of the anonymous-looking Ford Minibus in the sterile area between the external and internal prison gates. They waited there in silence, apart from the murmur of the breakfast radio station, which only just managed to break the uncomfortable atmosphere in the stuffy van.

'So where to then, Davie?' said DS Maxwell, who was sitting next to Davie at the rear of the van, his wrist shackled to Davie's with an old-fashioned set of link handcuffs.

'You need to know now?'

'Aye, of course we do. We have Marine Support Unit ready to meet us there, and I don't want to piss them about.'

'The White Loch,' said Davie. He felt tense and on edge, but was trying as hard as he could not to show it to the bastard cops, or the slimy Leo. He couldn't let them know how he was feeling, or they'd see it as a sign of weakness.

'Where's that?' asked Maxwell.

'Near Newton Mearns, not far from East Kilbride.'

'I know it, right enough, I sometimes paddleboard there. It's about an hour there this time of day. Lovely spot,' said the driver, whose name badge read 'Constable Clegg'.

'Nice and low profile, guys. I like it, you know how my fellow prisoners would take me helping you guys out, eh?'

'Snitches get stiches,' said DC Laithwaite.

'Aye, at best,' said Davie, chuckling.

'Well, you see, Davie. Your former empire is no more, so there are no grounds for an armed escort, hence it's just us five in the van, as agreed.'

'Well, I'm obliged, dudes,' said Davie with a sarcastic smirk.

Leo Hamilton sat in the back in front of his client, a leather-bound notepad on his lap, and Laithwaite was in the front passenger seat.

The driver flipped and swiped on the sat-nav and nodded. 'About forty-five minutes, so we'll be there by eleven,' he said in a rich, sing-song Highland accent.

Laithwaite reached for her radio. 'Destination: White Loch near Newton Mearns in East Kilbride.'

'Marine 1, all received,' was the crackly reply.

'MIT support 1, all received,' came another reply.

'Who're those bastards?' said Davie, sharply.

'Who?' said Maxwell.

'MIT support 1?'

'A DI and a DS from the murder investigation team. They want to be there, don't worry, they're following at a discreet distance, Davie. This operation is as low profile as a set of BMW M3 run-flats.'

'Well, let's hope it's a little more comfortable. I had an M3 once, and it was a right spine shatterer,' said Davie.

'Your driver, Cleggy, is an advanced driver, pal. Smooth as silk,' said Laithwaite as they drove off through the gates that almost seemed to be inching open.

The journey was slowed by the heavy traffic, but the morning was pleasant enough and Davie was enjoying seeing the familiar streets begin to whizz by as the van gained speed. They left the built-up Shotts and came into the more attractive Lanarkshire countryside.

'Ten minutes away,' Laithwaite said into the radio as they entered the open and bleak countryside of East Kilbride and onto the narrow road winding through the tussock grasslands, which were punctuated by lazily turning wind turbines.

'You ready for this, Davie?' said Maxwell.

'Aye, and isn't it a lovely day for pointing out where dead bodies are?' said Davie, smiling, as the late morning sun shone through the windows and danced on the ice-crusted grass.

'Davie?' chided Leo, turning to glare at his client.

Davie just chuckled. 'Along this road, straight for a wee while longer. You'll get to a metal gate at the edge of the loch. Pull over there and I'll direct you in.'

They drove along for about another mile, the sweeping road carving a path through the low, featureless hills until they rounded a bend, and there it was. The White Loch sparkled like a sapphire against the stark countryside, the watery winter sun reflecting off the glass-like surface.

'Just here, by the gate,' said Davie, pointing at a metal farm gate that was secured with some blue baler twine. A solitary paddleboarder was silhouetted on the water.

'So where, Davie?' Maxwell turned to face Davie.

'I need to get out. We need to walk along the shoreline towards the trees you see in line with the wind turbine. Once I'm there, I'll recognise it.'

'Okay, but nae tricks, man. Any shite, and you're on the deck, twisted up in rigid cuffs, ken?' Maxwell said, his accent broadening, as if to add authenticity to his threat.

'Sergeant, my client has cooperated all the way. There's no need for threats,' said Leo, superciliously.

'No threats, just a friendly warning,' said Maxwell.

'An unnecessary one.'

'Aye, right. Let's go then, how far are the marine unit?' said Maxwell.

Laithwaite spoke into her Airwave handset. 'Marine 1 and MIT 1, ETA at White Loch?'

'Marine 1, ten minutes.'

'MIT 1, fifteen.'

'Okay, you ready then, Davie?' said Maxwell.

'Like a coiled spring, Sarge,' said Davie with a broad smile.

DC Laithwaite got out of the car, unhooked the twine from the gate and swung it open. PC Clegg eased the van through the gate and brought the vehicle to a stop on a patch of compacted earth. 'I don't really want to take the van much further; we'll get bogged down. Marine guys have a four-by-four, so they'll be grand,' said Clegg.

'We're fine, we'll walk from here,' said Maxwell.

They all got out of the van and began to walk along the edge of a fence that ran alongside the shoreline. After about a hundred metres trudging in the heavy tussock grass, Davie stopped by two small conifer trees right by the water's edge and looked across the glittering surface. He wiped his face with his free hand and looked out towards the centre of the loch. It was a peaceful scene, almost totally silent other than the whisper of a gentle breeze and the slow, rhythmic whooshing of the nearby wind turbine that spun slowly in the sun.

'About a hundred yards out. In a direct line with where we are now and she's weighted down with a big chain, so she'll be near the bottom. That's where Beata Dabrowski is.'

20

MAX WAS IN the garden dressed in a thick hoodie and wielding a large wooden-handled axe against a beech log, which he was splitting into sticks for his wood burner that he was going to light as soon as Katie got home. The pile of cut logs was soon reduced to decent-sized burners, ready to keep the kitchen and sitting room warm during the long winter evenings. He was humming along to Radiohead's 'Paranoid Android' as he swung the axe, and the large log split in two. When his phone began to ring, connected to his earphones by Bluetooth, he set down the axe and looked at the screen. Nutmeg sat on the grass, watching him with apparent interest.

'Barney, what's up?' he answered.

'Ayup, do you want a bit of inside info, on the QT?' said Barney.

'Are you working?'

'Nay, lad. Just a bit bored, in me van parked up at a nice little spot just outside Glasgow, but I thought I'd keep me ear to the ground, if you get me.'

'Not really.'

'Well, I know we got warned off the Hardie job, but I thought I'd have a poke about.'

'Barney, was that wise? Our name is mud right now, and in particular, your name is mud right now with the electricity stealing in front of the DCC.'

'Well never mind. Hardie is out and about right now, did you know that?'

'I may have heard a whisper from a mate.'

'Would that be the same mate who managed to obtain backdoor access to a locked phone a while back?' said Barney, and Max could hear the smile in his voice. On a previous investigation, Bruce had managed to get a covert access route into a phone that Barney had failed to access. He had been full of curiosity as to how Max had managed it, and had always been frustrated by Max's reluctance to share.

'No idea what you mean, Barn. Now what do you know?'

'They're at the White Loch by Newton Mearns, leastways DS Maxwell is there, so I reckon that's where the missing lass is.'

'Barney, how do you know this?'

'Monitoring the channel they're using. Also, marine support are on the way, so it looks like they're diving for the body.'

'How have you bypassed the encryption on the Airwave?'

'The handset I managed to liberate from my former employers can access all channels.'

'Jesus, Barney.'

'Ah, don't fret, man. Just keeping an ear out. They sound pretty excited, like they expect to find something.'

'How close by are you, Barney?' said Max, suspicion rising in his chest.

'I'm parked by a right bonny place by Harelaw Dam.'

'Barney, that's right by the White Loch, isn't it?'

'Well, not right by it.'

'How close, then?'

'About two clicks?'

Max paused, unsure whether to reprimand Barney or admire his ingenuity. 'Barney, you're gonna get us all in the shit. Stay out of it, please.'

'Max, Max, don't worry about it, mate. Just doing a bit of camping in't van. Barbie's on right now for a bacon butty, come and join me?'

'It's close to bloody freezing.'

'Aye, hence the barbie. I'm fine, and warm. Heating runs on gas, mate, don't fret.'

'Haven't you got anything better to do than this?'

'Not really, but I do have my new toy to play with.'

'What's that?'

'Best don't ask, pal. Any road, just thought I'd keep you in the loop. I'll monitor the radio, see ya.' The phone went dead.

Max rubbed his temples with his fingers, a sense of dread beginning to rise. Something was going to go wrong; he could just feel it. Something always went wrong whenever the Hardies were involved.

He looked at his phone again, and went to the contact marked 'BF' and dialled. Nothing happened. No ring tone, no automated message, nothing. Just silence. Max frowned, the anxious twinge he'd been feeling for some time worsening. He took a deep breath, shrugged and tucked the phone away, staring out across the long, sweeping lawn and onto the wide expanse of the Firth of Forth that stretched away in front of the cottage. He sighed again, trying to force away the gnawing feeling of doubt. Nutmeg whined and moved closer, nudging his hand with her nose. Max responded by tickling the little dog's ears, and her tail started thrashing. 'Good girl,' he murmured, before picking up a small stub of wood, and throwing it as hard as he could. Nutmeg's ears pricked and she raced off after the missile, with a delighted bark. Max picked up his axe and set at the pile of logs with vigour. As always, hard, physical labour helped, and he began to feel better. Not all better. Just a bit better.

21

DAVIE, LEO HAMILTON and DS Maxwell were all sitting in the marine unit's liveried Toyota Hilux, which had arrived towing a black RIB on a trailer. It looked powerful and sleek with beefy-looking outboard motors at the rear. It had taken a couple of hours for them to get set up, get the boat into the water and get a couple of officers ready to enter the frigid waters of the loch.

Since their arrival, the loch had gone from being quiet, peaceful and deserted to a hive of activity. Various vehicles drove up, generators were started, and control vehicles established. The thrum of the generators was now competing with the whooshing of the nearby wind turbines.

'Looks like they're ready to go in. Are you gonna give them the final pointer, Davie?' said Maxwell.

'Aye, whenever they're ready. She's there waiting for you guys to find her,' said Davie from the backseat, where he was still shackled to Maxwell.

A uniformed sergeant walked up to the vehicle and opened the back door. He was a solidly built balding man, with a wide smile and crooked teeth.

'Okay, the RIB's in the water, you ready, man?' he said in a broad Glasgow drawl.

'I'm ready,' said Davie.

'Okay, tell us where, and we'll send the RIB out, and you just direct us in,' said the sergeant.

'Right, a hundred metres from the trees, towards the centre of the loch. Set your boys running, and I'll shout when you hit the spot, although I only ever saw this on video, you understand?'

'Aye, well. Whatever.' The sergeant lifted his radio and repeated Davie's instructions, shaking his head, the distaste for the convict evident in his face.

The engine notes of the RIB's powerful motors picked up, and the craft carved through the glassy surface at a slow speed, the two divers sitting at the sides, with a coxswain at the rear.

'A little to the left,' said Davie. The sergeant relayed this by the radio.

The craft adjusted its course slightly, maintaining a slow and steady speed.

'Another thirty metres,' said Davie, quietly.

'Thirty metres,' relayed the sergeant.

'There, stop there,' said Davie, his face a mask of total concentration.

'Stop there,' radioed the sergeant.

Davie looked at the RIB, stationary on the calm surface, bobbing gently side to side. 'That's it. That's where she is.'

The sergeant looked at Davie long and hard. 'You sure?'

'Aye. That's where she was put in, a chain around her legs. I've seen the video, and that's where she was dropped in. My old pa always kept receipts, and that's where she was thrown in. She'll still be there.'

'She'd better be, Davie,' said Maxwell.

'Or what?' said Davie.

'Or you're going straight back to jail. No body, no case, no early parole and no Castle Huntly. That's what the Crown Office said, eh? Do not pass go, do not collect two hundred quid.'

'She'll be there.'

'When do you tell us who put her there?'

Leo Hamilton cleared his throat. 'You know this, DS Maxwell. Once she's found, we do a limited interview to cover this part of the evidence, and then you go to the Crown Office. Once they've signed off the full agreement, we'll give you the rest of it, not before. This shows good faith on our part, and allows you to be sure my client is telling the truth.'

'Well, we'd all best hope she's there, or this will have been a big waste of resources,' said Maxwell.

'I'm telling you, Len. She's there. Any chance of a coffee?'

'Aye, we've makings in the van, help yourself. Now, if you'll excuse me, I've divers to supervise.' The sergeant moved off down towards the waterline.

'I'll go and get the coffees,' said Clegg.

22

BARNEY DRAINED THE last few drops of tea from his chipped tin mug, and washed it in the small fold-out sink at the back of his van. He was parked in a rough gravel car park by the reservoir, the end of a barbeque smoking away at the side of the van. He shivered at the biting cold as he threw the water onto the gravel and folded the sink back into the rear compartment and slammed the back door shut.

He slid the side door open, intending to get back in the van and get the Calor-powered heating going again, and maybe use some of his battery to watch a bit of TV, but his eyes fell on the compact case that the postie had delivered earlier. It was tucked under the reversed driver's seat and he reached down to pull it out, pausing for a moment. He'd chosen this spot to park up, as he'd overheard on the radio that the White Loch was the site of the apparent body dumping. As Barney had no particular place to be, he decided he'd scope it out, and he'd actually found a really picturesque spot. He'd been eavesdropping on the recovery operation, more out of general interest than any desire to get involved. If, as Max and the team thought, this was something dodgy, he didn't think it'd be a bad idea to have someone nearby. The radio sitting on the bed crackled. He'd had an Airwave set for a few years, since before leaving MI5, and it hadn't been hard to hold onto it, particularly as he'd been working freelance across other government agencies. The fact that he had access to all channels was a bonus, and any time encryption was changed, he had enough contacts to update the encryption in the set.

'Searching now, two divers down, and fingertip going on. Just ten metres deep, but bad visibility, stand by,' came the tinny voice from the handset.

Curiosity pricked at the old spy. This was why he still did what he did. Curiosity to learn new stuff, to try to defeat the bad guys who were always trying to outwit them. He slid the door shut, sat down, and switched on the heater, grateful for the sudden blast of warm air that came out of the vents. He enjoyed being in the van, but in winter it could get a bit chilly. He reached for his thermos flask, poured some hot water into his cup and threw in a tea bag.

The radio crackled again. 'We have something. We have something, definitely, exactly where he said it would be, secured by a chain. Yes, it's a body. A body in a tarp, stand by for further info.'

'Well, bugger me. He was telling the bloody truth,' he muttered. Looking again at the black, hard plastic case, he made a snap decision. He flipped open the fastenings and lifted the lid. A small, compact drone was flat-packed inside the case in tightly fitting compartments cut from high-density foam. He smiled looking at the sleek bit of kit which he'd been sent by an old pal from the service, who now worked for the manufacturer and wanted Barney to field test it. It was the latest model from the company and was packed full of new tech. It was reputed to be the quietest drone on the market, with a x32 zoom, 4K resolution video, long battery life, active tracking and the ability to live-stream imagery over 5G, as well as record to a one terabyte SD card.

Barney sipped at his tea, wondering if now was a good time to field test such a nice-looking piece of kit. His thoughts turned to Hardie, currently under two kilometres away. It was probably unlawful surveillance, but then it could just be considered that he was testing a bit of new tech that could be of use to the cops.

'Bugger it, why not,' he said, pulling the unit out of the box. Quickly he attached the rotors and extended the four quadcopter arms. He then slotted the battery that he had freshly charged overnight into the back of the unit, which was about the size of an A4 pad. He slid the van door open and stepped out, ignoring the niggle of discomfort where his prosthetic leg rubbed against his stump.

He set the drone down on the gravel, switched on the controller and slotted his smartphone into the bracket, making sure it was tight. He navigated to the app, linked up the phone with the controller and woke the drone. The blades began to buzz as they spun. It was uncannily quiet compared with other drones he'd used in the past. Still audible, but once it was over 100 metres in height it would be out of earshot, and with the long zoom, he'd be able to read a car registration plate, or even check if someone had shaved that day. Barney chuckled with pleasure. This was when he was happiest. Ever since he was a kid, playing with gadgets, electronics or whatever tech was new made him smile.

'Come on then, let's see what you've got.' The drone shot off the scrappy gravel and zoomed into the air, gaining height quickly, the whine of the motor and the rotor blades fading fast as it ascended. The image from the camera was pin-sharp, and panoramic, giving an incredibly detailed high-definition of the sweeping countryside. He tweaked the controls sending the drone across the open, barren countryside towards the White Loch.

'Right, Hardie. Let's see what you're up to, you bugger.'

23

JANIE WAS SPRAWLED on the sofa in her Edinburgh tenement reading a Hilary Mantel novel whilst the soft, sensuous sounds of a Stan Getz saxophone solo drifted out of the hidden speakers in the large, open-plan space.

'Janie, this sounds like lift music to me,' said Melissa, who was sitting at the kitchen island, her laptop and a pile of textbooks open. Curiously, she was dressed in football shorts, a hairy jumper and fluffy slippers in the shape of a shaggy dog. Her hair was held back with a spotted bandanna.

'Why is it that people always dig me out for my music taste? Stan Getz is the master.'

'Master of Muzak, maybe. It's shite. Coffee?'

'Aye, why not, philistine,' said Janie, throwing a cushion across the room. It missed by almost a metre and fell onto the polished wooden floor.

'I'm not picking that up, by the way,' said Melissa, moving from the stool and switching on the coffee machine.

'I'm not bothered,' said Janie, pretending go back to her novel, but unable to stop herself looking at the cushion. She tried to tell herself that she wasn't a clean freak, or possibly someone with some type of OCD, but the cushion on the floor now loomed in her mind, almost taunting her.

'I bet you are. I bet you're wondering when you can go and pick it up without me noticing,' said Melissa, with a giggle.

Janie smiled back sarcastically, trying to repress the urge to return the cushion to its rightful place. She'd been with Melissa for some time now, by far her longest relationship after a series of short-lived, and mostly disastrous attempts with both men and women. Melissa was kind, ditzy and funny, and Janie was happier than she could ever remember being.

Melissa busied herself with the coffee machine, and within a minute there were two steaming cups of cappuccino on the breakfast bar. Melissa took one of them and crossed the room, stooping as if to pick up the cushion from the floor, but deciding against it at the last moment, stepping over it theatrically.

'You're a horrible girlfriend,' said Janie as Melissa bent down to kiss her on the top of the head, and placed her coffee on the table in front of her.

'You know that's not true.' Melissa ruffled Janie's short, choppy hair and returned to her stool, busying herself at her laptop again.

Janie shook her head, and returned to her book, casting a sideways look at the cushion, which seemed to be taunting her. Her phone buzzed on the table in front of her, and she saw that it was a WhatsApp voice call from Barney. She frowned when she saw that it was a group call with Max included.

'Barney, what are you up to?' said Janie as she picked up the phone.

'Yeah, Barney, spill the beans,' said Max, his voice full of suspicion.

'Ayup, team. I'm messin' with me new toy. Click on the link in the chat function, and put me on speaker, this is a belting bit of kit,' he said.

Janie looked in the chat and clicked on the hyperlink, which opened a browser page, and a video feed began to load, clearly aerial footage of an open, barren land with a smallish loch way below.

'What are we looking at?' said Max, his voice tinny from the speakers.

'That, down there, is the White Loch, and the small boat you can see in it is currently pulling a body out of it which has just been found by some police divers. So, it looks like Hardie was telling the truth.'

'I can't see, Barney, it's too far away to be clear,' said Janie.

'Aye, I know, it's half the reason I called. Just watch this.' The loch began to grow quickly, as the footage zoomed in. The wide, panoramic view was replaced with a pin-sharp view of a black RIB, occupied by two uniformed cops with life vests on, hauling a black, greasy-looking form from the water.

'Jesus, is that a body coming out now?' said Janie.

'Looks like it. Cracking imagery, in't it?'

'Aye, but you're gonna get us all in the shit, Barney. Won't they hear it?'

'Nay, lad. Zoom's so bloody good, I'm way out of audible range. Look, here's Hardie.' The footage panned across to a liveried pickup truck and a small group of five individuals standing by it. The video feed zoomed in a little tighter, and there he was. Shackled to a stocky man in a suit was Davie Hardie, dressed in prison sweatpants, and a thick coat, looking out to the centre of the loch, a smug grin on his face. Janie felt her cheeks flush at the sight of the gangster.

'Bastard,' came Max's voice over the handset. 'And his scummy leech of a lawyer, as well,' he continued as the image stabilised on the pudgy form of Leo Hamilton standing next to Hardie.

'Looks like he wasn't lying though,' said Janie.

'Maybe,' said Max.

'Shall I patch Ross in on this?' said Barney.

'Christ, no. He'd go bloody doolally, and we're better off giving him plausible deniability. How long can you stay on them for, Barney?'

'Not too much longer. Battery life is good, but I've been up half an hour already, and I don't want the bugger to plunge into the loch. My pal is on the R and D department at the company, and this is a new model, so he'd be miffed if I lost it. Ayup, looks like they're off,' said Barney, panning out slightly as the group turned and began walking back towards the road where a minibus was parked up.

'Want me to keep filming?' said Barney.

'Aye, give it a minute, you've already smashed the law to pieces, so we may as well be hung for an ox as a lamb,' said Max.

'Speak for your bloody self,' said Janie.

The group arrived at the minibus and they all got in, a uniformed officer getting in the driver's seat, and it slowly moved off, and turning right, before gathering speed on the road alongside the loch.

'Where are they going? Wrong way to get back to Shotts,' said Janie.

'A local nick, I'd guess. They'll want to interview him, to capture this evidentially. Kilmarnock is just down the road, isn't it?' said Max.

'Aye, you're probably right. This is looking to be a bit of an anti-climax, right? Hardie telling the truth, just to get to a cushy nick, maybe he's developed a conscience?' said Janie.

'You believe that?' said Max.

'Not really, but I can't see what the angle is, otherwise,' said Janie.

The drone seemed to be moving in sync with the van, smoothly and effortlessly as it headed along the small road.

'Cracking camera work, Barney,' said Janie.

'Not me, love. Active track. I've locked it onto the van, and I don't have to do owt. It just homes in on it. Brilliant bit of kit, this. Wish I'd had it in the Northern Ireland days, would have saved loads of hanging around in boggy fields.'

The van swept along the road, and was heading towards a junction when it suddenly lurched and came to a halt, a puff of dust billowing up from the front, off-side tyre.

'What's happened?' said Max, an edge in his voice.

The driver's door opened, and the uniformed cop got out, and walked to the front of the van. He just stood there for a few moments, before returning and climbing back into the driver's seat.

'Looks like a tyre problem,' said Barney, zooming in tighter on the van. Even on the screen they could see that the tyre was completely flat.

'Shit. What's happening?' said Janie, feeling her heart begin to pound in her chest. Something was wrong.

Suddenly a black BMW screeched around the junction from behind some shrubbery that had been obscuring it. The doors flew open, and three balaclava-clad figures in dark clothing got out, all clutching handguns.

'Shit, they're breaking him out. Fuck, call for help on your radio urgently, Barney, and keep the drone going.'

'I'm on the radio now, but the drone battery's failing. I'm not sure how much flight time I have left.' His voice was typically unemotional, as if he was describing a chess match, not a prison break.

Janie could hear Barney calling it in on the radio, his delivery relaxed and unhurried. 'Urgent message, vehicle with Davie Hardie is under attack, repeat under attack, three hostiles, all armed with handguns, a mile south of the White Loch on the B769. Armed response required.'

'Keep it going, Barney, keep it going. This is crucial evidence,' said Max, his voice cracking with the stress of the incident.

Melissa stood up, her hand covering her mouth in shock, as she listened to the unfolding drama.

Janie looked at the screen, her heart in her mouth as the sliding door to the van was ripped back and Davie Hardie was pulled out, a large man, presumably a cop, dragged along with him because of the handcuffs securing their wrists together. Another gunman was by the driver's door, pistol levelled at the driver, and a third was standing back, a pistol in one hand and what looked like bolt croppers in the other.

'Battery's gonna fail, guys. I'm putting it in emergency landing mode,' said Barney.

Then the screen went black. Dead, and inert. There was total and complete silence as the shock landed. Like his brother, Davie Hardie was free.

24

'**PLEASE, DON'T SHOOT,**' said DS Lenny Maxwell, his voice surprisingly calm despite the abject terror that was coursing like molten lava through his veins, as he stood there at the side of the open van door, his wrist still shackled to Davie Hardie's.

'Shut up. You don't need to say or do anything, we're just here for Hardie. We've not been paid to kill any cops and I don't kill anyone I've not been paid to kill. However, you'd better believe that I won't hesitate to put a bullet straight through your head if you do anything stupid, am I clear?' His voice was low and even with a flat English accent. His eyes were flashing through the holes in the balaclava. He seemed contained, crisp and efficient, with a military bearing.

'I'll not do anything, I promise,' said Maxwell, feeling his bowels begin to loosen and his stomach lurching, as he looked at the large-calibre pistol that was pointed directly at his centre mass. With the attacker's distance, he'd not miss. No chance.

'Good, now my colleague over there is covering the driver and your mate in the front of the car, so you shout to them that they're to keep their hands where we can see them, okay?'

'Aye.'

'Tell them, then,' he goaded.

'Ann, Cleggy. Hands up where they can see, eh. No heroics,' Maxwell said, trying to keep the wobble out of his voice. He looked into the car: Clegg had his hands on the wheel and Ann was in the front seat, looking out of the side window at the gunman, her face pale and her eyes full of fear. Leo Hamilton was in the back of the van, fully exposed by the wide-open sliding door.

'You, Leo Hamilton. Just stay there cowering away, this doesn't concern you,' the gunman said to Leo, who didn't look up, his head covered by his hands.

'Hey, dickhead, I'm talking to you. Look at me!' barked the gunman.

Leo poked his head up, and nodded, his face pale as alabaster, his eyes wide in sheer, unadulterated panic.

'Right, my other associate is going to cut through the handcuffs. If you try anything, I'll shoot you in the gut, do you understand?' he said, lowering the gun to Maxwell's midriff.

Maxwell nodded rapidly, feeling the acrid rise of bile in his throat.

The gunman nodded, and the third masked attacker approached, bolt cutters in his hand. He efficiently and wordlessly cut through the handcuff link as easily as a knife cutting through butter.

'Nice one, boys,' said Davie with a cackle as he massaged his wrist and stepped away from Maxwell, a huge grin on his face. 'It's been a pleasure, Len. You fuckers must have been crazy to think I'd actually help the polis, but we needed to keep you all busy, and an old body in the loch will keep everyone out of mischief and distracted enough for this. No hard feelings, pal. I'm happy poor old Beata can get a proper burial, but you'll never know who put her in there. Now, can we get the fuck out of here?'

'Get in the car,' said the lead gunman.

'Nice knowing you, Lenny.' Davie's smile widened into a triumphant leer before his head quite literally exploded in a shower of blood, bone and brain. His body, already utterly dead, dropped to the floor as if his legs had suddenly vanished, every vestige of life gone in the blink of an eye. A microsecond later, there was the boom of a high-calibre rifle. The lead gunman's mouth opened in shock, his mind not catching up with what was happening.

There was another huge report, and a metallic crash followed by a wet splash, as a bullet struck the van. Maxwell fell to the floor, instinctively, and covered his head with his hands. He looked up quickly and heard the gunman shouting, 'Sniper! Let's get the fuck out of here,' as he sprinted to the BMW, followed by his two colleagues. The doors were slammed shut, and it screeched off, wheels spinning in the dust.

Sniper, thought Maxwell. He had served in the Army many years ago, and he recognised the report he'd heard twice. A big heavy ballistic round. *A sniper, here in fucking Kilmarnock!* His heart was beating almost hard enough to leave his chest, but deep inside himself, he realised that if the sniper had wanted him, or anyone else other than Hardie or Hamilton dead, then they'd already be minus a head. He tried to control his breathing, which was still escaping him in gasps. *Come on, Len, fucking sort yourself out.* He was the sergeant; he'd have to see if the others were okay.

'Guys, are you okay?' shouted Maxwell, his voice shaking.

There was just silence, beyond the fading noise of the BMW that had disappeared over the crest of a hill.

'Ann, are you okay? We need to call it in,' repeated Maxwell, more urgently.

There was no response.

With his heart beating frantically, Maxwell realised he was going to have to move. He lifted his head and glanced behind him, feeling a drip, drip, drip on his wrist. He saw the dark crimson of blood. His heart lurching, he stood up, and looked in the back of the van. Leo Hamilton was slumped in a mix of blood and gore. Well, he assumed that it was Leo, but he couldn't tell for sure, owing to the fact that the head was almost entirely missing from the utterly lifeless corpse, apart from a sliver of jawbone that held some smashed teeth.

Laithwaite and Clegg were stiff as boards in their seats, faces pale with shock, mouths agape and their clothes and hair all smeared in blood, brain and shards of bone.

'Ann, we need to call it in,' said Maxwell, gently.

She closed her mouth, her pale face a total contrast to her gore-encrusted hair and shoulders, and handed the radio to Maxwell.

'Cleggy?' he asked the silent driver, who just nodded, his right cheek splattered liberally with the detritus from Leo Hamilton, indicating he'd been turning to face the back of the van when the solicitor had lost his head.

'Let's get the fuck out of here, we might be next,' said Clegg.

'We're safe, man.'

'How . . . how can you be so sure?' stammered Laithwaite.

'Because he shot those two, from God knows where, with a head-shot and within about two bloody seconds. He made no effort to take out the bastards that held us up, either. If he'd wanted us dead, we'd be dead already. Let's call it in.'

The distant wail of sirens growing ever louder suggested that help was already on its way.

25

THE SNIPER SMILED from his position in the lightly wooded copse, four hundred metres up the gentle slope, as he looked through the powerful optic sight at the scenes of utter pandemonium on the small intersection of the road. The first shot had been child's play. Perfect conditions, just a slight breeze and a slightly sloping landscape. He'd watched with satisfaction as the bullet had slammed into Hardie's forehead, and had enjoyed seeing the pressure wave, caused by the big .338 Lapua round taking the gangster's head almost clean off.

Then it was a simple case of working the bolt action, moving the barrel just a few inches to the left and engaging the fat lawyer. He'd originally planned for a centre mass shot, but as the fat bastard was just sitting there, in the van with his mouth open like a goldfish, the head was too tempting a target, and a bullet straight through the gaping orifice was just too much of an opportunity to pass up. All that practice on ranges over the years, followed by the real thing in Afghanistan, Chad and Northern Mali, had made it childishly simple. He literally couldn't have missed. He chuckled to himself, feeling the familiar elation after a successful shot. 'The thrill of the red mist' was a real thing amongst snipers. Once experienced, never forgotten.

It had been almost comical watching the idiots who'd been tasked with rescuing Hardie react to his shots. Their initial ambush had been solidly planned, with the scattering of sharp caltrops on the road to take out the van's tyres, and then a decent intervention once the vehicle was disabled, but their reaction to his effective fire was laughable. He could have taken them out just as easily, but he hadn't been paid for that, so he didn't bother.

He'd been given word yesterday that Hardie was coming to the loch, and he had planned to engage once he was lochside, but the terrain was challenging, and concealment and egress would have been tricky and risky. When he saw the other team performing a recce, he decided that they were almost the perfect bait. They'd been so bloody obvious about what they were planning. Just three gorillas, in a gangbangers BMW, dressed in designer gear openly scouting the area. He'd been more careful: wear fisherman's camouflage clothing, hold a rod and tackle bag over his shoulder, whilst sitting on a collapsible chair by the loch. They'd forgotten the golden rule of camouflage. Blend into your environment. Whilst they stomped about, all furtive, tough-looking and threatening, he'd been pretending to fish, remaining in sight but anonymous. Just a fisherman doing what fishermen do.

Using the gangbangers as bait would mean that there would be only the escorting cops in the car, rather than the whole group of them if he engaged the target whilst they were lochside. He smiled at the irony that it was Hardie's rescuers who had actually made the operation much simpler. This location for the engagement offered a perfect stalk point, and more importantly, a perfect route for exfiltration.

He picked up the spent case that had been ejected from the rifle with his gloved hand and shoved it into his pocket, and took one last look through the scope at the van. Hearing the wail of sirens getting closer, he made the call. He had plenty of time, but it was best to move now, before they got organised and put helicopters up. Even worse, they would almost certainly get the dogs out, once they'd figured where the shot had come from. No matter how well he was hidden, a dog's nose would find him. It was time to go.

He kept low; belly pressed against the soft soil in the small copse of trees situated in the middle of the scrappy fields. He kept his movements slow and considered as he retraced his steps. As he reached the far edge of the copse, out of sight from the road, he slung the rifle over his shoulder to keep his outline unthreatening and headed down the slope towards the expanse of water that was the deserted Corsehouse Reservoir, where his fishing rod was set up alongside his tent and tackle box. He quickly went inside the tent, and within a few moments had reduced the long rifle into its component parts, and despite never having touched the weapon with bare hands, he used an antibacterial wipe to clean each component.

Once done, he went back outside and after checking the coast was still deserted, he threw each piece far into the loch. Satisfied, he reached for the packet of cigarettes in his pocket and pulled one out, putting it between his lips as he lit it. He inhaled deeply and with extreme satisfaction. It was always like this, and had always been like this. After a big operation in Afghanistan or Chad his unit would always celebrate with a cigar, and it resonated with him as an almost cleansing or ritualistic action. Together with his comrades, sharing a moment with a decent stogie. He didn't have time for a cigar, so a fag would have to do, but the ritual was important.

He dropped the cigarette on the soft soil and ground it out with his heel. Once satisfied it was extinguished, he used the heel of his boot to create a divot in the ground, and dropped the butt in the depression. He quickly covered it with the soft soil. Leave no trace was the sniper's watchword. It's why he got paid as well as he did. Within a few minutes he'd collapsed his camp and was ready to go. Just a few final tasks and a check that he'd left nothing behind, and he'd be on his way before the cops had even had chance to work out what had happened.

He smiled when he thought of the very tasty sum of money that would soon be hitting his off-shore account situated in the Cayman Islands. Easiest money ever.

26

MAX'S HEAD WAS reeling. An attempt to break Hardie out, followed by what sounded like an execution of him and then his solicitor by a sniper with a weapon system big enough to remove heads. After the drone had failed, Barney had relayed the radio transmissions. Max needed to speak to Ross, they needed to get in and amongst this, and soon. This whole thing had been messed up by idiots not listening to them, and a DCC in some stupid power-grab whilst the Chief was away. Max felt his phone vibrate in his pocket.

'Max, what the fucking fuck is going on, for fuck's sake?' Ross's voice blasted down the receiver as Max was grabbing some things and jamming them in a bag. He knew that their much-needed week off was gone.

'What have you heard?'

'Don't start bullshitting me. Where's Barney? Somehow the conniving bastard called it in, and Miles is going fucking tonto about us being involved.'

'He has his own radio, and was monitoring. What have you heard?'

'A load of garbled and confused shite from Miles about Hardie busting out, and snipers and the like. Apparently, we now have two fucking headless corpses in Newton Mearns. A dead Hardie, and a dead solicitor, so don't play that fucking game with me. What haven't you bastards told me?' Ross's building rage was palpable down the line.

'Barney was testing a drone up at the White Loch, and was just watching the body get recovered when Hardie and the others left. We saw them getting sprung, but then the drone went dead, but he was able to monitor the radio traffic. It sounded really grim, Ross. Heads removed by a sniper weapon. That means military-grade ammo.'

Strangely Ross didn't explode, in fact if anything his tone was suddenly calm. 'Ah fucking hell, man. I'm gonna catch bastard hell over this. We need to get together. In fact, fuck it. We told those daft bampots that this was a ruse to break Hardie out, and they didn't shitting listen. I say we go to the scene, apparently the DCC is shitting a brick, and is deploying everyone, all over the place.'

'Where's Miles?'

'On his way to the scene. Firearms teams are on standby, but the feeling is that the sniper has fled. They put the helicopter up, and have swept the immediate area, but there's no sign.'

'That's because they're not looking properly. Anyone capable of headshots like that knows what they're doing. When are you heading to the scene?'

'Now. Where's Janie?'

'At home.'

'Does she have a car?'

'Aye, she took the Volvo.'

'Okay, I'll get Norma to the office, and I'll meet you at the scene. Get Janie to pick you up. And, Max?'

'Aye?'

'Pack a bag, you know how these jobs go.'

Max sighed and looked at the scrappy rucksack as he threw some bits and bobs into it, ready for what could easily turn out to be many days of long hours.

He was pulling some socks from a drawer when he stopped dead and a name popped into his head. Bruce Ferguson. Ex–Special Forces Regimental Sergeant Major and no doubt a well-qualified and battle-hardened sniper. His words spoken just a day ago at the airport floated back to Max. *'I'm not letting those bastard Hardie boys get out of prison a minute before they're due out.'*

Max just sat there, lost in his thoughts. Surely Bruce wouldn't do this, but memories of what he'd done to Tam Hardie surged in his mind. A voice in the room dragged him from his reverie.

'Going somewhere?' said Katie, appearing from the en suite bathroom, her face pale and wan and her eyes lacking their usual sparkle.

'Looks like it. Hardie and his solicitor have just been shot dead during an escape attempt.'

'What by cops?' she said.

'No. It looks like someone else did it. A sniper.'

'Oh my God!' Her eyes flared wide with alarm.

'Aye, I know. It's all hands to the pump, and I bloody warned them. I told them that there was no way Hardie would cooperate with cops,' Max said, continuing to jam things in his rucksack.

'Do you have to go now? What can you achieve?' Katie suddenly looked sad.

'Janie's on her way to fetch me. You know how it is.' He looked up at his lovely wife, whose eyes were damp with emotion and just a touch of fear.

'I thought you were having a week off,' she said, sitting on the bed with a sigh.

'Things change, babe. This is a big deal, and we warned them that Hardie was planning something, but we didn't expect this.' Max reached out to touch her hand, but she withdrew it, her face blank and unfathomable, her eyes flinty as she stared at him.

'Katie, what's up?' said Max, trying to join the dots in his head. She usually accepted his absences stoically, but this seemed different.

'It's this fucking job, Max. It's always the fucking job. You left London to try to gain some balance, and I followed you here, but it's as bad as ever, in fact it's bloody worse. You're always at work.'

'But this is urgent . . .'

'It's always fucking urgent, Max. It's always the next big urgent job that takes you away from us, and I have to stay here, wondering if my husband is going to come home at all.' Katie's tone was hard, and her jaw was set tight.

'But . . .'

'But nothing, Max. When will your lot understand that when everything's urgent, nothing is fucking urgent? It's just so unfair. I want my bloody husband back, just sometimes. I want us to spend time together, do stuff together that isn't about you being a bloody cop.' She folded her arms defensively, pink spots dappling her smooth cheeks.

Max paused for a heartbeat, searching for the right words, the silence between them almost solid. She turned to look at him, a solitary tear spilling from her eye and running down her cheek.

'Katie, love . . .' Max began, but then stopped when he realised that he didn't have the words.

Katie held out what at first Max thought was a blue-and-white pen, her eyes wet with tears. 'I'm pregnant, Max.'

27

MAX, JANIE, ROSS and Barney were all standing in the White Loch car park where a police control vehicle had been established.

There were cops everywhere, all competing to have their say and to contribute. A police helicopter hovered overhead, police dogs barked excitedly and white-suited crime scene staff were all being briefed by the control vehicle. A panicky-looking inspector was talking to a middle-aged officer in a badly fitting suit, his face red and flushed.

'I reckon "clusterfuck" is the best descriptor for this scene, what do you reckon?' said Ross, swigging from a bottle of mineral water. His face was haggard, and his blue suit badly needed a press.

'Looks like it to me. You reckon we can get a look at the scene?' said Max, shaking his head to try to clear the fog that was swirling. The baby news was huge, but he still had a job to do.

'We can try, they're down there filming and photographing. At the very least I reckon I can swing a look at the images and footage, once Miles has got here. He's gonna need to eat some humble pie, after giving me shit about our involvement, the fud.'

Max just stared towards the tent and the clutch of crime scene investigators beavering away, but he really wasn't taking it all in. His mind was on the bombshell that Katie had delivered just a short while ago. A baby. He was going to be a father. He'd hardly been able to speak when she'd shown him the positive test; he'd just sat there on the bed, open-mouthed, his brain acting like a cog had been removed. He'd lost his parents many years ago, and so he was now full of self-doubt. Could he be a good dad? How would it work with this stupid bloody job? He felt his insides churning at the whole concept, but despite this, he felt a smile begin to spread across his face.

He was going to be a dad. He desperately wanted to speak to Katie. He wanted to tell her that he was happy.

'Max, fucking tune in and wipe that daft-arse smile off your face. What do you think?' Ross's brusque voice pierced Max's reverie.

He looked up, and nodded. 'I want to see the scene. I can't tell where the sniper would have fired from here.'

'Were you a sniper in the Forty Twa?' said Ross.

'Aye.'

'Sorry, "Forty Twa"?' said Janie, confusion across her face.

'The Black Watch. We both served, just at different times, Ross being so many years older than me,' said Max.

'Not that much older, you cheeky bugger. You being a sniper explains many things,' said Ross.

'Like?' said Max.

'Ice cold, detached and calculatingly evil, I'd say.' Ross smirked.

'Is he coming?' said Max.

'Who?'

'Mr Wakefield.'

'Imminently, I'm told. He wants to talk to us as soon as he arrives. He sounds a bit stressed.'

'How about the DCC?' said Janie.

'Not sure. I think as it was her call to ignore us, she'll be getting her ducks all in a row. I suspect, she'll be looking to shift the blame our way. Well, she can piss off. I know how to defend myself, and I keep records.'

'You reckon the Chief is aware?' said Max.

'He is. He's messaged me to say that he's keeping abreast of events and wants updating later. He never switches off, and I suspect he's watching the news with a G and T in his mitt. He won't be happy; in fact, it wouldn't surprise me if he's currently looking at flight options.'

Max just shrugged, his mind still on Katie's last words. She'd eventually hugged him and told him to go to work, but the atmosphere had been thick and tense between them. Pregnant. He was going to be a father. A dad.

'Max, what's up with you? Away with the fucking fairies, man.' Ross's sarcasm-laden voice jolted him back to the present.

'Sorry, I was miles away, what was that?' said Max. He knew he had to focus on the task at hand. Personal matters would have to wait.

'Switch on, man. I need you firing on what few rusty and corroded cylinders you have left operational. I was saying that you're going to have to have all your answers ready about where you got the initial info from, you know that, right?' Ross stared at him with hard eyes.

'Aye, of course,' he said, wondering if it was true.

'Anyway, look out, here comes a rather pissed-off-looking DCS Wakefield,' said Janie, nodding towards the makeshift car park that was already overloaded with marked and unmarked cop cars.

Wakefield was a lean, grey-haired officer, who was wearing a well-cut blue suit and carrying an A4 notebook. Trailing in his wake was a harassed-looking officer whom Max recognised as Malky Douglas, a short and stocky cop in his late thirties whom he'd worked with when he first came to Scotland. Max nodded at Malky, who nodded back, his face flushed as he almost juggled with various notebooks, and preformatted logs. Being the Chief Superintendent's 'bag man' could be a good career move, but it wasn't without its share of problems.

'Ross, what the hell is happening here? I hear one of your people was up here with a drone of all fucking things. Didn't I make myself clear that you were to have no involvement in this operation?' His face was hard, but his eyes told the real story. He was worried.

Ross clearly wasn't in any mood for a dressing-down.

'Shall we take this conversation elsewhere, Miles?' said Ross, the picture of icy calm.

'Ross, I just want to know how your man, whoever he bloody is, knew to be here,' said Wakefield, nodding at Malky and making a writing gesture with his hand, indicating that he needed his bag man to start logging. The old adage 'if it isn't written down, it didn't happen' was never more relevant in high-profile cases such as this one. Malky uncapped his pen, opened one of the log books and began scribbling.

'Well, Barney is actually a freelance technical expert. Just by coincidence he was testing a new drone in the area, as it's pretty bleak here. He saw the activity on the loch so decided to use it as an exercise to ascertain the drone's performance and capabilities. It works great, if you want to see the footage.' Ross nodded to where Barney was standing, a roll-up in his mouth and smoke wisping from his nostrils.

Wakefield's eyes narrowed, clearly planning his next move. 'I'm not happy about this, Ross,' he said after a pause.

'Can't say I'm ecstatic either, pal, but we are where we are. Now do you want our help? I don't want to pull the "we told you so" card, but I think that it's on record that the Policing Standards Reassurance Team made our suspicions clear that Hardie wasn't playing with a straight bat. What we didn't expect was a fucking sniper to blow his and his solicitor's heads off.'

Wakefield exhaled despairingly, and rubbed his temples with his free hand. 'The press are gonna go mad for this, Ross. Gangster taken from jail to expose high-level corruption gets murdered with his lawyer during escape attempt. It's like something from an implausible Hollywood film.'

'Shall I add the murder of Jack Slattery at Saughton into the mix, as well?' said Ross.

'Oh, bloody hell, that gets more significance in the light of this, doesn't it? One of Hardie's people murdered within twenty-four hours of this even if it looked like a typical hit on an ex-cop by a con with nothing to lose.'

'Sorry, nothing to lose?' said Janie.

'Aye, you not heard? He had inoperable cancer, a year left at most,' said Wakefield.

'Christ. This job just gets worse,' said Ross.

'It's gonna be hard to contain,' Wakefield said, his face ashen.

'What's the DCC's take on it?' said Ross.

'I'm at point on this, but operationally reporting directly to her whilst the Chief's away. I'm setting up two MITs. One for this, and the other for Slattery is up and running now.'

'What about us?' said Ross.

'She doesn't want you involved. Sorry, Ross. I know we should have listened, but she was adamant from the outset. I think she views you as usurping her position as lead for professional standards.'

Ross said nothing, just shrugged.

'How did your man know to be here?' said Wakefield.

'As I said, coincidence?' said Ross, his face displaying nothing but pure innocence.

'Coincidence, my arse,' said Wakefield, his belligerence returning.

'Look, Miles. How and why he was here is kind of irrelevant. It's hardly the world's best kept secret that the recovery operation was here, as it was all over the radio, divers involved with all their entourage and every other bugger. Police Scotland is a small playground. Let's just say that he was here, and be thankful that you have high-quality bloody footage of the whole thing.'

Wakefield sighed, even more deeply than he had done previously. There was a tone from his pocket, and he reached in and produced his phone, looking at the display.

'Yes, ma'am?' he said, his eyes closing resignedly. He paused and listened, the voice on the other end almost audible to Ross.

'Aye, I'm just here, and getting a briefing from DI Fraser now.'

There was another pause, and his eyes flicked up to Ross, his eyebrows raised in mild surprise.

'I understand completely, ma'am. We'll get right on it.' He hung up and tucked his phone in his pocket, a smile replacing the frown on his face.

'That sounded interesting,' said Ross.

'Aye, a hundred-eighty-degree shift. It seems that we'd be delighted if you could assist us on this inquiry in any way you can. It seems that Mr Macdonald has made his feelings clear from Tenerife. He's currently at the airport, and anticipates being back at Tulliallan first thing tomorrow, where he's going to want the fullest of briefings from all of us.'

'Stoatin. We'll pull out all the stops for you, pal.'

Wakefield shook his head resignedly. 'Okay, what do you need?'

'Firstly, a look at the scene, once it's been photographed. We need to know where the shooter was sited, and Max here was a sniper in the Army, so may have observations. It sounds like it was a big bore weapon, so that suggests military.'

'Fine. As I understand it, photographer has almost finished, so as long as you stay out of the way of the CSIs, I can't see why you can't see the scene. Can we get a copy of the drone footage?'

'No problem. Unfortunately, the battery cut out at an inopportune moment, but it has the attempted rescue captured beautifully.'

'Great. I can get the whole team to watch it.'

'I don't think that's a great idea, Miles,' said Ross, shaking his head ruefully.

'Whyever not?' said Wakefield, his eyes narrowing.

'Let's look at what actually happened here, and at the intelligence that Hardie was spouting off about. He accurately led your people to a submerged body, probably and correctly thinking it would keep you all busy whilst he got busted out. The body being recovered was never the real pull though, was it?'

Wakefield looked at Ross intently, clearly wondering how much to reveal. 'No. The suggestion that she was killed on the orders of someone more significant to protect them. We want whoever killed her, and more importantly, who ordered her death.'

'Exactly. So, two points arise from this. Firstly, how did the rescuers know exactly where he was gonna be, when he hadn't even told the cops the location until they set off this morning?'

'It's prison, Ross. Do I need to explain about prisoners having mobiles in jail?' said Wakefield.

'That's very true also. But how did our sharp-shooting friend know exactly where they were going to be, and what time? It's not likely that Hardie told his own executioner, is it?'

Wakefield opened his mouth to answer, before thinking again and closing it, his face pale.

'So, if the info didn't come from Hardie, it must have come via someone involved in the operation. I reckon we have a leak.'

28

THE SILENCE THAT followed was deep and cloying, and only just offset by the whisper of the wind and the thrum of the generator.

'A leak. Not again. Please not again,' said Wakefield, shaking his head slowly. There was a longer pause as the realisation sunk in, that corruption was at the centre of their world.

Ross broke the silence. 'Hardie had no intention of telling you about Mr Big. He was happy to give up a missing body, but giving up who put her there, especially if it was organised by his pa, is another matter completely. That'd make him a grass, which he'd never be, as we said to you a couple of days ago.'

'What's your point?' said Wakefield, his patience clearly wearing thin.

'Whoever shot Hardie and his lawyer was clearly a professional, but not just because he can shoot straight. He wasn't bothered about the three cops, or even the bad guys that were trying to bust Hardie out, despite the fact that he could have wasted the whole bloody lot of them. He'd clearly only been paid to shoot Hardie and Leo Hamilton, and a pro wouldn't shoot anyone he'd not been paid to waste. I mean, why would he?'

'So, whoever is ordering this has access to one thing, right?' said Janie, speaking for the first time.

'What?' said Wakefield, irritation bristling at him.

'Information, and money. What's the going rate for a professional contract killing, ten, twenty grand?'

'Absolute minimum, especially for a high-profile target like Hardie, then add the lawyer in and it's serious cash.'

'But why Hardie *and* his lawyer, then?'

'Well, it seems to me, that whoever had that poor wee lassie put in that loch was keen to get rid of anyone else who knew anything. They probably assumed that Hardie may have told his lawyer, which was too much of a risk. Whoever is behind this is killing anyone who may have any knowledge of who he, or she, is.'

'I think you could be right,' said Janie, looking at the screen of her phone.

'Why?' said Wakefield.

'Norma's been researching Hardie associates from the time Beata went missing, and one of them, a guy called Steven Mitchell, was shot in his garden in Newcastle yesterday. He was part of a crew that was suspected of doing wet work for Hardie, although he was supposed to have got out of the game, and was working as a joiner. It's only just filtered through, and the details aren't fully clear, but it's looking very much like a professional hit. Single bullet to the head.'

'Any connection to Slattery?' said Wakefield.

'Some. Obviously, Norma's still working it up, but there was phone traffic between them back in the day, and we know that Slattery was Hardie's middle man for shit like this,' said Janie, scrolling on her phone.

Ross exhaled, his cheeks puffed out. 'Jesus suffering fuck. Davie Hardie, his lawyer and two former henchmen all killed in a couple of days. This is bad. This is really bad, just what the hell are they protecting?'

Max said nothing. He just stared down the hill to the clutch of police vehicles at the scene of the carnage and thought of Bruce Ferguson, and his words to him just a few hours ago. *'Do something about this, Max. If Hardie gets out, I'm not just gonna let it lie, you know that, right? He's part of the reason my brother ended up dead, and if they got a chance, they'd kill me.'* His mind was whirling as if a cog had worked loose, and he just couldn't organise his thoughts properly. Would Bruce do this? He certainly had the capacity and the skills, and he had made it clear that he wouldn't stand by idly and let Hardie escape. But would he kill Leo Hamilton? The lawyer was sleazy, and no doubt not ethical in the slightest in his protection of the Hardies over the years, but would Bruce kill him too? Sweat began to bead on his spine as he thought of the consequences, and where that left him personally. His mind flashed back to the video sent to him by Bruce, of Tam Hardie being tossed into the North Sea, a thick chain around his ankles pulling him down. He was mulling this over when Ross's barking voice cut through.

'Max, for fuck's sake, will you switch on, you nugget? I asked you a question, and you're stood there like a bastard mute.'

Max shook his head to clear his thoughts. 'Sorry, Ross. I was just contemplating.'

'Aye, well, stop contemplating, and bloody tune in. We all need to bring our A game, here. What do you think?'

'I think we need to see the drone footage again. Barney, can we do this now?' said Max, suddenly back and focused.

'Sure. It's backed up on my laptop in't van. I'll get the kettle on, nay bother. But I reckon there's summat else to consider,' said Barney, exhaling a cloud of smoke from his roll-up.

'What?' barked Ross.

'Well, bearing in mind they seem to be rubbing out anyone connected to the Hardies, has anyone thought of how Frankie Hardie is getting on?'

There was an almost simultaneous intake of breath from the group, followed by a brief pause where the only sound was the wind and the distant thrum of the generator that the underwater search teams were using.

'Malky, make the call to Shotts now. Have Frankie Hardie informed about his brother's death, and then get him safe.'

29

MAX, JANIE AND Ross were all standing by the open door of Barney's van whilst he fiddled with the screen of his laptop. Within a few moments it was showing the footage that they'd seen earlier of the police van driving down to the ambush point.

'Shite, I know I gave you a row about putting the bloody drone up, but this is red-hot imagery. Kudos, Barney,' Ross congratulated.

'Thanks, I'm honoured and surprised at the positive feedback,' said Barney, adjusting the image on the screen with the trackpad.

'Aye well, don't get bloody used to it. Spin on, I want to watch it at normal speed.'

On screen, the van screeched to a halt, the dust and smoke puffing up from the front tyre and the uniformed cop driver exiting the vehicle to look at the shredded tyre before returning to the driver's seat.

'What did they use?' said Ross.

'I'm hearing caltrops. You know, like four-edged nails that always land spike up however you throw them. PolSA team have recovered a load on their fingertip search of the approach,' said Janie.

'Properly planned then. Here we go,' said Ross as the BMW swept into the picture and the masked raiders exited the vehicle. One of them dragged the shackled Hardie and DS Maxwell out of the car. They watched wordlessly as the cuffs were cropped, before Max interrupted the silence.

'Pause there, Barney,' a sense of urgency in his voice.

'What, the action is just happening now?' said Ross.

'Back up slowly, frame by frame.' Max stared intently at the screen, his face rapt with concentration, as the scene went into reverse, and Hardie and Maxwell disappeared back into the van. 'Stop,' said Max, his voice tight.

'What are you looking at, you dafty?' said Ross, his voice exasperated.

'There.' Max pointed to a point in the field beyond the road.

'What, for fuck's sake?' said Ross.

'A point of light, in that copse of trees, probably at least five hundred metres away.'

'Craigie, I'm gonna bloody swing for you in a minute, what is it?'

'Scope glint. I'm sure of it.'

'Ah, right. That makes sense then. Shit, he must be a bastard good shot.'

'Not that good, or we wouldn't see the glint. A real pro wouldn't have been in that location where glint was likely,' said Max, looking up from the screen.

'Anyone want to interpret this conversation for me, chaps?' said Janie, a touch of frustration in her voice.

'Any sniper shooting from that range would need an optical zoom sight to make the shots that killed Davie and Leo. I reckon that's where the shot came from, but I need to get down to the scene to make sure it's a viable location. Come on, let's get down there.'

'If you don't mind, I'd like to remind you all as to who is in bloody charge, and I'd like to see the rest of the footage if that's not *too* much trouble,' said Ross, his voice dripping with sarcasm.

'Rolling.' Barney activated the footage again.

Ross stood and watched impassively, with rapt attention until the screen went blank. 'Is that all?' he said.

'That's all we have. Battery life is limited, and it was in limp home mode. Don't want to lose the bugger, it's not mine and it's worth a packet.'

'Aye, and we know what your financial situation is, don't we?' Ross gave Barney a sideways look.

'Harsh,' said Janie.

'Cruel, I'd say,' said Max.

'Aye, no respect for your elders, who risked life and limb for their country over many years.' Barney looked down at his lighter and lit the roll-up that was between his lips.

'Ach awa' and bile your heids, ya bunch of fannies. Come on, let's get down there,' said Ross, stifling a smile.

30

THE CRIME SCENE was a hive of activity cordoned off by blue-and-white scene tape on all sides, and guarded by a uniformed cop clutching a scene log. A large white forensic tent had been erected around the van and a small clutch of crime scene examiners, dressed in white coveralls, overboots and surgical masks, were being briefed by Jimmy Duggan, whom Max knew from previous cases. Jimmy was experienced and thorough, and as crime scene manager he would exercise his cast-iron control over the scene once it had been handed over to him, as was clearly happening now.

'What ya saying, Jimmy?' said Ross, cheerfully.

'Grand thanks, Ross. Nasty one, must have been a great big bugger of a bullet. Practically taken their heads off,' he said from behind his surgical mask, his accent rich with the tones of Dublin.

'Where are we with the scene?'

'Just handed to me now. Photog's done the business, and Miles has had his first glance. He said Max wanted a quick lookie, and he's okayed it, is that right?'

'Aye, it'd be helpful. Max used to waste people from very long distances when he was in Afghanistan, and we think we may have seen a possible firing point on the drone footage, which I hope you've seen.'

'Seen it. Nasty business, and what would we have given for five more minutes battery,' said Jimmy.

'So, is Max good to go?'

'Aye, but just Max, suit up, touch nothing, and name with the loggist, yeah?' He nodded at the uniformed cop.

'Done. Go for it, Max,' said Ross, nodding.

Within a few minutes, Max was dressed in a white Tyvek forensic suit, black overshoes, nitrile gloves and a surgical mask, and he was ducking under the tape that was being lifted by the uniformed cop. He felt his stomach begin to tighten as he moved towards the tent, where the door flap was gently fluttering in the light wind. As he approached, the familiar smell began to hit him, slowly at first. Just a mere waft on the breeze, but growing in strength as he neared the synthetic material. A creeping dread gripped him, and beads of sweat prickled on his back. He rounded the tent but kept his back to it, looking outwards into the stretch of rough, scrubby grass beyond the low fence at the edge of the road. Looking up towards the copse of trees he estimated that it was between four and five hundred metres away, with a reasonable elevation, maybe fifty metres up in total. For a great sniper, it would be an easy shot. For a decent sniper, it would be a little trickier, and Max thought it unlikely that they were dealing with a great marksman. A properly skilled sniper would have considered the position of the sun, and the risk of scope glint. Even with the simplicity of the task it would be in the DNA of a well-trained sniper to pick a better position than the overly obvious copse of trees.

But the shot was on, and it was easy. He could have made it from twice the distance, and he could see several far better positions, from longer distances. His thoughts flitted back to Afghanistan, years ago: the head of an insurgent, framed in the Schmidt & Bender 5-25x56 PM telescopic sight, suddenly vapourised by the .338 Lapua sent by a simple squeeze of his finger on the trigger of the Accuracy International sniper rifle. He felt his skin chill at the memory, and nausea begin to rise in his throat.

Max shook his head to clear the image. He had to look at the scene properly, to see what he was dealing with. What damage had been caused to the victims would tell its own story. He took a deep breath, the flimsy material of the mask being sucked inwards as he did, his head reeling, knowing that what lay within the scene tent would be as bad as anything he'd seen before.

His heart pounding in his chest, he took another deep breath and drew back the door flap.

Davie Hardie's body lay on the floor, face up, limbs splayed. Max could only identify the headless corpse because he knew Davie had been outside the van when the sniper struck. Now he was just a gory stump with the glint of a shattered vertebrae and a sliver of jawbone still attached to a portion of the skull. Max forced down the bile in his throat, and looked to the van. A slumped corpse sat in one of the seats, arms by its side, with a similar level of devastation where the bullet had struck, except a little more skull had been left in place.

Max stood stock still, almost frozen to the spot, as he took in the scene of unimaginable horror, trying to process it. He felt his face flush, and a sudden burst of heat began to make his head swoon as the blood surged. *Breathe, Max. Breathe*, he ordered himself. He inhaled deeply, holding for four seconds, before exhaling for four, feeling the sense of panic beginning to ease. He turned on his heel and left the tent, his head reeling at what he'd seen, trying to force the image of Dippy from his mind. This always happened. Scenes of violent death transported him straight back to Helmand Province. The searing heat, the baked earth, the stench of death. He shook his head again.

'Not now,' he muttered to himself as he walked back towards Ross and all the others. 'Not now, I've a job to do.' His eyes shut tight as he moved.

'Are you talking to yourself, you bloody fruit loop?' said Ross, his jeering, piss-taking voice jerking Max into the present again.

'Aye, only way I get to have a sensible conversation around here, pal. I'm confident that the sniper was in the copse of trees up the slope. We need a dog, and we need armed support in case he's still up there, although I doubt it very much. He's had plenty of opportunities to leg it.'

Ross nodded, reached for his radio and began to bark orders into it.

'Max?' Janie's voice was soft to his side.

'Aye?'

'Are you okay?' she said, her eyes full of concern.

'All good.' He smiled, weakly.

'Sure?' she said.

'I am now. It's all good. I just needed to see the bodies, and I still have a job to do.'

'Well, as long as you're sure.'

'I'm fine.' He raised his voice. 'Military-grade ammo, Ross. Both of their heads have been practically removed. Best case is a .338, worst is a .50.'

'Fuck, so a pro, then,' said Ross, eyes wide.

'Competent, rather than an expert, I'd say. Come on, let's get up there, he may have left something behind,' said Max as a dog van pulled up by the cordon.

A lean, tough-looking uniformed cop clutching a carbine got out of the car. He was followed by another more solid, but equally grey-haired cop, who went to the back of the van and opened the door. An excited whining came out, followed by a couple of low barks, and suddenly a large dog jumped out, ears back, tail wagging.

'Quick work, boys, quick briefing, and we're on our way,' said Ross, cheerfully. Ross had many faults, including bumptiousness, a short temper, foul language and very little in the way of sensitivity. He wasn't a panicker, however, and was at his best in moments of high stress.

Max looked at his boss, pensively waiting for one of his typical briefings that either went down well, or rather badly, depending on whom he was addressing. The two new officers both looked like no-nonsense, experienced cops and they stared expectantly at Ross, as the dog strained at the leash, tongue lolling, ready for action.

Ross cleared his throat. 'Right, fellas. Some bad bastard's tooken the heid's off the two unfortunate buggers, currently camping in that forensic tent, with a big, fuck-off rifle. Max here was a sniper in Afghanistan, which his icy, and possibly evil, demeanour demonstrates. He thinks he knows where the bastard's shooting point was, but as almost ninety minutes have passed, the chances of him being there are bugger all. We need to search the copse of trees to see if we can locate his firing point. Fido here can do the sniffing, and you can shoot anyone who tries to kill us. Any questions?'

'No, boss,' they said almost in union, eyes glinting in amusement.

'Excellent, Barney, get the drone up. I want eyes on that wood before we get up there.'

'On it,' said Barney.

'We all set?'

There were nods all round.

'Let's roll.'

31

FRANKIE HARDIE WAS prone on his narrow bed, watching some terrible programme about antiques, when there was a tap at his open door and Mr Jeffries, one of the more friendly screws, poked his head around the door.

'Frankie, you're needed in the office.' There was something in his voice that made Frankie's hackles rise.

'What is it?' he snapped back.

'Best come, pal, someone to see you,' said the screw, his voice unusually soft.

'If it's a fucking cop, I'm not interested, boss,' he said, his voice hard.

'It's not a cop, Frankie.'

'Well, fucking who, then?'

'Just come, eh?' The screw's voice was almost sad, and Frankie felt a grip of tension in his gut.

Sighing, he swung his legs off the bed, slipped his feet into a pair of sliders and stood up. He followed the screw onto the landing, through one of the chipped and painted steel gates and along to the reinforced glass box that served as the supervisor's room.

The sense of foreboding that was pulsating in his temples morphed into a rushing of blood in his ears when he entered the drab office. Mr Cole, the senior screw was sitting behind the desk next to a short, stout man wearing a clerical collar. Frankie wasn't a religious man, and had never been to a church service at the prison, but he'd seen the prison minister on the wing once or twice, and it was always for the same reason. Delivering bad news.

'What's going on?' he said, actually feeling the colour draining from his face, followed by an explosion of butterflies in his stomach.

'Sit down, Frankie, do you know Mr James?' said Mr Cole.

Frankie felt weak, the dread beginning to overwhelm him. He sat in front of the desk, breathing heavily. 'I don't. What's happened to Davie?' he said, his voice low and with a slight tremor.

The minister cleared his throat, and in a light English accent, said, 'Frankie, I'm Stanley James, I'm the prison minister, and I'm sorry, but I have some terrible news. Your brother Davie was shot dead this morning, together with your solicitor, Leo Hamilton. I'm so sorry.'

Frankie sat back in his chair, feeling like the wind had been knocked out of him. He just sat there for what seemed like forever. Stunned. First his big brother, and now Davie was gone. Wee Davie. His little pal. Confusion swirled in his head like thick fog on a Scottish hill. 'Just back up a second here. What do you mean, shot?' His voice was monotone as he tried to stop the rage that was starting to chase away the fog in his mind.

Cole stifled a cough. 'Details are sketchy, Frankie. Davie left this morning with a couple of police officers, to help with an investigation of some type. During that time, there was a confrontation, and he was shot.'

'But how? Did a cop shoot him?' His voice rose, as the bubbling anger began to surface.

'I don't have details, but what I do know is that the shot came from outside the vehicle they were in, and that the cops are searching for the gunman,' said Cole.

'Wee Davie,' said Frankie as tears welled in his eyes.

'I'm sorry, Frankie. I'm told that the cops are appointing a family liaison officer, who will be coming soon today to update you.'

'Who?'

'Pardon,' said Cole.

'Which cop? I want a name.'

'I've no idea, sorry.'

'No way. No fucking way am I speaking to any random fucking cop. I need to get out of here, I can't bloody stay here, that's for sure. They've killed Davie, and they'll be coming for me next.' Frankie felt the familiar rage surging as he spoke through gritted teeth.

'We'll be doing a threat assessment now, Frankie, but we have no identified or actionable intelligence of a threat against you, personally. It looks like someone wanted to stop Davie escaping.'

'Bollocks, it's not that. If it was that, why isn't every fucker dead, eh? They wanted Davie and Leo dead for a reason, which means they'll want me dead for the same reason.'

'What reason is that?' said Cole.

'Because of what I know, or at least what they think I know,' said Frankie, sitting back in his chair and massaging his temples.

'Frankie, you're safe here . . .' began Cole.

'Shite. No one can protect me in here. I'll be fucking dead before the end of the week. Now listen, Mr Cole. I'll speak to the cops, but I'll not speak to no random bastard. You tell them, I'll speak to DS Max Craigie, but no other bugger, eh?' he hissed, his neck tendons quivering like high tensile steel cords.

'I can't influence who'll come, Frankie. Why this particular cop?'

'Craigie's a bastard, but he's good, and he has one thing in his favour,' Frankie said flatly.

'What?' said Cole.

'He may well be the only straight cop in Scotland.'

32

THE WIND WAS sweeping down the gentle slope from the copse of trees, and the dog was on it like a flash, nose up in the air, riding his leash up onto his hind legs and barking furiously, his handler struggling to contain the animal. Ross, Max, Janie and the armed officer were almost having to jog to keep up.

'Now . . . I'm nae dog expert, pal . . . but it seems like el-poocho . . . has something in its nostrils, and it's not my aftershave,' said Ross, huffing and puffing as they ascended the slope, the armed officer sweeping ahead of them.

'Aye, boss. She's wind scenting from the trees, but not strong enough. I don't think anyone's there, or she'd be really wanting off the lead,' said the dog handler, straining to hold the big dog back.

'Jesus, that's one angry Alsatian. I wouldn't want her biting my arse, you want to let her go? I wouldn't cry if she ripped the fucker's throat out,' puffed Ross as he struggled to keep up with the quickening pace.

'Nah, we're good, and she's a Belgian Malinois, not a shepherd.'

'What's the difference?'

'The SAS use these buggers to kill Afghan insurgents, so maybe keep her on, eh?' said Max.

'She's good as gold, pal. Hasn't bitten a cop for ages.'

'Define "ages"?' said Janie.

'Well, not this week. Settle, girl,' the handler said in a soothing voice, before pausing and looking at Janie, a slight frown on his lean face. 'You know I was talking to the dog, right?'

Janie laughed. 'I was about to report you for a microaggression.'

They were soon close to the trees, the high whine of Barney's drone hovering ahead of them. 'No signs of life either side of the loch, or the trees. Clear to proceed, I'd say,' came Barney's voice over the radio.

'Okay, I'm gonna cast the dog out and quarter her into the woodblock and see how we go, stay back from me, and if she decides to rush towards you just stand still, and I'll call her off. She normally stops,' said the dog handler, with a smile.

'Define "normally"?' said Janie.

'Ach, eight out of ten times?' said the handler, with a puckish grin, releasing the dog's leash, with a command of, 'Go on, Wendy, where, where?'

She streaked off like a bullet, towards the trees, ears flat against her head in a cheetah-like bound, the picture of pure, unadulterated commitment.

'Wendy?' said Ross, looking at the handler, with his hands on his knees breathing deeply.

'Aye. I didn't name her; she was a gift dog from a member of the public who got fed up with her eating the sofa and biting delivery-men.'

'But fucking Wendy? Why not Lucifer, Beelzebub or Exocet, or maybe even Crook Killer? Look at the bugger go!' Ross said, admiring the speeding dog that had begun to cast left to right, searching for the scent of her quarry. She suddenly eased her pace, her ears pricked up, and she then changed direction, directly towards the copse, with a bark of excitement before she disappeared into the treeline.

'She's got something,' said the handler, beginning to jog towards the woods, Max and Janie in hot pursuit, Ross just picking his pace up as much as his hefty frame would allow.

A torrent of barks came from the trees, and they rushed as quickly as they could until everyone apart from Ross entered the wood line, where the dog was circling behind a small hump in the ground covered by an elder shrub. The dog's body language was one of pure excitement, as she circled around the shrub, nose to the ground, tail wagging.

'Right, he was here, I'm sure of it. It's a real strong signal. Wendy, come,' the handler commanded. Immediately the dog returned to his side and sat, panting with her tongue lolling. The handler reached down and touched the dog's ears reassuringly. 'Shh, good girl,' he whispered.

'I agree with Wendy,' said Max, pointing at the scrubby grass behind the shrub. 'The fronds are all flattened in the same direction, and look.' He stooped and picked up a few thin twigs that were next to the flattened grass. He held up the ends of the elder twigs, and pointed. 'See how these have been cut? That was done by our sniper to clear his view, probably with a multitool or similar, which is really shoddy tradecraft. Leave no trace is the mantra, so whilst I'd say that our man can shoot reasonably straight, I don't think he was a properly trained sniper. Well, not British military trained, anyway.'

'How can you be sure?' said Ross, puffing as he entered the woods.

'Too many mistakes that are drilled into you. Shite location and he's left signs all over the place. He may have slipped up. Mate, can you track his egress route out of here?' Max said, looking at the handler.

'Aye, she's already looking in the right direction, let's go.'

'I'm calling PolSA up here now, so I'll stay and brief them. If he's as much of an incompetent as you think, Max, then there may be something relevant here,' said Ross.

'Okay, don't talk to any strangers. Let's go,' said Max, nodding at the dog handler.

'Where, where, Wend?' said the handler, and the dog took off, her nose to the ground, as the lead was extended. They were off again, trailing in the wake of the excited Malinois as they were led through the woods and out the other side onto some more grassland that sloped down towards a deserted loch.

'He definitely came this way, and not that long ago, either. She's really indicating to the loch edge; I'm letting her go. Go on, girl,' he said, slipping the dog's lead once more. She took off again, but at a more considered pace, her nose down until she reached the edge of the loch, where she circled, sniffing, her tail fanning side to side until she just sat, stock still and looked at her handler, mouth agape, panting with her tongue lolling.

'Massive indication there, I'd say he spent a whole load of time at that point.'

They caught up with the dog, and Max dropped to his haunches and looked at the ground. He noted the depression in the middle of the scrappy ground, which was littered with stones, apart from a patch in the middle. He looked left and right, noting the small holes around the edge of the cleared area.

'Evidence of a tent here. Look, he's cleared the stones away, and the holes are where the pegs went in.' Max lowered his head and sniffed at the earth, wrinkling his nose. 'I can smell a trace of smoke as well. He may have had a small fire, or a cooking stove.'

'Jesus, he's a brazen bastard. Are we saying he stayed the night?' said the armed officer as he scanned all round, his carbine butted into his shoulder.

'It's actually quite sensible, especially if he stashed the weapon first. A fisherman camped by the loch, what could be more natural?' said Max.

'How do you know he was fishing?' said Janie.

'A hole close to the water's edge, and a depression just behind it. I'd say that was his rod rest. Makes perfect sense to me.'

'Jesus, Max. Were you a hunter-gatherer in a former life?' said Janie.

'Just a bit of tracking training in the Army,' said Max, sniffing again, closer to the water's edge. 'I can smell cigarette smoke, it's faint, but it's definitely there. We need PolSA up here, there could be cigarette ends about. I don't think he's smart enough to take them with him. Can you call it in, Janie?' said Max, looking towards another copse of trees a few hundred metres away.

'On it.'

'Right, let's find the egress route from here, as he's bound to have had a vehicle nearby, unless he got picked up, which I can't see. I'm betting he's gone to that next tree block around the loch. Can you send the dog over?' said Max.

Within a second, Wendy was off again, nose down, tail swaying, as she headed around the loch towards the trees, before she began fussing with interest just on the leading edge of the trees by a large gorse bush. As before, she sat, looking at her handler expectantly, until they joined her. Max peered into the shrub, noting the broken and bruised evergreen branches, and studied the ground, spotting the single tyre track that headed away from the muddy ground and the woods towards the farm track, where it disappeared completely on the compacted, hard surface.

'He's on a motorbike, off-road style, I'd say. Looking at the skinny, knobbly tyre prints I'd say it's a fairly low-power one, as the tracks haven't decayed at all, yet. Reckon he left here no more than ninety minutes ago. He's gone, and he could be bloody miles away by now.'

'Shit,' said Janie.

'Indeed. Make it clear, we need divers in the loch. A weapon capable of firing that size of round would be hard to conceal, particularly on a motorbike. I'm betting it's in there, and it'll not be far from the edge.'

33

DROOPY WAS SITTING behind the wheel of his anonymous Ford Mondeo as he navigated the busy Edinburgh traffic when his phone rang on the seat next to him. He indicated and pulled off the main road and onto a small side street before stopping and picking up the handset. He always did this. Droopy had stayed well off law-enforcement radar for as long as he had by not doing stupid things, like driving and talking on the phone. No need to get loads of penalty points, it just put you in the bastards' sights. A ban for someone like Droopy would be inconvenient, to say the least.

'Aye?'

'It's me.' The accent was a curious mix of Manchester with just a hint of something European, yet somehow flat and devoid of any emotion.

'Any problems?'

'Nope. Easy as owt, mate. Like shootin' ducks at a fairground.'

'Both?'

'Yep. Both now have a case of missing head syndrome. When can I expect the moolah to be transferred?'

'As soon as there's official confirmation.'

'Well, I'm confirming it, mate. I watched it happen through me scope.'

'Well, nice of you to say, pal, but funnily enough my employer likes official confirmation from independent sources. Nae disrespect, like.'

'None taken. It'll be all over news soon. Straight away, yeah. I've onwards travel booked.'

'It'll be done. Make sure you ditch this phone, okay?' said Droopy. It shouldn't have been necessary to say this, but the sniper, whilst efficient and a decent shot, wasn't the brightest.

'Of course. I'll watch my bank.' He rang off.

Droopy slid the SIM card out of his cheap smartphone, and slotted in another. He didn't immediately dial, but navigated to the BBC News page.

Breaking news: Police at major incident at Scottish loch, unconfirmed reports of two fatalities.

Droopy smiled and dialled again. The phone was answered immediately with a hoarse whisper. 'Yes?'

'Any news for me?' said Droopy.

'Your man did the business.'

'Both?'

'Aye.'

'A permanent solution.'

'As permanent as it's possible to be.'

'Any other casualties?'

'A couple of cops need to change their underwear, maybe.' There was a slight chuckle at this.

'The other firm?'

'They legged it pronto, no sightings, but your man was careless.' The voice was low, and almost a whisper.

'How so?' Droopy's voice sharpened.

'Somehow there was a drone up, and it caught his firing position. A couple of cops tracked it down with a dog. I'm not a hundred per cent sure, but there's talk of some evidence being found up by the loch. They're putting divers in there now. Will they find anything?'

Droopy was silent for a full ten seconds, and looked at his reflection in the rear-view mirror. As always, his face was totally expressionless, his hooded eyelids and sagging cheeks giving nothing away as to what he was feeling. It was wholly possible that the sniper had thrown the rifle in the loch, as he wouldn't want to be lugging it about after a double hit. Would it matter if the cops recovered it? He doubted it very much, but it would be careless, and for the money paid, that really wasn't good enough.

'Are you there?' said the voice.

'Aye. Don't worry about it.'

'Theory is that the gunman camped by the loch, but surely, he wouldn't have been that obvious. What if he'd been seen?'

Droopy paused again, churning this information over. 'Keep me informed of any developments.' He hung up, and removed the SIM from the phone before slotting in another fresh one. He quickly composed a message.

Objective achieved. Transferring fee to contractor now.

The response came back almost immediately.

Acknowledged. Final objective?

Droopy tapped the keys on the phone again and replied. **In hand and imminent.**

The reply was immediate. **Good. ASAP pls, there's too much riding on this.**

He navigated to the new banking app on the phone and opened it, logging in with his thumbprint. He smiled at the brand-new account in the name 'H MacFarlane', sat there with just one deposit in it of tens of thousands of pounds. Money laundering rules were so draconian now that moving money was tricky, but ID theft made it far easier if you knew what you were doing. Everyone knew about burner phones but Droopy was equally hot on 'burner bank accounts', particularly the newer app-based accounts. All you needed were scans of ID documents, and an account could be set up in minutes. Just use the account for one job, and then abandon it. Any suspicious activity reported to the NCA would almost certainly come to nothing, and even if it did, so what? They'd just find a new account set up and a couple of transactions to numbered accounts, or other burner accounts. The

National Crime Agency was so swamped with suspicious activity reports that it would probably just be ignored. No bags of cash any more. No risk of the cops taking the lot with the cash seizure laws. Just a series of computer code instantly sending money from one account to another. Anonymous and untraceable.

Droopy pulled out the final SIM card and threw it with the others in the cup holder. He'd ditch them all separately, best not to get caught with them if he was stopped by the cops, not that that was likely. Droopy never got stopped, mostly because he never did anything that would result in cops noticing him, and secondly because his hangdog face was just so unassuming that he didn't look like what, or who, he really was. He engaged the gears and moved off, happy at the nice percentage of the sniper's fee that would now swell his already healthy finances, and all for making a few phone calls and knowing the right people. He turned up the music, and Matt Monro began to seep gently out of the speakers as he moved off, a smile stretching across his heavy face. Soon this whole situation would be wrapped up for good.

34

DCC LOUISE CAMPBELL was sitting in her office, her gut heavy with anxiety as she took in the report that DCS Miles Wakefield had sent her about the previous day's drama, which didn't make good reading. The phone call from the Chief Constable just now hadn't helped at all. Despite his calm manner, she could sense the tension in his voice. He wanted DI Fraser and his team assisting, no arguments. And he was on his way back from holiday early, which couldn't be a good thing.

The level of scrutiny was going to be forensic in its detail, and the Police Investigations Review Commission were already stomping all over it, with investigators still at the scene and early interviews of those present underway. She knew without a shadow of a doubt that she was going to be questioned about her decision-making processes, so she needed to get her story tight, and ensure that she had recorded everything.

Hardie and his solicitor both executed by a sniper who had vanished almost into thin air. What was also disturbing was how and why Fraser and his team had all arrived on scene very quickly, despite her insistence that they remained uninvolved. She'd read with incredulity about the technical surveillance freelancer who was actually monitoring the whole thing by a drone, which was frankly astonishing, even though he had captured the first-rate evidence of the attempted breakout.

She really wanted to carpet Fraser for this, but she knew that tactically she had to tread carefully, particularly as they had warned her so vehemently about Hardie's intentions. They had been proved right, and also Fraser was close to the Chief. Much too close as far as she could see, but this was made worse as Wakefield's interim report made clear that it was Craigie who had not only managed to trace the sniper's firing point, but also his laying-up point from the night before and where he had stashed his getaway bike. The fact that the dive team had pulled out rifle components from the loch and PolSA had found a cigarette butt likely to have been smoked by the sniper would only make her job more difficult. It certainly seemed like they were competent officers, and the Chief would no doubt be singing their praises when he returned from his holiday, whereas she was going to be on the defensive from the first moment.

It had been a mistake to be so closely aligned with the decision-making process, which in retrospect she hadn't needed to do. She could have handed this straight back to Miles Wakefield to manage, overseen by one of the ACCs who could have liaised with the Crown Office. It was a tactical error, and she really needed to think about limiting the personal damage to her, and perhaps shifting some of the attention towards Ross Fraser and his team. She had seen teams like this in the Met for so many years and knew how to handle them. Small squads of specialist cops who get a few good results, and then are left without any proper, strategic oversight and often a toxic, overly macho environment. Nothing she had seen from that oaf, DI Ross Fraser, or DS Max Craigie had persuaded her that they were any different, and how the Chief could justify having them outside her control, now that she was lead for professional standards, was still a mystery to her. Also, 'Barney', or whatever he was called, was seemingly vital to the team, which was troubling bearing in mind his financial difficulties. She had no idea why he was being utilised when they had a perfectly good technical team available. She made a note in her daybook to check on the man's vetting status, and vowed to raise it further when the Chief returned.

She clucked her tongue as she sat back in the chair, her fingers steepled as they often were when she was in deep thought. She recalled the meetings with Finn Townsend at the Crown Office. She had probably said too much in her dealings with him, particularly over the boozy lunch they'd shared. He really needed to know that their conversations about their future mutual relationship were kept between themselves. If Macdonald knew exactly what they had discussed, it probably wouldn't be very well received. She opened her laptop and composed a brief email.

LC-Campbell, Louise <Louise.Campbell@scotland.police.uk>
To: <Finn.Townsend@copfs.gov.uk>
Subject: David Hardie – Debrief and immunity exploratory exercise

Dear Finn,
You'll no doubt have seen the news re Hardie. Maybe we should meet to consider any ramifications?
    How about lunch?

Warmest regards,
Louise

35

THE ATMOSPHERE IN the packed incident room at Gartcosh was febrile and crackling with tension as Chief Superintendent Miles Wakefield, a sour look on his face, entered with Malky Douglas in tow, carrying a sheaf of documents and files. The low hum of conversation stopped as if a switch was flicked. The room was full of a mix of uniformed cops and detectives in suits, their tie knots slackened and their faces weary. All clutched A4 books, or ring binders, and all looked tired. It was almost eight o'clock and they had had a hard day scene processing, and generally running about shaking trees, speaking to informants and scanning CCTV for the missing BMW that contained the three raiders who'd attempted to spring Hardie.

'Fuck me, Miles looks bastard scunnered,' said Ross to Max in a hoarse whisper that could be heard across the incident room.

'You say something, Ross?' barked Wakefield, eyeing Ross balefully.

'No, boss. All good with me.'

Wakefield stared at Ross with an expression that looked like he'd had a sudden twinge of toothache. He shook his head, just slightly, firmed his stance, and then spoke. 'Right, we don't have long as I'm needed at Tuliallan, urgently. The DCC wants a face to face, and I want to leave here assured that we're all over this, am I clear?' His voice was as sour as the look on his face, which seemed to be carrying more lines than earlier in the day.

There were murmurs of assent.

'Okay, I have direct oversight of this case, which as of now is wholly focused on the attempted breakout of Davie Hardie, and then the subsequent fatal shooting of him and his lawyer, Leo Hamilton. We will also be considering if and how this interacts with the discovery of the submerged corpse in the loch. No assumptions, okay? DCI Heather Davies is SIO, but under my direct supervision, deputy SIO is Acting DI Mark Bryan, who is joining from MIT 3. Jimmy Duggan is crime scene coordinator. Can we hear from you first, Jim?'

Jimmy scratched at his heavily stubbled chin and spoke, his Dublin accent rich. 'Body from the loch has been recovered, but very little for us to do there, boss. She's well decomposed, so it'll have to wait for the post-mortem. We have a DNA profile on the database for Beata Dabrowski, so once we extract whatever DNA is available from the corpse, we should be able to make a positive ID. She was naked, it seems, but no chance of cause of death at the scene. ID will have to be via DNA, or maybe dental, she was using a dentist in Glasgow, so we'll have comparators. No suggestion that the raiders touched anything, although we've taken all the clothing of the cops in the van. Bodies were photographed in situ, but were quickly removed, and PM is scheduled for tomorrow, not that cause of death is going to be much of a surprise.'

'Aye, loss of a nappa tends to ruin your day. Any bullet recovery?'

'We got lucky. The one that took out Leo Hamilton was deflected by the metal of the van after passing through his skull, and it was buried into the ground. A big old lump of lead. It'll be going to ballistics straight away, once the forensic budget is approved.'

'Consider it approved. What about the bullet that took out Hardie?'

'Well, as he was stood when it happened, it would have passed straight through his skull, and into the countryside. PolSA are returning in daylight with metal detectors, but it's unlikely, and to be honest, not vital. If I had to choose one to submit, it'd be Hamilton's.'

'Who's attending the PMs?' asked Wakefield.

'That's me, boss, together with Doreen Urquhart who's handling productions,' said Bryan.

'Lucky you two. Okay, I'm on a real tight timescale here. How about the sniper's firing point and lay-up point? Good work from your team there, Ross,' said Wakefield, eyeing Ross, his voice laced with sarcasm.

'All part of the service from Crocodile Dundee Craigie here, boss,' said Ross, cheeks bulging as he chewed on an apple, a small fragment of the fruit flying out of his mouth. There was a ripple of laughter in the room.

'Indeed . . . and remind me that we need a chat about how your man conveniently found himself nearby with a state-of-the-art drone, although the footage that's been shared with me has made it a fortunate coincidence.'

'Barney has a Zen-like ability to sniff out trouble, boss,' said Ross, shrugging.

'Aye, well, that's for later. Are we sure it's the firing point?'

'I'd say so, there are signs in the foliage, and scrapes in the dirt where his boots dug in. I also think he cut some of the fronds away with a knife, or more likely snipped with something like a Leatherman.'

'No sign of a shell casing?' Wakefield said, turning to a uniformed inspector in the overalls often worn by the PolSA teams.

'No, sir. Nothing there at all, but we did recover a cigarette butt, which doesn't look too old. It'd been crudely buried at the site where DS Craigie thinks he camped.'

'Has that been submitted, Jimmy?' said Wakefield.

'Yep, fast track. Costing a fortune, but we'll hopefully have a profile by tomorrow, if it's there to be found,' said Jimmy Duggan.

'Anything to add, Max?' said Wakefield.

'Well, someone certainly camped there, I could still detect a whiff of cigarette smoke and there was evidence of pegs, a rod and plenty of footprints. Someone stayed there, that's for sure, and with the rifle components in the loch, I think we can make the assumption it was the sniper,' said Max, his thoughts returning to Bruce. He looked at his phone, wondering whether he should call.

'Ah, right. The weapon, what do we have?'

Doreen Urquhart spoke for the first time. 'Divers have recovered the barrel, the stock and a small piece of the working parts. A firearms officer has had a look, and he thinks that it's military grade, and probably chambered for a .338.'

'Is that big?' said Wakefield.

'It's very big, boss,' said Max.

'Just how big?'

'Big enough to remove heads. Snipers use them, in fact the British Army main sniper weapon is chambered .338.'

'I hear that we also think that he used a motorbike? Tyre tracks recovered, Billy?' Miles turned to the crime scene manager.

'We got a decent cast, may be able to narrow the bike brand down with some tyre company manufacturers,' said Billy.

'Already in hand,' said DCI Davies.

'Okay, thanks everyone for your hard work. I really need to get to Tulliallan, or I'll be very unpopular with the DCC. Anything on the rescuer's car?'

'The drone didn't capture the plate number, and no sightings nearby. Still combing what CCTV there is, but it's sparse,' said Davies.

'Is that all the main parts before I go?'

'Lots more happening, but that's the salient lines of inquiry we've been concentrating on,' said Davies.

'PIRC?'

'They sniffed about a bit, but seem happy to leave it with us. They'll be looking at the planning and tactics of the operation in slow time, as it's a death in police custody.'

'Lastly, before I go, how are DS Maxwell, DS Laithwaite and the driver?'

'Shocked, but okay. We sent them away after they gave initial accounts, and seized all their clothing, which look very much like a Jackson Pollock piece after the spray caught them,' said Davies, with a grimace.

'Okay, thanks all. We need a big push on this one, as the scrutiny is going to be intense. Keep at it one hundred per cent, am I clear?' There were nods and murmurs of assent.

'One thing, boss?' said Ross. 'The deaths of Steven Mitchell and Jack Slattery.' His voice was almost hesitant.

'What about them?' said Wakefield.

'Both Hardie henchmen, and both killed within hours of this going down. It must be connected, no?'

'No one has told me anything that suggests that. Slattery being ex-cop was hardly going to be popular in jail, and Mitchell was a career criminal living in Newcastle, I was told. We've enough on right now, and I don't want us distracted by minor coincidences. As I understand it, Slattery was killed by a psychotic criminal, who daubed about pigs in his victim's blood, and Mitchell was a criminal shot dead in an unconnected fashion. Unless you have evidence, we won't be distracted by that.'

'That feels like a mistake to me, sir,' said Ross, politely.

Wakefield's face darkened, the stress showing in his lined, pale features, as a silence descended on the room, which was thick and uncomfortable.

'Well, it's my mistake to make, DI Fraser. Now, unless you have tangible evidence linking the cases, we carry on as agreed under Heather's direction.' He straightened his tie, nodded and left the room, Malky in tow, shrugging as he walked past Ross.

Ross just smiled back, his eyes twinkling with amusement.

The murmur in the room increased in volume, and people began to stand, stretching their backs and loosening ties.

'Okay, folks. Once all your submissions are in, and evidence and statements handed into the receiver, I want you all to head home, ready for a long day tomorrow. We have to be ready to deploy urgently if we get a DNA hit on the fag butt, and the PM's at 1 p.m. I'll be handing out all the actions in the morning, and there'll be a lot of them. Ross, do you have a moment?' Davies said.

Ross nodded and they moved over to the corner of the room.

'Mitchell and Slattery, do you actually have anything at all?' said Davies, in a whisper.

'No, but does anyone not think that's a coincidence too far?'

'I agree. My core jobs are all allocated, so if you don't mind, maybe your guys can sneakily look into it, despite what Miles just said. I think his decision is bollocks, so if there's a connection, we need to find it. I wish you could concentrate on that.'

'Ach, maybe we'll have a wee poke about, there'll be something linking it all, there always is. Miles only likes to investigate what he can see and touch. He doesn't like theories.'

'You may cop some flak?'

'I'm used to it, Heather. Don't worry about Miles, we'll find the link before he realises that we've been looking for it, and then he'll have no choice.' Ross nodded, and smiled, and then walked over to Max and Janie, who were chatting conspiratorially in another corner of the room.

'What are you two buggers planning?' said Ross as he approached them.

'Nothing. Talking about boxing,' said Janie, but her eyes told a different story.

'Bollocks. Spit it out.'

'Galbraith at the jail.'

'I thought as much, is your pal on prison liaison? Phil something or other?'

'Yeah. I spoke to him about our concerns for Frankie.'

'Shit, I'd forgotten about that. Tell me he's not dead, please,' said Ross.

'He's not dead, in fact they have him locked down tight, waiting for us to advise. There's something else.'

'Go on,' said Ross, eyes narrowing.

'Frankie wants to see a cop, and he'll only see Max.'

'What?'

'I know, that's what I said.' Max shrugged.

'Is Galbraith gonna go after Frankie as well?' said Ross.

'No, Galbraith's been moved to double A cat and he's at a different nick, anyway. He'll never get near anyone again, but Frankie thinks it's only a matter of time before someone else makes a move. He wants to speak to us, and he wants to speak to us straight away.'

'Can your mate set that up for tomorrow, covertly?'

'He normally covers Saughton, but he's making the arrangements with Shotts as their liaison cop is on leave. He'll be waiting for us and only needs an hour's notice,' said Janie.

'Okay, as soon as you can tomorrow morning. We need to know what Frankie knows. You also said something about Galbraith?' said Ross.

'Aye, Janie was thinking. He's terminally ill, nothing to lose, but Norma went off and used her initiative.' Max scratched his head.

'Shite, I hate it when she does that. What did she do?'

'She nobbled a pal of hers in the NCA to do some basic financial checks on Galbraith's family members, and it turned up something interesting.' Janie paused.

'Shite, woman, stop being so bastard obtuse, just spit it out, it's not am-dram.' Ross's eyebrows bristled.

'His mother received a large amount of money, from a new bank account, yesterday.'

'How much?'

'Fifteen grand . . .' Max interjected. 'It was marked as a car sale, but guess what?'

'Stop pissing about and tell me, ya fud.'

'No cars registered at her address, she's never had a licence and she lives alone.'

'Shit. That's the motive right there. We need to tell Heather and get this moving.' Ross picked his phone from his pocket, and started to dial.

'Hold up, don't touch that dial. That's the last thing we should do, Ross,' Max said quickly. 'This is a direct lead into who ordered Slattery's killing, and I would say who ordered the killing of Davie and Leo too. Look at what's happened. How did they know precisely where and when Hardie would be? Someone clearly tipped off Hardie's rescuers, and someone *else* told the sniper about it. That someone is a cop. We keep this to ourselves. The boss is back tomorrow, we tell the Chief that we want to handle Frankie, and we investigate who paid to have Slattery and Davie whacked. We get the answers to that, and we probably get closer to the source of the leak if we can get him lumped up, bugged up, tracked and traced, eh?'

Ross knotted his face in a frown as he pieced it all together. 'Good call. So, what do you suggest?'

Max waggled his fingers in an approximation of quotation marks. '"Thematic review." Speak to the Chief, his ears only, and get the green light to do our thing. With the DCC in the picture and flexing her muscles we need to be authorised, or it could get intensely political,' Max said.

'Ah, bugger it. Okay, make arrangements to go and see Frankie, and start poking around, subtly. Get Norma to get her pal to dig into that new account as well, any other transactions will be interesting.'

'Of course, Ross. Always subtle we are.'

'Aye, which is what worries me. I've seen your subtlety; it normally ends up with people getting shot in the face.'

'I promise that won't happen,' said Max, grinning.

Ross opened his mouth to counter, but a ping from his pocket stopped him. He picked out his phone, and his eyes creased in amusement.

'Something funny?' said Max.

'It's gonna get lively. The Chief's back and wants to see me at Tulliallan right now. Whatever you guys had planned, best cancel them, I suspect we're gonna get even busier.'

36

CHIEF CONSTABLE CHRIS Macdonald looked pale and wan behind the suntan as he sat behind his large desk in his open and airy office at Tulliallan. Unusually, he wore a yellow polo shirt and creased linen shorts. 'Now, Ross, you can probably tell from my casual attire that I've come straight here from the airport, and I suspect that my wife is as pissed off as Mrs Fraser gets when you're burning the candle on both ends, as you often do.'

'That's not possible, sir. In fact, to be able to grasp Mrs F's mood today, you'd have to imagine Satan himself with a bad case of piles and an ingrown toenail that he's just stubbed.'

'That bad, eh?' said Macdonald with a smile.

'Worse, boss.' Ross's head shook almost imperceptibly.

Macdonald's smile widened. 'Then I'll consider myself fortunate. So can you give me everything you have? All of it. I understand from Miles that there may be some slightly non-standard evidence-gathering going on from your team?' His well-trimmed eyebrows raised at this point, the meaning clear.

'What do you want to know, boss?' said Ross, his eyes narrowing. He and Macdonald had a long shared history, joining the police at around the same time, and working together on many occasions. They had few secrets, and each knew when the other was bullshitting.

'The lot. Unvarnished, good and bad.'

Ross told him. He told him everything, including the fact that Max's original source was a little 'off-books'.

'So, it was DCC Campbell's decision to exclude you?'

'Aye. I think the fact that she's the lead for professional standards makes our existence a little confusing to her,' said Ross, carefully.

Macdonald steepled his fingers together and supported his chin with them. 'Well, suffice to say that as far as I'm concerned, you are still operational, and you remain under my direct control, is that clear?'

Ross just nodded.

'I'll speak to DCC Campbell now, but what's the deal with Barney? She got quite upset about him. "Disrespectful, misogynistic and a potential security threat" were the terms used.'

Ross chuckled. 'I don't think she liked him calling her "love" but he's an old Yorkshireman, boss. He sometimes calls me "love", and occasionally "pet". As for a security threat, that's utter nonsense. Barney has been at the centre of the covert world since we were in short breeks. His integrity is beyond reproach, he's just skint.'

'House repossessed, I'm told.'

'Aye, but I think he basically just forgot to pay his mortgage, or something. He enjoys a wee flutter, but really, he just has no time for what most people call a traditional life, having lived out of a suitcase for about fifty years. He seems to actually quite like living in his daft van, tinkering with his gadgets. In another life he'd have been a hippy. But he's highly decorated, and moreover he's the bravest and most skilled operative I've ever worked with. He's vital to us, as he's demonstrated time and time again,' said Ross, his voice firm.

'Must be cold in that van,' said Macdonald, a smile playing on his lips.

'Baltic, but he's okay. One thing he doesn't do is moan. We didn't even know until recently that he's had a prosthetic leg for years after getting shot. He's actually registered disabled, and has a blue badge for the van, hence parking it out the front of this place, much to the chagrin of the DCC.'

Macdonald guffawed. 'I did hear about that. Okay, here's what we're going to do. I will personally tell the DCC that Barney is my responsibility and my risk, is covert in nature and that she isn't to pry any more. I've already heard from the vetting department that there are no flags on him; quite the contrary, he's held Developed Vetted status for more years than the both of us have been alive without so much as a single red flag. Would he like temporary accommodation for the winter? There's a flat available if he would.'

'I'll ask him, but if I know Barney, he'll jump at the chance of something that's free, but I'd steel yourself for a big electricity bill.'

'Excellent. I'll make a call. So, what's next?'

'Max is going to see Frankie Hardie in prison tomorrow. We may need a quick move on that with the Crown Office, depending on what he wants, and what he knows. If he really wants to spill the beans, we may need to look into moving him into a covert and secure location. If this is as big as we suspect, they could get to him, wherever he is.'

'I'll need proper convincing if that's the case, and any operation to debrief him outside of the prison estate will need serious planning, and a detailed risk management plan.'

'We can discuss that once we know what he's got to say. I'm still hesitant to believe any Hardie would help the polis.'

'Agreed. Anything else?'

'We'll still chase the money, that's a big part of this. Norma can keep digging as it looks like it could be a burner account that paid money into Galbraith's mother's account. It may have been used elsewhere.'

'And you want to limit the dissemination of this, I assume?'

'Aye, of both Frankie and the banking lead until we can bottom them out. The fact that the sniper knew exactly when and where the van would be could only have come from someone on the inside, and we're going to find out who it is. Bent bastard.'

'More bloody corruption. This is a bad situation, Ross. Miles is going to brief me on the reactive investigation tomorrow, but I want you to look at the covert side, and keep it locked down tight. See what

Frankie has to say, and chase up this banking. We'll decide how we approach it from there. We may get a DNA hit on the sniper after all.'

'I want us to be involved in any arrest op on him. Max was a sniper, and he may know how to get into his head, plus we have to consider how he was paid. He's definitely a pro, although Max is being critical about his tradecraft. He'd have been expensive.'

'Always the key to anything like this, eh, Ross,' said the Chief, stifling a yawn.

'Follow the money, boss. Always follow the money.'

37

FRANKIE HARDIE WAS in his cell, staring at the TV which was not switched on. His thoughts were rushing like static electricity as he thought of his brother, dead on a slab somewhere. Just over a year ago, Frankie was part of a big family. A respected family with serious influence and plenty of money, and now look. He was the only one of them left, and he was in this putrid fucking cell in the shite-hole that was Shotts jail. His pa died in a shitty old graveyard. Tam Junior was gone, presumed dead having escaped from jail, and his wife and kids had heard nothing from him since then. Now Davie was gone. Shot by a fucking sniper during an escape attempt, and all because someone thought he was going to drop the dime on them. Something about someone big and powerful who was tying up loose ends. Frankie knew things that the cops would want to know, but he didn't know everything. There were gaps. He knew his old man had some big bit of evidence stashed away somewhere, but was he going to help the cops? Could he be that person? It had been imprinted on him from day one that you never grassed, and you never helped the police, but things had changed. He was the last of the Hardies, and if he didn't help the cops, then the bastard who put his brother in the morgue would get away with it.

He didn't look up at the familiar rattle of keys in the cell door. 'Grub's up, Frankie,' said Mr Jeffries, his head poking around the cell door.

'Awesome,' said Frankie, standing up, his voice flat and laden with sarcasm.

'Stovies again, unfortunately, but most of the guys are back in their pads now. Grab your food and then straight back in, eh?' said Jeffries, who opened the cell door wider.

'Jesus,' said Frankie, shaking his head, the cloud of depression thickening around his head. He couldn't even have his bloody food out of his cell, since they'd risk-assessed him after his brother got topped. No new intelligence of hostile intentions, no need for full segregation, but meals in his cell and only out for necessities like showers and healthcare had been the decision by Cole, the head screw. They'd offered him rule 43 with all the nonces, but he'd told them to fuck off. He was a Hardie. Hardies didn't hide away with all the paedos.

He had to turn to one side to get past a silver-haired, tattooed elderly con he'd not seen before, who was disconsolately pushing a dirty mop along an even dirtier floor, a tiny roll-up somehow attached to his lower lip. What sounded like twenty types of music, from rock to hip-hop to country, was blaring out from twenty cells. It all made for an unpleasant and febrile atmosphere, only made worse by the sour and unpleasant stench of the spice that was clearly reducing his co-inmates into whatever oblivion they were seeking. Spice had replaced heroin as the inmates' choice of 'bird killer', meaning that if you were out of your box, your time passed so much quicker. A brief mental escape from the hellhole that was HMP Shotts. He sighed deeply, the depression biting even harder.

Frankie descended the iron staircase where he found the meal hall almost empty, apart from one of his pals behind the counter nodding at him.

'Frankie, man. How ya doing?' said the server.

'Fucking stoatin, Charlie. Twenty-three hours bang-up, and now it's stovies for dinner again.' Frankie tried to lighten his voice, to chase away the deadening fog that was seeping into his brain.

'Aye well, we spoil ya, eh?' Charlie guffawed as he ladled a big pile of the grey-brown stew on his proffered plastic tray with compartments for pudding and a big hunk of stale bread. Another ladle, this time of some kind of sponge and a watery custard, was deposited into its space on the tray. Frankie picked up the plastic bag containing his breakfast pack, which he knew would contain two Weetabix, a carton of UHT milk and a bruised apple. All the food he'd get in the next eighteen hours was now in his hands. He was thankful for the stack of noodles and packets of biscuits that sat on the shelf in his cell, which acted both as currency and as sustenance for the putrid diet.

'Straight back to your pad, Frankie, eh?' said Jeffries as Frankie made to sit at one of the long trestle tables.

'Ach, come on, Mr Jeffries. I'm sick of the fucking place, just give me twenty minutes.'

'Sorry, Frankie. You know the drill, straight back up. I'm just doing the phone checks and then it's bang-up, pal,' said Jeffries, shaking his head, with no trace of a smile.

'Fuck's sake,' muttered Frankie, standing up again and heading to the staircase, clutching his tray and bag. He ascended the steps, where the old con was still mopping, his head down, lips moving silently, the roll-up bobbling between his lips, the wooden handle of the mop clutched between his calloused hands.

'What ya sayin', old fella?' Frankie greeted as the old guy looked at him through rheumy eyes, his face unsmiling.

'Working,' he said gruffly, and shrugged as he continued to swish the mop on the scuffed floor.

Frankie shook his head at the grumpy old bugger's attitude. He'd only appeared at the jail a short while ago and had somehow managed to blag himself a pad on the 'ones', prison slang for the preferred ground floor. Probably because the old bastard's knees were so creaky.

'Frankie, dude. What's happening?' came a voice from Logan McGill's cell, his small and wizened face pressed against the hard Perspex of the cell wicket, the sliding door that the screws used to check on prisoners without opening the door. Logan was a bit claustrophobic, so the screws always kept his wicket open during the daylight hours, as long as he behaved.

'Fucking partial lockdown, Logan. Have to eat this shite in my pad. I'll never get rid of the fucking smell, man,' said Frankie.

Logan cackled, showing stained and broken teeth, his muddy brown eyes full of amusement. He was a total junkie, and mad as a box of frogs, but he was a likeable enough guy. 'Aye, I'd give this place a two-star review on Tripadvisor, maximum.'

'I may stretch to three, Logan, if the stovies don't give me the shi—' Frankie stopped mid-sentence, as Logan's eyes flared wide open with alarm, staring beyond him, just as a shadow fell across his shoulder.

'Frankie, look out!' yelled Logan, in what was almost a high-pitched squeal.

Time seemed to slow, and it felt like Frankie was wading through treacle as he turned. The elderly con, who seconds ago was working his mop on the floor, now had the wooden handle held high, like a spear, the pitted tip flashed bright white with something jammed into it as he drove the makeshift weapon with surprising speed at Frankie's neck. The man's face was set firm, teeth bared. Frankie fell to the floor, instinctively, feeling the disturbed air as the makeshift spear passed over his head, ramming with a clatter into the heavy metal of Logan's cell door. The tip broke, and the man stumbled. Immediately Frankie's martial arts training clicked in. He'd been a proficient cage-fighter in his time, and a big part of that had been jiu-jitsu. He rolled onto the floor, scissoring the old man's legs with his, bringing him to the hard, wet ground. He went straight on the attack, and within a second, had him restrained, his forearm pressed into the old man's throat.

'Who fucking sent you?' hissed Frankie.

The man said nothing, so tightly was his airway constricted by Frankie's forearm, but his eyes sparkled.

'Who fucking sent you?' Frankie repeated, letting some of the pressure off the man's throat.

The man coughed wetly, a smile stretching across his face, showing a mouth totally devoid of teeth. 'You dead man, Hardie. Not today maybe, but soon. You say a fucking word, and you'll be dead within a day. You can't stop it. No one can, he has people everywhere,' he said, his voice crackling with phlegm, and his normal mumbled timbre replaced with a harsh and thick Eastern European snarl. The crudely worked tattoo on his corded neck of a two-headed bird stood out harsh and stark against his skin.

A piercing tone split the silence as the alarm began to sound, and there was a sudden uproar, as the cons behind their doors erupted in shouts and catcalls.

Frankie felt strong arms pulling him away, and in a second he was secured, in an arm lock, his face pressed to the hard floor, whilst the prison raged around him.

38

MAX AND JANIE sat across the worn and chipped desk in the healthcare office in the far wing of Shotts jail, a turgid silence in the room as they looked at the lean form of Frankie Hardie. He leant back in his chair, his chin cupped in his hands, as he returned their stare. He still wore his customary contemptuous glare, but it was marred by something else. It was visible in his eyes by the slight downturn at the corners, and by the flush in his cheeks.

Vulnerability. Max could see it as clear as if it was tattooed on his forehead. Frankie was scared. He barely looked like a Hardie any more. He looked what he was: a man in fear of his life. A man with nothing to lose.

Max didn't speak, and neither did Janie. They both knew that as Frankie had requested to speak to them, the obligation was his. They were happy to wait and allow the uncomfortable silence to continue until Frankie was ready. There was just the three of them in the poky and depressing room, the wordless prison officer had left after escorting Frankie in with just a nod. The room was silent apart from a slight whir from the fan in the old desktop computer that sat at the side of the room next to a medicine cabinet. Frankie's eyes were downcast, and his face radiated a mix of fear and despair. He looked like a man who had lost everything. Still Max and Janie said nothing.

Predictably, Frankie broke first. 'Who tried to spring Davie, then?'

'We don't know yet. Inquiries are ongoing,' said Max.

'And who killed him? I'm hearing a sniper.'

'Same answer, Frankie. Inquiries are ongoing, but we have some leads. It was a sniper, but he's not been that careful.'

'What leads?'

'Items from the scene where he fired from. He's not been as meticulous as he could've. Can you think why or by who he was shot?'

'I would'nae be asking if I knew, would I? He knew lots of folk on the outside, though. Davie was always better connected than me, and Pa and Tam always favoured him. He'd have had people to call. I don't, which is why we're talking now. I need help, or I'm gonna get killed. Maybe not today or tomorrow, but no way will I last ten years in gen pop, and I'm nae going rule 43, either. Nonces and grasses are just as dangerous if they think they can curry favour with someone. Killing me could get a nonce a powerful ally and get them off 43 and back in gen pop, or at worst a few quid to their family on the out. I want a deal. I know things about why Davie and Slattery were killed, but I need assurances.' He sat back in his chair and exhaled, the relief at having said what he wanted to say was almost palpable.

Max held Frankie's gaze for a beat. 'So what happened on the landing last night?'

'You not heard from the screws?' said Frankie, narrowing his eyes.

'I want to hear it from you.'

'Some old con went for me with a fucking makeshift spear. His mop handle had a toothbrush handle sharpened to a point attached. If a pal hadn't shouted, he'd have fucking brained me, man.'

'Who is he?'

'I've hardly even spoke to the guy. He turned up on the wing recently, no one knows anything about him, other than he got straight onto the ones, and got a plum cleaning job that got him out of his cell when we were all banged up. He sounded foreign.'

'He is. His name's Almir Duka. He was in here awaiting an extradition hearing to return him to Albania. Someone hadn't done the proper intelligence checks, and didn't know that he had been connected to the New York Rudaj cartel before the Yanks deported him. He'd fled Albania after a bit of strife with a rival gang and ended up in Scotland.'

'Why did the Albanians want him back?'

'Attempted murder.'

'Fucking hell. See what I mean? They have people everywhere, and wherever I am in the system they'll get to me. They've too much to protect, Max.'

'Well, you need to talk to us, Frankie. What are they trying to protect?'

Frankie scrubbed at his scalp with his fingers, his eyes wide and looking hunted. 'Not what are they trying to protect, it's *who* they're trying to protect.'

'Who then? We can't help you unless you give everything you know,' said Janie.

'Are we on the record?' said Frankie, glancing side to side, worry in his eyes.

'Frankie, there's no lawyer, no tape machine and we haven't cautioned you. This is intelligence gathering, not evidence. Now you called us here, so who are you talking about?'

'I don't know who it is.'

'Then you're no use to us, Frankie.' Max made as if to stand up.

'No wait. Look, I don't know, right. I promise I don't have a bloody clue, but my pa did and my brothers did, and they'd have it safe somewhere, and I might know where, leastways I may be able to find out.'

'Maybe it'd be easier if you just tell us what you do know, Frankie, eh?' said Max, settling back into his chair.

Frankie sighed deeply. 'Look, seriously I don't know who ordered that poor wee girl to be killed but I know why she was killed and I know who killed her, but they're just the hired help. You want the mannie at the top, yeah?'

'Of course. We want the bloody lot, Frankie. We go after corrupt individuals, bent coppers, bent lawyers and the like. We don't go after the hired help.'

'The killing was organised on behalf of someone my pa had in his pocket. He always referred to him as The Ace. Someone who wasn't always big and important, but he became so. My pa had something on him and had done for years but I'm not sure what. The Ace ended up having an affair with the Polish girl, who started causing problems, so whoever he was went to my pa for help, and he used a contractor to take her out.'

'So, your pa sorted it for him?'

'Jack Slattery was the middle man, and he made the arrangements, you remember Jack?'

'How could I forget?' said Max with a straight face remembering his last confrontation with the bent ex-cop.

'Aye well, Jack reached out to a proper nasty bastard who does this kind of thing. I don't know his proper name, but he's known as Droopy because he's a right miserable-looking bastard, like the cartoon dog character – know who I mean?'

'I know the cartoon character, but I don't know another Droopy.'

'You'll be able to find him. There were also another couple of guys, one called Billy Watson, who's no longer with us – died in jail – and another dude called Mitch. Mitch got out of the game totally and went straight, but Droopy is still active and is a fucking evil bastard. I know this because Pa was scunnered with him; after the hit, somehow Droopy started working for The Ace. Pa thought this was cheeky as fuck, but didn't want to rock the boat, as Droopy is such a difficult bastard to keep on top of. Pa ended up allowing it in exchange for a bit of tax from him. Droopy's ex-army, keeps out of normal trouble, and just sorts out problems for rich bastards who can afford to pay. And I mean proper pay. He makes a fucking fortune. Whoever is behind this will be rich, as Droopy charges big dough. Slattery will know who he is, for sure. You could ask him.'

Max and Janie exchanged a glance. 'You've not heard then? I thought the prison grapevine would be buzzing,' said Max.

'No, what?' said Frankie, his eyes widening and the colour draining from his face.

'Jack was murdered in his cell by a lifer called Galbraith, and Mitch was shot in the face at his place in Newcastle.'

'What?' His mouth was agape, his eyes like saucers, and the remaining colour leached from his face.

Max just shrugged.

'When?'

'Very recently.'

Hardie leant forward, head in hands. 'No, no, no, no,' he said over and over again, his voice tight and harsh. 'This won't stop, Max. It won't stop until everyone who knew about the murder of that girl is dead. This is housekeeping. I'll never be safe, and I had fuck all to do with this, you get me?' He suddenly looked up, his cheeks stained with wet tears, and his pale face full of fear. The once fearsome Hardie, now reduced to this. A terrified surviving member of a once powerful criminal family.

'You need to go on record with all of this,' said Max.

'Aye, I know, but I need some bloody assurances.' Hardie's voice was suddenly firmer and more assertive, his face harder and resolute.

'Like what?'

'I need out of this shite-hole now. Like today, okay? Then I'll want my parole brought forward with no more time in a normal jail. I need out of gen pop for the rest of my bird, then once I'm out, full witness protection, forever. If I get that I'll come on board fully. I'll need a decent lawyer, one who won't grass me up and one who'll make sure I don't get screwed by youse lot.'

'We can arrange that. There's a list of vetted solicitors who do terrorism cases, I don't know who they are, but they're dead straight.'

'Aye, that's fine. The other thing is, you and your pal here can do the interviews. I don't trust any bastard. I don't like you much,

Max. You ruined everything for me and my family, but when all's said and done, I get it was just your job, and I know for a fact that you're straight, unlike half of your colleagues.'

Max smirked. 'I'm flattered.'

'Fucking don't be. You're still the polis, we're no' pals,' Frankie said, scowling.

'But you still haven't given us the man at the top. If I'm to get the Crown Office to sign off on deals like that you'll need to give us chapter and verse.'

'I don't know who, but Davie will have known. Pa would have handed over dynamite like that before he died, either to Tam or Davie, so it'll be somewhere. Also, if you find Droopy, you'll find this dirty bastard who ordered that poor wee girl killed.'

'What makes you think Davie would have known, Frankie? You only know all this second hand, so why do you think Davie was more closely involved than he said he was? He claims he had an alibi.' Max sat back in his chair.

Frankie guffawed harshly. 'Aye, he would say that, wouldn't he?'

'Well, I never spoke to him, but that's the report I had from those that did.'

'Aye right. How do you think Davie could point the cops to the exact point on the loch where that lassie was put?'

'He said he saw film,' said Janie, looking sideways at Max.

'Aye, did you know what Davie's hobby was?'

'Can't say I do.'

'He loved boats, jet skis and RIBs. He knew where that wee lass was put because he was there when she was dropped in the loch from his RIB. Pa farmed out the hit, but Davie was in charge of losing the body. I knew it was happening, but Tam Junior told me to keep out of it and leave it to Davie. It was him, Droopy and Billy who threw her in there.'

There was a long pause in the room, as all three looked at the others in turn. Eventually Max broke the silence. 'Do you know anything about the big man at all? Even the smallest detail would be helpful.'

Hardie's eyes turned to Max, and they were open wide, and displaying no trace of duplicity, no tics, nothing. 'Not a thing. I may have been the best fighter in the family, but my brothers always excluded me from the business side of it. The only thing I know for sure was that they referred to him as The Ace.'

'The Ace? What, because he was amazing, or something?'

'Nah, my pa was a gambler. Loved poker, and was really good at it. He meant Ace, as in "ace in the hole". A card in his back pocket that could get him out of any trouble, no matter how serious.'

39

'SO, WHAT DID you think of Frankie's performance?' said Janie as they approached their Volvo in the car park at Shotts.

'He's scared, that's for sure. The difference in him now and when we last encountered him is stark. I'm minded to believe him. Want me to drive?' Max nodded at the car.

'Is the Pope a Scientologist?' said Janie, blipping at the big car with the key in her hand.

'I can't imagine he is.'

'Then you have your answer. You're a shite driver,' said Janie, opening the driver's door and sliding in behind the wheel of the immaculately clean car.

'You're a shite driver, *sergeant*,' corrected Max as he climbed into the passenger seat.

'Fine, you're an absolutely garbage, shite, crap, bollocks, incompetent, indecisive, slow and awful driver who makes my teeth itch when I'm forced to be a passenger in any car you're driving, *sergeant*,' Janie retorted, returning his smile.

'That's better, constable. A little respect for the rank isn't hard, eh?'

'Indeed. I tend to agree with you. Frankie is as shite-scared as a dog in a thunderstorm, how're we going to play it?' she said, exaggerating her normally cultured Edinburgh brogue.

'I need to speak to Ross. I'm a little out of the witness protection loop, but we need an urgent, secure and highly covert debrief premises. It's true what he says. They can only protect him for so long. In the Met there were suitable facilities, which I used once for a supergrass. I'm assuming there's the same up here.'

'NCA run witness protection now, on a national basis, UK PPS, as in Protected Persons Service. I had some input from them on the last course I did for my accelerated promotion programme, which I'm bloody way, way behind on, mostly thanks to you and Ross not giving me the bloody time to study for the sergeant's exam,' said Janie, pulling her seatbelt on.

'Nonsense, you manage to sleep, don't you? You've plenty of time, but you waste it listening to odd music and playing your trumpet.'

'Saxophone.'

'Anyway, we digress, constable, can we get back on topic?'

'Fine. Yes. NCA manage the process.'

'Of course, I remember now. NCA, though? With our recent experiences with NCA officers, we need to be careful. This case is so bloody sensitive, maybe I best call Ross and get him to push it up the food chain.' Max pulled out his phone and dialled, the ring tone audible out of the vehicle speakers that it was connected to.

'What did the dirty, amoral, evil shite-bag say?' was Ross's opening gambit, without preamble.

Max summarised what Hardie had said.

'Aye, sounds plausible, I'm sorry to say. I've already alerted the Chief to the possibility of this, and he's flagged it up to the NCA. Who the hell is this Droopy character?'

'No idea, but he must be traceable if Slattery was in contact with him at the time of Beata being murdered. He was obviously an associate of Mitch, Billy and Davie as well. Can you get Norma working on this? We need to get to him urgently. If we can identify him, we're halfway there to tracing "Ace".'

'Fucking hell, "Ace"? What is this, *Top Gun*?'

'Ace in the hole, is how Hardie Senior referred to his big asset.'

'I get the analogy. Shit, this could be big. We'll need to get into the Crown Office if he's looking for any immunity deal, and any reduction in sentence. I'll flag that up, but the DCC seems to be wanting them to herself. I'll see what the boss says. What else do you think you'll need?'

'A secure debrief facility with accommodation attached and armed protection. We don't want to be pissing about with moving him back and forth to a jail with armed convoys, it leaves far too big a footprint. A full research package on Droopy and his links. Any phones, cars, addresses, the whole lot. If we get Droopy, we can chuck in an initiating incident, and watch what he does.'

'I'll get Norma on it now. Our favourite tactic, eh? Chucking a big bastard stone into a pond and watching the ripples, eh?'

'Indeed. We can do this, Ross, but we can't go noisy on it. If it gets widely known, it'll leak. We need to keep a sterile corridor between us and the MIT team reactive investigation.'

'I'll talk to the boss, but he won't want Miles being in the dark, and I suspect that he won't want Heather Davies excluded. She's SIO, after all.'

'Do we trust Miles? After all it was the slimy solicitor going straight to him that was the problem, don't you think?'

Ross sighed, his voice through the car's speakers crackling. 'I can't see Miles being bent. He's too much history, and surely the last time we had Hardies on the rack, he'd have fucked up?'

Max said nothing.

'Fuck's sake. I'll talk to the boss. The PPS may want to handle the debrief, they don't like sharing their sweeties.'

'They can't. For some reason, Frankie trusts me and won't deal with anyone else. We'll also need a vetted defence lawyer for him.'

'On it. What's the timeframe?' said Ross, and Max could hear tapping on a keyboard.

'Yesterday. The big Albanian old geezer got very close to slicing Frankie open. If he could get to him, someone else could. We need to move fast. This is big enough already. We have the murderous

Droopy topping people left, right and centre, and seemingly with the ability to get to anyone in jail.'

'Okay. I'm on it.'

'Any other news?' said Max.

'Aye, literally this second, an email has come through from Heather Davies. They've a DNA hit from the fag butt by the loch. A team's being scrambled now. He's a nasty bastard, by all accounts. Name is Kyle Ellis, aged thirty-five. Born and raised in Manchester, a few juvenile convictions before joining the Army, where he served in the Grenadier Guards. He then got in the shit for topping an Afghan in questionable circumstances, went AWOL and then ended up in the French Foreign Legion, where he was a sniper and paratrooper. Was discharged from them with honour after serving his five-year contract and then went to ground, was thought to be somewhere in Europe, but clearly not right now, it seems.'

Bruce Ferguson popped into Max's mind, and he felt a strange sense of relief. It was still possible that he had employed the sniper, but it didn't feel likely. His first instinct that Bruce may be responsible had been strong, but looking at the mistakes that the sniper had made, it had been less and less likely. No way would ex–SBS sergeant major leave such a big trail of breadcrumbs, and he couldn't see that Bruce would employ anyone so incompetent. It didn't make sense. He pushed the thought away. 'Where's he from originally?'

'Yorkshire, but not for a long time. MIT team are handling it, they'll call us if they need us, but our priority is Frankie. Get back here now, we need to plan this properly, okay?'

'On our way.' Max hung up.

'This is all gonna happen quickly, isn't it?' said Janie, starting the car.

'Looks that way,' said Max.

'An on-the-run Légion étrangère, soldier and a maniac fixer killing people all over the place to protect a mysterious Mr Big.

It'd be nice to have a small, simple and easy-to-manage job now and again, wouldn't it?' Janie engaged the gears, and moved off.

Max thought about Katie, sitting at home newly pregnant, as he was about to rush off on another hyper-urgent job. He closed his eyes and sighed, his beautiful wife's face in his mind.

'Aye, it would be nice. Let's go.'

40

DROOPY SAT BACK in his Mondeo at the other end of the Shotts prison car park and watched as the Volvo containing DS Craigie and DC Calder moved away. One of his police contacts had told him about them both. Part of some covert team that looked into police corruption, but no one seemed to know much else. They smelled like trouble to him, and he'd learned to trust his instincts over the years. He wondered if they were the cops that brought the Hardies down. It would make sense, bearing in mind what had happened. He'd had no contact with any Hardie since the Polish girl, and he hadn't closely followed the demise of Tam Hardie and his boys.

He smiled at the fact that his instinct was, once again, correct. After that idiot Almir Duka failed to finish Frankie, he knew that the cops would be called in, although he didn't necessarily expect these two. His source in the police didn't seem to know much about what was going down, so it seemed that Craigie and Calder were working on the downlow. That was bad news, as it almost certainly meant that Frankie was either talking, or was thinking about talking. This could make things far more difficult if they moved him to a secure facility to debrief him, but he doubted that Frankie knew that much, really. Davie had certainly known more as his boat had been used, but the kompromat held by old man Hardie would hopefully be out of reach now. He felt ninety per cent certain that they were in the clear.

Ninety per cent wouldn't be good enough, that's for sure. He needed to speak to The Ace.

He pulled out his phone, slotted in a new SIM card, and composed a message on WhatsApp. **Need to speak, urgent**.

The reply was instantaneous. **What?**

Final objective failed.

Within a minute, Droopy's phone began to buzz with an incoming WhatsApp call from a totally new number.

'Yes?'

'What happened?' came the voice. Deep and smooth, almost like melted chocolate.

'Man on the inside failed. He's locked down now, so no chance of a repeat and I have no more assets in Shotts. What can he know, anyway?'

'I don't know. Old man Hardie had proof of my involvement, which he would have handed on to Tam Junior, who may have passed it on to Davie. I can't be sure of what Frankie knows. It's too much of a risk, you need to sort it permanently.'

'It'll be expensive. If they move him out of jail to a covert facility, we may struggle to get to him.'

'It costs what it costs. Get it sorted, how you do it is your business. This is the last link back to what happened six years ago, we need to excise this tumour, right now.'

'As I said. Expensive. If he's in a secure facility I won't be able to do it on my own, even if I can find out where he's being held. I'll need a team.'

'Listen, I don't give a fuck. I'll keep my ear to the ground. I'll be getting some degree of a briefing on it at some point, and I may be able to assist, but you need to be ready to act. Know this, though. If I have to dig around and find out where he's being held, it will affect your fee, so get on it, and find out where he is.'

'I will,' said Droopy, smiling. The man's pugnacious attitude. He was easy to play, this idiot.

'One more thing,' said The Ace, his voice tight.

'What?'

'I just heard through the grapevine. The sniper has been identified. The idiot left a cigarette butt, and it's been DNA matched. Some Foreign Legion man, or something. Every resource is being thrown at getting hold of him.'

'They'll not find him,' said Droopy, his voice confident, but feeling a small flip in his stomach.

'You said that about the girl.'

'If Davie hadnae cliped, they wouldnae have. They won't find him. Not that it matters, he knows nothing. Hired help,' he said, his mind whirring as he considered all the ramifications.

'Right. I have to go. Get this sorted.' The three beeps in his ear indicated that the call was over.

Droopy stared out of the window at the drab prison, thinking of Frankie Hardie tucked away out of reach just a few hundred metres away. His thoughts switched to the sniper, Ellis, whom he'd used a few times on other jobs he'd managed overseas. He'd always been efficient in the past, but he'd really made a pig's ear of this one. He looked at his phone and composed a message. **Have you left UK, yet?**

The reply came back almost immediately. **Tomorrow.**

Droopy's fingers flashed across the screen. **Cops found your DNA at loch, they're looking for you. Don't travel on real passport.**

There was a long pause before the reply flashed up. **No problem. On different passport, and no one will recognise me.**

Where are you flying from?

Not flying. Ferry from Newcastle. Keep tabs, yeah?

New name? I can monitor if you're being searched for under alias?

The reply came back immediately. **French ppt Davide Arbon. Benefit of speaking French. They'll never find me.**

Where are you staying?

Shite hotel by the ferry terminal. I'll lay low.

Good. Be lucky. Droopy minimised the message screen, pulled out the SIM and slotted in a new one.

As always, he was one step ahead of the idiots. He had enough contacts to stay one step ahead of the law, and make sure he got the job done for The Ace, even if they did move Hardie to a secure location. The benefits of planning, contacts and experience. He'd been doing this kind of work a long time, and he knew how to roll with the punches.

He'd get the job done, of that he was certain.

41

'WHAT GIVES?' SAID Max as he and Janie walked into the office at Tulliallan. Ross looked up from his screen, face red, tongue protruding with his two index fingers poised above his keyboard. Norma gave a little wave from behind her large screens.

'I'm doing all the fucking work, as usual, that's what. You tardy buggers swanning in here like prima donnas. You know how bloody weary it is trying to get a violent, major gangster out of jail and into secure and covert facilities. I'm bloody carrying this team.' He scowled as he turned back to his screen, his fingers beating a steady rhythm on the keys.

'Tea?' said Janie, with a smile.

'Aye, first sensible thing you've said for a week or two,' said Ross, without looking up.

'Anything on the sniper?' Max asked.

'No. Not a thing. No bugger has anything on him, so we're leaving it to the MIT team. We're better served concentrating on Frankie.'

'How about the covert debrief venue for Frankie?' said Janie.

'In hand. PPU have reluctantly allowed us to deal with our own bloody witness, and have a covert premises for us in an old single officer station in a wee village in the far north. It still has an operational cell, so we can keep the bugger secure. I'm just negotiating now about transport and armed support. We also need a sign-off from the prison to agree to it all with a decent cover story about a hospital appointment for some tests or shite like that, so we can justify an overnighter, I'm waiting to hear now. Norma also has some news which, no doubt, she is about to smugly tell you about.'

'It's true. I've been remarkably brilliant on several fronts,' said Norma, her ever-present smile widening.

'Go on then, hit us with it,' said Janie as she busied herself with the cups and a kettle.

'Remember the fifteen grand payment to Galbraith's mother from a brand-new internet bank account in the name of Hector MacFarlane?'

'I didn't know that was the name, but yes, what about it?' said Max.

'My pal at the NCA quickly managed to get a monitoring order on the account by adding it onto another bulk application, on the basis that they're supporting the debrief of Frankie. It was opened very recently, and immediately received a deposit of fifty thousand from an overseas registered account. Straight after that it transferred a thousand pounds to an account in the name of Mairi Malone.'

'Who's she?' asked Ross.

'I'll get to that, be patient. The next payment we know about, 15k to Mrs Galbraith, right after her son kills Slattery. Then, just an hour after Hardie and his lawyer have their heads removed, the account transferred another 30k to a numbered overseas account.'

'Shit, 30k feels about the right amount for a contract kill like that, possibly even a little cheap. Feels really slack to use the same account,' said Max.

'Maybe not if the account is ditched after the job in the same way that they would a phone. As Norma says, no one from the NCA would even bother with it. Fraud's almost been given up on, recently,' said Janie, shaking her head.

'What about the grand to Mrs Malone?' said Max.

'Aye, a strange one that. I've looked into her background, and she's clean as a whistle. Glasgow woman, lives in a scheme on the west of Glasgow. Regular payments into the account from Alba-Care, a private company that provide home care, mostly for the elderly, from what I can see,' said Norma.

'So, if she's stealing IDs of elderly folk, she must have a connection to Droopy, who we know is at the centre of this, according to Frankie at least. It's not coercion if she's doing it for money. A grand for an ID is decent enough cash for just scanning or photographing some documents off old people. Are there any other deposits in similar circumstances?' Max enquired.

Norma looked at the screen, her lips pursed in concentration as she scrolled. 'She's very much living beyond her means, that's for sure. Her only obvious source of income is her wages from Alba-Care, and some benefits. I can see at least eight payments of a thousand pounds over the last couple of years, from similar internet-based bank accounts. This will take a fair bit of unpicking.'

'Well, that's both good and bad. We can't approach her, because if they're connected, then she'll just go straight to him, and we lose our advantage, but it's a lead. Do we have a phone number for her?' said Max.

'Aye, just the one, shall I send off for the data on it?'

Ross looked up from his screen. 'Yeah, do it. Mark it as urgent, and I'll get it authorised as grade 1 by the boss. I'm betting that she's photographed it in the old boy's house, and then she'll have sent it to whoever set up that account. If we can isolate the day that she was at her client Hector MacFarlane's place, we may be able to work out where she sent it. Nothing else makes sense. Whoever she sent those bank details to is our man.'

'Aye, want to know something else interesting?'

'Go on.'

'Mr MacFarlane is almost ninety. A widower and local cops have returned him home once or twice when he used to go wandering. Dementia, apparently. What do you make of that?' said Norma, sipping her tea.

Ross sat back in his chair, and sighed. 'So she's swiped his details and someone's opened an account in the poor old boy's name. The grand into her account is payment for services rendered. It's so simple a moron could set up one of these accounts, it apparently just takes a few minutes.'

'Could you set one up, Ross?' said Janie, a smile playing on her lips.

'Could I fuck, but Mrs Fraser set up one of these accounts recently. I have no bastard idea how it works, but it just took her a minute, and she took the piss out of me because she said I looked confused.'

Max, Janie and Norma all laughed.

'You lot can all piss off. I'm the DI, no bloody respect,' Ross muttered, turning back to his screen, scowling.

Norma was still chuckling as she continued. 'As I understand it, you just have to scan in proof of ID and residence and you're done. It's a smart way of avoiding money laundering regulations, especially if you just use it for a few transactions. By the time that the suspicious activity report lands with the NCA the account will be ditched and left fallow, probably with a nominal sum in it to keep the bank from making a fuss. It's a good idea, but how does it help us?'

'I don't think we should approach any of them. It would bound to get back to whoever is running this. Do we all think that it's this mysterious "Droopy" character?' said Max.

'Almost certainly,' said Janie.

'We need the intel quicker than the phone unit can supply, even at the quickest. We'll need a subscriber check on it first, followed by data and cell sites. That's too long. Also, if we just get the data, all we get is a list of numbers called, and texted together with the cell sites, which won't be accurate enough for our purposes. How will we know what house she was in, especially if she lives and works in the same locality, which most carers do? They don't get paid enough to commute. Cell sites aren't accurate enough. Where's Barney?'

'At his temporary flat,' said Ross, his face flushing.

'What?' said Max.

'Aye. Bloody Chief took pity after the DCC bollocked him and he was worried the old codger would get cold. He's letting him use one of the old police flats that they've held onto for emergency accommodation. He's only up the road in Dunfermline. He's as delighted as you'd imagine a tight-arsed Yorkshireman would be to be getting free board and lodging. He's already got a full load of washing on and he called me ten minutes ago to tell me he was planning to use the tumble drier. You'd think he'd won the bloody lottery.'

'I'll call him. I've an idea.'

'When for?'

'Probably early tomorrow morning, we'll need it authorised.'

'Probably for the best, you know you won't get the tight-arse away from free telly, and a cooker he doesn't have to pay for.'

'He'll be fine. We need his skills, and we need them tomorrow, he can enjoy being warm for once.'

42

KATIE WAS ON the phone to her mother when Max arrived home a few hours later, to Nutmeg's total delight. She'd obviously imparted the news of her pregnancy, and there was clearly much excitement at the other end of the phone. She smiled wanly, her face pale as Max handed her a cup of herbal tea, which she took and set on the side, but shook her head when he asked if she wanted any food.

Max quickly made some cheese on toast, to go with his tea. He was hungry but had no interest in cooking something significant, and clearly his wife wasn't hungry, her pale blotchy face giving some indication of the nausea she was feeling.

'Hey, how are you?' said Max, chewing his cheese on toast, as Katie placed her phone on the side.

'Tired, and constantly feeling nauseous,' she said, shaking her head but stroking Nutmeg's ears. Nutmeg clearly wasn't interested, giving all her rapt attention to Max as he ate.

'Sorry, is there anything I can do?' he said, unsure what else he could say.

'Why are you apologising?' She looked up from Nutmeg, and her beautiful eyes bored into him with an unusual intensity.

'Because . . .' He paused, unable to find the words.

'Maybe because you have a job that means you're rarely at home? Because I'm stuck here, feeling sick and tired, and lonely and wrung out that my husband always puts his work first?' Katie's eyes softened, and she reached out and touched Max's cheek.

'Aye, all of that. I'm really sorry. I want to be here, but . . .' Max just couldn't find the words, and he just sat there, mid-sentence, his mouth gaping. The silence in the room was thick and awkward. He looked at his wife, taking in her choppy, dirty-blonde hair and kind smile, and he was gripped with a sudden, almost overwhelming love for her.

'Max. I understand. I realise how much your job means, and I know I can't ask you not to go to work. As much as anything, we'll need the money once I'm on maternity leave. I have a doctor's appointment in three days, please tell me you'll be able to come?' Her eyes were wide and almost pleading.

'Aye, I'll come.' Max curled his fingers around Katie's, lifted her hand and kissed it, gently.

'Promise?'

'I promise. I'll do everything I can to be there, Katie.' Max smiled, but his insides were churning at the prospect of letting her down.

'When are you working tomorrow?'

'Earlyish,' said Max.

'How early?'

'Pretty early. It's a big job,' he said, shrugging.

'They're all big jobs, Max. That's always the problem. I take it a long day in store?' She pulled her hand away from Max's, and rubbed at the bridge of her nose.

'Probably, we're getting Frankie out of jail to a debrief site.'

'But you'll be at the doctor's appointment, yes?'

'I promise.' Max stroked her hair.

'Good. Give us a bite on your cheese on toast, then,' she said, her smile wide and genuine, and the glint returning to her tired eyes.

Max offered the plate and she took one of the slices and bit into it, chewing with relish. Within about thirty seconds, the colour drained from her face, and she stopped chewing. She handed the plate back.

'I hate you for making me pregnant, you bastard,' she said, leaning against his shoulder, a tear appearing in her eye.

'Sorry.'

'You should be. You made me hate cheese.'

43

KYLE ELLIS, OR more accurately, as the passport in his pocket declared, Davide Arbon was feeling mildly buzzed, most likely because of the decent bottle of red wine he'd consumed in the Newcastle restaurant a short while ago. He threw the taxi driver a twenty-pound note and told him to keep the change, and climbed out close to the hotel in the flat and open area close to the ferry port by the Royal Quays outlet centre. He zipped up his coat and flicked up his collar against the cold evening air. He wasn't staying at the hotel, as experience had taught him that it was a good idea to always get dropped off away from your actual destination. There was hardly any traffic or pedestrians about, being as it was almost midnight as he set off, burping and grimacing at the stale garlic aftertaste in his mouth. He couldn't wait to be back in a country with decent cuisine . . . as always, his visits to the UK reminded him of how godawful the food was.

He set off yawning extravagantly, and scratched at his chin, still raw after shaving his beard a few hours earlier, as he walked past the hotel towards his true destination, the bigger hotel a few hundred metres away. Davide Arbon's smooth face, heavy rimmed spectacles, neatly trimmed hair and smart suit with crisp white shirt were a stark contrast to the bewhiskered, long haired, scruffy Hans Graumann, who had entered the UK at Glasgow Airport a week ago. The documents for Hans Graumann had been parcelled up and sent by courier to a PO Box in London for safekeeping until he next needed them.

He wobbled along the pavement heading towards the chain hotel close to the ferry port, yawning again, suddenly realising how tired he was. His ferry to Amsterdam left early the next morning, he needed some sleep. He wasn't worried about what Droopy had told him just a few hours ago about the DNA the cops had found. They would never find him, with the level of incompetence in the UK police force. He was a ghost. He could move across the globe with impunity, with multiple identities in different nationalities that he currently held, all backed up by impeccable documentation.

He was also at an advantage when travelling across Europe, being as proficient in languages as he was after his years in the Legion surrounded by the multiple nationalities of his comrades. His French was faultless, his German was accented but fluent, his Dutch not perfect but adequate, and his Spanish and Italian more than conversational. That was one of the big bonuses of the Légion étrangère. You found yourself plunged into this huge melting pot of nationalities and were forced to learn French from day one, it being the default language spoken by all. From there, if you wanted to survive and then flourish, learning the other widely spoken languages was essential. Comrades were always flattered when he as an Englishman, always known as Johnny, wanted to learn their language.

He pulled out his phone and navigated to the banking app as he made his way along the pavement, only pausing to light a cigarette. He was delighted to see the thirty thousand pounds had been deposited as Droopy had assured him it would be. He hadn't doubted the fixer, as he'd always paid on time after previous jobs he'd done for the Scot. With just a few flicks and swipes on the phone, he moved the money again into his account in the Cayman Islands, way out of the reach of law enforcement. Once the transfer had been confirmed, he deleted the banking app from his phone, and returned it to his pocket with a chuckle of satisfaction. A good night's kip, then this time tomorrow, he'd be in the air from Schiphol Airport en route to Corsica, where Davide Arbon planned to relax for a few months before looking for some more work. He loved Corsica, being full of current and ex Legionnaires, it was a great place to pick up contracts for work. Plus the weather was wonderful and the food even better.

His sinews suddenly stiffened as a large BMW cop car swung into the road ahead of him, a small pump of adrenaline in his blood system chasing away the buzz of the alcohol. He didn't look up, and just continued along the cracked pavement towards the purple sign of his hotel, desperate to be inside and off the streets and between the crisp sheets. He was confident that any photo that the cops had of him wouldn't be worth worrying about being at least four years old if they'd got hold of his Legion discharge papers, but it paid to be careful.

The note of the engine told him that the car had stopped, but he didn't look behind him, instead he knelt down and pretended to tie a shoelace. His hand went to his pocket where he felt the comforting presence of the small lock knife, which he'd purchased in a fishing shop just a few hours ago. He heard a heavy door slamming. He risked a glance behind him, and saw that the cop was out of the car and looking straight at him, the light reflecting off his shaven head. He noted that the cop had a side arm mounted in a thigh holster, and the heavy ballistic body armour of an ARV crew.

'Shit,' he muttered, and stood up, before picking up his pace again towards the hotel, walking along the building line of the Royal Quay. Instead of continuing towards the purple sign, he took a sharp left along the side of the smaller hotel, and leapt over the low fence into the small kids' play area, keeping his back to the rough brick wall of the hotel. He risked a peek around the corner, in the direction of the cop car. The armed cop was still standing, legs planted firmly on the tarmac, his hand on his side arm, head swivelling left to right. '*Merde*,' muttered Ellis, defaulting to his customary French. Had they made him? He couldn't see how, but he was a lone man walking in a deserted, closed retail area so maybe it was inevitable that he'd attract some attention. There was a sharp, metallic squeak behind him, which made him start, his heart began to pound in his chest, and his skin was prickling with fear, his synapses firing on all cylinders. He turned, but saw nothing, apart from dark shadows amongst the dark shapes of the play equipment as an empty swing moved in the soft breeze. He turned away, and decided to risk another peek around the wall at the cop car.

The cop was leaning against the car, a lit cigarette between his lips glowing brightly in the gloom, his attention on the phone held in his hands, which lit his stubble-laden face. Ellis exhaled, the relief flooding through him like a gentle, warm wave.

He leant against the wall and wiped at his brow, which was damp and clammy despite the chill of the night, a smile forming on his lips, as he realised that he was home and dry. A decent night's sleep on a comfortable bed, and then he was gone. Out of this shit-hole country.

Then, out of nowhere, a shadow loomed, huge and dark as the night that surrounded it. There was a metallic flash as the swinging axe caught the streetlights, and Ellis barely felt anything as the blade was buried deep into his forehead, and he fell to the ground like a dumped sandbag, still and inert.

44

MAIRI MALONE WAS late as usual, as she rushed out of her small flat in the West End of Glasgow, her hair askew, a piece of toast clutched in her hand. She pulled the door shut and set off towards the staircase. A minute later, she was letting herself back in to retrieve her phone which she'd left in the bathroom. She'd already had a call from one of her moaning bloody clients, who had contacted Alba to tell them that she was late.

She tried to stem the rising panic that was bubbling in her chest at the words that that sour-faced bitch Anya had said to her down the phone. 'You already on warning, Mairi. Any more and we have let you go,' she had said in her Polish-accented English. She was a bloody tyrant, but Mairi had to agree that she did have a point. Mairi was awful at getting out of her bed in the morning, particularly if she'd been on the cider the night before, which she had been, evidenced by her pounding head and the unpleasant metallic taste in her mouth. She was very late for Mrs Henderson, that was for sure. She was supposed to be there to get her out of her bed by eight, and it was almost ten past already. Thankfully she was only a five-minute drive away.

Her car, a little blue Renault, was a few moments' walk away from the block of flats, and within a minute, she was in the vehicle, seatbelt on, and was moving away, off the side road and turning left onto the main street, still chewing her toast. The phone on the seat next to her pinged again, and she could see a message from Anya. She picked it up and looked at the message. **How long?**

Five minutes, she typed out with one hand whilst trying to eat toast, steer and change gear all at the same time, which just resulted in her stalling the car as she tried to negotiate her way into the stream of heavy traffic.

'Shite,' she said as she tucked her phone under her leg. She needed to get herself together, that was for sure, or she was going to be out of work, and then what would she do? No cider tonight, not even one, she promised herself, already realising that it was probably untrue.

The traffic was heavy as she turned onto the Great Western Road and headed towards Mrs Henderson's tenement in a side street close to the Botanic Gardens. She felt her panic begin to subside along with her headache, as she reached for the old bottle of water that was in the centre console. She took a deep swig of the thankfully cold water, and then grabbed a stick of chewing gum that sat in the pot next to the bottle. The minty nugget instantly freshened her mouth, and she almost began to feel human again. She sighed. She'd be fine, it was only a couple of minutes to Mrs Henderson, and she was actually quite sweet, if sharp at times. Her phone vibrated under her leg on the seat.

'Ah, bugger it,' she said, looking at the screen, seeing 'no caller ID', which almost certainly meant it was Anya again.

'Hello?' she said, trying to hold the phone in place between her shoulder and ear.

There was nothing. No voice, just three beeps indicating someone had hung up.

A sudden squeal emitted from behind her, and she jumped in her seat as she looked in the rear-view mirror and saw the strobing blue lights of a cop car, its headlights flashing, the shape of a stern-faced cop at the wheel. Fear gripped her like a vice. Had they seen her on the phone? 'Jesus suffering fuck,' she hissed under her breath as she indicated and pulled to the side of the road. She just sat there, her eyes briefly closing thinking of the three penalty points she already had on her licence and the fact that her MOT had run out three weeks ago. Would they know this? She sighed again, even more deeply. Of course they'd bloody know.

She started again, as there was a rap on the car window, and a small and wiry young cop wearing a white-topped police cap made a winding gesture with his hand, indicating that she should lower her window. She pressed the button, and the window descended agonisingly slowly.

'Morning, miss, would you be so kind as to switch off the engine and join me on the pavement?' he said, a small smile on his smooth face. A white hat, Mairi thought. That meant they were traffic cops. They were known for being really harsh with motorists, particularly ones on their phones. Maybe they had not seen that and had seen on the computer that she had no MOT. She'd seen on the myriad of cop shows that they had computers in their cars, maybe that was it.

'Aye, of course, what's wrong?' she said.

'Driving's a little erratic, madam. If you'd join us that'd be great,' he said, smiling in what to her seemed a genuine manner. Maybe it wasn't the phone then. She slid the phone from under her leg and slipped it into the driver's side pocket on the door. If they didn't see it, maybe it wouldn't occur to them.

She opened the door, and within a second had joined the officer on the pavement, where stood a much bigger and much older cop, who wasn't smiling at all. In fact, he looked properly scunnered.

'Yes, officer?' she said, forcing a smile.

'Morning, madam, we noticed that your driving looks a little raggy this morning, and we just wanted to have a word. Where are you off to?' said the young cop.

'Work, I'm a home carer. I've a client needing help just around the corner,' she said, tapping at the ID card on her lanyard.

'Your car?' said the older cop.

'Yes.'

'What's your name?'

'Mairi Malone.'

'Address?'

She told him.

'Driving licence?' he said.

'Not with me, sorry.'

'Tell us about the MOT?' he said, jabbing his thumb at the old Renault.

'I know, I'm sorry. I only realised this morning, I've been so busy with work,' she said, forcing another smile.

'Three weeks is too long, madam. Now about your driving, I noticed you stalled it coming out of the road . . . ?' He left the sentence hanging, but the meaning was clear.

'I know, rushing and late. Sorry.'

'Had a drink?'

'What, in the morning? No,' she said, eyes widening, but her stomach tightening. She had sunk a fair amount of cider last night, but surely she was clear now. She looked at her watch, her last drink was well after midnight. The fear bubbled up even stronger, please no, she thought.

'How about last night?' said the younger cop.

'I had a couple of drinks, but no' many.'

The cops looked at each other, and something passed between them. The older one nodded.

'We're going to require a breath test, madam. Alcohol can remain in your system for some time, and as your driving is below par, we need to check. Come and sit in the back of the car and we'll get a check done.'

'No machine in the car, Shug,' said the older one.

'I'll radio for it,' said Shug, reaching for the handset that was affixed to his body armour.

The rear door of the cop car opened and another officer stepped out, wearing a hi-vis jacket and the same white cap as the other two. He was small and wiry and looked seasoned and tough, although his eyes twinkled with amusement.

'I'll get out of the way if you're doing a breath test, but I'll have a look at the car. I don't like the state of your tyres,' he said, walking up towards the Renault.

'PC Jones is a qualified vehicle examiner, and as your MOT has expired, I think we could make sure it's road-worthy, okay?' said the older cop.

'Aye, no problem,' she said, her voice wobbly.

'Why not take a seat in the back of our car whilst PC Jones does his exam, and we wait for the machine, it'll no' be too long,' the younger cop said, his eyes kind and a reassuring smile on his face.

She sat silently in the back of the big cop car, the door open as the third cop was busying himself inside and outside her little Renault, whistling tunelessly.

It took about ten minutes for another car to arrive and a breath test machine was handed to the older cop, who in turn handed it to his colleague who explained the procedure to her. Within a few moments she had blown into the tube as directed, a sick feeling clutching at her stomach. If this was positive, she was done for. Her job was done, and she'd not be able to pay rent. She felt the blood drain from her face as she stared at the inscrutable cop's face for a sign.

'Right, Miss Malone. You're very lucky. I'm detecting alcohol in your breath, but you're below the limit.'

Mairi felt hot tears well in her eyes. 'Oh thank God,' she said.

'A good lesson, eh. Booze can linger about, so be careful,' he said, snapping the tube from the machine and handing it to her, his kind eyes twinkling.

'Aye, I'll be careful. How about the MOT?' she said, relief flooding through her as she stepped out of the car.

'PC Jones?' said the younger cop.

'Tyres are on the edge, handbrake has too much travel, and your number plate light is dicky, but nothing to get our knickers in a twist about,' said PC Jones as he passed by and sat in the back of the car.

'Thank you. I'll get them all sorted, I promise,' she said, feeling lighter as she skipped over to the car, the feeling of relief almost overwhelming. That was too close, she thought as she caught sight of her phone in the door pocket, before she started the engine and drove off, ready to incur the wrath of Mrs Henderson.

45

'PLEASE TELL ME it worked, Barney. That was a bastard to organise in that timeframe. The surveillance commissioner thought we were going fishing, and I promised the miserable bastard that we weren't, despite the fact that Max may as well have been wearing sodding waders and a hat with flies in it when he presented the case for property interference and intrusive surveillance to the Chief. You look a right tit in a police uniform, by the way, go and get changed before I nick you for impersonating an officer.' Ross's cheeks bulged as he chewed upon a large doughnut, his lips plastered in sugar. He surveyed Barney, who was dressed in blue serge trousers, a black wicking T-shirt and a high-visibility jacket that was unzipped. A cap was perched on the back of his head at a jaunty angle.

'I'm guessing by your overly chuffed demeanour that Max has already told you. Aye, it worked a treat, she were that nervous in the car getting breathed that she didn't even notice me messin' with her phone, which she didn't think we'd seen her on and had stashed in't door. I reckon she's a right pisshead, that one. Stinkin' of booze at this time of the morning. Full download, easy as, and I resent that remark. I think I cut quite the dash in a uniform,' he said, clutching an SD card between his finger and thumb.

'Anything on it?' said Ross.

'Nay idea. That's not my job, I get the data, you buggers can analyse it. Any chance of a tea?' said Barney, sitting down in the lone, scraggy armchair in the corner of the scruffy office that had become his default place to sit.

'Aye, if you make it. Two sugars,' said Ross.

'You've the equivalent of two sugars around your bloody lips. You'll give yourself diabetes, you soft bugger, and woe betide Mrs F finds out.'

'Is that a threat? I'll get you evicted from your free flat if you grass, you old sod. Mrs Fraser is being uncharacteristically pleasant to me at the moment, because I got home fairly early last night. Now make the bloody tea. I'm having to justify a frankly weak intrusive surveillance operation to a sceptical gatekeeper, and I'd like some peace from your blether.' Ross wiped his lips on a grubby handkerchief that he had pulled from his pocket.

Barney laughed as he pulled himself to his feet and flicked the kettle on. 'Will you look at the state of the bloody mugs? Full of bloody penicillin.'

'Aye well, you can wash them whilst you get changed out of that bloody uniform, you're making me nervous. You look like an elderly stripper about to hit a hen do.'

Norma chuckled in the corner, behind her monitors. 'Chuck us the SD, Barney, and I'd love a tea whilst I get on with it. Where's Max?'

'On his way, just making phone calls. Sounded like he was having a difficult one with Mrs Craigie, to me. Is everything okay with him?' Barney tossed over the SD card, which Norma failed to catch, and it skittered across her desk and landed on the floor. 'Poor shot,' said Norma as she stooped to pick it up, pulled it out of its small plastic case and slotted it into her computer.

'What's up with Max?' said Janie, who had appeared almost out of nowhere into the office.

'Dunno. Fractious phone call with his better half as far as I could hear,' said Barney as he loaded up the putrid-looking mugs onto the battered metal tray and left the office.

Ross looked at Janie and shrugged. 'What's happening with Frankie?'

'All in hand. Phil at the prison has been brilliant sorting it all out and the NCA PPU team have been helpful. The PPU manager is handling it, nice bloke called Mal Crookston, and it's locked down to only those who need to know the location and identity of Frankie. Cover story is set as a minor operation for a hernia, and beyond Phil and the prison doc, no one else at the prison knows.'

'That's great. How about security?'

'Well, it's on the real downlow, so we're keeping it simple and low profile. Mal Crookston has briefed four armed NCA escort and protection officers to transport him and then provide security during the debrief, so we can keep it away from Police Scotland. They've only been briefed as much as they need to do the job to limit exposure.'

'That's good. What's their ETA?'

'Late afternoon. We have a custody officer ready to take charge of him and make sure he abides by prison standards and the lawyer is ready to meet us there once we're all ready to start the debrief, probably tomorrow.'

'Where's he going, then? I should know all this, but everything else has taken over,' said Ross, rubbing his temples.

'Lochinver cop shop. Single man office with an unused cell, it's being reinstated to hold Frankie for a couple of nights whilst we do the job,' said Janie.

'Well, that's hardly convenient. West coast midge hell, that place.'

'Not this time of the year, it isn't. Anyway, you're a Highlander. You should be used to all that.'

'Aye, but I stayed around Dingwall, and never go back. I'm a townie now, like yourself. How far away is it?'

Janie smiled. 'Four to five hours.'

'That's going to spank my overtime budget, you money grabbing shysters. Couldn't the NCA have picked somewhere a little closer?'

'They're the experts, Ross. It's suitably remote, and a cell is being cleared ready for Frankie having been a store for years. There's only one cop there with it being a single man station, he's apparently a decent sort with an impeccable record and is well vouched for. Plus, any incomers will stand out a bloody mile up there at this time of year. Too cold for tourists.' Janie sat down behind her desk and opened up her laptop.

Ross just stared at his screen, muttering something about overtime.

'Any news?' said Max as he walked into the room, his face blank of any expression.

'You're late,' said Ross, not looking up from his computer.

'For what?'

'We've got an imminent meeting with the Chief, the DCC and some gadgies from the Crown Office about the debrief and what we can offer Frankie and limitations associated.'

'I didn't even know about that, so how can I be late for it?' Max looked puzzled.

'Not that, you're late for not telling me what happened with soppy bollocks in the ill-fitting cop uniform when you stung Mairi Malone. I had to listen to that smug old bastard telling me how brilliant he was at impersonating cops.'

'Aye, all true. He was impressive, I even watched from over the road. No way did she suspect anything, she was just too relieved not to be over the drink drive limit, although it was close, she must be a right pisshead. Anything jumping out of the download, Norma?' said Max, sitting at his desk with a sigh.

'Give me a chance, I've only just imported it into spreadsheets I can search. I'm not a miracle worker, you know,' said Norma, huffily.

'I bet you've found something already, haven't you?' said Max, chuckling.

'No.' Norma's voice was sharp.

'How about if I tell you that I have Tunnock's products in my desk?'

'Okay, maybe I've identified the photographs of Hector MacFarlane's ID, which she stole, and have the number she texted them to. There are also a number of other photographs of ID documents that she's sent. Each time to different numbers, so it's either to different people, or our man is careful with his phones. I'll mark all the checks to be done cross-network in case he just changes SIMs and not handsets. Is that worth a teacake?' Her eyes sparkled mischievously.

'A teacake and a caramel wafer, I'd say. Can we expedite the checks on those numbers, including cross-network handset checks?' said Max.

'Already authorised. Telephone unit are waiting,' said Ross.

'Any obvious connections between Mairi and Droopy beyond the phone call?'

'I'm scanning now. I have the e-discovery software running, and I'm just inputting the data now. We should be able to get some link, particularly if I compare against other occasions she's sent ID docs, of which there are a good few. There has to be a link somewhere, this has been a busy phone, and she's active on social media. She has Facebook, Insta, Twitter and TikTok. I'll also use some open-source aggregator sites I have access to. If the link's there I'll find it.'

'I have no doubt you'll find it, Norma.' Max grinned, handing over a foil-wrapped teacake and a caramel wafer, which she accepted with a beaming smile.

'Just need a tea to go with it, and as if by magic, here's Barney with the clean cups,' said Norma, nodding at the door, where a scowling Barney, now dressed in his customary cargo pants and polo shirt, was clutching a tray of clean mugs.

'Well, I'm not bloody making them. Those cups were a disgrace and I want a proper coffee, someone else can do it. Man of my years scraping mould off mugs. I used to fight the IRA, you know,' he chuntered, putting the tray down on top of the fridge with a clatter, snapping the kettle switch down, and then slumping in his armchair, arms folded defiantly, bottom lip jutting.

Ross, Max and Janie all began to titter.

'You buggers can all piss off. I've a good mind to sod off home. I put a wash on, it needs tumble drying and I feel that the Chief Constable owes me clean clothes,' said Barney and the tittering became louder.

'Err, guys,' said Norma, but no one heard her because of the laughter that was becoming louder.

'Guys,' she repeated, looking up, her brow furrowed. Still, no one noticed as the chuckling continued.

She exhaled, the frustration clearly boiling up in her. 'Oy!' she shouted, eyes flaring.

The room went silent, and every eye swivelled to the analyst.

'Sorry, Norma, what?' said Ross.

'Our man is apparently called Droopy, right?' she said.

'Aye, that's what Frankie said, because he looks like the cartoon dog, why?' said Janie, wiping tears from her eyes, a huge smile still splitting her face.

Instead of answering, Norma turned her screen around so it was facing the rest of the office. A black-and-white photograph of a boy and a girl, both aged about eleven, was displayed, seemingly a school portrait. They smiled widely at the camera, wearing matching white shirts and striped school ties. The girl was clearly Mairi Malone, whereas the boy had a round, sad-looking face with nothing of the beaming smile the girl wore. His eyes were heavy and hooded, sloping downwards at the corners, his cheeks soft and flaccid.

There was complete silence in the room, only punctuated by the ticking of the radiators.

'Shit,' said Max, eventually.

'Shit indeed,' said Norma.

'Where's the picture from?' said Janie.

'Facebook. It just says, "me and Gordy, St Brides School, Primary 7 school pic. Can you even believe we're twins?"'

'That's not conclusive, he just looks a miserable fucker,' said Ross.

'True but look at the third comment down under the picture.'

Everyone moved closer to the screen, and at the entry that Norma's painted nail was pointed at. '*I wonder why he was called Droopy, lol x* 😌'

'Okay, that's a bit more conclusive,' said Max.

'Aye, and how about this?' said Norma as the image switched to a faded colour photo of the same man, now an adult but with the same hangdog face and sad eyes, dressed in military fatigues and sporting a maroon beret with the badge of the parachute regiment. '*Proud of my bro*' was the comment under the photograph.

'Shit, he was airborne,' said Ross.

'Not always,' said Norma as she swiped to the next picture from the Facebook account. A picture of the same man, no doubt about it, but on this occasion, he was wearing plain olive-green fatigues and a white-topped cap, and cradling an assault rifle. Again, there was no smile, and just the same jowly, fleshy face and heavily hooded eyes.

'What's with the weird cap?' said Norma.

Max spoke, his voice low, his eyes fixed on the screen. 'It's called a képi, or to be more accurate, le képi blanc. The headdress of the French Foreign Legion.'

46

THE CONFERENCE ROOM was silent when Ross and Max burst in. Chief Constable Chris Macdonald was at the head of the table, sitting alongside DCC Louise Campbell, who glared at them as they entered the room. Opposite were two men, both smartly dressed, one with a shorn head, a shadow of stubble and horn-rimmed glasses. The other was smaller, with tightly curled black hair that was so dark it just had to be the product of Grecian 2000 or Just for Men. His face was soft and doughy, and a distinct double chin hung down like a wattle. Both men surveyed Max and Ross with an element of disdain, and one looked pointedly at his watch.

There was also a tough and stocky man sitting at the other end of the table, in shirtsleeves which were rolled up showing wiry and knotted-looking forearms. His face was tanned and lined and he looked ex-military.

DCS Miles Wakefield sat at the side of the room, trying not to laugh at the dishevelled pair. Ross's tie was slack, and a button on his shirt was unfastened, revealing pasty white flesh beneath.

'Ross and Max, I'm glad you could both join us. Eventually,' said Macdonald, with a trace of levity.

'Sorry, sir. It's all been happening in our wee office,' said Ross, slightly out of breath.

'May I introduce Finn Townsend, Crown Agent, and Mark Jacobs, Advocate Depute from the Crown Office. Finn has oversight of the deal with Frankie Hardie and is reporting to the Lord Advocate on any immunity and sentence adjustments, and Mark would lead in any prosecutions arising from this case, and is to be the primary source of legal advice at this stage, okay?'

'Aye, boss. Nae bother,' said Ross, nodding at Mark Jacobs, who nodded back, his shaven head reflecting the harsh overhead light.

'We also have Mal Crookston from the NCA PPU team who is liaising directly with your team on the safe transportation and security of Hardie.'

Crookston nodded and smiled, showing white, even teeth. 'Pleased to meet you, Ross.'

'Of course, you know DCC Campbell and DCS Wakefield. Miles is, of course, here as he has oversight of the murders of David Hardie and Leo Hamilton as well as the suspicious death of Beata Dabrowski. He will monitor for the purposes of ensuring that the MIT investigation isn't hampered, and can also disseminate any new lines of inquiry to DCI Davies. I don't want them hamstrung by our need for a covert approach in the debrief of Frankie Hardie, I hope that's clear?'

'Crystal, sir. Once we've Frankie safe, via Mal's team and debriefed, we can get the evidence out, but he's going to want to know what's in it for him.'

'That's why we're here. Heard a lot about your team, DI Fraser,' said Townsend, nodding. His wattle trembled as his head moved and Ross had to work hard not to grin.

'All good I hope,' said Ross, sitting at the table. He reached for the coffee flask and poured two mugs, but mistimed it, and a big splodge of scalding black liquid splashed on the polished wooden table. Ross reached for his grubby handkerchief and mopped up the mess with an apologetic grin.

'Mostly. Some significant successes, I understand,' said Townsend.

'Aye, I'm proud of our record, sir.'

'So you should be.' He nodded, and Ross just couldn't help but stare at the flabby fold of skin as it quivered.

'So, where are we, then?' asked Macdonald.

'How much do you want? Lot's happening right now, and leads are developing as we speak,' said Ross.

'Well, how about Hardie for a start?' said Macdonald, looking at Crookston.

'I have four of my guys signing him out of HMP Shotts and transporting him to a secure and covert location this afternoon, where we'll hand him over for debrief by DS Craigie and DC Calder starting tomorrow. I understand that there was a serious attempted attack on him in jail, by an Albanian prisoner just recently, so he's being held in solitary at the moment until we can remove him for his debrief.'

'Initial account from Hardie, Ross?' said Campbell.

'He's given one, but not under caution and no lawyer, so we can't rely on it yet. Essentially, he's alleging that his late brother was involved in the disposing of Beata Dabrowski's body as ordered by his father, who was working for an individual who is now in a position of power. He claims that the murder was carried out by a man he knows as Droopy, assisted by someone else called Mitch, and another called Billy Watson, all facilitated by Jack Slattery, who I think we all know about. It's of course now noted that Jack Slattery and Steven Mitchell were murdered within the last few days. Slattery was killed by a man called Galbraith in Saughton, and Mitchell was shot dead at his home in Newcastle.'

'How about Billy Watson?' said Campbell.

'Died some years ago, of natural causes.'

'Anything linking them to this case other than coincidence?' said Jacobs.

'Nothing direct, but it's far too big a coincidence for me,' said Ross.

Wakefield cleared his throat. 'Far too big for us on the MIT as well, Ross. We're keeping an open mind, and all the investigative teams are talking to each other, but no obvious and firm links from us, as yet. We really need you guys to pull it out of the bag, Ross.'

'We'll do our best, boss.' Ross paused to sip his coffee, and grimaced just a touch.

'Can Hardie assist on this?' said Jacobs.

'Not directly.'

'How about this Droopy character?' said Macdonald.

'We believe we've identified him as Gordon Malone. An ex-soldier from Glasgow, no criminal history, some weak intelligence linking someone called Droopy to major crime as a fixer, but this is hot off the press, and we're still developing the picture as we speak,' said Max.

'Any actual solid evidence?' said Campbell.

'Less than we'd like. We'll get witness testimony from Hardie, but we need Droopy. We need him quick.'

Townsend cleared his throat and spoke, his voice clear and authoritative. 'Well, I'm happy to recommend to the Lord Advocate that in return for a full witness statement from Frankie Hardie that details his knowledge of the death of Beata Dabrowski, and the involvement of his father, his brothers and others as yet unidentified, we will consider an immunity deal for Hardie. I'll also recommend that in the event of solid evidence or intelligence leading to an arrest and prosecution of those responsible, his parole will be considered early, and authorised removal out of general population. It'll be in writing by this afternoon once I've had chance to brief the Lord Advocate. This will be reviewed after his interviews, and nothing is promised until his evidence has been evaluated. Clear?' he said, his head held high, stretching the wattle taut.

'Crystal clear. We can proceed then?' said Max.

'Hardie will require independent legal advice to make this solid. Does he have his own solicitor?'

'He did, but he's now minus a head.'

'Of course. We really can't do this without him receiving independent advice, but you'll want someone who's security cleared, I imagine?'

'Already in hand, we have Shona Devlin from Devlin and Bird in Glasgow acting for him, he was happy to leave it to us. She's appropriately vetted, but we still won't brief her until she arrives at the location, we need to be so careful,' said Ross.

Townsend and Jacobs looked at each other and smiled knowingly.

'Shona is highly respected. I've encountered her more than once over the years. She's pretty ferocious, you know,' said Townsend.

'No bother for us. We want him properly advised,' said Max.

'Excellent.'

'Anything to add, Mal?' said Macdonald.

'No, sir. We'll handle his transportation and security, and my guys are great at what they do. You guys just need to get the evidence from Hardie, I hope you can handle it, Max,' said Crookston, his blue eyes holding Max's.

'We're ready, and he's ready to talk. Let's get this done.'

47

'THAT TOWNSEND IS a snidey little cockwomble, isn't he? What's with his neck? He looks like a fucking turkey,' said Ross to Max as they walked the dusty corridor back towards their office.

Max just grunted, weariness seeping into his bones, and his thoughts were split between Katie and, since their latest discoveries, Bruce.

'What's up with you, Max? You've been as crabbit as a bear with a sore arse,' said Ross, glancing at Max.

'It's nothing, just tired.'

'Well, liven up, man. We're about to get busy, so if you've shit to sort, get it sorted, pronto, eh?'

'Like what?'

Ross held his arm in front of Max, stopped suddenly and turned to face his friend. 'Look. You'll have noticed that Mrs F and I have occasional differences, and that this job is fucking shite for relationships, so if there's anything you need to do, get it done now, before things gets chaotic, okay?'

'I'm okay,' but even as Max said the words, he knew that he wasn't being convincing, and the look on Ross's face made it clear that he wasn't buying it, either.

Ross's eyes softened. 'Look, pal. I get it. Things can be rough. Is Katie okay?'

Max opened his mouth to protest, then closed it again, and leant against the scuffed and scraped wall, rubbing his face with his hands.

'Max—' began Ross.

'Katie's pregnant,' interrupted Max.

The silence in the deserted corridor was tense and thick, as Ross stared open-mouthed at Max.

'How far gone?' he eventually said.

'No idea. Only just done a positive test a couple of days ago. She's got an appointment with the doc soon.'

'Is she okay?'

'Aye, gone off cheese, is throwing up a bit and is pissed off at me for being at work all the time.' Max sighed, but forced a smile that no doubt looked unconvincing.

Ross's big face switched from its customary scowl, and he broke into a big, wide grin that showed his uneven teeth. 'You lucky bastard,' he said, extending his hand and shaking it with genuine warmth.

'I thought you'd be all sarky, or tell me how kids and this job don't mix, or how you'd always assumed I couldn't get it up,' said Max, a smile arriving on his face as Ross clapped him on the shoulder.

'Normally I would, pal. You're in for a treat, and I'll tell you something for free, man to man. I've had a full-on career, done all the big crime stuff, nicking bad guys and bent cops, but being a dad is the best thing I've ever done in my life. My kids mean everything, pal. This job gets in the way, but you can do it. You can still be a good cop, you can still make a difference and still be a great dad, but it takes some work. So yeah, I'm calling you a lucky bastard, because you're about to experience the ride of a lifetime. Have you spoken to her today?'

'No, I got up early, and she had her head down the toilet when I left.'

'Well, go and give her a call, and give her my best wishes, eh? And tell her that Mrs Fraser will be delighted, and that if she ever needs someone who knows the score, including moaning about husbands being at work, then I'll pass her number on.' Ross thumped Max on the shoulder again and chuckled.

Max didn't quite know what to say, but was almost shocked to feel a tightness in his throat, and emotion beginning to stir.

'Now don't get fucking emotional on me, ya fud. Go and speak to your missus, sort shit out and make sure she knows you're there for her, even if it is over the phone, until we've got this current load of shit under control.' He grinned again, turned on his heel and stomped off, whistling cheerily.

Max just stood there, breathing deeply at how the normally brutally sardonic Ross Fraser could go from being sarcastic, impatient, foul-mouthed and crass to understanding and kind in the blink of an eye. Max felt himself grinning. He reached for his phone and dialled, as he pushed a door open and stepped out into the cold, fresh air.

'I bloody hate you for making me pregnant, Craigie,' was Katie's opening gambit. Her voice was gummy and thick, and she sounded tired.

'So, I guess, "how are you" wouldn't be a welcome next line for me?'

'Only if you want a punch in the face when you get home,' she said, and Max was relieved to hear the humour returning into her voice.

'Ah well, maybe it's a good thing that I'll be a while, then.'

'Why aren't I surprised.'

'How are you feeling?'

'Honestly?'

'Of course.'

'Like a bad hangover, but without the good memory of a decent night out. I've been throwing up constantly.'

'Shit, sorry. Have you called the doc?'

'I called. Appointment day after tomorrow. You remember, the one you've faithfully promised to come to with me, where we're discussing me being pregnant with your child. You'd not forgotten, had you?'

'As if. I'll be there, don't worry. Have you called in sick?'

'Well, I'm technically working from home, but in reality, I'm sat on the sofa in my dressing gown, with the fire on, not eating cheese, and trying to not scare the crap out of Nutmeg with the puking noises.' She coughed wetly.

'I'm sorry, babe. You want me to come home?'

'You're doing something urgent, right?'

'Aye.'

'How urgent?'

'Very.'

'As urgent as the other urgents?'

'More. If we don't get this right, things will get very bad.'

'Then get back to it, then. I'm off to get rid of the tea and toast I managed to get down half an hour ago.'

'Katie, I'm so . . .'

'Don't apologise, Max. You're a total and complete bastard, and I hate you. Although I actually love you. Promise me two things.'

'Of course.'

'You don't know what they are yet.'

'Aye, sorry.'

'Just promise me that you'll be careful, and that you'll be at the doctor's in two days' time.'

'I promise.'

'Good. Now piss off.' Katie hung up.

Max walked across the wet grass and to the small knot of conifers that were in the grounds of the castle, his gut churning after the call. His mind was whirring at everything that was happening. Becoming a dad, the prospect of beginning a complex debrief of a major criminal that he truly didn't trust and above all, that it felt like someone, somewhere was pulling strings that had resulted in multiple deaths recently, and that if they didn't do their jobs properly the number would grow. It felt like a ton weight of responsibility was on their shoulders.

And Bruce Ferguson. The shadowy ghost that was Bruce Ferguson. Two former French Foreign Legion soldiers had made Max suspicious again. Could Bruce have employed them to stop Hardie escaping? Would he act against Frankie? Max's stomach churned at the prospect.

He scrolled on and dialled when he reached Bruce's number. As usual there were clicks and beeps, before an electronic voice simply said, 'Leave a message.'

Max stood and looked at the large turrets of Tulliallan Castle for a moment, before pocketing his phone and heading off, back to the office.

There was work to do.

48

THE OFFICE WAS buzzing when Max walked back in, with Ross, Janie and Barney all crowded around Norma's screens.

'Where've you been, you idle sugg,' said Ross, not taking his eyes from one of the screens.

'Sugg?' said Max, walking over and joining them.

'Man, you've really spent too long with bloody cockneys, you've forgotten your roots. Old Scots word meaning you're a lazy bugger and you're missing important evidence that my inspired leadership and foresight have led to being recovered that proves Drippy is at the centre of this.' Ross nodded at the screen, which showed a large, open-plan visits room at a prison. Prisoners all wearing red tabards were sitting at tables, mostly women and children opposite them.

Janie groaned with exasperation. 'It's Droopy, Ross. Phil at the prison has been scanning through recent visit records at Shotts and Saughton. This is the visits hall at Saughton. Look at the big gorilla sat in the middle of the hall with the yellow tabard, and shaven nappa.' She tapped the screen.

Max moved closer and took in the powerful-looking man, sitting back in the chair, his long arms almost touching the floor, and he had to admit that there was something of a silverback about him. He was opposite a smaller man, wearing a dark cap with hair poking out from the back and sides and thick-framed, slightly tinted glasses, and sporting a heavy beard.

'Looks like Galbraith to me. Who's the beardie he's talking to?'

A metallic voice came out of the speaker and Max immediately recognised the rough Glaswegian voice as being that of Phil, the DC from the prison liaison team. 'That's the interesting part. Hi by the way, Max.'

Norma clicked her mouse and Phil's face appeared in a small box at the top of the screen.

'Hey, Phil. So, who is it?' said Max.

'Well, the visiting order said it was someone called Tom McDaid. He produced a driving licence in that name. Here's a scan of it.' The screen switched from the visits room to a blown-up image of Tom McDaid's driving licence. 'Look closely at the picture.'

Max studied the stubbled face, thick, tousled dark hair and glasses. He wasn't that surprised to see the heavily lidded eyes and jowly cheeks. 'Hello, Droopy. I guess that explains what we were all wondering. Shit, he's got some balls going into a jail with a fake ID, decent though it looks. Going in and talking direct to Galbraith, he must have had solid intel and seriously good connections.'

'I guess he didn't want to use an intermediary, and the phones are risky. Cons are all convinced that they're listened in on, even though they rarely are,' said Phil with a shrug.

'I'm sensing there's more?' said Max.

'Aye, there is. Check out this next still taken from Shotts prison visits the very next day. This one's taken at reception when he booked in. His back was to the camera in the visits hall, but the VO makes it clear that he did visit Almir Duka.' Phil vanished from the screen, and a crystal-clear image appeared, seemingly taken in the reception area where visitors book in before going through to the visits hall. Once again, it was clearly Droopy, but this time just sporting a heavy moustache, and with his hair neatly cut and styled. He looked different from the photograph taken at Saughton, but there was no mistaking the same heavy features, and downturned, sad-looking eyes.

'Another ID used, looks genuine to me,' said Phil as a scan of a passport biodata page appeared on the screen in the name of Matthew

Simons. 'Interestingly, these visits were conducted on consecutive days, so he totally changed his appearance in that time. As the Shotts photo is the most recent, we can be fairly sure that's an accurate representation of how he looks now, unless he's wearing a wig.'

'Christ, this is something else. Droopy has managed to stay off law-enforcement radar for this long, and yet he has the connections to be able to get two cons at two different nicks to kill a fellow inmate. Who has that level of clout?' said Ross.

No one answered him, and there was a heavy silence in the room, only disturbed by the slight hiss from the speakers.

'Janie, I hope there's a solid plan to safely get Frankie to the debrief location,' said Ross, not taking his eyes off the screen.

'There is. Very solid, trust me, and the risk management plan is in your inbox already,' said Janie.

Ross just nodded, grimly.

'I hate to add to the plates that you're spinning but there's something else,' said Phil.

'Go on,' said Max.

'These visits were over four weeks ago.'

'What?' said Ross, incredulously.

'Aye. I know. Droopy solicited these hits weeks ago, well before Hardie approached his lawyer,' said Phil. 'But why, for Christ's sake? I mean why now, after all this time, does the decision get taken to murder Hardie and the others. Did the person behind it suddenly have more to lose? Or did they realise that Davie was gonna grass?'

'Find that out, Ross, and we can clear this whole thing up,' said Max.

'But for fuck's sake, how the bastarding hell could he know that Davie was going to approach the cops? Now, I know I'm no rocket scientist, but this makes no shitting sense,' said Ross, throwing his pen on the desk.

'I may have something on that front,' Phil said. 'When we were going through Davie Hardie's stuff, we found a letter from Jack

Slattery to Hardie, sent a week before the visits, but not through the normal mail system. Must have come through a back channel. There was plenty of normal blether in there, as you'd expect, but it's safe to say that Jack sounded a little worried.' Phil picked up a piece of A4 paper and slotted a pair of spectacles on his nose as he read from the sheet, '"Keep your eyes open, Davie. I heard a whisper that we're viewed as being a potential problem to someone because of something we sorted for your pa years ago. Maybe watch your back, eh?"'

49

Ace: They know who you are, and they're looking for you. They also know who the sniper is.

D: He won't be a problem, and they know nothing. All in hand.

Ace: Get it sorted, and fast. They're moving Hardie out later today to a safe house.

D: Where?

Ace: No idea, it's being kept need-to-know. That's for you to find out.

D: Is Craigie doing debrief?

Ace: Yes with the female DC.

D: Calder?

Ace: Yes, that's her. There's going to be a solicitor present as well.

D: Name?

Ace: Devlin, Glasgow firm. You need to sort this urgently.

D: In hand. No problems.

50

FRANKIE WAS SITTING in reception at the prison, not surprised by the knot of nerves he was feeling, almost like someone had punched him in the gut.

Two stocky and tough-looking plainclothes cops entered the grim and dusty space, and nodded at him. Both wore police ID on lanyards, and Frankie couldn't help but notice the significant bulges on both their waistbands. Normally the sight of an armed cop would have caused him some angst, but on this occasion, he was thankful.

'Frankie?' the older one said.

'Aye?'

'I'm Jim, this is Danny, and we're your lift to the debrief location, you all set?'

'Aye,' said Frankie.

'Got everything you need?'

'Is it just you two? You know that there's a bad bastard out there who wants me dead, right?' He nodded at a clear bag with 'HMP Shotts' printed on the side in bold blue lettering, but the feeling of anxiety just got stronger.

'Don't worry, this is what we do, Frankie. We're in a covert car, with blacked-out windows, so you'll be invisible from the outside, and we have another car with us that's got three firearms officers in it, with carbines, shotguns and pistols. Anyone trying their luck with us would get a shock, trust me,' said Jim.

'They could follow us,' said Frankie.

'Leave it to us, pal. We've done this before, and I've never lost anyone. We've a plan.'

Frankie looked at the tough-looking man, with his short, wiry grey hair and muscled forearms, and suddenly felt a little better. He radiated professionalism.

'Right, let's get going. We've a decent drive ahead of us, give us your hands, we have to cuff you, but as I'm a nice guy, we'll use nice cuffs, not the horrible new rigid ones that always end up sore,' he said, brandishing a pair of old-fashioned chain-link cuffs.

'Where are we headed?'

'Honestly, I don't even know yet. Need-to-know principle applies, and I don't need to know, yet. You'll find out as soon as we do. Let's go.'

Frankie sighed, but he didn't complain. He just held his wrists out compliantly as the cuffs were snapped into place.

51

DROOPY WAS SITTING in his Mondeo at the far end of the prison car park, watching the vehicle entrance through a pair of binoculars. He'd seen the two cop cars turn up forty minutes ago, the black BMW X5, with the darkened rear windows, had gone through the gates and out of sight. The Lexus saloon had remained outside in the car park, right by the gate. One of the occupants had got out of the car, cop lanyard around his neck, and smoked a cigarette, and even from this distance, Droopy could see that the cop was armed. Good tactics, he'd thought. The BMW would have Frankie in it, and the chase car would probably contain two or three armed cops. It was a shame that they'd stayed with the car, as he'd have liked to have snapped a tracker underneath it, but it was just too risky. He'd no doubt start making his way once Frankie arrived at wherever they were planning to take him.

His being here was belt and braces, as he knew he'd find out where they were taking Hardie, one way or the other. He always found a way of making things work, which was why he could charge the rates he did. Once he knew where they were taking him, he'd be able to plan how to take him out. He had some guys at the end of the phone waiting, but they'd need to plan carefully. Whether to take him out at the debrief location, or intercept the return convoy, was the decision he'd make once there was more actionable intelligence.

Then, movement caught his eye, as the external gate began to slide open, and the BMW eased its way out pausing by the Lexus for a moment, before both cars moved off, in convoy and heading towards the car park exit.

Droopy picked up his phone and dialled.

'Yeah?' a heavily accented voice said.

'Piotr, they're moving. Two cars, one a BMW X5, the other a dark blue Lexus. Heading towards the exit now.'

'Okay, I'm ready,' said Piotr.

Droopy watched as the cars headed out of the car park and onto the service road, eventually stopping at the junction that led to the main road.

'They're at the junction. I see a right-hand indication, and they're off onto Newmill and Canthill Road, south towards Glasgow. Are you ready?'

'Yeah, I'm ahead and waiting.' Piotr, an old comrade from the Legion, was a good man, who like so many had left after his time, and gone into the specialised private security sector. Specialised really meaning that he was essentially a mercenary. Piotr was a good surveillance operative, as was Droopy, so he was confident that between the two of them, they could follow the convoy to the destination, and from there they could make a plan. Hopefully this job could be all wrapped up in a couple of days. Droopy started the car, and moved off, steadily and smoothly, a smile stretching across his face. The money was great, but it was the adrenaline rush that he really did it for.

'I have them in sight, they're driving hard, I suspect they'll be putting in some anti-surveillance,' said Piotr, his voice coming out of the speakers.

'Stay with them, I'll move up and be ready to take over from you and we can rotate the visual on the convoy.'

'Roger, heading towards M8 and generally towards Glasgow. I hope they don't use a big central police station.'

'They won't. Too many leaks at big police stations,' said Droopy as he drove hard until he could see Piotr's Vauxhall ahead of him.

Looking beyond he could see the escorting Lexus, driving hard towards the M8, the traffic was getting heavier and heavier, and Droopy knew that this wasn't going to go well. He was hoping that they'd stay under the radar and attract minimal attention, but it looked like they were intent on shaking off any possible followers. He felt his gut tightening, with the realisation that they may not be able to follow them without getting compromised, which he couldn't let happen.

Droopy eased past Piotr as they joined the motorway, keeping a few cars back from the Lexus, a sense of inevitability beginning to bite as the BMW accelerated again.

Then it happened, and Droopy knew it was all over. An arm snaked out of the window of the Lexus, and a blue light with a curly flex snaking from it was stuck onto the roof, and began to oscillate. This was made worse when the familiar howl of a siren erupted from the car. It was over, he couldn't follow any more, as they'd be spotted in seconds.

'Break off, Piotr. We can't follow. Go back to the safe house, and I'll join you later.'

'Roger,' said Piotr.

Droopy eased off the accelerator, a sense of disappointment rising. It would have been ideal to have followed them to the secure location, but it wasn't worth a compromise.

Droopy turned up the radio, and Elvis Presley blasted out of the speakers. A setback, that's all. Nothing to worry about.

Frankie Hardie was still a dead man walking.

52

MAX AND JANIE were sorting out their kit in the office ready to head north whilst Ross and Norma were poring over phone and financial evidence that had been filtering through after all the applications had been submitted.

'Much in any of it?' said Max, hoisting his ballistic vest and stuffing it into a kit bag.

'Well, Droopy ditches his SIMs daily from what I can see, sometimes multiple times, but he keeps the same handset.' She paused, and looked across the room, her glasses a little askew. 'A bit slack that, eh?'

Max paused, furrowing his brow. 'Yeah, it is, I'd say. He's not a traditional villain though, is he?'

'What, apart from all the murdering?' said Ross.

'What I mean is he hasn't come to this by the traditional criminal route, has he? Normal upbringing, military service, no criminal convictions, he's never even been arrested,' said Max.

'There's another option,' said Janie.

'What?'

'Encrypted phone. They cost a fortune. Like thousands. Maybe he doesn't care much about the data, as switching as often as he does, it's complicated to interpret, and cell sites are only of limited value. The big benefit of an encrypted phone is that if we get our hands on it, even Barney couldn't crack it, right?'

'Fair point. What does his cell site suggest?' asked Max, looking across at Norma.

'It's complex, but it is of value. We'll need to share this with the MIT team soon. It puts him close to the prisons on a few occasions, and he does hit a cell mast heading south around the border that may tie in with the murder of Mitch in Newcastle, but the phone seemed to be offline around the timeframe for the murder. It'll take ages for me to sort this though, if I'm to check all the numbers called. I've just got one back for a number he communicated with that was cell-siting in Newcastle, but that was only yesterday. I wonder who that was.'

'Say that again?' said Ross, looking up from his computer.

'Droopy communicated with a number that cell-sited in Newcastle yesterday, so can't be connected to Mitch's murder.'

'What cell site did he hit?'

'One at the ferry terminal.'

Ross's mouth gaped open, his eyes wide. 'There was a murder at the ferry terminal last night. I saw it on the news this morning. Axe in the head, which made me sit up and listen because of the corrupt cop case in London in the 1980s.'

'Could it be connected to this case?' said Max.

'I'll make a call. There was a MIT team number on the TV, it'll be a direct line.'

'I have it here on screen,' said Norma, and read it out. Ross picked up the phone and dialled.

'Christ, this job gets more and more convoluted. Any news from the MIT?' said Max.

'Nowhere fast is what their analyst is telling me. No witnesses, nothing on the car that tried to spring Davie and no trace of the sniper who left the fag butt,' said Norma.

Ross was speaking quietly on the phone, having clearly got straight through to the right person and was talking amiably to whoever was on the other end. He clamped his hand over the handset. 'Apparently a French bloke called Davide Arbon got an axe in the heid right by a shite hotel by the ferry terminal. No suspects and no witnesses.'

'How'd they ID him?'

'Passport in his pocket allegedly, which has been examined and is forged. Dodgy photo, it seems. They're waiting for his DNA to come back, no trace on fingerprints, so far. They're sending a photo of the passport, and of a distinctive tattoo, it'll be here anytime. In fact, here it is.' Ross clicked on an email that had popped up in his inbox. There was a photograph of a biodata page of a passport, of a clean-shaven man staring blankly at the camera. His hair was neatly shorn, and he was smartly dressed. The name read Davide Arbon.

The next photo was of a pale forearm, which bore a tattoo of a winged arm clutching a dagger. Ross and Max looked at each other, eyebrows raised.

'This is the sniper. Almost certain that's him,' said Max.

'How can you be so sure?' said Norma.

'That tattoo is the badge of the second parachute battalion of the French Foreign Legion. That's Kyle Ellis, he was the sniper that killed Davie Hardie and Leo Hamilton, the DNA will confirm it.' Ross spoke into the phone.

'Shit. We'd better tell Miles Wakefield, Ross,' said Max.

'Aye, I'd best, but you and Janie get heading north. I think there'll be some shite coming our way, I saw Miles a while ago going to the DCC's office. I want you up there getting on with it. The sooner we have Frankie debriefed, the better. Is he there, yet?'

'No but getting closer. They did much of the journey on a blue-light run. Last I heard they were expecting to get there in an hour. Shall I get onto the lawyer and get her making her way? She's just waiting for the word,' said Janie.

'Aye, get on with it, and get going. I've a nasty feeling this is going to get political very quickly and there's only so much the Chief can do.'

Max and Janie stood up, and hoisted their heavy bags.

'And guys?' said Ross.

They both stopped and looked at their boss.

'Be vigilant, okay? It seems like he's come over to the side of the angels, but when all's said and done, he's still a Hardie.'

Max and Janie just nodded, and left the room.

53

THE ATMOSPHERE IN the conference room was tense and febrile as Ross sat at the far end of the table, DCC Louise Campbell and DCS Miles Wakefield both staring at him accusingly.

'I must say, I really don't like being kept in the dark here. Policing Standards Reassurance are assisting, but I have responsibility for solving these murders. And now out of nowhere, you reveal strong evidence against this character Malone, and also identify the sniper, who is now conveniently dead. The body count is bloody ridiculous in this case and we're no closer to getting who's responsible for them.' Wakefield glared.

Campbell shifted in her seat, and nodded. 'I'm minded to agree, Ross. It feels to me like Miles is being forced to do his job with one hand tied behind his back. He should be the decision maker on all aspects of this case. Why are we just learning that you have new and significant evidence against Gordon Malone from the prisons team?'

'Only just found out ourselves recently,' said Ross with a shrug.

'And the sniper. When did you learn of this?' she added.

'As I said, just minutes ago. Is the Chief coming to this meeting?' asked Ross.

'He's at Holyrood at the moment, so it's me you're dealing with, DI Fraser, and I'm not happy about your progress here. When is Hardie being debriefed?'

'Starting today. Max and Janie are on their way to the debrief site, and Hardie will be there soon with his NCA armed escort team.'

'I'd like to have sight of the risk assessment for this. We can't afford another cock-up like the last one,' said Campbell.

'Well, we had nothing to do with that one, ma'am. I'm satisfied that the risk management processes are tight. We have four armed officers, and the site is secure, and covert. Hardie is still being kept according to prison rules, and we have a trained and experienced custody officer who will be managing his detention.'

'I'd still like to see it, make sure it's forwarded to me.'

'Of course, ma'am,' said Ross.

'And I want all material your team holds forwarded to Miles. He's overseeing all MIT activity so it's imperative he's not kept in the dark.'

Ross nodded, his face blank.

'Where is the debriefing site?' said Wakefield.

'Lochinver Police Station. It's been set up with a custody officer, the cell has been reinstated and we have a video-enabled interview room.'

'I hope this is being kept on the proper downlow,' said Wakefield, scrawling in his notepad.

'It is. His lawyer doesn't even know fully, yet. She's been told enough to get on her way, but that's all.'

'I'm not happy about this, DI Fraser, and I'll be speaking to the Chief Constable as soon as he gets back,' Campbell said, her cheeks spotted pink and her eyes flaring with indignation.

Ross just shrugged, trying desperately not to smile, but his eyes twinkled with mischief.

'Make sure all evidence, and intelligence is shared with Miles, as a matter of urgency, and don't go home. I'll need to speak to you once Mr Macdonald returns. Now, get out of here.'

54

THE BMW AND Lexus swept into Lochinver, on the northwest tip of Scotland, on the edge of, predictably, Loch Inver after a four-hour drive taken for the most part at eye-watering speeds. It was late afternoon when they eventually pulled up outside what looked like a typical whitewashed semidetached house opposite the loch, and a stone memorial of a kilted soldier. It was only the presence of a marked police van, and a small blue-and-white sign over the door marked 'POLICE' that gave any indication as to the building's purpose.

The afternoon winter sun was dipping down towards the horizon over the loch, casting burnt orange colours across the flat, calm surface.

'So, this is what we've spent four hours in the car for? A shite whitewashed house that looks like it belongs on a scheme in Paisley?' said Frankie, stifling a yawn.

'Perfect for our purposes, Frankie, and look how bonny the sunset is, eh? Ya dinnae get this in Shotts,' said Jimmy.

'Aye, man. Low key, dead quiet at this time of the year and it has a cell we can house you in. It's nice and secure, and we even have a friendly custody sergeant to look after you,' said Danny, unbuckling his seatbelt and stretching his back with a wince.

'Well, I'm fucking delighted,' Frankie replied, with maximum sarcasm.

'Ach, don't moan, man. Proper mattress on the bed, a decent bog, and the sergeant will order whatever food you need brought in. There's even a telly. Think of it as a holiday, eh? Think of us, pal, having to stay awake and make sure you're safe, and it'll be Baltic tonight, as well,' said Danny, cheerfully.

Frankie was surprised to hear himself chuckle, and he realised that the journey, whilst fast, had included some truly spectacular scenery as they'd negotiated the winding Highland roads, around vast lochs and snow-capped munros. After his time in jail, this had proved to be almost cathartic, and now the prospect of a quiet location, decent food and no homicidal prisoners trying to kill him was actually quite attractive, even if it did mean doing a deal with the polis.

'When's my lawyer getting up here?'

'I'm told she's heading up here now, although the location is only being shared with her a bit at a time for security reasons. I don't think she'll be so long as she's staying in a B and B close by and will need to check in. Janie said that she was going to pop in and see you before she got settled, and then I think you're having a quick initial chat with her and Max before you're bedded down for the night. It'll be a full day of it tomorrow,' said Jim.

'Cannae wait.'

The door that was under the sign swung open, and a uniformed cop stepped out, and looked left and right before approaching the BMW. He was a well-fleshed, grey-haired man in his forties, his physique really not suited to the black nylon wicking T-shirt and cargo trousers that he was wearing. Jim lowered the window and pulled out his ID badge. 'Sergeant McCallister?'

'Aye, that's me. Is this Frankie?' he said in a sing-song Highland accent that was pure west coast.

'Certainly is, sarge. I'm Jimmy from the NCA PPU escort and protection team, are we all ready?'

'Certainly am. I've spent all day making it proper nice like. Decent mattress on the bed, it's plenty warm and I think you'll have a good night. Come on, let's get you in and settled,' he said, his smile widening, showing surprisingly white and even teeth.

Both cars were parked up, the BMW at the back of the house, the Lexus on the hardstanding in front of the office door. The driver remained in the car.

'We'll always have one of us outside, once the sun goes down, we'll be nicely discrete,' said Danny.

'I'd no worry about it, pal. It's dead of winter here, no bugger about after dark, apart from the occasional person making a foray for a drink,' said the sergeant.

The station was essentially an office with a small counter, and a lone computer on a desk. There was a filing cabinet and a radio tuned to a local station, and it was pleasantly warm and cosy after the biting cold outside.

'Frankie, your room is through here,' said Sergeant McCallister, walking through a small corridor to a heavy wooden door, with a solid lock on the outside, and tellingly no handle or keyhole on the inside. 'I've tried to make it as cosy as I can, pal, but when all's said and done, it's still a cell.' He stepped to one side, and extended his arm, as if ushering a guest into a hotel bedroom at The Ritz.

Frankie wasn't too disappointed. It was still a cell, but it had a small reinforced window, a low platform bed, but a decent-looking mattress on it, and a TV in the corner on a low table. There was a new-looking duvet and pillow on the bed. A toilet was behind a screen at the back of the room.

'It's no top luxury, but it's cosy enough, and there's a shower in the corridor with everything you'll need.' The sergeant almost seemed proud of his efforts.

'Thanks, sarge. Looks fine, and I appreciate you making it as nice as possible for me,' said Frankie, initially intending to be sarcastic, but the man was so calm and diffident that he didn't have the heart.

'Nothing of it, man. I'm getting paid a heap of overtime for this.

Anything you need, just give me a shout, yeah? There's a button by the door. Cuppa?'

'Aye, that'd be great.' The sergeant nodded and wandered off, whistling tunelessly, leaving just Danny in the cell with him.

'Right, Frankie. We're here to keep you safe, so if there's any drama we'll be right in to get you away, so for God's sake, if we seem like we're acting with urgency, no daft questions, and just do as you're told. This is our full-time job, protecting you, and we've picked this place because it's easy to protect. Understand?'

Frankie nodded, and Danny turned on his heel and left the cell, shutting the door with the all-too-familiar thump. Frankie sat on the bed, and sighed. He was doing it. The thing he'd always said he'd never do. Help the police. Strangely he felt nothing. No regret, no fear, no shame. He'd had his fill of this life, which had cost the lives of all his family. He was the last of the Hardies, and he was hoping he'd have the one thing he'd always secretly wanted. Normality.

He was determined that he'd get this thing done, and then he'd find a way to live a normal life. He picked up the remote control from the bed and flicked on the TV.

55

Ace: Lochinver. Now.
D: I know. We're travelling up. Will update when objective completed.

56

IT WAS THAT deep, almost velvety dark that you only get in the remote Highlands of Scotland when Max and Janie pulled up around the back of the police station in Lochinver as they'd been instructed to do by Danny. Janie yawned as she switched off the engine, and turned to look at Max.

'Sometimes I think that I should get a job in a control room, or something, rather than working the bloody stupid hours we do. Melissa is moaning. Look, five bloody texts. And it's your fault.'

'Why?' said Max, looking at her shadowy face, only just visible in the gloom.

'Because you attract trouble. Commonly known as a shit magnet.'

'You're not the first to say this. Come on, let's go inside, did you clock the cop in the Lexus at the front?'

'Aye, not that subtle I'd say. Are we sure this is the best place for this kind of job?'

'Less chance of a leak, I guess.' Max opened the door, flooding the car with light, and got out. He opened the back door and grabbed his hold-all and they walked around to the front of the tiny police station. The Lexus window buzzed as it wound down, and a well-muffled face spoke from the inside. 'Max and Janie?'

'That's us.' Max and Janie both passed their warrant cards through the open window, and he studied them briefly with a small torch.

'Cool, chap the door, and Danny will let you in.' He picked up a radio handset and spoke. 'Two expected arrivals here, coming to the door now.'

Max nodded and they approached the door, which swung open, and a sturdy-looking man appeared in the doorway. 'You guys okay?' he said as they entered.

'Aye, all good, I'm Max and this is Janie.' Max extended his hand.

'Danny. Jimmy's over there, and Baz is out the back sleeping, and manning the custody desk, making sure Frankie's looked after, is Sergeant McCallister.' Danny pointed at a uniformed cop, who smiled across.

'Steve, please. All informal in here.'

'How's Frankie?' said Janie.

'In good spirits, I'd say. Nae crabbit at all, and seemed delighted with the food I gave him a ways back. A local lady from the Lochinver Larder sent some pies over. There's some for you in the wee kitchen, and you'll not eat a better pie, I'm telling you.'

'Sounds great, I'm starving,' said Janie.

'You've the run of the house attached as well. There're camp beds upstairs and everything you need.'

'Is there a local cop?' said Max.

'Not this week. Mannie from Lairg is covering in case of anything else, but we have old Tavish in the village,' said Steve.

'Tavish?'

'Aye, he's a local fisherman, and he's also a special constable, reserve fireman and on the shout list for the lifeboat. A busy boy and a real character is Tavish. He'll help out if we need anything, like.'

'That's good to know. How about the lawyer?'

'Gave her the final directions an hour ago, so she'll be here quite soon, I imagine. She sounded quite haughty, I must say.'

'Haughty?' said Janie.

'Aye, like she no' suffers fools gladly, an' that.' The sergeant grinned.

'You're stuffed then, Craigie,' said Janie and everyone chuckled.

'Right, a quick word with Frankie, just to say hello, and then we'll wait for his solicitor. All I intend on doing today is going through the agreement with him, letting his solicitor consult, and then we'll get a proper start tomorrow, and have a full day of it,' said Max.

'Sounds fine to me,' Steve said, standing and reaching for the keys hanging from a hook on the wall.

The three of them went into the corridor, and Steve opened the door. 'Frankie, visitors.'

Frankie was sitting on the bed, a mug of tea in his hand and an empty plate with a knife and fork on it next to him.

'How are you, Frankie?' said Max.

'I'm fine, especially after that pie, Steve. That made the whole bloody trip worth it, despite four hours in that car with a flatulent, but fast driver.'

'I did tell you, best pies in Scotland. I'll leave you to it,' said Steve.

'Is the lawyer here, yet?' said Frankie.

'No, but on the way, expected any time. We have the immunity agreement here, no prosecution for minor matters, and early parole decision and removal from gen pop once statement given, okay?' said Max.

'I'm not signing until she's seen it.'

'That's fine, once she's spoken to you about it, we'll knock it on the head for the night and start fresh in the morning. It's after eight now, and I don't want to be interviewing through the night. Now that your safety is taken care of, there's no mad rush and we'd rather get it done right.'

'Fine by me,' said Frankie, turning back to the TV.

'Happy with the accommodation?'

'It's fine. Four stars on Tripadvisor, and three of those are for the pie and the cheery desk sergeant.' Frankie smiled, and it seemed genuine.

There were noises outside in the corridor, and Steve appeared. 'Solicitor is here, Max. Ms Devlin, DS Craigie and DC Calder.' He nodded and left.

A sturdy-looking woman appeared at the cell door, dressed in jeans, Timberland boots and a Barbour jacket. Her hair was short and neat, her face sharp and devoid of even a trace of humour, which showed in the deep brown eyes. 'I hope you're not interviewing already?' Her voice was strong and cultured, and she showed not even a trace of trepidation at the unusual situation.

'Evening, Ms Devlin. We were literally explaining to Frankie what was going to happen, and giving him a copy of the agreement ready for you to consult with.'

'Yes, yes, of course. Now if you'll give us a minute, I can explain my role and talk through the document. Then I intend on going back to my guesthouse. I'm decidedly tired, officer, and I want a bath and some food. It was a long drive made all the more tedious by the refusal of the NCA to disclose the location at the outset of my journey. I estimate that it took me almost twice as long as it needed to.' She puffed out her cheeks, her eyes flinty. She clearly wasn't happy.

Max opened his mouth to explain, then realised there was probably no point. 'Fine. We'll just be in the office, ring the bell when you're ready.' Max nodded to Janie, and they left the cell, shutting the door behind them.

*

Max and Janie were sitting with Steve in the office, eating a large meat pie each, washed down with strong tea that the sergeant had brought to them with his customary easy smile. As predicted, they were delicious, meaty and hearty and perfect fare for a cold winter evening.

A buzz made Steve look up. 'That didn't take long. I reckon she's looking forward to a gin in her guesthouse,' he said, standing up and then returning within a few moments with Ms Devlin.

'All good?' said Max with a smile, his mouth half full of a pie crust.

'Yes. All explained and he'll sign the document in the morning at the commencement of the interview. I want it read to him on tape first, is that okay?'

'Fine by us. Fancy a pie?' said Max.

Miss Devlin's lip curled. 'No, thank you. I'm a vegetarian, and anyway, pies aren't really my thing.'

'Dinnae know what you're missing,' said Steve.

Her stern face turned to a sickly smile. 'I'm sure, sergeant. Now, I'll be off, and I'll be back here at nine in the morning.' She nodded.

'I'll show you out,' said Steve, who stood and followed the lawyer as she disappeared into the night.

'She seems fun,' said Janie, chewing with relish.

'She'll be fine. I've dealt with many a haughty solicitor in my time, and remember, Frankie needs us more than we need him.'

'Fair point.'

Max's phone buzzed on the table in front of him. He picked it up, a message from Katie.

Miss u oxo.

Max tapped out a reply. **Miss u 2 x**.

He stared at the screen, feeling his heart lurch at the thought of Katie sitting at home, Nutmeg probably snoring next to her.

'All okay?' said Janie.

'Aye. I'm fine.'

'Katie?'

Max nodded, but didn't elaborate. Now wasn't the time.

A voice came from outside, and Steve appeared at the door, a touch of a grin on his face.

'Max, you'd best come. Lassie has just reversed her Beemer into your Volvo.'

'What?' said Janie, her face suddenly hard. Janie had a particular obsession with cars being clean and serviceable, and Max knew that this would be a major stress for her.

'Settle down, constable. It's just a car.'

'Aye, I know, but it's just been bloody serviced. This means it'll have to go in again and we'll get that shite Ford. Honestly, it's such a pile of bloody junk, and it smells.' She stood up and followed the sergeant out of the door at almost a jog.

It wasn't much of an accident. Devlin's car was a compact BMW and the rear bumper had crashed with the much bigger Volvo's rear end. The Volvo was barely marked, but one of the BMW's rear wheel arch plastics had bent and cracked inwards, and a shard was pressing against the tyre. Max pulled out a penlight from his pocket and shone it on the damage.

Ms Devlin looked suitably chastened. 'Sorry, it's just so bloody dark up here, and your car's black. I just didn't see it. Is my car driveable?'

'Ach, it's fine. I can just pull the plastic away, and you'll be okay.' Max reached down and pulled the shard away from the tyre, whereupon it cracked and sprang back. Max gave it a shake, and the plastic snapped clean off, a piece of it falling to the ground. 'Oops. Sorry, it just came away in my hand, but it would probably have needed replacing anyway. It's clear, though. You can drive it.'

Max shone his torch where the piece had fallen. A small oblong box lay on the rough tarmac. About the size and shape of a tobacco tin, but made out of hard plastic. Max picked it up, and turned it over in his hands.

It had a magnet on the base. He'd seen something like this before in the past. Something almost identical had been attached to his motorbike by a corrupt ex-cop.

It was a tracker.

A tracker that had been attached to Frankie Hardie's solicitor's car that was displaying precise coordinates to someone, right now.

Max felt the blood in his veins turn to ice as he turned the hard plastic device in his hands.

'Janie, we have a problem.'

57

'**WHO THE HELL** put a tracker under my car, and more importantly, why me?' said Devlin, her eyes wide with alarm, and her face ghostly white.

'We can't be sure, but we suspect that it's someone who's being employed to take out Frankie to stop him talking to us.'

'But why me? I'm just a bloody solicitor, I didn't sign up for this, I'm just here to represent the interests of my client.' She ran a quivering hand through her hair. All her earlier spiky demeanour had gone, replaced by something else. Fear. She looked utterly terrified.

'Because they couldn't get this location any other way. What we know now is that they know where we are, so we can't stay here,' said Janie.

'But this has nothing to do with me. I haven't even taken instructions from Frankie, yet. I should just go,' she said, her voice several octaves higher than it had been a while earlier.

'I wouldn't advise that, Ms Devlin. Whoever's after Frankie won't know what you do or don't know, and we know they aren't averse to targeting lawyers.' Janie's voice was gentle, but there was certainty in her delivery.

'Oh, Jesus. This is bad, this is really bad.' She sat heavily in one of the chairs in the room and buried her face in her hands.

'No need to panic yet, what we don't know is where they are, or what they're planning, and we have four highly trained armed officers here ready to protect us. Right, Danny, can you get two of your guys out, armed up and in positions front and rear whilst we make a plan.'

'On it, I've called it in, but the nearest NCA armed support is three hours away. I'll call into Police Scotland control to see what they have, but I suspect there won't be an ARV closer than Inverness.' Danny began issuing instructions to his team, as they were strapping on body armour and checking their pistols and carbines. The picture was one of practised efficiency of cops whose job was protecting people under threat.

'Ms Devlin, we'll get you to your guesthouse as soon as we can, but we need some info. Janie, you've been liaising with Norma, what's happening with the phones?'

'Urgent live-trace has gone in on the handset we know Droopy has been using. As soon as we have a new number the phone will be pinged. Should be imminent, I'll call her back now for an update.' Janie pulled her phone from her pocket and dialled, moving to the corridor.

'Ms Devlin, who knew you had been instructed in this case?' said Max.

'I have no real idea. I was approached via Police Scotland Legal Services, and we had some contact with the Fiscal's office on the broad brushstrokes of the deal, but that's it.'

'How about in your office?'

'Well, yes. It was known I was to represent Hardie, but I trust my staff.'

'Okay, that's fine. No need to panic here.' Max turned to Steve. 'We may need to prepare Frankie for an evacuation, can I leave you to tell him? And we'll need someone to escort Ms Devlin to her guesthouse, and keep an eye on her.'

'I could call Tavish, he's only a minute or two away. He'll be her bodyguard, I certainly wouldn't want to get on the wrong side of him, I know that. He's a big bugger.'

'Okay, do it. I need to speak to my boss.' Max dialled.

'Max, talk to me,' said Ross, with none of his usual sardonic and sarcastic tone.

Max quickly briefed Ross of the situation.

'Fucking shite. A tracker on the lawyer's car is next level sneaky shite, but at least we have the advantage that they won't know you've found it. What have you done with it?'

'I've put it back on the car.'

'Sensible. What would your instinct be on any attack?'

'If it was me planning this, I wouldn't do it straight away. It's quiet here, but there are still civilians about, and they won't want that as we know these guys are professionals who won't kill people they've not been paid to. We've guns front and rear, so I think we're safe in the immediate future. I'd say they'd leave it a while until this place is dead, and then try a sneaky approach, before a noisy storming of the cop shop. Any word on armed support?'

'On their way, but from Inverness, ETA is two hours.'

Max looked at his watch. It was 9 p.m. now. 'Too long, Ross. They could easily hit us in that timeframe. These guys are all soldiers, Droopy was airborne, he'll know what he's doing, and we know he has access to other ex-soldiers, bearing in mind he killed one of them in Newcastle.'

'Then just all get in cars and evacuate. Drive like fuck south, and leave the tracker in place. I have a strategic firearms commander on the other line, he's going to liaise with Danny on the protection team, so you just need to concentrate on making sure Frankie's kept in one piece. Has Norma updated you on Droopy's phones?'

'Janie's on the line to her now.'

'I'll save time. We've just had an update, the handset Droopy's been using had a new SIM put in earlier today. Only one message ten minutes ago at which point they were hitting a mast in Ullapool which is an hour away from you. You've time to get out, Max. Get everyone loaded up and get the fuck out of there and to Inverness, Burnett Road will at least be secure. I'll start making my way now, and I'll also bring Grandpa with me in case his sneaky skills are required. Someone's been chatting, that's for sure, and we need to get all over it, but in the meantime, just get to bloody safety. We can't let the last Hardie get topped without knowing what he knows at least.'

Max's mind raced, thinking through all the possibilities. If they ran now, they'd all be safe, and could live to fight another day. Leave the tracker here on the car, and head off at top speed by a circuitous route to the Inverness station. It made total sense.

'Aye. I guess so.' Max paused, his mind turning all the possibilities over, as the door opened, and a huge figure strode into the office. He was wearing blue fisherman's overalls, with a hi-vis Police Scotland jacket over his shoulder, and a flat cap at a strange angle, perched on his enormous head. His face was massive and cracked and creased, which all spoke of a life spent outside. He nodded at Max, with a huge smile that split his heavily bearded face.

'Tavish, you were quick,' said Steve.

'Aye, nae bother, Stevie. I hear there's trouble afoot, eh?' he said in a thick Sutherland accent.

'Max?' Ross's voice was impatient on the end of the line.

'Yeah, I got you. We'll start getting ready for extraction, priority is to get rid of the lawyer, and then get Frankie out. We're on it.'

'Aye, make sure you do. No buggering about.'

Max hung up.

'You'll be Max then.' Tavish extended his hand, calloused and the size of a large joint of ham. The handshake was powerful, yet came with none of the expected crushing squeeze.

'Tavish, good to meet you. I hear you're also a fireman?'

'Aye, that I am, watch manager for fifteen years, noo. I'll do anything for a bit of coin.' He chuckled, and his Baltic blue eyes sparkled with mischief.

'Glad you're here, we need all the help we can get.'

'Whatever I can do, pal.'

'That's great, we need to get out of here soon. There's trouble heading this way.'

58

DROOPY MOVED HIS body position in the gorse bush on the opposite side of the river Inver, and put the night vision monocular to his eye, allowing the green images to settle.

Across the small expanse of water was the white building with the blue-and-white police sign over the door. There was a marked cop van parked to the side of it and in front on the hardstanding was a Lexus. By increasing the zoom to the maximum he could just make out the shape of someone sitting in the driver's seat, wearing the chequered baseball cap often worn by firearms cops. He shook his head at the incompetence of it all. Literally sitting right outside the target premises for everyone to see. He could even see the vapour coming from the exhaust pipe, indicating that the lazy bugger had the engine on to keep warm. Light was coming from the windows in the office and main house, all diffused by Venetian blinds.

He reached for the pressel switch for his radio, pressed and spoke in French into the mic that was clipped on his tactical waistcoat. 'Piotr, I've a long view of the front from the opposite side of the river. One target at the front of the premises in a Lexus. A lone cop from what I can see and he has the engine on. Can you see the rear?'

Piotr replied, also in French, his voice a hoarse whisper in Droopy's earpiece. They always spoke French on operations, just in case they were overheard. Unless, of course, they were in France, in which case they used German.

'One at the back, in a BMW X5, I can't see inside it from my angle, but the engine's on. Lights on at the back of the house, but I can't see in because of the blinds.' After being dropped off by Droopy, Piotr had taken a tactical position on the small hill at the rear of the police office, also carrying a night vision monocular.

'Roger that. Looks to me like they're sitting ducks. I'm told that the single cell is via the office door, and then in via a corridor. Keys kept by the desk sergeant. Chico, you receiving?' Droopy whispered. Chico was the third member of the team. A Spaniard, also ex-FFL, and a good man, if a little impetuous. Chico tended to shoot first and then ask questions later. He was on foot in the kids' playground just to the left of the war memorial, about fifty metres away.

'Yeah, I got you.' Chico's heavily accented voice was tight with anticipation.

'Any movement along the front?'

'Negative. All quiet. I'm ready.'

Droopy looked at the illuminated dial on his watch, noting that it was almost eleven, a good time to engage. 'I'm going to move to the forming up position now. When I give the go ahead, Piotr, move in and neutralise the threat at the rear. Chico, you drive up and engage hostile at front, I'll then effect entry from the front with the breacher and neutralise any threats in the office, and then forward to the cell to take out the objective. Are we all clear?'

'Piotr, clear.'

'Chico, clear.'

'Wait for my command, I'm moving up now.' Droopy eased back out of the gorse bush, and jogged over to his Mondeo, which was parked across the river from the objective. Before getting into the car, he did his final mission equipment check, as he always did before action. He knew that his kit was in order, but it was almost cathartic to perform the ritual. He removed his Glock from the holster, and worked the action, putting a round into the chamber, before returning the polymer weapon back and checking it was secure. He checked his spare magazines were secure in his ops waistcoat, and that the retaining flaps were tight. He then reached into the car and pulled out the matte black Mossberg 500 tactical shotgun. He'd already preloaded the five-round magazine. Two breaching rounds, designed to defeat the door, no matter how tightly it was locked, followed by three rounds of buckshot designed to flood a space with a devastating spray of shot. He returned the shotgun to its space alongside the driver's seat. He took in three cleansing breaths, eyes closed, holding each for four seconds before exhaling. His eyes snapped open, and he was filled with a sense of anticipation at what was to come. And peace. As always, during these moments just prior to a violent incursion, he felt more at peace with himself than at any other time. It was why he did it.

He slid into the Mondeo, started the engine and then headed off, north towards the crossing point, just two clicks away.

The journey took just three minutes and soon he was heading to the centre of the tiny village where Chico had moved away from the kids' playground and up to the road edge. Droopy eased to a halt, and Chico jumped into the Mondeo, and reached under the seat where his pistol, a Glock 19 was stashed. He worked the action, checking it was ready to fire, and held it in his lap, ready to go.

'All good?' he said, looking at Droopy.

'All good. You ready, my brother?' Droopy held out his hand.

'*Legio patria nostra*, bro,' he replied as they shook hands. His eyes shone with excitement and anticipation. '*Legio patria nostra*. The Legion is our country.'

'*Honneur et Fidélité*,' replied Droopy, and they both laughed at the motto, which translated as 'Honour and Fidelity', just as they were about to go into the police office and slaughter everyone in there. They didn't care, not even one bit. This was a job, nothing more, nothing less. Droopy nodded, and both men pulled on tactical gloves, with Kevlar knuckle protectors, and lowered the cotton balaclavas that they'd been wearing rolled up as hats.

Droopy pressed the radio pressel again.

'Final approach, are you ready, Piotr?' he said, feeling the knot of excitement in his gut, his synapses firing with the pre-battle buzz.

'Ready and waiting.'

'Okay. Masks down. Moving up now, counting down, and engage on my mark.' Droopy engaged the gears and began to move steadily down the road towards the station. The final advance to contact.

'Counting down, five, four, three, two, one. Mark!' Droopy said, his tone not changing, his demeanour relaxed as the Ford pulled in front of the Lexus, blocking it in. Their doors flew open, and both men exited the car with deliberate, almost methodical movements. Acting at speed, but not rushing, not panicking, and ready to engage. Droopy had grabbed the Mossberg 500 and hefted it to his shoulder as he made for the door of the police office. He didn't stop to engage the driver of the Lexus, being totally focused on his objective, which was breaching the door, hence the Mossberg. Chico's Glock was bucking, sparks shooting out of the barrel, as he unloaded five rounds through the side window and door of the Lexus, immediately shattering the glass, and punching holes through the metal. Droopy caught sight of the chequered cap jerking as the bullets entered the driver's body, but he didn't pause. He heard, but barely registered the four or five reports from the back of the house, as Piotr was taking out the cop at the back.

Droopy strode without hesitating to the door, raised the Mossberg and shot directly at the handle. The frangible breaching round smashed into the mechanism, disintegrating, and totally destroying the lock without causing lots of rebound buckshot that could have injured him. Droopy racked another breaching round into the weapon, and hit the top of the door with another blast. Racking the weapon once more, he kicked open the door, the Mossberg in his shoulder, ready to engage whoever was inside, but this time with the heavy-grade buckshot strategically loaded into the weapon. He'd planned the loading of the shotgun with exactly this scenario in mind. Two breaching rounds for the door, followed by buckshot that would tear anyone inside the office to pieces.

The office was empty. Completely and totally empty. Droopy pressed the button on the transmitter. 'Office is clear, begin sweep of the rest of the building whilst I find the keys to the cell.'

'Received,' crackled in his ear.

Droopy looked about the room, his eyes halting at the main desk, which was empty apart from a laptop computer, and a clipboard with a pen next to it. A half-finished cup of tea sat on the desk. Droopy picked it up and held it against his cheek. It was still warm.

He swivelled his eyes, until they landed on a chunky bunch of keys hanging on a wall hook. He marched over, grabbed them and jammed them in the pocket of his cargo pants. He hefted the Mossberg again into his shoulder, and set off for the corridor.

The lights were low in the corridor, which stretched towards a solid wooden door with a heavy lock and a spyhole in the upper centre. He approached carefully and ignored the cell door, instead making for an opening in the opposite wall that was covered by a shower curtain. He whipped back the curtain, only to find an empty and dry shower tray. He let out a soft breath, listening to the sounds of Chico and Piotr clearing the rest of the property with a rising sense of unease. They'd taken out the two cop guards, but where was everyone else? Where was Craigie, and Calder? Had they gone somewhere else? A hotel, maybe, and just left Hardie in the cell with no one other than the now dead guards? It didn't add up.

Droopy advanced slowly and cautiously towards the cell door, and briefly put his eye to the spyhole. The bed was covered with a new-looking duvet, and there was a body shape under it, at least six feet in length, with the feet poking out of the bottom, clad in a pair of brand-new slip-on gutties. He looked again at the footwear, noting that it was the type given to detainees so they didn't have laced shoes in the cells. He had no choice; he'd have to enter.

He picked out the keys from his pocket, and selected the simple iron key amongst the others, which were all brass or chromed steel. He slotted it into the hole, and it turned, easily and smoothly.

Leaving the key in the door, Droopy's hand reached for the handle, and turned it. The door swung inwards on well-oiled hinges. He raised the Mossberg to his shoulder again, feeling the adrenaline surge as the door continued on its path into the cell.

As soon as the bed was visible, he fired. The buckshot slammed into the duvet, the shotgun's report roaring deafeningly in the confined space, and the duvet almost immediately turned red with blood, which sprayed from the body in a shower of gore. He racked again and fired once more. The shredded duvet flew up with the blast, revealing a ripped trouser leg. Blood splattered all over the cell, decorating the painted brick wall. Droopy roared with delight, an almost primeval victory cry, as the mess slid down the wall behind the bed.

He lowered the shotgun and moved towards the bed, took hold of the duvet and ripped it away.

A shredded mannequin torso was on the bed, the type used in first aid to practise CPR, the abdomen tucked into a pair of grey joggers that had been stuffed with something and jammed into the gutties. A mangled plastic bag that was spilling deep red blood slid from the bed and onto the floor with a wet splat. Panic surged in his chest, and he reached for his pressel. 'Exfil, exfil. It's a set-up,' he screamed into the mic that was clipped to his tactical vest.

59

'**WHAT THE FUCK** is going on?' said Piotr as they all arrived back at the office.

'Report?' said Droopy.

'Whole building's clear, no one anywhere. There are beds set up upstairs, but no trace of anyone. What happened in the cell, did you shoot him?'

'No, I put buckshot into a fucking mannequin that someone had set up under the covers, even with fake blood, or some kind of animal blood. What the hell has happened? Has Frankie escaped?' Droopy's mind was racing.

Chico went to the window, and peeped through the Venetian blinds, looking up and down the street. 'All clear outside, come on, let's get the fuck out of here,' he said.

'You guys took out both guards, yeah?' said Droopy.

'I pumped five rounds into that Lexus, you saw me firing, bro,' said Chico.

'Same in the BMW. I saw the body flinching and jerking, come on. Maybe someone's rescued him, and he's gone,' said Piotr.

Droopy stood there, still cradling the Mossberg, trying to make sense of it all, but he just couldn't. 'Okay, let's go, straight to the car, and we get the fuck out of here. Piotr, you go first, and clear the outside, Chico you take the rear exit, and then we just sprint like hell to the car and get moving.'

All the men looked at each other and nodded. 'Okay, go,' said Droopy, and they all went, sprinting for the doors, and bomb-bursting out of the tiny police office. They made as fast as they could across the pavement and jumped into the car. Droopy reached for the keys that he'd left in the ignition.

They weren't there. His fingers brushed against the cold metal of the empty slot. He roared with rage-filled frustration.

'Droopy, what the fuck, man? Get moving,' yelled Chico.

Suddenly there was a deafening explosion, and a figure appeared in front of the car, a shotgun raised at his shoulder as he pumped what Droopy knew were tyre-disabling Hatton rounds into the tyres of the Mondeo.

And then there were laser sights dancing around the car interior coming from the war monument a few metres away, and a figure popped his head over the bonnet of a car parked opposite.

'Armed police, stand still and raise your hands,' he roared, the shape of a carbine pointed straight at Droopy.

'Armed police!' came another demonic yell from the other side of the low wall that was in front of the police station.

'Fuck this,' yelled Droopy, feeling utter, total and complete rage gripping him, his face suffusing with blood and pounding between his ears. He reached for his holstered Glock. Years of anti-hijack training, and operations in Afghanistan and other war zones kicked in, and he began firing straight through the door of the car, the high-powered 9mm round smashing through the thin metal towards the figure crouched by the monument. It was no contest. Pistols against high-powered carbines being fired from cover will only end one way. What felt like a hammer blow caught him in the side of his shoulder followed by another that struck him in the neck, then another pierced the skin of the vehicle and entered his body, into the ribcage and lodging in his lungs. He felt no pain, no panic and no regret. Droopy always knew that it would end this way, he cackled softly as mayhem raged around him. Suddenly, there was a massive, overwhelming, and devastating impact into the side of his head, and then there was nothing but deep, impenetrable, inky blackness.

60

IT TOOK ANOTHER twenty minutes for the backup to arrive in the form of two armed response vehicles, an unmarked police CID vehicle occupied by a DS and a DC, and two prisoner transport vans that had been summoned.

The two surviving prisoners, neither of whom had uttered a single word since being dragged out of the car, were prone on the cold ground, their wrists secured with zip ties. They'd surrendered immediately after challenge, unlike Droopy who was still in the car, slumped over the steering wheel his Glock pistol still in his hand. His eyes were open and vacant and yet somehow still full of the rage he'd displayed whilst firing the Glock through the door of the car. They hadn't performed any first aid on him; once the prisoners were secured, there was little point. Whilst the wound from the bullet that had entered the side of his head was small and neat, the exit wound was the size of a tennis ball. Bone and blood were congealing on the windscreen, and also on the hair, face and clothes on one of the prone prisoners who was currently shivering on the tarmac, next to his cohort with several firearms still trained on them by the newly arrived ARV crew.

Max, Janie and Danny were sitting on the wall outside the police station, all the energy sapped from them after the adrenaline rush of the ambush. Jim emerged from the police station clutching a tray laden with steaming mugs and a pack of biscuits.

The CID officers soon got things moving and within a few minutes both of the surviving prisoners had been thoroughly searched and loaded into the transport vans. The DS had words with both the drivers, and then they moved off, blue lights strobing in the gloom.

The newly arrived DS was a relaxed-looking man in his late thirties, casually dressed in jeans, trainers and a bomber jacket.

'That's the prisoners on their way, straight down to Burnett Road, reception committee waiting for them to get them processed and banged up. A news blackout has been authorised, and no details have been released beyond that there's been a shooting.'

'Nice one, cheers,' said Max.

'Shite, bit of a state here, eh? I'm Nige Jones, by the way. On-call DS,' he said, accepting a mug from Danny.

'You could say that. We need to keep it as tight as a drum until we can assess properly what's happening, so no updates on the radio, yeah?' said Max, also taking a mug.

'Anyway, duty inspector is on his way, as is DCS Wakefield, DCI Davies, CSI teams, the PIRC and no doubt half the bloody world. I'm told post-incident procedure is to be fully in place as of now, and once everything is secure you guys are relocating somewhere until PIRC authorise your release.'

Max shrugged. 'Nae bother.' This was typical procedure after a police shooting, even one as clearly justifiable as it was. The PIRC would have to come to the scene to oversee the investigation to ensure accountability, seize firearms used, view the video footage and decide the next steps. In this case, Max was totally certain that there was no issue. They'd gone by the book, consulted the firearms commander, and had prepared the ambush. It had been Tavish's idea to utilise the mannequins from the fire station. 'It'll either put them off, or it will at least make the fuckers' intentions clear if they shoot up the dummies, eh?' Max was almost shocked when the superintendent firearms adviser, and detective superintendent had agreed.

'Did the armed officers have BWV?' Nige asked, referring to body-worn video cameras that uniformed cops routinely wore.

'Aye, fortunately, as they had about thirty minutes to prepare. I'm bloody glad they did. You'll never see a more righteous shooting, Nige. Mannie was unloading his Glock through the skin of the door. It's still clutched in his hand.'

'Mate, the panic on the net is something to behold, particularly as details are so bloody scant.' He sniggered and took a sip of tea. 'I have to say the fire brigade rescue dummies was a genius idea, who came up with that?' said Nige.

'Tavish.'

'Who?'

'Local special constable, reserve firefighter, and lifeboat crew member. They had a couple of the mannequins, and one of the CPR trainer dummies. He also had a shit load of blood he was saving up to make black pudding, which was really sneaky of the bastard,' said Max with a chuckle.

'He sounds a character, where's he gone?' said Nige.

'Fire station around the corner together with the custody officer, keeping Frankie Hardie out of the way.'

'Is that not risky? He's a bloody Hardie, after all.'

'You'd not say that if you'd seen Tavish. He's a man-mountain, and to be fair to Frankie, I think he's feeling safer hanging with us.'

'Fair one, and he's probably right, bearing in mind these bastards were willing to execute two cops. They didn't know they were dummies, that's for sure.'

'Have you looked in the car?' said Nige.

'Not properly, just a cursory check once the surviving gunmen were dragged out. They both had phones in their pockets, which we have seized,' said Max.

'How about the dead man?'

'Gordon Malone was his name, known as Droopy. It's a bit of a mess in there, but there's a chunky phone in the centre console, which I'm confident will be encrypted. It's certainly not like any phone you see regularly.'

'Anything else in the car?' said Nige.

'As I said we've been covering the prisoners, so haven't looked properly, and being honest, I'm reluctant until any of the bosses are here. Miles Wakefield may well go fucking doolally,' said Max, looking at the car and the five holes in the driver's door. He knew he really shouldn't look, but something was telling him that this may be the last opportunity before half the world arrived, and they wouldn't get access for a while. Once the PIRC were here, all bets were off. They'd never let them within a mile of the car.

'Max, you look like you're thinking deeply. That's always a worrying sign,' said Janie.

'How about a quick visual scan of the car's interior? Droopy received a call on the way here, but just the one on the encrypted phone, that doesn't seem right. You saw the assault, they planned it meticulously, Droopy went straight into the office, breaching the door with the shotgun. That strikes me of planning and pre-existing knowledge. How would they know the layout like that, if someone hadn't told them? They didn't have time to do a detailed recce.'

'Why would he use a simple burner when he has an encrypted phone?' said Janie.

'An encrypted phone still leaves a trace and will still use the same IMEI and IMSI numbers. If he uses a brand-new burner with a new SIM for each job, then it's another level of confusion, I guess. And he can just toss the burner after the job. Encrypted phones cost a fortune.'

'I guess. PIRC are gonna go mental, Max.'

'Aye, maybe. So, we film what we do on BWV, and justify it as we urgently need any comms data from in that car. Some bent bastard fed them the name of Frankie's solicitor whose car was lumped up, and I'm betting that someone gave them the layout of the cop shop. We know that someone influential has been at the top of this, but it couldn't be just Droopy. How did they know when and where Davie would be to shoot him? How did they know the layout of this place? We can't wait for the PIRC to release this, they're too slow.'

'A wee shufti can't hurt, but glove up, yeah?' said Nige, producing some nitrile gloves from his pocket and handing them to Max and Janie, who snapped them into place.

'Okay, let's do it. Danny, can you switch on your BWV?' said Max.

Danny reached to the small dark box secured to his body armour and pressed a switch. It began to flash with a red light. 'We're filming,' said the armed officer.

'Okay, this is an urgent flash search of the suspect's vehicle, for safety reasons. Primary aims are any communications devices on which evidence may be available, but could be at risk of auto deletion after a certain amount of time has elapsed.'

Max pulled his penlight from his pocket and switched it on as he approached the car.

Janie was on the passenger side and began shining her torch through the open window. 'I'm going to give a commentary for the benefit of the camera. Lots of gore here, presumably has come from the deceased, who is currently sat in the driver's seat and is pretty encrusted, fortunately window being open is allowing a good view. I can see the large and chunky phone in the middle of the centre console. It appears to have a flashing light on the screen, possibly indicating notification. Something in the cupholder, Max.'

'What is it?'

'It's closer to your side, but I think it could be a SIM card.'

Max approached the driver's side window, which was also rolled down, trying not to look at the lolling head of Droopy, whose eyes were still wide open and seemingly staring at Max. His heartbeat beginning to accelerate as the stench of death assaulted his nostrils, Max felt his stomach tighten. 'Not now,' he muttered to himself, as the beginnings of familiar nausea started to bubble. He bent down, his head close to the open window and saw what Janie had seen. It was a single micro-SIM. So Droopy had changed SIMs on this trip, meaning that there could be evidence available on it.

Maybe a new number? 'Aye, it's a SIM. How far away are Ross and Barney?' said Max.

'Last I heard an hour, but that was about half an hour ago. What are you thinking?'

'I'm thinking we get Barney to download the SIM.'

'Will that help us if it was in an EncroPhone?' said Janie.

Max considered this. They knew that Droopy changed SIMs regularly in his phone, and now it seemed clear why. Ditching SIMs after every call made it almost impossible to follow phone data, and if the EncroPhone couldn't be cracked, which was likely, then the phone wouldn't help them at all. If that SIM had been removed from the EncroPhone after being used, they'd know about it from the data obtained via Norma.

'Maybe we leave it. We can get the data from Norma.' Max looked around the inside of the car, trying to ignore the oozing blood, brain and shards of bone on the roof, dashboard and windscreen.

He sighed, a sinking feeling in his gut. 'This is a waste—'

A green wink of a light from the driver's door pocket caught his eye, and the words died in his throat. He shone his torch down into the black space, and his heart lurched.

A tiny, dark plastic mobile phone was nestled in the door pocket. It flashed again, a pinprick of light on the top of the handset.

'Janie, phone Barney, and find out how long they'll be,' said Max, reaching down into the door pocket and picking out the phone with a thumb and forefinger. He pressed a key on the side of the phone, and it lit up, the greenish hue casting a ghostly shadow on Droopy's ruined head, the crusted blood almost black in the half-light. There was a preview of a message on the screen.

I need an update urgently. The message had been received just thirty minutes ago.

Max withdrew his head from the car and looked across to Janie, who returned his gaze with a frown. 'I'm just on the phone to Barney now, who's twenty minutes away with Ross, what's up?'

'Get Ross to make all the calls. This job needs locking down tight as a drum. No press release, no comments, nothing at all, and in particular, "need to know" in force, we have a leak, but we have an opportunity, as long as we control the flow of information.'

'Ross is swearing a great deal and asking what the devil is happening? Although he may have used more salty language,' said Janie.

'We've a burner phone, and I think that The Ace messaged Droopy half an hour ago. We have a live phone for him.'

61

ROSS AND BARNEY arrived, as promised, within twenty minutes, Barney at the wheel of his camper van, and Ross scowling in the passenger seat, as they pulled up outside the police station.

Danny and his team had left in a marked car and were on their way to Ullapool police station, which had been designated for the post-incident debrief and holding location. As they'd used lethal force, clear cut though it was, the post-incident procedure was now in full swing. They'd be confined to the debrief location until the initial investigation had taken place, BWV had been viewed, firearms seized for examination and initial accounts recorded.

The crime scene manager had arrived and the cordon was in place around the police station, the car containing the body of Droopy and the two police cars that had been shot up with the mannequins inside them. There was still no sign of the PIRC investigators, and Max was confident they'd be some time yet.

'Fucking hell, Craigie, here we go again, you're a bloody Jonah, you are. I'm starting to think that working with you may be detrimental to every facet of my bastard life.' Ross had appeared as if by magic at Max's side.

'Hi, Ross,' said Max, and he was surprised to feel a smile stretching across his face.

'I've had Miles on the blower just a few minutes ago, he's about fifteen minutes away and, I was surprised to hear, sounding rather sanguine,' said Ross.

'Sanguine. That's not a word I'm used to hearing you use.'

'Because you never listen, and underestimate me all the time,' said Ross.

Barney snorted with amusement. 'Miles was on speaker phone, and he actually used the word. He then had to translate for 'im.'

'Shut up, you old get, I had to put up with your shite driving for bloody ages, and worse your overactive bowels. Honestly, a canary in a bloody cage would be a good idea, man.'

'It was the battered sausage and chips with curry sauce, what can I tell you?' said Barney, rubbing his stomach.

'Aye, eating that shite and I had to suffer.'

'You had a bloody full fish supper, with a sausage on the side, so don't give me gyp about health food, or I'll tell Mrs Fraser.' Barney shot him a warning look trying to suppress a smile.

'All right, settle down you two. We have a burner phone with an unread message, but first, Ross, is this information being locked down? It's imperative that what has happened doesn't leak,' said Max.

'Aye, totally. Miles knows that there's been a shooting and an assault on the cop shop but as he was on his way here, he's happy to wait for an in-person briefing.'

''Ow about the phones?' said Barney, looking at Max.

'We've a simple Samsung, and there's a weird-looking EncroPhone in the car. What do you suggest, Barney?'

'I should be able to download the Samsung easy enough. Shite password protection on those. The Encro is a different matter.'

'Will whoever sent the message to the Samsung know we've read it?'

'Maybe. Hard to tell,' said Barney, taking the phone, which was sealed in a bag, from Max's hand and studying it, his face rapt with concentration. 'If I just download the handset, it may remain unopened, depends what you want to do.'

Max frowned in thought. 'If we wait too long, he'll start to get suspicious, does Miles know about it, Ross? He's the boss, and we don't want to piss him off.'

'He knows you have it, and he appreciates the urgency. We need to come up with a plan. Can we use the phone to reply to the sender?'

Barney thoughtfully turned the burner over in his hand. 'Again, possibly, but it's risky and whilst I can bypass the password to download, I may not get access to the actual handset. Also, if Droopy had something installed in the phone, it may auto-wipe, and we'll lose the lot. If it's a dirty phone, there may be something vital on it. I say we should just download it first, that way I can safely bypass the security. Once we have a safe download, we can make a decision.'

'Okay, fine. We'll do that, Miles will be fine about it. He accepts that this is our best opportunity, and he accepts the need for immediate action. It's fortunate that we're in the arse end of nowhere, or the press would be all over this. In fact, I'll get onto the boss about this now,' said Ross.

'Yeah, good call. We can't totally stop this getting out, but if we leave it suitably brief then our man may assume that their operation was a success, but time is of the essence, let's get this phone sorted,' said Max.

'In the station, I could murder a cuppa,' said Ross.

'Sorry, no good. The crime scene manager has cordoned it off, no more entrance into the station.'

'I'll get kettle on in't van then, lads,' said Barney with a snort.

'Oh shite, more of your irritable bowel, haven't I suffered enough?'

*

When the kettle began to whistle, Max tipped the boiling water into four mugs with teabags in, while Barney sat in the reversed driver's seat of the van, now parked a hundred metres away from the police station, in a small petrol station.

Barney had inserted a cable into the phone and connected it to a metallic square box. A few moments later he unpacked an SD memory card from a blister pack and slotted it into a small slit on the side of the box. He pressed a few keys on the box, and smiled when a green light flashed.

'That was a quick download. There'll be sod all on the phone, I can tell you that,' he said, handing the phone back to Max, who returned it to the evidence bag.

Barney accepted a steaming mug from Max as he slotted the memory card into his scuffed and battered laptop that was festooned with Leeds United stickers. He whistled tunelessly as he tapped at the keys.

He paused to sip his tea and screwed up his face. 'Too much bloody milk. Bloody non-Yorkshire folk 'ave no bloody idea how to make a cuppa. Anyway, here we are. Right. No photos, no internet, but he's been using it for sat-nav. Phone was switched on somewhere north of Inverness and they sat-navved all the way here. He received a WhatsApp en route from someone he'd obviously saved as "Ace".'

All four sets of eyes exchanged looks as the implications landed.

'What'd it say?' said Ross.

'Just "Lochinver. Now." To which he replied, "I know. We're travelling up. Will update when objective completed."'

There was silence in the van.

'So, let me get this straight. He already knew Lochinver was the destination,' said Janie.

'Yes. He knew because he was tracking the solicitor, but he hadn't told The Ace.'

'So, who told The Ace?' said Ross.

'That'd be nice to know. There's our bent man on the inside. How well was the location locked down?' asked Max.

'Fairly tight. Obviously NCA PPU operational head knew, as he had to deploy his staff for the escort, but they didn't even know final destination until they were almost there.' Ross sipped his tea, and grimaced. 'Any biscuits?'

'Who else?'

'Well, I was basically forced to tell Miles and the DCC when I was getting my arse chewed a few hours ago.'

'Miles again? His name keeps cropping up all the bloody time,' said Janie.

'What, Miles? You can't think it's Miles Wakefield? He's a bit of a stuffed shirt, but shit, he's a decent bloke. I've known him my whole service.' Ross shook his head, but there was hesitancy in his movements.

Max just shrugged. 'Who would have thought some of the bent cops we've brought down were actually bent before we got the evidence? Not like we've never been surprised, is it?'

'There's another message in here. A standard SMS message that was delivered a few hours ago. New number I've not encountered before,' said Barney, looking up from the laptop.

'Go on,' said Ross.

'"It's a small one-man station with police house attached. Public entrance leads to small office. Corridor off the office at the end of which is a shower and a small cell. Hard wooden door with spyhole, steel key on main station bunch, normally on desk or on a hook. Fire exit to the rear."'

The silence in the van was overpowering.

'Get both those numbers to Norma, now. Urgent search required, including live-trace cell sites, okay?' said Ross, rubbing his face with his hands.

'Droopy had someone else on the inside, and it seems that neither The Ace or the contact know about each other. Droopy was playing them off against each other,' said Max.

'What next then? Can we use Droopy's phone, put a call or a text in to The Ace and flush him out?'

'Phone's still locked, and if I try and bypass it, it may cause a problem, but we know the number and I've an idea,' said Barney.

'Sure, you have, old timer, but we still have to brief Miles, and we still have a lot of shit to deal with up here.'

'I know, but we have a live phone for The Ace, who is currently waiting for dead Droopy's call. Surely, we can do something with that?' said Max.

'There is, but we also have another problem, we have a bent cop close enough to cause problems. We need to sort that first,' said Janie.

'Okay, Miles will be here imminently, so we can sort the strategy for the press. We need The Ace to think that the operation was successful, he can't know that Droopy is no longer with us, okay?' Ross picked up his phone from the desk which was buzzing like a demented bee. 'Speak of the devil. Miles, my dear boss, what's happening?' He paused for a moment. 'Fine, we'll join you, there in a jiffy.'

'Jiffy?' said Barney, his face incredulous.

'Aye, jiffy. Come on. Miles is here and he wants a chat.'

62

Breaking news: Shooting in remote Highland village

There are early reports of a fatal shooting after an attack on a police station in northwest Scotland. A Police Scotland spokesperson said, 'An incident is ongoing in Lochinver in Sutherland during which firearms were discharged and an individual was sadly killed. The public are strongly advised to stay away from the area, and local officers will be engaging with residents for reassurance purposes.

'This is a live investigation and there will be no further updates until family members of the deceased have been informed.'

More to follow . . .

The Ace looked at the scant report and smiled. WhatsApp showed that Droopy had been online quite recently. Maybe this whole bloody situation could soon be over.

63

ROSS WAS ON the phone to Norma about the recently received phone data when DCS Miles Wakefield had arrived with Malky Douglas at the wheel of a small Hyundai saloon.

Ross listened to Norma's report, feeling a tightness in his stomach, as he looked around him. 'Thanks, Norma. Miles and Malky have just turned up, can you relay everything you just said to me to Max? He's in the van with Barney and Janie.'

He hung up and surveyed the busy crime scene as he approached Wakefield. CSIs were working under the harsh lights that had been erected. There were cop cars enforcing a strict cordon, which fortunately was simple enough to manage, as the village was essentially a long road, with the sea to one side.

As soon as they had arrived, Miles had sent Malky off with a list of questions to get answered for his briefing with the Chief.

'How about the media?' said Ross.

'The Chief and the press office have sold the usual line. "Ongoing incident, public warned to be vigilant, no more updates until families of victim updated."'

'That's nicely vague. Is the DCC handling the press?' said Ross.

'No, Chief's on point from home, DCC is out of range on her phone, but she's not on call tonight. She'll hear about it when she wakes up. The press release will keep them at bay for a while, but we need to move fast.'

'Okay, look, Miles. We clearly have a bent cop on the inside and close to the investigation. We've kept any details of what's happened here totally quiet, but we have to go further. Whoever is on the inside here needs to believe that Frankie Hardie is dead. So, we keep the press release brief and anodyne, and keep what happened here totally off the radar, yeah?'

'We're on it already. Chief's press strategy is tight, and nothing has gone out on the net, and there will be no further info releases either inside or outside the force without my authorisation. Can't be any clearer than that, eh?'

'Good, my guys are ready for the next phase.'

'Fortunately, with the geography of this place we can easily have big cordons and keep any press who venture this far north at bay. So, what is it that you couldn't say earlier?'

'We have a live phone for The Ace. I've just heard from Norma now that it's cell-siting in Edinburgh.'

'What?'

'Aye. Droopy had a burner, and it had received a message from it. Looks like he was giving the location away.'

'But I thought that Droopy tracked the solicitor's car?'

'Aye, he did, but it seems The Ace found out directly from someone else as well, and they're not talking to each other. Droopy wasn't satisfied with just getting his info from The Ace, he's got someone on the inside of the investigation as well.'

'What?' Miles looked at Ross, his mouth agape and eyes wide.

Ross just shrugged, pulling out his phone that had buzzed in his pocket, just as Malky joined them. 'I've a report for you, boss,' Malky said.

Ross looked at the DS, who had his phone in his hand as he ran through a list of actions that were in hand at the scene. 'Scene's under control, the body is staying in place until daylight and arrival of PIRC and pathologist. Forensic tent is up, and scene cordons are all in place. I'm hearing that one of the raiders is dead, where's Frankie?'

'Thanks, Malky. Who's doing production retention?' said Wakefield.

'Not sure yet, but DCI Davies isn't far away, and she's with the core team.'

Ross looked towards the petrol station at Barney's van, visible in the low streetlights. He tapped his fingers on the phone and composed the message. **Now.**

Ross pocketed his phone and looked at Miles and Malky as they spoke. Suddenly there was a buzzing that came from Malky's pocket. He flinched, just a touch, but carried on speaking, but his eyes gave him away as they flicked from side to side. He was scared.

'Why don't you answer the phone, Malky?' said Ross, his eyes flint-hard, his voice low and menacing.

'I . . . it's my personal phone, I'll leave it for later, boss,' he said, his voice cracking.

'Nah, I think you should answer it, pal.' Ross fixed the DS with a glare, just as the buzzing stopped. There was a cloying silence as Ross eyed the man.

'Ross?' began Miles.

Ross didn't take his eyes from Malky. 'You're a legacy northern constabulary man, that's right, Malky, eh?'

Malky looked at Ross and Miles in turn. 'Aye,' he said, eyes wide, and face ghostly pale in the dark.

'Ex-paratrooper as well, I'm hearing?'

'Ross, what the hell's going on?' said Miles.

'Served at this station, right? This tiny, wee place just here. Spent four years as the village bobby, no?' Ross nodded towards the white building, which was bathed in an artificial glow from the scene lights.

'Aye, but that was years . . .' He stopped dead, just as the buzzing started up in his pocket once again.

'Answer the fucking phone, Malky. Answer it fucking now, or I'll get it out of your pocket and jam it up your bloody arse.'

Max and Janie suddenly appeared almost out of nowhere, Max

holding his phone up, the screen illuminated as it showed the number being called. 'Your phone number, Malky. The same number that texted Gordy Malone, also known as Droopy, just a few hours ago, giving him the precise layout of this police station.'

Max and Janie each seized one of Malky's arms, and Ross went to the man's jacket pocket and pulled out the phone. 'Hello, Max,' he said.

'Hello, Ross,' said Max into the handset.

Miles just stood there, mouth agape, and looked at his DS. 'Oh, Malky, what have you bloody done?'

64

'**HOW THE HELL** did you know it was Malky?' said Miles as Max and Janie were escorting the handcuffed DS to a marked police car.

'I didn't. But it was either you, Malky or the DCC, and I didn't think it was her, she's too much of a nugget. Has Malky made any calls on the way up, or sent any messages?' Ross said.

'No, he was driving, so I think we can be sure he's not tipped off anyone.' Miles scratched his head, his face a picture of disbelief.

'That's a relief. We have to keep it that The Ace believes Frankie is dead.'

'So, you suspected me?' Miles's voice was hard.

'You and the DCC were the only people I told about the location, and I just couldn't see it being her. I'm no' keen, but she's only just arrived, and my Met source assures me she had a reputation for being dead straight, if a little bit up her own arse.'

'By Met source, I assume you mean Max?'

'Aye well, he made the call, so I prefer "Met source, once removed". So that left you, Miles, but I've known you a long time, and whilst you can be a bampot at times, you're no' a bent bugger. I figured that Malky would have access to your stuff, and I saw you writing down this location when I was getting a bollocking from you and the DCC earlier.'

'I should give you a row for calling me a bampot, but in this instance, you're correct. Fucking Malky Douglas, what was the ex-para thing?' Miles scratched at his scalp; the stress was leaching off him almost in waves.

'Malone was ex-para before the Legion, so I figured that it wasn't beyond the realms of possibility that they served together. Who knows what shite they got up to, eh? When I found out about the burner with the details of the station, I thought it had to be you, but I didn't buy it, so I just wondered who else had access to your logs, and Malky was the only real choice. Norma quickly researched him, and found out that he'd served at Lochinver, and had been a paratrooper for a few years as a young man. It struck me then that he and Malone could have served at the same time, and you know how the airborne stick together.'

'I wasn't a soldier, so no.'

'Two things drop from the sky, Miles. Birdshit and paratroopers. Anyway, enough blether, we need to crack on. Can we carry on with identifying The Ace?' Ross sat on the wall, wincing.

'How about Malky?'

'We let the bugger stew in a cell somewhere and we'll interview him when we're ready, but he's incommunicado, much as I'm confident that his contact is now leaking brains in a car over there. Even so, not so much as a bloody phone call, even though I don't think he's a link to The Ace. All the evidence is that Malone kept them unaware of each other, as both supplied this place.'

'Yes, get on with it, you have a plan?'

'I need to get together with my people, and come up with something, fast. The Ace will be expecting information, and the only person he or she would be getting said information from would be Malone.'

'So, what do we need to do? We've no idea who The Ace is, and our main link is now dead. At least we've plugged the leak in the team.'

'I'm not so sure about that.' Ross's eyebrows bristled, and his eyes were hard.

'What?'

'Who told The Ace that the debrief location was Lochinver?'

Miles just stood there, stunned. 'Could it be Malky?'

'Unlikely. Two messages into Malone's phone, one we know is from Malky, the other is from The Ace. I'd say they don't even know each other exist. We can check phones and the like, but there's no doubt about it, someone told The Ace that the location was Lochinver. Malky was just giving Malone the layout of the place. We still need to keep this as tight as a duck's arse, Miles. Literally no one outside my team, the Chief and you can know about it. There has to be another leak, somewhere, either a cop, or the NCA. No one else knew about the debrief location.'

'Ach, fucking hell. I'm getting sick of constantly chasing our tails here. Whenever we think we're making inroads there's another corrupt bastard trying to screw things up. What do you suggest, bearing in mind we have no time at all to play with?' Miles loosened his tie and undid the top button of his shirt.

'We'll come up with something, don't fret. I've a psychologically damaged ex-Met DS, an uptight, ex-public-school DC, a potty-mouthed analyst and an ageing, freeloading ex-spook on it. We're bringing this bastard in, boss. That's a promise.'

65

MAX AND JANIE were sitting in the crew room at the fire station, just over a mile away from the police station. Frankie was sitting in front of them, a mug of tea in his hand and the imposing form of Tavish next to him. Frankie looked pale and tired, but he stared open-mouthed at them when they explained what exactly had happened.

'So, fucking Droopy actually came for me. He was going to bust in the cop shop and fucking waste the lot of us?' His face was white as a sheet, which only accentuated his blood-shot eyes.

'Aye. We're lucky that we got wind of it, and were able to get you to safety. We need your help, and we need it now, Frankie. Shit's happening, and we need to know what you know.'

'How about a solicitor?' he said, but Max could tell his heart wasn't it.

'Frankie, we just need what you know in quick time. We need to find out who the bloody "Ace" is, and we need to know now before he gets wind that Droopy is dead. What evidence did your dad have on The Ace?'

'Look, I want to help. I really do. You lot saved my life, and you've been dead straight, but Pa and Tam never really trusted me. I've never seen it, but I know he had something huge on someone who became big and powerful, but I don't know who it is.' He took a long sip of his tea, and rubbed his cheeks with trembling hands.

'You must know something, no matter how small. We have to find this bastard, Frankie. He had an innocent woman killed, he's killed your brother, he's killed Slattery, Mitch and others. He won't stop. You'll never be truly safe with The Ace willing to pay out serious money to have you silenced.'

'But I don't know anything,' Frankie said, his voice rising several octaves.

'That's as may be, but he doesn't know that, does he?'

'Oh fuck. I'm screwed.' Frankie buried his face in his hands.

'Come on, man. There must be something,' said Janie, a touch of irritation in her voice.

'Look, all I know is what I heard. Pa telling Tam about some kompromat that he had on The Ace. Something that would finish them off for good, as it was proof that he ordered that lassie killed six years ago. I'm sure he'd have handed it to Tam once he knew he was dying.'

'Where was it kept?' asked Max.

'I don't know where he kept it, but I saw it once. Just a small computer card in its wee plastic case with "Ace" written on it in Sharpie. I heard him saying something along the lines of, "contents of this will really fuck the bastard up". Pa was really careful with his computer, and his secrets generally. He would tell Tam stuff, but never me. I was just muscle. Being the best fighter in the family didn't mean I had status.'

'Kompromat?'

'What?'

'You used the word "kompromat".'

'Aye, that's what Pa called it, and so did Tam Junior.'

'How about Davie?'

'I heard him say it, but I don't think he even knew that much either. I certainly don't reckon he knew the identity of The Ace. All he did was dispose of the girl's body.' He paused to sip from his tea.

'You're sure he used the word "kompromat"?' said Max.

'Aye, a hundred per cent. I didn't even know what it meant, so I googled it. Compromising material for blackmail, I seem to remember.'

'When did you overhear them talking about it?' said Janie.

'Not long before Pa went missing.'

'Where were they?'

'In the kitchen at the old house, I think.'

Max nodded at Janie. 'We need to go. Frankie, you're going somewhere safe with Tavish and Steve. We'll come and see you as soon as we can.'

'And then what?'

'Then we do this properly, with a lawyer, and somewhere properly safe.'

'Is the deal still on?'

'Aye, of course.'

'Even though I know nothing?'

'You know plenty, Frankie. You just don't know what you know,' said Max, clapping him on the shoulder.

'Despite being polis, you two buggers are okay, really.' A smile stretched over Frankie's face, which was pale and lined with fatigue.

'Get some sleep, we'll see you later,' said Max.

He and Janie stood up to leave.

'Max?'

'Aye?'

'Get the bastard, won't you? Not just for me, but for that poor wee lassie. She deserves justice.'

66

JANIE DROVE THE Volvo with her customary skill as they hit the Slochd Summit on the A9, the main route linking the Highlands with the central belt of Scotland. The sun was emerging from above the horizon, the light hitting the summits of the ice-capped munros, transforming them from dull grey to bright, burnished orange. They were heading south towards Edinburgh.

Max sat in the passenger seat, his notepad open in front of him, his phone clamped to his ear. Barney was in the back of the car, his laptop open, Droopy's bagged phone at his side, as he tapped away at the keyboard, a look of intense concentration on his face and an unlit roll-up in his mouth. 'Sure I can't light this? I work better with a tab on the go,' he said, looking up from the keyboard.

'No, you bloody can't,' said Janie.

'I can't believe you even asked, Barney. How's it going?' said Max, through a yawn.

'Worth a punt, mate. I'm almost ready to go with this phone malarky, it's all set up.'

'Okay, hold fire a minute, I'm just waiting for Ross to answer.'

'He'll be struggling with hands-free in't van, which, incidentally I can't believe you persuaded me to let him drive,' Barney said, shaking his head.

Max was chuckling when Ross eventually answered with a load of background noise, and muffled curses. 'Fucking shite thing. Ah, fucking . . . how's this piece of crap work?' This was followed by some beeps before Ross managed to answer the phone. 'What's so fucking funny? Bloody blueteeth system is shite, whatever happened to a radio, eh? Max, what's bastard going on? I'm stuck on my own, driving this hunk of shite that stinks of pish and rich tea biscuits, why couldn't I come in the Volvo?'

'You know why, we need Barney with us, and you're not known for your running ability in case we need to chase the bugger. Just saying that we're ready to send the message,' said Max, grinning at Janie.

'Are we sure this'll work? It's our only shot.'

'Barney thinks so.'

''Course it'll bloody work, I'm a borderline tech genius,' said Barney from the back of the car without looking from his screen.

'Okay, when are you sending?'

'I'm ready, and it's almost eight-thirty. As good a time as any. I'll send the message, and we can stop for a bit of brekkie at Ralia services. I'm chuffin' starving,' said Barney.

'Right, get on with it, and keep me in the loop, I may stop for a bite myself.'

'Don't break my bloody van, Ross.'

'Ah, get fucked, you MI5 reject.' The three tones on the phone indicated that Ross had gone.

'Remind me how this works, then?' said Janie.

'I use voice over internet protocol, and deploy a piece of software that will mimic Droopy's number on WhatsApp. A bit of jiggery-pokery from this end so once I send whatever you want me to send, it will appear as if it's come from Droopy's phone.'

'And you're sure it'll work?' said Max.

'Aye, easy as. It's a two bob fraudster's trick. You know, phone or message an old dear and pretend to be from her bank.'

'Okay, let's go for it then.'

'I'm ready.' Barney looked up, fingers paused over the keys.

67

D: Mission successful.

Ace: Thank God for that, where have you been?

D: Keeping my head down. It got noisy and we needed a comms blackout.

Ace: Any problems?

D: No. I have the kompromat. It was with cops.

Ace: What is it?

D: Frankie had it all the time. Just an SD card marked 'ace'

Ace: And now you have it?

D: You want it?

Ace: Of course I do. When?

D: How much is it worth? No other copies, they didn't have chance

Ace: I've paid you already.

D: We had to take big risk. People are dead. I need more money. Or I can send to cops. Or newspaper.

Ace: How much?

D: Fifty

Ace: . . . Which account?

D: New one. J Callender. Kwik Bank 11-09-88 20909828

Ace: Where for handover.

D: I'll send location when funds received.

68

'NOW THEN. THE soft lad's only gone and bought it,' said Barney after he'd read the messages out from his laptop.

'Needs the funds transferred, that proves intent, and hopefully gives us an account to work on.' Max looked at the display on his phone, which had just buzzed. A message from Katie.

2pm tomorrow. Don't forget :-)

He tapped out a reply, **as if.** 'Pick up the pace, Janie. We need to get this done.'

'Are you going to write the tickets off, sarge?' said Janie, mashing down on the accelerator, and switching on the siren and blue lights that were concealed within the radiator grille.

'Not if you call me sarge again. We need to be in Edinburgh quick as we can.'

'What's the rush?' said Janie as she expertly overtook a long line of cars, all of whom had been abiding by the speed-camera-enforced limit of sixty miles per hour.

'Let's say there's somewhere I need to be at a particular time tomorrow.'

'Do tell?' she said as she dived back into the correct lane, and smoothly pushed the car over a hundred, her voice never deviating from calm and collected. This was Janie at her happiest. Driving the big car at big speeds with immunity from prosecution.

'Never mind. Tell you another day.' His phone buzzed again; it was Norma. **Hitting cell tower in Portobello. No other calls in or out. Been there all night**. 'Looks like he's Portobello way, keep up the pace.'

'Blimey, he's not buggering about,' Barney said from the back. 'Fifty grand's landed in the account I just opened. I'm forwarding the sending bank account details straight to Norma. He really must want that kompromat back. What now?'

'Just reply to him on WhatsApp. Funds received, standby for dead drop location.'

'On it. What time?' said Barney, tapping away.

Max looked at his watch. It was just after 9 a.m. Plenty of time. 'Let's make the bugger sweat. If he asks what time, just say. "Await instructions."'

'On it like a car bonnet, lad.'

'Shall I keep this breakneck speed up?' said Janie, hopefully.

'You want to keep driving like this?'

'Damn straight I do. I want this job done.'

'Then crack on.'

69

D: 55.95171838347938, -3.1663923174757547.

Ace: What's that mean?

D: Coordinates. Copy into Google Maps and it'll take you to kompromat. Bottom right of sign, taped to rear. It's there now, so I'd hurry up before someone else finds it. You wouldn't want that.

Ace: Leaving now. Will I see you there?

D: No. We'll watch the well from a distance for thirty minutes, then we're off, I'd make it quick in case anyone saw us put it there. After that I'm gone.

The Ace copied the numbers from the message and pasted them into Google Maps. He smiled; the location was familiar. In fact, it was very familiar. A twenty-minute walk, or a five-minute drive. The sun pierced a shaft of light through the window, bathing the room in a pleasant warmth.

It'd be a nice walk at this time of day, and the park would be quiet.

The Ace stood and grabbed a coat from the stand in the corner of the office and set off, a warm glow replacing the gnawing anxiety.

70

'ARE WE ALL set?' said Max, looking at Janie and Barney across the surface of the table in Barney's van, which was in a quiet spot in the car park that sat at the beginning of Holyrood Park in the centre of Edinburgh.

'I'm all set. Are we good to go?' said Barney.

'Give it a minute, can we finish our tea first? I don't know about you guys, but I'm bloody knackered,' said Max, yawning extravagantly.

'Goes wi' the turf, mate. We're almost there now.' Barney drained his cup before reaching down and bringing out the drone case, flipping the catches open and pulling out the gadget. He quickly extended the arms and slotted the propeller blades in place, then the battery.

'How long can it stay up?' said Janie.

'This is a new battery, so forty-five minutes, especially if I get a decent height and go into a steady hover.'

'We need good images; I want it lurid and in four K,' said Max.

'It will be, lad, don't fret.'

'Go for it.'

Barney slid the van door open and laid the drone on the ground. He fiddled with the control unit, and the blades began to spin. The drone shot straight up with a familiar whine. Within a few seconds, the sound had gone.

'Bloody remarkable, I wish we'd had these in Afghan, it would've saved a lot of smashing down of compound walls.'

'Same here. Wish I'd had them in Crossmaglen, would have saved being up to my knees in peat bogs. Right, hovering over target location now. Footage is streaming to the iPad on the side.' Barney nodded at the worktop.

Max leant over, picked up the tablet and woke the screen. A pin-sharp image of Holyrood Park was displayed. The few pedestrians were like small dots of colour in the wide-open expanse of vivid green grass, with the grey hues of the city to the east.

'Okay, tighten in. Let's see what view we've got,' said Max.

'Zooming in now.' Barney fiddled with the controls once again, the wide image narrowing sharply until it focused in on a small path that came off Queen's Drive, the long, straight road that bisected the north of the park.

'Tighter, I want to be able to read the sign, Barney.'

'Wrong angle. I'll never get the sign.'

'I was joking, Barney, as tight as you can.' The image zoomed in again on a small square of concrete, close to the shape of a leather patch.

'This is as tight as I can go without getting lower.'

'It's fine. Now we wait. He'll be here soon.'

'Why here?' said Barney.

'What, St Margaret's Well? That was Janie's idea.'

'Close to the car park so we can sit here without standing out, close to the city so The Ace doesn't have far to come and easy to fly the drone at a decent height and pick out the corrupt bastard,' she answered.

'Any other reason?' said Max, his voice laced with sarcasm.

'No,' said Janie, a little too quickly.

'Fibber,' said Max.

Janie shifted uneasily in her seat. 'Well, the water flows from a pipe in a carved grotesque mask. It just seemed a little symbolic to me. I mean The Ace has been shielding behind a mask of respectability for years, right?'

'You are such a bloody geek,' Max said, chuckling.

'Piss off.'

'Piss off, *sergeant*.'

Barney cleared his throat. 'Whilst you two are bantering really badly, I think we have a customer.'

Max and Janie grinned and then turned back to the screen. A lone figure was walking along the path towards the well. He was dressed in a black jacket and wearing a woollen beanie hat. Barney adjusted the position of the drone and zoomed in tighter. The figure stopped, looking all around him, his hands going to his face.

'Well, *hello* there,' said Max.

Janie looked up and smiled at Max. 'This is the best bit, isn't it?'

'Aye. The moments before the strike. Come on, you corrupt bastard; we're waiting for you.'

71

THE ACE LOOKED over each shoulder as he walked along the path towards the well, a spot he'd been to on a number of occasions in the past, being a student of history as he was. On this occasion, he had no interest in the ancient well, and his sole intention was to get the kompromat that Tam Hardie had shown him six years ago. Hardie had always been an evil, ruthless bastard and The Ace had almost danced with delight when he'd died, and then his even more evil son had disappeared without trace. He'd had no idea that fucking Davie and Frankie would start causing the problems they had from jail.

Fortunately, Droopy was a resourceful bastard, and scary though he was, he was glad to have had him on his side even with the small fortune it had cost him. Now hopefully, he could carry on living his life without this shit hanging over him.

He stood on the setts at the front of the well, stamping his feet to try to get some blood to them, and wishing he had more appropriate footwear on. He took a last look over his shoulder, thankful that it was quiet and the freezing cold weather had kept the tourists away. Had it been summer this place would have been crawling with Americans, all cooing and taking photographs of the old well. He looked at the ancient grotesque mask with the water dribbling from the pipe, and gritted his teeth as he stretched out his hand to the bottom of the black metal sign, with its perfunctory explanation of the well, which had been moved to its present location in 1860.

His finger went underneath the raised edge of the sign, where it sat proud from the granite. They caught on something smooth and plastic, and his heart leapt as he pulled it away with a snap as the gaffer tape holding it in place gave way. He stood there, looking at the small SD card, with 'Ace' scrawled on it in marker pen. The kompromat that had been hanging over him for the last six years like the sword of Damocles. A smile stretched over his face, and he felt the weight of anxiety and dread suddenly lift from his shoulders.

He was free. Droopy was an evil bastard, but he had morals, and his word was his bond which was why he charged so much money. And with all the Hardie boys now out of the way, he was home free. He chuckled as he turned the card over in his fingers. He'd check it out when he got back to the office, and then, he'd get rid of it forever. The whole story would be as dead as Beata Dabrowski.

He tucked the card into his pocket, turned on his heel and hurried off, looking at his watch. He had an important meeting with the Chief Constable in an hour and he needed to prepare. It'd be too easy now. He was safe.

He picked up his pace, almost feeling like his feet were barely touching the ground as he strode off, enjoying the warming rays of the winter sun.

72

'BOOM,' SAID BARNEY, his eyes glued to the screen, as he steered the drone ahead of the figure that was striding along Queens Drive back towards the city centre.

'Okay, he's got it. We now need to see if we can get a facial shot,' said Max.

'Right, I'll fly ahead of him and wait, how low can I go?'

'How low before it becomes audible?'

'Hundred or so?'

'What, feet?'

'No metres, but with a decent zoom we should be able to clock his fizzog.'

'Okay, do it.'

The picture shifted as the drone swept off and then settled, static and still, above Queens Drive. It zoomed in tight on the approaching figure that walked, head down, at a quick pace, bristling with a sense of purpose.

'He needs to look up a bit, or we're just getting the top of his head, and the hat isn't helping at all, I think it has a small peak on it,' said Barney, his voice tight with frustration.

'Go lower,' said Max, his eyes glued to the screen.

'He may hear us,' said Barney, looking up.

'Doesn't matter, drones are common enough, just go lower, I want him to hear it.'

'You're the boss.' Barney adjusted the controls again and the picture shifted as the drone lost height.

'Do a bit of swooping, so you look like a dodgy amateur, but keep active track on him, we just need him to look up once,' said Max.

'Come on, you bastard, look up, look up now,' said Janie, her eyes fixed on the iPad.

'Dick about, Barney. Swoop all over, acting like you're an ASBO hooligan with a drone, you'll fit right in.'

'Goes against all my instincts, Max,' said Barney as he started to swoop the drone sharp left and right, but the active tracking kept the camera fixed on the striding figure.

'Go on, more. Dive bomb the bastard,' said Max, his voice rising an octave.

Barney pushed both control sticks down, and the drone dropped like a stone; the whining of the drone was suddenly audible to them in the van.

The striding figure looked up, his face a white splodge against the black of his coat and dark beanie.

'Right, zoom off again, acting like a dickhead drone owner, don't worry about being seen. And screenshot the face.'

'Max?' said Janie.

Max sat there, his eyes fixed and hard as he stared at the frozen image of the face looking up at the drone. He grabbed his phone and dialled.

'About time, you bastard, I'm with the Chief and he's having fucking kittens. What's happening?' said Ross.

'I know who The Ace is.'

'Right, nick the bastard right now.'

'I don't think that's the best idea. We have a better opportunity. Barney, how much time do we have left on the drone?'

'Half an hour, easy,' said Barney.

'Remind me what happens if he puts that card in a computer?'

'It'll ruin his day for a start.'

Max stared at the figure, now from a much higher altitude, but the active track kept the camera focused on him. 'Follow him, but gain height, stay out of sight, and see where he goes.'

'Careful you don't lose him,' said Ross.

'It doesn't matter if we do. He's toast, but let's give him the chance to really tuck himself up.'

73

THE ACE WALKED quickly back, head up, a feeling of elation coursing through his veins as he passed the Dynamic Earth visitor centre, sparkling blue-white in the bright sunshine, almost like a huge chrysalis about to pupate.

He continued on to Holyrood Road, keeping his pace up, aware of his meeting that was due very soon on working protocols, and budget transparency, which was more boring than he cared to think of at this particular moment.

The streets were getting busier as he crossed onto Cowgate, with more and more tourists poking around and gazing with awe at the familiar architecture that he rarely even noticed nowadays, after years of working in the city.

His phone buzzed in his pocket as he turned into Chambers Street. It was Maureen, his secretary, asking how long he'd be. He shook his head, she was very efficient, but had crossed that line where she felt that she was the sole custodian of his time and diary.

Within five minutes he was walking back into his wood-panelled office and shutting the door, having more or less ignored Maureen, who just blurted, 'Don't forget the appointment.' He walked straight past her desk and into his office, saying, 'No calls, and no visitors,' before shutting the door.

He removed his coat and hat, and threw them on the stand. He sat at his desk, rubbing the disk in its case between his palms, as if expecting a genie to erupt from it.

He opened up his laptop, and it sprang to life, displaying the logo of the organisation as a screensaver. He took a deep breath, retrieved the card and slotted it into the slot on the side of the laptop, and waited.

```
Run SanDisk programme GR4-9-a-j-7546n9?
Y/N
```

He extended his finger, and paused it over the Y key, his stomach in his mouth. Part of him wanted to see what was on the disk, but part of him didn't, such was his shame at what had happened six years ago. He closed his eyes, and pressed the key.

Nothing happened. Frowning, he pressed again. Still nothing. He searched in the open files section and located the removable disk icon. He clicked on it. The screen went totally blank. Literally dead, and totally inert. He felt a sudden chill descend on him, as if he'd stepped into an industrial freezer. What the hell was happening? Where was the kompromat?

He picked up his phone and went to the WhatsApp icon and looked at the last message from Droopy. He looked at the display, and it showed that he was still online. He began to compose a message, but then thought better of it. He needed to speak to the bastard.

He dialled, and listened to the tones in his ears. The phone diverted to the standard voicemail.

'Please leave a message.'

He spoke in a hoarse whisper, ever aware of the nosy Maureen. 'Droopy, what the hell is going on? The memory card is empty, and now my computer has gone blank. Call me urgently.' He slammed the phone down on his desk, feeling his pulse beginning to whoosh in his ears, and beads of sweat forming on his top lip.

Suddenly the door burst open, and a shaven-headed man and a slim, younger woman entered the room with Maureen hot on their heels.

'Mr Townsend, they just walked straight past me,' her voice was laced with anger, 'how dare you, I've a mind to call the police,' she spat as they totally ignored her and approached.

'I've no idea who the hell you think you are, but I'm the bloody Crown Agent, and I will have you both remov—' He stopped mid-sentence and looked at the shaven-headed man standing in the middle of the room, totally relaxed, appraising him with a look of amusement on his face.

'DS Craigie . . .' he began, but then the words died in his mouth, as the phone began to buzz on his desk. He glanced at the screen, and almost shrivelled in his clothes when he saw that it was Droopy calling.

'You not going to answer that, Mr Townsend?' said Max.

'How dare you burst into my office? I'll be sure to speak to the Chief Constable,' he said, but his voice carried no authority whatsoever.

The phone's buzzing was almost deafening in the stultifying silence of the dusty office.

'It's Droopy, isn't it, Finn? It's Gordy Malone, yeah? Go on, answer it,' Max said. The buzzing suddenly stopped as the phone went to voicemail. Max pulled a phone from his pocket and raised it to his ear. 'Hello, this is a message for the Crown Agent, the principle legal adviser to the Lord Advocate on prosecution matters. You're under arrest on suspicion of the murder of Beata Dabrowski, and conspiracy to murder Jack Slattery, Steven Mitchell, David Hardie, Leo Hamilton, and soliciting the murder of Frankie Hardie.' Max pressed a button on the phone, and then placed it back in his pocket. 'Unfortunately, Droopy can't come to the phone, Finn.'

74

FINN TOWNSEND SAT on a fixed chair next to his solicitor, who had introduced herself as Moira Dougal. She was soft-spoken and friendly, but Max had detected a core of steel in her from the set of her shoulders, and dark, firm eyes. She opened a MacBook on the table, and nodded at Townsend.

'Have you understood the caution, Mr Townsend?' said Janie.

He nodded just once.

'For the tape, please?' said Janie.

'I understand,' he said, his eyes cast downwards.

'Tell us what you know about the murder of Beata Dabrowski,' said Janie.

'No comment.'

'Tell us about your relationship with Beata Dabrowski.'

'No comment.'

'How about your relationship with Gordon Malone, also known as Droopy?'

'No comment.'

'What were you expecting on that computer disk? What was the kompromat?'

Moira Dougal cleared her throat. 'Just to reiterate, officers. My client has been advised to answer no comment to all questions. Now do you have any evidence of his complicity in the murder of Miss Dabrowski? I'm sure you realise that you must disclose it to us, yes?'

'We've given the fullest appropriate disclosure, Ms Dougal,' said Max.

'So you say. Now I must say that beyond proving an association with Mr Malone, by communications data, I've had no material disclosed to me that constitutes evidence of my client's complicity with any of the homicides. It is debatable that the evidence of a phone message allegedly from my client to the man you call "Droopy" constitutes sufficient evidence of any criminality. I'd venture to suggest that the evidence against Malky Douglas clearly puts him at the forefront of this inquiry, wouldn't you say?'

'That inquiry is ongoing. We have clear evidence that Mr Townsend is closely linked to Malone. He was witnessed collecting what he believed was compromising evidence against him.'

'And that was a set-up by you.'

'We just opened the door, he walked through it,' said Janie.

'Well, it strikes me that you've gone to a great deal of trouble to prove my client has a dubious relationship with a man, who has no previous convictions, and it seems that beyond my client sharing the location of Lochinver Police Station with Malone, you – and correct me if I'm wrong – have nothing?' She paused, and smiled again. Not triumphant, not snidey, just mildly querulous.

Max and Janie just looked at each other, the tension in the room crackling like static electricity.

The solicitor sighed and sat back in her chair, steepling her fingers in front of her chin. 'I see. Perhaps let me know if you have evidence that my client has done anything other than, perhaps unwisely, release information about the location of a debrief. Now, that's not particularly desirable behaviour from a man in my client's position, but it's hardly evidence of the grave crimes for which he's accused by yourselves, is it?'

'Let's take a short break, shall we?' said Max.

75

'SHE'S RIGHT, THE bastard. We have him bang to rights for corrupt practice, but not for the murders,' said Max as they walked down the corridor at Edinburgh central police station.

'Well, that's better than nothing,' said Janie, following in Max's wake.

'No chance, it's nowhere near good enough. All this. All the murders, all the dead bodies, all the carnage is down to that bastard. The evidence is out there, we just need to find it. We find the kompromat, and we have him.'

'Are we even sure it exists?'

'It exists.'

'Where do we start, though?'

'Where's Frankie?' said Max, suddenly stopping in the corridor.

'Glasgow city centre custody.'

'Right, let's go, we need to speak to him now. He knows where that fucking evidence is, even if he thinks he doesn't. Let's go now.'

*

Frankie was in a bullish mood as he sat in the interview room at Glasgow central station. It was too busy for anything covert, but the security at the station was tight, and with Droopy out of the picture, it all felt a little safer.

'Come on, Frankie. You must have something. Anything on where the bloody disk is. We need it, or that corrupt bastard is looking at five years, rather than bloody life. He'll essentially walk from this shit that cost your brother his life, as well as all the others. We can't let that happen.' Max sat back in the chair, feeling exhaustion creep up on him like a cloud crossing the sun.

'I've told you. I wasn't trusted, I never saw what was on it, other than I knew it was on some big bastard, even though I couldn't have dreamed it was for the bloody Crown Agent. Shit, my dad was good at this, wasn't he? . . . A top cop last time, and now the top dude at the Crown Office.' He smiled in admiration at his father's achievements.

'Aye, and he's gonna walk unless you can get us to that fucking kompromat. Now think. Where did he keep it?' said Janie, banging her palm on the desk.

'Okay, settle down, hen. Look, he always kept his computer on him, and anything else he locked in his safe.'

Max opened his mouth to retort, then stopped. 'What safe?'

'I don't know. He'd refer to it, but I don't know where it was, I didn't live with him, he lived at Tam's after Ma died. He'd been there a few years before he went missing.'

'Was it at the house?' said Max, referring to the sprawling Glasgow mansion he'd visited when Tam Hardie Senior had first gone missing.

'Most likely.'

'And you've no idea where it was in the house?'

'None. We went to the house for dinner sometimes, and to see Pa and Tam, but I never lived there, and nor did Davie. I had my own flat in the West End, and Davie had his place in Kelvingrove. I do know one thing though.'

'What?' said Janie.

'It'd have been a decent one. Pa never scrimped on shit like that, and he liked a gadget.'

'Any safes at the clubs?'

'Nah. He'd never have had one there, he did'nae trust any bastard, and stayed away from the clubs.'

'So, at the house then?' said Janie.

'Probably, but the house was sold after the asset confiscation. Sold by court order after all Tam's cash was seized. Most of it went back to the Crown. Fucking shame, eh?' He smiled, but then paused and opened his mouth, realisation arriving like a truck.

Max paused as it hit. 'If the safe was well hidden by your pa, and was then cleared by Tam's wife before selling, would she have known where it was?'

'Doubt it. She stayed well out of all the business and was mostly in Cyprus.'

'So, the safe could still be in the house?' Janie's eyes flared open.

'I guess it may be. But you've a problem there.'

'Why?' said Max.

'You know who bought the place, right?' said Frankie, amusement twinkling in his eyes.

'No, I'd moved onto the next case, asset confiscation dealt with all that.'

'The house was bought by Angus McCall.'

Max suddenly felt nauseous. 'What, Angus McCall, major international money launderer, financier and a close associate of most of the big crime gangs across the UK?'

'Aye, apart from us, of course. We didn't get on, which is why we think he bought the house. Just to annoy Tam Junior.'

Max and Janie stared at each other. 'It could be in that house, right now,' said Janie.

Max picked up his phone and dialled.

'How you getting on?' said Ross.

'I think the kompromat is at Hardie's old house in Glasgow.'

'What?'

'Aye, exactly. Look, time is tight, where's Barney?'

'At his free flat, probably with the tumble drier and dishwasher on.'

'Okay, we're heading back to the office. The place is now owned by Angus McCall, so we need to know exactly where he is right now.'

'What, *the* Angus McCall?' Ross sounded incredulous.

'The very same. We need to know exactly where he is, and who's in the house right now. Also get Norma to link into the financial teams that investigated the Hardies, they'll have six years' worth of accounts on file. They need to search for anything to do with security, or having a safe installed. We also need a blueprint for the place, including all the services, it's a new place so they'll be with the planning department.'

'Right, I'll sort out a warrant from the on-call Justice of the Peace.'

'Yeah, we'll need it, but we also need to box clever.'

'Go on.'

'What if it leaks?'

'Shit. You're right, Angus McCall has fingers in many bloody pies, more so than Hardie did. It leaks, we'll be met by an army of lawyers who'll frustrate the hell out of the process. We'll need to plan for that.'

'I've an idea, we can talk it through when we get back, but what I really need is the details of the safe. We need where, and what type.'

'Norma's on it now. What's Townsend saying?'

'No comment, although his lawyer is indicating that her client won't deny an improper relationship with Droopy, but she's almost taunting us that we don't have direct, admissible evidence of his complicity in the murders, and you know what?'

'Go on.'

'She's right. We get this wrong, and the bastard is looking at five years for corrupt practice, but walking for the murders. He'll be out in two.'

Ross exhaled heavily. 'No fucking chance, not happening, not on my bastard watch. Get yourselves back here, and we'll come up with a plan. How much of Townsend's detention clock is left?'

Max looked at his watch. 'He arrived at the nick at half two, and it's 6 p.m. now. I don't want to interview him again tonight, as we'll only get the same result, and in any case, he'll need to go into a rest period.'

'Shit, it's gonna be tight, if we don't interview until the morning and the clock expires at two thirty, I'll get the custody extension in place, we're gonna need every second of the twenty-four hours. Fucking shit situation. I much preferred when lawyers had to serve habeas corpus writs on us before we'd tell them where the clients were.'

'If you can pause swinging the lamp for a minute, we'll head back. We've sneaky shit to plan.'

76

HELENA MCCALL WAS sitting in her huge, beautifully plush lounge in the palatial home on the outreaches of Glasgow, a flute of Krug Champagne in one impeccably manicured hand, as she only half watched the enormous TV that was set into the wall.

Once again, she was home alone. Her husband had gone away on 'business' in London, doing something, she knew not what, and frankly she didn't care. She reached into the ice bucket and refilled her flute with the straw-coloured liquid, and watched the tiny bubbles lazily rise, the anticipation of the drink hitting her tongue increasing as she raised it to her lips. She sighed as the cold, crisp Champagne washed over her tonsils, soothing her as it did. She knew that she really did drink too much, and drinking Krug at two hundred quid a bottle on a Tuesday evening wasn't a great look, but fuck it, she thought. She knew that Angus would do that annoying head shake if he could see her now, before he disappeared into the gym in the basement for yet another workout.

She knew her role in the relationship was as arm-candy for Angus, and the fact that she was literally half his age was further evidence of this. Essentially, she was there to look good at social events, so Angus could enjoy the envious stares he got from his contemporaries when he arrived with his arm around her narrow waist. It was basically a business relationship, and it always had been, ever since he'd wooed her when she was working in one of Glasgow's lap-dancing clubs, and she was mostly okay with this. A wardrobe full of designer clothes, lots of jewellery, plenty of holidays, and an Aston Martin on the drive came with the small cost of having to shag him every now and again. She looked at the Rolex on her wrist, and saw that it was almost midnight. She sighed and took another deep draught of the Champagne, and was just in the process of refilling the glass when a piercing shriek erupted.

'Fucking alarm,' she said, leaping to her bare feet, and running out of the lounge and into the marble-floored hall. She keyed the code into the alarm keypad, but the hideous noise continued unabated. She tried again three times without success, the screaming seeming to get louder. She looked at the control panel, something she rarely did, and saw the words on the LCD display. 'Error code 754'. Jamming her fingers into her ears, she went to the lounge and picked up her phone, scrolling for the number of the alarm company. The alarm was dodgy, to say the least, and she'd almost rather not have one. It wasn't as if the feared Angus McCall was likely to get burgled, was he?

The phone vibrated in her hand, and she saw on the display that it was her husband calling.

'Angus?'

'Is everything okay? I'm getting an alarm message on the phone,' he said, his voice mildly slurring and gummy.

'Fucking alarm, darling. Went off for nothing, I hadn't even set it.' She had to yell to be heard over the squealing.

'I'll call . . . company . . . fix . . .' said Angus, although she only caught half of his words such was the volume.

'What?' she bellowed.

His voice was drowned out by the racket. The phone buzzed in her hand again, she looked down to see a text from him. **I'll call the alarm company**.

She ran up the marble staircase to the master bedroom, went to her bedside drawer and pulled out a small box, where she kept some earplugs, and jammed them into her ears, sighing at the sudden respite from the din.

The phone buzzed in her hand again. **Engineers are close by on another call, be there soon. Love you xx**

Helena sighed with relief, as the noise seemed to get even louder. 'Come on, you bastards,' she yelled at the top of her voice.

Fortunately, the alarm engineers were as good as their word, and within ten minutes a small van had swung into view on the CCTV screen by the gates at the bottom of the long, sweeping drive. She pressed the button on the panel, and watched as the gates swung open and the small white van passed through.

Helena went to the front door and stood there, as the van pulled up outside the house and two people jumped out. One was a small, wiry older man, the other a taller, lean guy with a shaven scalp. Both wore sweatshirts with a logo and the name 'AGF-Home Security Solutions'.

'Mrs McCall?' bellowed the younger one.

'Yes. It's been going off for fifteen minutes, and I hadn't even set the bloody thing,' she yelled back.

The younger man nodded towards the house, and she led the way, her hands over her ears, trying to keep the overwhelming noise at bay.

They went into the house and she pointed to the alarm control panel in the far corner.

The older one reached into his bag and came out with some kind of meter, with wires attached, and he plugged one end into a small port in the white box, and looked at the readout.

'We have an error code, and it's showing some faults upstairs. We'll need to physically check them. There's one in each bedroom, are we okay to go and check?' the older man said.

Helena nodded. 'Please. I'm getting a migraine. I'm going to go and sit in the car whilst you do what you have to do, but please make it stop,' she shouted, her voice beginning to tire. Her head was swimming with a mix of the racket, and the bottle of Krug she'd consumed.

The older man nodded, and the pair headed upstairs. She grabbed the car keys, and ran outside where she was soon grateful to be cosseted by the soft leather and decent sound-proofing of the Aston.

77

'RIGHT, WE DON'T have long, Barney, let's get going,' said Max.

'Shit, this is a noisy bastard, it's giving me a reet bonce-ache,' shouted Barney.

'Leave it, it's keeping her in the car. Straight up to his room as per the building plan, yeah?'

Barney nodded, and they ascended the double-width staircase, two steps at a time, before they arrived at the room that Frankie had assured them was his father's. The door wasn't locked, and when they entered, they found that the room was clearly not in use. The bed was pushed to the side of the room, and there were a number of suitcases piled up in the centre, all covered with a plastic sheet. There were several paint pots in the corner, along with a selection of brushes, rollers and a bottle of white spirit.

'Decorating by the look of it, over by the en suite bathroom. Look a small step, just as the plan showed.'

Barney nodded, and reached into his bag, coming out with a flat-headed screwdriver. He knelt down and inserted the blade of the driver at the top of the step, where the riser was. A quick flick, and the front of the step fell down on a low recessed hinge. A flat metal surface was revealed with a digital pad and a blank readout on it. A small safe, similar to the type you'd find in a chain hotel. Barney pulled out a smaller cross-headed screwdriver, which he slotted into a grub screw at the side of the control panel, and within a second the fascia of the keypad came away in his hand, exposing a computer chip and some wiring. Working quickly, but without even a trace of haste or panic, Barney went to the side of the main unit with the flat screwdriver, and in a second had flipped out a cartridge that contained two small batteries. He pulled out two similar-sized batteries, replaced the ones in the unit and dropped them into his bag.

'Flat as a bloody pancake, those are. Hold up.' Barney reached into the bag again, and pulled out a small black plastic box, with a keypad on the front. He went to the wires in the open control unit on the safe, and disconnected two wires which he attached to some crocodile clips that he'd pulled from a slot at the top of his box. He pushed the buttons on his box in sequence 1-2-3-4-5-6.

The safe sprang open. Max and Barney looked at each other and smiled, and Max raised a thumb. He opened the safe door, his heart pounding in his chest as he reached his hand inside. First out came a thick roll of cash, easily five thousand, thought Max. Next came two scratched and battered mobile phones, followed by a new-looking automatic pistol. Max reached back in and pulled out a small file containing documents, and then a couple of passports. He reached in again, feeling into the almost empty space. Almost empty, but not quite. His fingers closed around a small self-seal plastic bag, which contained just one thing. A square SD card. Scrawled in pen on the outside was one word.

Ace.

Max held it up for Barney to see, and smiled.

78

FINN TOWNSEND LOOKED pale and broken as he sat next to his solicitor Moira Dougal, who had the same easy-going look on her face as Max and Janie, who entered the interview room carrying a small file and a laptop computer.

'I must say you're pushing it timewise, officers. By my watch we have two and a half hours before the detention clock expires.' Her tone wasn't smug, but was more curious.

'I think we'll have plenty of time,' said Max.

'Well, I hope so, as I'll be making the strongest of representations of discontinuance should the custody clock expire,' she said, scrawling on her legal pad, before fixing them with an intense stare that was only softened by the suggestion of warmth in her eyes.

Max switched on the tape machine, and waited whilst the familiar beep stretched on, as always seemingly interminable.

'Okay, we have a continuation of the interview of Mr Finn Townsend, same persons present as the last interview. Can you confirm this, Ms Dougal?' said Max, sitting down as Janie opened the laptop and began to tap at the keys, her face blank and unfathomable, and possibly a little pale.

'Yes, I can confirm that. Can I make the point that I've had no additional disclosure prior to this interview. Is any coming?'

'Yes, more coming now. Mr Townsend, you're still under caution, you don't have to say anything, but what you do will be noted and may be given in evidence. Understand?'

'Yes,' Townsend said in barely a whisper.

'Janie?' said Max, looking at his colleague.

Janie reversed the laptop so that the screen was visible to Townsend and his solicitor.

'What are we looking at?' said Ms Dougal.

'Last night we searched a property that used to belong to the Hardie family and seized an SD card. This video clip was found on it.'

The screen was frozen and filled with a female face that was ghostly white from an unseen torch. Everyone in that room knew who it was. It was Beata Dabrowski. A masked man had her held in a firm grip with a gloved hand around her shoulders. Her eyes were wide with absolute, sheer and unmitigated terror.

'Officer, I must protest. This should have been disclosed to me . . .'

'Ms Dougal. Once we've shown this to you, we'll withdraw and you can consult but watch it for now, eh?' said Max, his voice low and tight.

Voices came from the tinny speaker.

'*Ye, cannae do this, ye ken, missie. Ye cannae threaten the boss.*'

'*I'm sorry, I'm sorry . . .*' Beata's eyes were full of tears, and her voice was thick with terror.

'*Dinnae want to hear it, lassie. He's no' happy, so what do we do, eh?*' The thickly accented voice was matter-of-fact, and almost sounded bored.

'*I'll say nothing, I promise, I promise I'll say nothing.*'

There was a pause before she spoke again, her voice pleading. Her eyes were wide, and the naked fear shone from them.

'*Where . . . where are you taking me?*'

Townsend turned away, his face pale, his mouth open and quivering.

'Watch it, Mr Townsend. You damn well watch it,' hissed Janie, her voice thick with emotion.

He returned his gaze to the screen, shaking violently as he looked at it. He yelped when the plastic bag was stretched over her face, and he began to sob as she struggled and fought for her life, until she slumped, and the camera was switched off.

There was a long pause, and a deep, thick silence descended on the gloomy room.

Eventually Ms Dougal spoke, her voice shaky. 'Is that all of it?'

'No,' said Max.

'Whilst horrific, that doesn't implicate my client—'

'Keep watching,' interrupted Max, who then nodded at Janie.

The screen cleared again, this time showing what seemed to be the inside of a grotty hotel room.

Townsend watched, his mouth wide open at the scene of him and Beata making love on the grimy bed, in the dreary room. He didn't take his eyes from it when they had finished, and the events that he remembered so well from that day six years ago played out in clear, well-recorded footage. The tears streamed down his face as she stormed out of the hotel room after the threats to him.

'*You'll be sorry. You'll be very fucking sorry, you think I don't know what you do, eh? You think I don't know that you wash money for big criminals? You think I'm always asleep, but I hear your phone calls. I know who you work for,*' she said, her voice laced with venom.

He just sat there staring, his body slumped watching himself pick up his phone from the bedside table and make a call.

When his voice came out of the speakers, his face told Max and Janie everything they needed to know. Finn Townsend knew it was all over.

'Mr Townsend, I'd listen to the next bit, if I were you,' said Max.

He watched, his head low, and fresh tears streaming down his face as his words came from the speakers, quiet, crackly but distinctive.

'*Droopy, it's me. She's just left, and she was threatening me. Deal with it, okay?*' he said, his tone matter-of-fact as if he was discussing the removal of some rubbish from his garden.

The same stultifying and thick silence descended on the interview room.

Eventually Ms Dougal spoke. 'I'd like to speak to my client, please.'

79

MAX AND JANIE were inside the office adjacent to the custody suite, whilst Townsend and Ms Dougal were consulting after the interview. Both were in total silence after what they'd just sat through. Their faces were lined and pale from lack of sleep, apart from the couple of hours snatched in the office after they'd secured the video evidence from the safe at McCall's house. They were exhausted. Bone-wearingly shattered.

Ross slammed his phone down on the desk, triumphantly. 'Yes, ya dancer. Lord Advocate himself has handed the case over to the lead Fiscal in Glasgow. He's authorised holding charges for the case of Beata Dabrowski, and a general conspiracy. Lots more to come, but the MIT team can handle that. I know I don't blow smoke up your arses much, team. But fucking well done.'

Max and Janie looked at each other and smiled, barely able to keep their eyes open such was their levels of fatigue. 'I'll take that, Ross.'

'Aye well, don't get used to it. Who wants to do the honours and charge him? MIT team have offered to do the necessary holding paperwork, as we've not slept for a few days, but one of you two should get the honours of charging the shithead.'

'Not me, Ross. Can't someone from the MIT do it?' Max shook his head.

'What? Biggest collar of your life and you don't want to charge him?' said Ross. 'How about you?' He turned to Janie.

'Nah, I'm good. If MIT are doing the paperwork, then they can charge.'

'What?' Ross looked at them both, perplexed.

'Who told Droopy about the debrief site?' said Max.

'We all saw the message. It was Townsend,' said Ross.

'Aye, but who told him?' said Janie.

The silence in the room was total and complete.

'Ah, bollocks. Anyway, that can wait. Let's get back to Tulliallan, get our stuff and piss off. The Chief wants to see us before we go. Tea and medals, and all that shit.'

*

The Chief was sitting in the conference room next to DCC Campbell, as Max, Janie and Ross walked wearily in and sat.

'Thanks for coming in, guys. Great work, I mean it. Really great. I've actually just had a message from the First Minister to express her shock at the arrest of the Crown Agent, but also adds her thanks and admiration for all your hard work.' The Chief looked at each of them in turn, his face full of pride.

Max, Janie and Ross just looked at each other, a knowing smile passing among them.

'Nae bother,' said Ross, shrugging, but wearing a huge grin.

'At least it's clear about the motivation for Townsend wanting them dead. He'd only been in the job for a few weeks, and his face was going to be regularly in the papers, so he wanted all those links to his dirty past obliterated. I still can't get my head around the fact that he'd have three people killed just to protect his career.' Macdonald shook his head in disbelief.

'Any skeletons in your cupboard, boss?' said Ross with a snigger.

'Piss off, DI Fraser.'

Ross chuckled and rubbed at his bristly chin.

'So, we're all wrapped up, then?' said Macdonald as he stood and poured out three coffees from a flask on the table.

'Well, almost,' said Max.

'What?' said Macdonald, a confused look on his face.

'Townsend texted Droopy about the location of the debrief. We still need to find the source of that leak, but it can wait a wee while. We all need some kip.'

'Any ideas?' he said, sitting down, concern in his voice.

'Well, it shouldn't be too difficult to pin down. The list of people who knew at that precise moment was really limited. The NCA escort team didn't even know the full location, as it was drip-fed during the journey. Miles knew. You knew, ma'am. You knew, sir, and the NCA head of the PPU would have been aware. Of course, we all knew, so I'll be looking at you, Craigie,' said Ross, and Max and Janie both chuckled.

Ross continued, apparently in full flow, 'I'm sure with a load of phone work, computer downloads, internet traffic, keyword searches, we'll get to the bottom of it. I have Norma working on it all now, so it shouldn't be too much to find out. You know what she's like when you set her a difficult task. She's bloody relentless, dog with a fucking bone.' He paused to sip from his coffee.

'Well, it's still really disturbing. I want a clean bloody sheet after all the issues. Louise, are you okay?' Macdonald turned to the DCC who had suddenly gone the colour of alabaster.

'It was me,' she said, her lip quivering.

'What? What are you talking about?' said Macdonald, eyes wide.

'I told Finn. After our meeting in here with Miles and the others. I met up with Finn later, and he asked me, but I didn't know he was what he was. Oh my God, what have I done?' she said.

'Louise, I don't understand. Why did you meet with the Crown Agent outside of the working day?' said Macdonald.

They looked at her face, pale and shaking, no longer the spiky, confident leader, but a broken woman.

Everyone in the room knew exactly why DCC Louise Campbell had told Finn Townsend.

80

'BLOODY HELL, THE DCC was shagging the Crown Agent? Now there's a scandal. I knew she was ambitious, but that takes the bloody biscuit,' said Ross as they walked down the corridor back to their office.

'How did you know?' said Max.

'I didn't, but there was something fucking odd about how she spoke to him during that meeting. Didn't smell right. The daft bint, it was fucking pillow talk.'

'So that's why you went on a big rant about how we'd find out who it was? You were flushing her out, you sneaky bastard,' said Max.

'You sneaky bastard, *sir*.' Ross smiled.

'Whatever. I guess it hit her like a ton of bricks. All this does is ruin her career, but if we'd had to find out the hard way, which let's face it, we would have, it'd be much worse. She can just disappear elsewhere now, but at least her and I now have something in common.'

'What's that?' said Max.

'Neither of us is getting promoted again. Anyone fancy a pint?'

Max looked at his watch. 'No, somewhere I need to be.'

'Janie?'

'Nah, I told Melissa I'd be home at a reasonable time.'

'Bloody detectives have changed, man. Time was we'd have all gone on a two-day bender after a job like this,' said Ross as they arrived back in their small, dusty office.

'Load of shite. You've always gone straight back home after a job to make things right with Mrs Fraser,' said Max.

Ross opened his mouth as if to make some cutting and sarcastic retort, but then paused and shrugged. 'Fair point, well made.' He grinned and clapped Max on the back.

They all stood in the office looking at each other, the familiar sense of pride passing wordlessly among them.

'Top team. Now fuck off home, all of you.'

81

MAX WAS THANKFUL that he had his motorbike at the office, as it made for a lightning quick journey between Tulliallan and Valleyfield, a village outside Culross where Max and Katie lived. He parked up outside a long, low building on a small green and pulled off his crash helmet, checking his watch as he rushed inside. It was just before 2 p.m. His stomach was churning when he entered the large room, with bench seats and chairs all around. A feeling of doom settled in the room like an early morning haar.

'Can I help you?' said a stern voice from behind a counter. Max looked at the woman, who had short, severe hair, and wore a blue cardigan, and she looked at him disapprovingly over her half-moon spectacles.

Max surveyed the room, which was about half full of people sitting on the chairs and benches, none of whom were acknowledging him. Then he spotted her on a bench, staring at her phone, her face drawn and pale. Max ignored the querulous woman at reception and went and sat next to his wife.

'Hey, babe,' he said, kissing her on the cheek.

'Blimey, that was close, matey,' she said, looking up, her face lighting up as she gripped his hand tightly.

'How're you feeling?'

'Bloody appalling, you utter bastard,' she said, but her smile gave her away.

'Mr and Mrs Craigie? The doctor will see you now,' said the receptionist, a smile having replaced the scowl.

82

Four months later, The High Court, Glasgow

ROSS, MAX, JANIE, Barney and Norma all descended the stairs in between the sweeping columns that adorned the grand granite frontage of the High Court of Justiciary, where the Chief Constable stood resplendent in his full uniform in front of a phalanx of reporters, TV cameras and photographers all clustered around the bottom of the steps waiting for his statement.

'Shite, too many cameras for us. Let's get out of shot,' said Ross, darting to one side as the Chief approached a microphone stand, bathed in harsh lights from the cameras.

Ross and the team all hustled to the side and joined the group of onlookers watching the proceedings.

The Chief cleared his throat and spoke.

'Good afternoon, ladies and gentlemen. Today's conviction marks the end of a complex and wide-ranging investigation into the activities of former Crown Agent Finn Townsend. The weight of evidence gathered by my officers was of such a high quality that he was met with no alternative but to plead guilty to these most serious of offences, and the weight and severity of the sentence imposed by Her Ladyship will leave nobody in any doubt that Police Scotland will not tolerate corrupt practice by those in positions of power. Finn Townsend will remain in prison for very many years. I hope that this serves as a warning to those who abuse positions of trust that the Crown will be relentless in its pursuit of justice. We will use all the tactics at our disposal to bring you down, and will devote all the expertise of my officers to make Scotland and beyond a hostile environment for your activities. We also make it clear that we never stop investigating murders, and we will never give up on those that go missing . . .'

'Fuck me, I like the Chief, but he can be a right corporate bastard, can't he? Shall we piss off to the pub and let the backslapping carry on without us?' said Ross, in a hoarse whisper that was probably almost audible in Edinburgh.

'Funny that they didn't mention Malky Douglas. I knew it would be old paratroopers sticking together. Did he ever clear up the link?' said Janie.

'Aye. Malky went full hands-up early on, and it turns out that they did some bad shit together in Northern Ireland back in the day, and Droopy used it as a sword of Damocles over his head. Crown Agent is the headline, pal. They don't want to detract from that. Come on, let's piss off.' Ross looked at the phalanx of reporters and shook his head.

'What, you don't fancy talking to the press?' said Norma.

'Do I fuck. Face for radio, come on. Whistler on the Green is just around the corner, and I'm buying.'

'What really?' said Max.

'Aye, I can stand you a cranberry juice, but I can't listen to this shite. Let's go.' Ross turned and stomped off, his scuffed shoes clicking on the pavement.

*

'Good work, team,' said Ross as they all clinked glasses in the small pub, just a few minutes away from the court.

'I must say, I wasn't expecting a guilty plea,' said Max as he sipped his cranberry juice.

'Me neither. I thought they'd attack the search of the old Hardie place. Let's face it, it was a little rushed,' said Janie, drinking a gin and tonic.

'Nah. This way he has a shot at getting out one day. Plead not guilty and he'd be screwed, and I suspect he's not going to have the best time in there, is he?' said Ross.

'Happen he'll have a miserable time. Can't say I feel bad for the bent bugger. Nice beer by the way, cheers, Ross,' said Barney, raising his dark beer.

'Aye well, don't get used to me buying you drinks. You've had enough largesse from Police Scotland with your free flat for four months.'

'Aye, right comfy in there. Shame he wants it back, but weather's getting better, so no big deal.'

'How's Frankie?' said Norma, who was sitting on a bar stool, eating a bag of crisps.

'He's happy. Settled into Castle Huntly, and isn't getting any grief from any of the other cons. Seems that sinking the Crown Agent has actually made him popular. He's working at a nearby wood shop and seems to be enjoying it,' said Janie.

'He'll not last. He's a Hardie, and one day the lure of the underworld will drag him back,' said Ross.

'You think?' said Max, draining his juice.

'Aye. Once a Hardie, always a Hardie. Want another squash?' said Ross, nodding at Max's glass.

'No, thanks, places to go, people to see.' Max placed his glass down on the bar and nodded. 'Great work, everyone.' He smiled at the team and left the bar to cries of 'boring bugger'.

83

MAX GOT INTO his car in the nearby car park and was securing the seatbelt when his phone began to vibrate in his pocket. Looking at the screen, he saw a familiar series of numbers and characters. He smiled and answered the call.

'Hello, Bruce,' he said as he put the phone into the cradle on the dash.

'Max, am I getting obvious?'

'Maybe a bit. I hope you have no bad news, as I've places to be.' Max started the car, engaged the gears and moved away, the phone transferring into the hands-free facility.

'None. I've been monitoring Frankie, as you'd expect, and I have nothing. He's working hard, seems to have made a friend in a woman from his wood shop and all his reports are of someone wanting to do his bird easily. He's even studying for a degree in history,' said Bruce.

'You sound disappointed,' said Max.

'Not really. I was doubtful of his intentions, but he brought a really bad man down, and I guess he deserves his fresh start. I'm all for rehabilitation. Are you satisfied now?'

'About what?'

'That I didn't shoot Davie or his slimy lawyer?'

'I was always satisfied, Bruce.'

'How so?'

'Sniper was too slack. If it was you, we'd have never caught you.'

Bruce laughed. 'Aye, well that's true. I guess that's it then. No more Hardie trouble, unless Frankie does decide that the dark side is more attractive, in which case I'll be waiting for him.'

'You serious?'

'Deadly serious, Max. If Hardie stays on the side of the angels, he'll get no interference from me.' His voice was tight and firm.

'So, is that it for us then?' said Max.

'Max, I'm always here. I owe you, and I won't forget what you did, and what you know about me. You always went the extra yard, and it makes me wish that we'd served together. You ever think I can help you out, just pick up the phone. Right, I gotta go. About to get on a plane.' The phone clicked in the car speakers. Max smiled and shook his head, feeling as he always did a sense of comfort at his guardian angel, the grizzled ex–special forces operator that was Bruce Ferguson.

Max looked at the clock on the dash, and his heart leapt. He was going to be late. He negotiated his way out of the car park and drove, his stomach tight as the nerves began to bite. He couldn't miss this, and the appointment was in just over an hour.

*

The journey took exactly an hour, before Max was parking and jogging through the grounds of the small complex. He went into the low-rise building that had a sign outside that read 'Radiology'. He burst through the doors and into the reception, where a young man in scrubs smiled.

'Mr Craigie?'

'Aye, that's me,' said Max, puffing at the exertion.

'Your wife's in room three. I'd hurry, if I were you, she looked a little scunnered,' he said, stifling a smile.

Max jogged down the corridor and tapped at the door with a '3' on it before easing it open.

'You cut it fine, you bugger,' said Katie, who was lying on her back on a low bed, a scrubs-clad sonographer using a doppler on her stomach that was smeared in a clear gel.

'I know. Sorry, traffic was awful.'

'Well, you're here now, pal. Come and have a seat. I've just started,' said the sonographer, a grey-haired man in his fifties, with twinkling eyes.

Max leant across and kissed Katie on the forehead, and turned to the screen that was just black and muzzy. The sonographer used the doppler on Katie's swollen stomach. At first there was nothing to see, just a haze of fuzziness against the black, but then it cleared.

A dome of a head came into view, and a shape of an arm suddenly wafted across the screen.

'He/she is a lively one,' said the sonographer as he moved the doppler.

Max said nothing. He couldn't as it felt like he'd swallowed an apple whole. His mouth gaped open as the shape of their child became more and more distinct on the screen.

'Lovely strong heartbeat,' said the sonographer.

'Fuck,' said Max, his voice hoarse and tight, feeling his own heart beating in his chest.

Katie reached for his hand and squeezed tight, smiling at the sight on the screen. Max felt tears begin to prick his eyes at what he was seeing. His child, heart pounding away, legs kicking, head moving. Their flesh and blood, just twenty weeks gone.

'Potty mouth, Max. Lively bugger, eh?' said Katie with a chuckle.

Max opened his mouth to answer, but couldn't find the words, his eyes just remained glued to the screen as he tried to take it all in.

'Will you want to know baby's sex?' said the sonographer.

Max looked at Katie, and almost as one they realised that they hadn't discussed this. Katie chuckled, her face serene in direct contrast to what Max knew he probably looked like . . . A rabbit caught in the headlights, maybe.

'I . . . I don't know,' said Max, his voice little more than a croak.

'Aye, maybe we should have talked about this, eh Craigie?'

Max just stared at his beautiful wife, glowing with happiness on the bed as she looked at their child. He knew that life was changing, and he smiled at Katie, who had turned to look at him.

'You ready for this, slugger?' said Katie with a beaming smile.

'Bring it on, babe. Bring it on.'

Acknowledgements

THIS BOOK WAS a lot of fun to write, and as always it wasn't just me that made it happen, and I'd like to extend my heartfelt thanks to the people who helped me along the way in making it as good as it could possibly be. Writing a book is a lonely old business, but making it into something worth publishing is a team effort.

My agent, Robbie Guillory at Underline. Literally none of this would have been possible without you taking a chance on me two years ago. I'm so glad to have you in my corner, and I value your steadying presence.

To all the team at HQ who graft away behind the scenes, making the magic happen. There are many whom I never get to meet, or speak to in sales, analytics, cover designs and many other areas, but please know that I appreciate you all.

To Belinda, my editor who has worked wonders making this book as good as it can be. I've loved working with you on this book, and can only wish you the best in your new role.

Audrey Linton, my new editor who grafts hard on making these books do all the good stuff. I'm so looking forward to moving Max and the team onwards and upwards.

Sian Baldwin, publicity ninja who keeps the books out there so that the public know that they (and me) exist.

Jo Kite. Marketing guru, who makes everything look beautiful and makes them stand out from the legions of other books on the shelves.

To Angus King. Master narrator, you turn these books into

something totally different on audio. You have a legion of fans, and I'm delighted to be sharing them.

A big thank-you to Iain Jane, a very clever defence solicitor from Peterhead who very kindly helped me out on getting a few things right about the legal processes that are written about in this book.

To Colin Scott, for the shits and giggles and helping me to stay sane.

Clare, love you always x

My brilliant kids, Alec, Richard and Ollie. So proud of you guys.

To all my family, in the UK and beyond, I love you all.

To all those that police the streets fairly and honestly. You're going through a rough time at the moment, but I know you'll come through. I am proud to have served, and you all should be as well.

As always, last but definitely not least, all the booksellers, bloggers, reviewers, enthusiasts, and of course readers, thank you. Without you guys, it really, genuinely means nothing.

EXCLUSIVE ADDITIONAL CONTENT

Includes an author Q&A with Neil Lancaster
and details of how to get involved in *Fern's Picks*

Dear lovely readers,

I am thrilled to be bringing you another Fern's Picks read. Prepare to be completely absorbed in this intense and gripping crime thriller by Neil Lancaster, *The Devil You Know*. This novel will plunge you into the deepest darkest depths of crime and corruption with a plot that unravels bit by bit, and with characters that are as complex as they are compelling.

Six years ago, a woman mysteriously disappeared. Now, notorious imprisoned crime boss, Davie Hardie, offers to disclose where her body is buried – in exchange for his freedom. But soon classified information begins to leak. And as tensions rise, DS Max Craigie and his team are thrust into this high-stakes case and are determined to outsmart those who will stop at nothing to keep their secrets hidden.

Every action-packed twist and turn will keep you constantly on edge. I can't wait to hear what you think of *The Devil You Know*.

with love
Fern x

Look out for more books, coming soon!

For more information on the book club,
exclusive Q&As with the authors and
reading group questions, visit Fern's website
www.fern-britton.com/ferns-picks

We'd love you to join in the conversation,
so don't forget to share your thoughts using
#FernsPicks

A Q&A with Neil Lancaster

Warning: contains spoilers

The Devil You Know – and many of your other books – have some incredible twists. How do you develop your plots and keep the suspense building throughout? Do you know how the story will end when you begin writing?

This is a great question, and the answer is simple. I don't really know. It's not particularly great for my blood pressure, but I really am the ultimate 'pantser'. Writers are generally considered plotters, i.e. they plan their books out and typically know what is happening at each stage. Or they're 'pantsers', as in they fly by the seat of their pants and see where the story takes them. I fall very much into the latter category. I start a book with a basic theme I want to talk about, and then I discover the plot as I go. Now that I have an established cast of characters, I trust them to show me the way.

In *The Devil You Know*, I pretty much knew that Davie Hardie was having the cops over in order to escape, and I hope that I led the reader up the garden path into believing that was the plan. A very nasty, returning villain from the earlier books, escaping into the wind. Then I hit them with what they expected as the breakout predictably happened. Here is where I then had the fun. A sniper takes out Hardie and his solicitor, turning the whole premise upside down. This then turned the attention onto Max's guardian angel, Bruce Ferguson. Was he the killer? It's such fun to write, to take the reader down one path, and then suddenly open another possibility. Other twists can come to me out of nowhere. I'm pretty chaotic, and sometimes I wish I planned more, but things seem to be going nicely.

I almost never know exactly how the book will end — other than we'll probably prevail. Good over evil, I reckon most readers like that. Most of my books are all about discovering who the mole or corrupt cop is, and I often change my mind at the last minute. It's such fun.

What was a particularly challenging scene to write and how did you approach it?

I'm not good at the sensitive stuff, but I am trying hard to make Max a rounded character and a family man. He loves his wife a great deal but is also married to the job of being a detective, and this causes real challenges in balancing work and family life. (I know this only too well from my time as a detective in the Metropolitan Police.)

During the book, Max discovers that his wife Katie is pregnant, which causes some difficulties, as well as happiness. I found dealing with the elements of their relationship and the emotional heft a little challenging. (I almost wrote an intimate scene between them but then chickened out.) The final scene in the book was actually pretty hard to write. Max sees his baby during a scan and I had to dig deep to remember how it made me feel to see that with my own kids. I hope I got it right. (I've had messages from readers saying I made them cry, so hopefully, I did.)

DS Max Craigie is an iconic detective, along with many of your other characters. Can you tell us more about your process when creating these amazing protagonists and antagonists?

I like the word 'iconic'. I'm not sure Max would, as I think he likes to be a little more under the radar, he's not a show-off. Most of the characters are amalgamations of people I've encountered during my life, both in and out of work. I've had a couple of old bosses message me and ask if Ross Fraser is based on them, with his sarcasm and terrible language. He's also a great guy, who would go to the wall for his team, so I suspect they are hoping I'd say yes!

I like to give them all quirks, which helps me make them more rounded and interesting. Barney, the tech expert, is an ageing Yorkshireman, who lives in a campervan because he's always skint. He's happy with his lot, and as long as he has enough money for his tobacco and a bet on a horse, he's content. He also really annoys Ross Fraser, which I find very funny to write. It's all about dynamics and the elements which make a good team, which is just as applicable in the real world.

Odd characters can often come together, and their differences are what makes them real, even if they do rub each other up the wrong way at times. I do play for laughs, and we need characters like this to keep us smiling during really tense, and sometimes horrifying, stories. That's how policing actually works, you really do have to find the funnies amongst the tragedy and horror to keep you sane.

In many ways, despite the books being marketed as 'DS Max Craigie books', he's really nothing without the team. Janie is super smart, dedicated, and brave, but she's also obsessive, quirky, and eccentric against Max's more relaxed persona. I think it makes them tight, and bigger than the sum of their parts. I view Max as the straight man in a comedy act. He knits it all together.

Bad guys are huge fun to write, and many have elements of criminals I encountered in my life, both in and out of the police. I met some of the worst people imaginable, and I can take elements of them, their mannerisms, their ruthlessness and cruelty, and use them to create believable, if horrible, protagonists. I feel really lucky to have had my experiences to help me.

Creating these characters, good or bad, is the best bit about being a writer. People come for the plots, the action, the tension, and the crime, but they keep coming back because they enjoy reading about what the characters are up to. I'm ageing Max and the team in real-time, so by the time you read the next book in March, Max will be becoming a dad for the first time.

Now I bet you can't wait to read about that, can you?

What inspired you to begin writing police procedural crime thrillers? Was this always the genre you wanted to write?

Is it too obvious to say that my former career as a homicide and serious crime detective wouldn't allow me to write anything else? It's probably a bit more than that, and in reality, I still consider myself to be a thriller writer who writes police procedurals. I always hope that I'm writing a police procedural novel that has the heartbeat of a fast-paced action thriller, like Alistair MacLean, or more contemporary writers such as Gregg Hurwitz with his *Orphan X* books.

I love all types of crime books, and the crime writing world is just so friendly and accepting. For a bunch of people who write about cruelty and murder, we really are a fairly friendly bunch.

I also have to admit that as a fairly lazy writer, being an ex-cop means I don't have to research a great deal, but that would be shallow. I love crime books, and I always wanted to be in this world. It's so much fun.

Max Craigie has taken on some intense cases, what do you think his greatest strengths and weaknesses are? How does this impact your writing and his journey throughout the series so far?

Max is dedicated, brave, relentless, and tough, and he has a real sense of 'justice'. I put that in inverted commas, as he has skirted close to the edge of illegality himself on a couple of occasions, particularly in his dealings with the mysterious Bruce Ferguson.

His biggest challenge seems to be the balancing of his family life. Unusually for crime fiction, he is pretty balanced, doesn't drink alcohol, loves his wife, and isn't a philanderer, as many other fictional (and real) detectives are. He has a lovely home, a loving wife, a lovely wee dog, and he's about to become a father. Getting his work-life balance right is the hardest thing for me to write, without stretching the bounds of plausibility too much. This is very true to life, as I often failed to get the balance right during my career, and I almost made myself ill on one occasion with my inability to switch off from the job. Thankfully I made the decision to retire early aged 49, and now live an idyllic life in the Scottish Highlands with my wife, son, and lovely wee dog. (Can you sense any inspiration here?)

What would you say is the most impactful case Max Craigie has taken on? How did this influence his character development?

I'm contractually bound to say, 'The next case, so you'll have to buy book 6 *When Shadows Fall* in March to find out 😉'.

In reality, *Blood Runs Cold* took Max to the very edge, as it brought his wife into harm's way. Mind you, there was a very tough encounter in *The Blood Tide* when Janie almost died. Also, I can't discount *The Devil You Know* when he was battling really corrupt forces from the police whilst on enforced leave. Now you come to mention it, *The Night Watch* took him very close to the edge, which was very nasty.

Have I made you want to read my backlist, yet? Good!

There are many great character dynamics within your books. Did any of your character relationships change in ways that surprised you as you were writing, or did you plan these out?

When I first started the series, there was distinct tension between Max and Janie Calder. She's fast-tracked promotion, university-educated, very intense, and somewhat 'quirky'. I intended them to butt up against each other when I began, but then things happened that really drew them together as partners, and now they really trust each other implicitly. Ross Fraser is probably my favourite character to write. He's rude, crass, foul-mouthed, hates bureaucracy and is something of a bull in a china shop. Sometimes his mouth runs away with him, and he ends up saying things that could be seen as a little 'old-fashioned'. (I don't want to use the word misogynistic.) However, his relationship with the team, and the fact that he has two dedicated and hard-working female team members, who are willing to challenge him on his poor use of language, is softening him a little. He'll always be Ross, but he's trying. We all know a 'Ross', and they're often good people who are trying their best to adapt to a changing world.

How do you handle the balance between realistic crime depiction and engaging fiction? Are there any challenges you face when writing about these sensitive topics?

For reasons of my pension (and national security), there are things I won't write about. The last thing I want to do is to give bad guys information they can use to make my former colleagues' lives any harder.

Crime fiction is just that. Fiction. My priority is to tell a story that is engaging, interesting, exciting, and compulsive. Making it realistic is secondary, but important. I can often do this, as much because I know what police procedures, techniques, and methods to not put in the story, as well as those to deploy. Much of police work is boring, repetitive, time-consuming bureaucracy. No one wants to read about that. I think the advantage I have is that I know how to take the short-cuts to make the reader believe that the story is really authentic, and accurate. Don't get me wrong, whilst it's fiction, the things I do talk about are accurate, I just leave a lot out that doesn't help the story rattle along.

Can you tell us more about what you're writing next?

Max Craigie 6 is out in March, and I'm just finishing the edits on that. I also have a new, and very exciting thing planned, that I can't actually talk about right now. So, stay tuned for more info on that.

Also, I'm very confident, in fact, I can guarantee that you've not seen the last of Max and the team. As long as you guys want to keep reading about him, I'll keep writing them!

Questions for your Book Club

Warning: contains spoilers

- There are many great action-packed scenes but also heart-warming and humorous ones throughout the book. What scene or moment stuck with you the most? Why did it leave an impact?

- How did the relationships between the team add to the story? Were there any dynamics that stood out to you the most?

- Max Craigie and his team were thrust into this complex case suddenly. Were there any moments where you questioned or disagreed with his choices? What would you have done differently?

- How did you feel about Max and Katie's pregnancy news? Was this shocking? Did this impact your opinion of Max at all?

- There are many great twists in the story. How did you feel about the revealing of the 'double agent' towards the end of the novel? Were you shocked? Or did you guess who it may be?

An exclusive extract from Fern's new novel

The Good Servant

March 1932

Marion Crawford was not able to sleep on the train, or to eat the carefully packed sandwiches her mother had insisted on giving her. Anxiety, and a sudden bout of homesickness, prohibited both.

What on earth was she doing? Leaving Scotland, leaving everything she knew? And all on the whim of the Duchess of York, who had decided that her two girls needed a governess exactly like Miss Crawford.

Marion couldn't quite remember how or when she had agreed to the sudden change. Before she knew it, it was all arranged. The Duchess of York was hardly a woman you said no to.

Once her mother came round to the idea, she was in a state of high excitement and condemnation. 'Why would they want *you*?' she had asked, 'A girl from a good, working class family? What do you know about how these people live?' She had stared at Marion, almost in reverence. 'Working for the royal family. . . They must have seen something in you. My daughter.'

On arrival at King's Cross, Marion took the underground to Paddington. She found the right platform for the Windsor train and, as she had a little time to wait, ordered a cup of tea, a scone and a magazine from the station café.

She tried to imagine what her mother and stepfather were doing right now. They'd have eaten their tea and have the wireless on, tuned to news most likely. Her mother would have her mending basket by her side, telling her husband all about Marion's send off. She imagined her mother rambling on as the fire in the grate hissed and burned.

The train was rather full, but Marion found a seat and settled down to flick through her magazine. Her mind couldn't settle. Through the dusk she watched the alien landscape and houses spool out beside her. Dear God, what was she doing here, so far away from family and home? What was she walking into?

When the conductor walked through the carriage announcing that Windsor would be the next stop, she began to breathe deeply and calmly, as she had been taught to do before her exams. She took from her bag, for the umpteenth time, the letter from her new employers. The instructions were clear: she was to leave the station and look for a uniformed driver with a dark car.

She gazed out of the window as the train began to slow. She took a deep breath, stood up and collected her case and coat. *Come on, Marion. It's only for a few months. You can do this.*

Available now!

The No.1 Sunday Times bestselling author returns

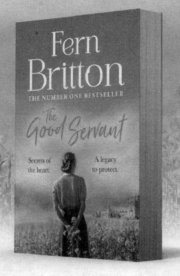

FERN BRITTON

THE NUMBER ONE BESTSELLER

The Good Servant

Secrets of the heart. A legacy to protect.

Balmoral, 1932

Marion Crawford, an ordinary but determined young woman,
is given a chance to work at the big house as governess
to two children, Lilibet and Margaret Rose.

Windsor Castle, 1936

As dramatic events sweep through the country and change all their lives
in an extraordinary way, Marion loyally devotes herself to the family.
But when love enters her life, she is faced with an unthinkable choice . . .

Available now!

Our next book club title

THE SUNDAY TIMES BESTSELLER
B A PARIS

THE PERFECT MARRIAGE OR THE PERFECT LIE?

THE RUNAWAY GLOBAL BESTSELLER · OVER 4 MILLION COPIES SOLD

BEHIND CLOSED DOORS

'Twists our expectations of the entire psychological thriller genre'
GUARDIAN

Everyone knows a couple like Jack and Grace. He has looks and wealth, she has charm and elegance. You might not want to like them, but you do.

You'd like to get to know Grace better.

But it's difficult, because you realise Jack and Grace are never apart.

Some might call this true love. Others might ask why Grace never answers the phone. Or how she can never meet for coffee, even though she doesn't work. How she can cook such elaborate meals but remain so slim. And why there are bars on one of the bedroom windows.

Sometimes, the perfect marriage is the perfect lie.

Dear Reader,

We hope you enjoyed reading this book. If you did, we'd be so appreciative if you left a review. It really helps us and the author to bring more books like this to you.

Here at HQ Digital we are dedicated to publishing fiction that will keep you turning the pages into the early hours. Don't want to miss a thing? To find out more about our books, promotions, discover exclusive content and enter competitions you can keep in touch in the following ways:

JOIN OUR COMMUNITY:

Sign up to our new email newsletter: http://smarturl.it/SignUpHQ

Read our new blog www.hqstories.co.uk

X https://twitter.com/HQStories

f www.facebook.com/HQStories

BUDDING WRITER?

We're also looking for authors to join the HQ
Digital family! Find out more here:
https://www.hqstories.co.uk/want-to-write-for-us/

Thanks for reading, from the HQ Digital team